The Weary Carry On

by

Bowman Wilker

A Constable Gus Albright Mystery

Cover Art by *Tina Lynn Stout*

The Wild Rose Press, Inc.
PO Box 708
Adams Basin, NY 14410-0708
Visit us at www.thewildrosepress.com

Publishing History
First Edition, 2025
Trade Paperback ISBN 978-1-5092-5933-5
Digital ISBN 978-1-5092-5934-2

A Constable Gus Albright Mystery
Published in the United States of America

Dedication

To the real Paul Stanley

Disclaimer:

This book is set in the 1920s and reflects the language and attitudes of that era. Terms such as Oriental, Indian, and Native are used in the historical context of the period and may be considered outdated or culturally insensitive today. The author acknowledges the evolving understanding and sensitivity towards these terms and emphasizes that their usage in this work does not reflect contemporary viewpoints or intentions to cause offense. Readers are encouraged to approach the text with historical awareness and to consider the context in which these terms are employed.

Prologue

Her first steps into the unfamiliar snow are painful, but her fear pushes her forward. It's clear that the world is against her: the frosty air attacks her lungs, the ice and slush bites at her naked feet. She forces her hand over her mouth to stop the sound of her gasps. They would show no mercy if they found her out here alone.

Across the yard, she hastens and throws herself over the low fence. A sliver of wood pierces her leg through her dress before she flops over to the other side. She makes no sound as she pulls it from her flesh. Here, at the tree line, she waits. She expects one of the men to burst through the door and chase her. But all is quiet.

Still watchful, she drops the stolen boots into the snow. For several seconds, she works to untie the stiff laces. The men always kick them off—such lazy men. If they weren't so lazy, she would not have gotten away.

One after the other, she places her frigid feet inside and then packs them full of the discarded fabric she was clever enough to stash. The boots are too big for her, but the extra material will allow her to walk. She pulls on the laces with all the strength she can muster from her frozen fingers, and with one final look at the doorway, she breaks off into the woods.

The pale moon sits low in the sky, giving scant light to the pathway through the trees. She moves forward. It was not just good luck that allowed her to escape.

Something told her to take this chance, to disregard the dangers. If she keeps the moon's light behind her, she will find the railway line, the guide to bring her back—first, the railway and then the ocean.

The cruel ocean.

Her first sight of the sea had paralyzed her. She knew then the men had tricked her, that she was trapped. For who could oppose the power of something so boundless? That great wash of nothingness that cared for no one?

They kept the girls imprisoned in the ship's hold for countless days, where the ocean strove to ruin them. Her body vomited everything she ate and drank. A violent fever bewildered her. She begged the ocean to consume her, but it was relentless. When they carried her from the ship, the suffering was only beginning.

The other girls guessed too well what would become of them. Back home, her aunties taught her to be careful of men, but these brutes, with their hairy faces and sour skin, were more animal than man. And their cruel appetites became more depraved with time and loneliness. Now she had found a way to escape, she would risk anything to return home. Let the ocean do what it wished. She had survived it once; she would survive it again.

As she picks her way through the trees, the branches snap back at her as if they are angry. Who knows what forest spirits lurk here? And what tricks they might use to confuse her? The tangled roots of the forest claw at her feet, making her stumble in her ill-fitting boots. She needs to find her way out. Surely, she must have gone far enough by now. A crow calls out in the darkness. It scares her. It sounds like a voice imploring her to move deeper into the forest. Instead, she turns the other way and finally sees the clearing.

Here, the rail runs straight, a band of frozen iron barely visible over the crust of the snow. She holds the thin man's stolen coat at the collar to protect her from the blowing wind as she hobbles along the track. Her feet throb; the adrenaline of her escape is extinguished. How far did the line go? And what sort of people might she find at its end?

The crusted snow reflects the half-moon's light in a crystal glow. The other girls marveled at the snow, but she hated how the coming snowfall turned the sky to a featureless white. How it lay flat on every surface, stealing any hope of warmth. Oppressive. Even now, it spelled out her destiny in her footsteps.

The narrow beams of their battery torches dance along the trees. The wind carries their brutish voices, harsh and hoary from too much drink—not angry but excited, and that scares her more. She chooses an angle and dashes toward the darkness of the forest.

The men must have seen her shape. Their heavy steps pound in the snow as she breaks inside the tree line. The branches slash her skin as she hurtles on. Breathless, she steps and jumps, curls herself around the trunks of trees, the world becoming dark and haunted as she dives deeper into the brush. She searches for hard ground where her path cannot show her progress, but whichever way she weaves, the men pursue. Their curses and laughter echo as they force their way toward her. They carry guns, but they will not use them. The men will catch her and hurt her, not even allowing death as an escape.

But in the dark, a strange voice bids her to keep

running. She slips and tumbles down a hill, then across a trickling stream. Her lungs struggle to take in air. Running, still running, her feet painful, the extra fabric bunched under her arches and between her toes. Something drives her on. Calls to her. She cannot surrender now.

Through the gray light, she uses what is left of her energy to ascend a rocky slope. There she slips inside a crevice and yanks on her coat so it will come with her.

She waits as her ear attunes to the sounds of the forest. A squirrel darts through the underbrush. Once caught in a branch, a melting mass of snow crashes to the ground. But all else is silent. No footsteps, curse words, or heavy breathing. She reaches into the coat pocket and brings a piece of their tasteless bread to her mouth, swallowing hard to drive it past the lump in her throat.

When the dawn's light breaks through the trees, she slides out. Stretching, she finds the aches and pains gathered in her pursuit. She climbs a little farther and finds the top of the ridge, tall enough to survey her surroundings. But as she pushes through a clearing, a nearby sound intrigues her. *Could it be a train?* What luck it would be to find the track again. Surely, it would lead to a settlement, somewhere she could hide and steal the things she needed.

She steps closer to the edge of the cliff. The sound is louder now; it is not a train but a turbulent river, whitewater in full force from the spring melt. This is good. Where there is water, there are people, towns, or even cities. A way back. The sun is rising in the east; this day will be as warm as the last.

She walks along the ridge but loses her balance and causes a tremor in the snow. The surface gives way as a sheet of snow collapses, tossing her on the ground as it slides from the cliff. She reaches out and grabs a rock. The snow rushes past her into the chasm. Her right boot, filled with snow, gives way. She clutches the rock, her foot naked to the cold.

Shaken, she pulls herself to her knees onto a stodgy sludge of slush and mud. She turns to search for her boot. The current had not borne it down the river. Instead, it stands upright on a small ledge, five feet below, as if someone had placed it there.

She needs it. Walking without it would not only be painful but dangerous. Lying on her belly, she stretches forward, but it is just out of reach. She finds a stick and tries to prod it but worries she will make it fall. The girl assesses her surroundings once more. Could she hold on to the roots of a tree growing out of the bank and reach from there? Would they be strong enough?

A shout rings out—a hate-filled voice approaches. It is now or never. Taking hold of the thickest root, she swings herself out and stretches her arm as far as it can go, but still, she cannot reach it. Loud curses! They have found her tracks. She grabs a thinner root and lowers herself, catching hold of one lace with her other arm. She pulls it and feeds it into her hand until she can grip the mouth of the boot. But is there time to climb, to fit the boot on her foot, and to run?

She shifts her balance to rise back onto the ridge, and the root twists with a crack. She grips it as she falls, crashes hard into the cliff wall, and tumbles into the rushing stream. Even if she knew how to swim, the current is too strong.

Three times, she lifts her head above the water to gasp a breath. There is no fourth time. When the panic dissolves, one final thought comes to her: it wasn't hope that called her. It was the ocean. It had reached its fingers into the mountains and plucked her out—to carry her into its unfathomable depths. To be lost forever.

Chapter 1

Clayton's Curse
Day One
Monday, February 21st, 1923
Chambers, British Columbia

Clayton Caufield was no one's idea of a trustworthy man. His face didn't help him much: long skinny snout, dark black eyes, and a thick knotted beard that never made it beyond stubble but always gave evidence of last night's dinner. A weasel's face, for sure. But his routine drunkenness and foul mouth were also part of his charm. And yet it was he whom I let drag me through the woods one hour after midnight in the full moon's light.

I'd made the journey twice before. Chasing a ghost I didn't believe in. But sometimes, you must swallow your pride and do difficult things to settle people's minds. That was part of it. But even more compelling was proving them all wrong.

Clayton grumbled about the cold, though he dressed well enough for it, a walking pile of furs, each one a different color, dirty, matted, and smelling of piss and spirits. But they weren't enough for him tonight. That was Clayton. If he wasn't full of drink, he was full of curses. After walking half an hour into the bush, I was just about willing to shoot him. The only thing to stop me was the badge on my belt—RCMP—though half the town would have felt it was a public service.

The truth was I should have sent Clayton home. I didn't need his help to see the tracks. This woman did not attempt to hide her footsteps. It hadn't snowed in a while, and while the temperature had fluctuated several times in the past week, the ground pack had begun to shimmer, taking on a slippery crustiness that made walking difficult and finding defined footprints even harder. But the moonlight and the snow's glare made it much easier to pick out details. And fortunately, there were enough other signs: torn branches, disturbed stones, packed moss, and dirt. No blood though or signs of chase or struggle,

This would be the third sighting of the ghost girl. Dutch Mosley saw her at his back fence, but she moved into the woods as he approached. Mosley was too old to follow. Too old to be out in the cold at all. The story came to me from Millie, who helped me at the detachment. She heard it from the young Mrs. Granderson, who cooked for Mosley from time to time.

Of course, at once, I suspected a local like Bea Brannon. But "No," I was told, "This girl was too short," and her clothing was all wrong: a tight black jacket with a heavy skirt that hung below the ankle, accompanied by a large hat and matching muff. "Somewhat fashionable," Millie told me, though I wasn't sure how she would know.

At this point, I counted the population of Chambers to be forty-eight, which included the outlying ranches and the Chambers Lodge. Of these, only ten were women, none known to wear such a collection of garments.

I put the first sighting off as fantasy, but when she

appeared a second time, I knew I would have to investigate. Mitch Blood saw her standing in a patch of grass outside his fence. Everyone considered the man a reliable source, a hunter and trapper who had journeyed here from Dawson in '17 and taken to raising cattle—a local fixture. I hunted with him in the mountains from time to time and was impressed by the accuracy of his shooting.

The girl showed herself to Blood at the first break of the sun three days previous. He described her as a smallish woman with long black hair. He saw it when she had turned to walk back into the woods.

He found it curious. Taking his rifle, Blood followed the girl deep into the pine. Not an easy trail, he said, over deep banks of snow, rough branches, and rock, skirting a mountain stream before beginning an ascent into the peaks. The rancher figured the trail went on for more than six miles and then stopped in the exact center of a clearing, with nothing to guide him in every direction. The only thing to mark the trail's end was a white handkerchief. Lacy and embroidered with the letter "M."

He brought the handkerchief with him when he came to tell me the story the next day. Mitch spoke few words but answered all the questions I had for him. Millie must have been eavesdropping as by the afternoon, the story had become a legend with a few additions thrown in. Many linked her to every mysterious sighting in British Columbia and the Yukon. And others gave her a role in every superstition and shadowy tale they could remember.

Since the Chambers mine had closed, gossip became the town's most productive industry. Millie prattled on that afternoon, unable to stop her speculation even after

I clearly showed her my irritation and disinterest. In his notes, the old post commander, Sergeant Deacon, told me she was level-headed and responsible. But ever since I arrived, she enjoyed yammering on to me about one fantasy or another. Lately, it was ghosts and spirits, but I didn't listen to half of it.

The next day, after my morning chores, I ran into Mayor Fox on the boardwalk. He mentioned the sightings and urged me to get to the bottom of it.

"Chambers doesn't need any more negative press," he told me, though I was unsure what he was going on about. The outside world forgot about this community soon after the mine closed. If anything, the sighting of a ghost girl might engender some interest.

"You need to start doing some work around here, Albright." He was close against me as he talked into my face. "You need to figure out what this is about. We can't have strange women appearing out of nowhere, spooking the population, can we? Time to show your mettle, Gus—to be the man you're supposed to be." He poked me with his finger.

Tom Fox was not my boss. Nor was he my father. I would have liked to put him in his place. But some of what he said was correct. In my seven months of service at the detachment, my most exciting task was locking drunks like Clayton in our jail cells to sleep off their booze. Besides, I was eager to check out the story for myself. I wanted to prove Millie's fantastical tales were poppycock.

I rode the forest trail five miles southeast to Mitch's ranch and found the man at his pump. Before darkness, we followed the path together for more than a mile. The footprints were small and curved to a sharp point at the toe. A woman's boot for sure, but they did little to tell why a lone woman would walk off the trail into the perilous bush, surrounded only by mountains. The dress she wore was an ill-fitting choice for travel. Besides, there was no place else to go. Chambers sat alone, without roads or walking paths to connect it to the outside world. River and rail were the only ways in or out. I suppose she could have disembarked in Plateau and walked the eight miles of track between there and Chambers. But why would anyone do that?

So when my unctuous neighbor Bernard came at the midnight hour to wake me, I removed myself from my warm bed to follow Clayton. The man had made enough noise to rouse the devil, but it was the detachment's dog, Lloyd George, who finally nudged me awake. I swear the creature's nose was the coldest thing south of the Arctic Circle.

I did not give the dog its name. Millie chose it because she thought it humorous, but I blame Sergeant Deacon for allowing such disrespect. I won't say our canine version of the wartime British Prime Minister didn't bear some resemblance, with his broad and disordered whiskers, but Deacon knew full well the dog by breed was a German Wiretailed Pointer. Usually, I wouldn't resent a man for spending the war years keeping the peace back home, but the frivolity of the dog's name served as a reminder that the Sergeant never faced Jerry across the battlefield.

As I waved the dog away, Bernard continued banging on the detachment door with his heavy fist. Next came a rattling of the front window pane furious enough, I worried the glass would break into shards. Bernard adhered to the philosophy of always doing the least he could in life, so his frenetic energy was uncanny in its own right. It was a strange piece of civic duty for a man solely interested in himself.

When I finally unlatched the door, Bernard needed to take a moment to regain his breath. "Clayton…ghost woman at the Hole,"

The Hole was the town's least respected drinking establishment.

"Calm down, Bernard," I told him. He stood on the porch outside as the cold air filtered into the detachment.

"Clayton saw the ghost woman at the Hole. He's going to follow her." Bernard's eyes were round with excitement. "They're holding him there. They're waiting for you."

"Who? Who's waiting for me?"

"The other men." Curious. The West had an unwritten rule to let others do as they wished. And the men drinking in the Hole at midnight were already working on their one wish—getting drunk.

I pulled on my outdoor wear as Bernard waited in my doorway. I checked to make sure my pistol was in its holster and then grabbed my large metal battery torch in case the shine of the full moon was not bright enough to light my way. When I looked up after tying my boots, Bernard was gone, disappearing back into the gloom of the stable yards, much like he was a ghost himself.

****

The Hole was a ruinous shack of a tavern in the old part of town. Outside it, I found five men at the forest's edge restraining Clayton as he sat in the snow. There was Sook, the barkeep, and four of the Hole's usual boozers; each one committed to pouring enough liquid down their necks as possible. Tonight, they banded together and restrained Clayton, presumably by a sense of camaraderie. To kill yourself drinking was one thing; to die from exposure in the woods was something else entirely.

While none were in the best shape for an interview, they all agreed with the general story. Just before midnight, the mysterious girl had shown herself outside the window, standing still and resolute before moving into the bush. They described her as wearing the same dark jacket, hat, and muff as seen during the previous two sightings. All agreed she must be white because of the way she stood. I'm not sure I understood this, but there was a feeling amongst these drunks that natives and white folk held their bodies differently. This town was always trying to teach me something.

Sook, the barkeep and the only man amongst them without a pickled brain, guessed the woman's wandering spirit chose Clayton as her victim. He implored both of us not to follow, asserting that such ghosts were known to coax the living into peril in the hopes of stealing their souls. I knew nothing about that except that it struck me as nonsense.

After this brief exchange, the four drunks disappeared back into the Hole; their charitable act was now over. I told Clayton I would follow the tracks on my own, but he was adamant in his desire to follow the apparition, a curse-filled diatribe proclaiming his freedom to do whatever he damn well wanted. Of course, he was correct. I couldn't put him in cuffs for threatening to walk into the woods. Besides, having a witness was a sensible plan, even if it was someone as unreliable as Clayton. It was time to put this matter of a ghost to rest.

It brought the two of us together—Clayton and I.

Clayton was intent on deciphering the mystery, like Mitch Blood before him. This time, though, the trail was hot—a curious word to use at any time out here. I was glad of all my woolen underthings and the non-regulation toque and scarf I had grabbed on my way out the door.

By the time we arrived at the clearing, we were both tired enough that not a word had passed between us for the last half mile. I stopped Clayton at the opening because I didn't want another pair of boot prints to confuse the scene. Before us, we saw a clear set of tracks leading to a large rock in the middle of the snowy glade. The exact circumstances the trapper, Mitch Blood, had described. Footprints that stopped dead in the middle of a clearing with no one around to make them.

The squarish clearing stretched no more than thirty yards on any side. The full moon shone overhead, giving everything a supernatural glow. But off to the west, I saw the arrival of an ominous cloud moving across the sky as if to catch the moon unaware. I took a moment to breathe and caught the whiff of a coming snow, the tension of it already causing a familiar throbbing in my left eye socket.

Clayton glared at me, pointing at the rock with an outstretched hand. I could smell his noxious breath as he cursed at me—a combination of cheap alcohol and gum disease. "What are you waiting for?" was the gist of what he was saying. Clayton pointed at the surface of the rock, and I could make out something soft and delicate lying open on its surface. A matching handkerchief to the one Blood had found when he had tracked the second sighting? But still, I didn't move.

The scene did not seem right. I knew plenty of men

believed in spirits and such. "There are more things in this world than you can understand" type nonsense. But my four years in Europe knocked the magic right out of me. Over there, I saw exactly what humanity was capable of. No magic at all was needed. We could do it all ourselves. And yet, I couldn't figure this out.

Clayton pushed past me into the clearing. He was walking backward, spitting profanities and waving his arms. That's when the bullet hit him. My eye caught the muzzle flash in the southwest of the clearing and the quick glow of the murderous face beyond it. I looked back at Clayton and saw him stumble toward me, his eyes wide, his mouth tight. I reached out to him and pulled him to the safety of the trees right before a second bullet blew past us, this one coming from the opposite corner—a missed shot.

"I think I got one," I heard a rough voice howl. Clayton was on his ass now, his eyes closed, a string of profanities rising from his lips with the steam of his mouth. His eyes darted toward me, and I could tell he was scared. He should have been.

"Who are they?" I whispered, my hands against his chest, trying to figure out in all those furs where they shot him.

"The Pickle brothers," was his mumbled answer. "They were drinking in The Hole tonight."

By Blazes! The Pickles! Damn, if I could remember their name or number. Cole or Dutch, maybe. But the names didn't matter now; it was the numbers that would get me killed. I sent my mind backward trying to remember, two or three?

"How many?" I whispered to him.

The time to make a plan was over. Clayton was in

no condition to run, and I never enjoyed the idea of being shot in the back. I gazed into the sky. That dark cloud drifting over was about ready to swallow the moon—a bit of good luck. I should have brought my Enfield rifle, but this was supposed to be a rescue mission, not an ambush.

My heart pounded. The situation looked bleak. Even if there were only two brothers, their guns outnumbered our own. I closed my eyes and envisioned the scene, trying to settle my breath for what I was about to do. The first signs of panic gurgled in my blood.

I turned to Clayton. Why had he been so insistent on following the girl? With a bullet inside him, he was even more of a hindrance. At least his curses were now only a mumble. I grabbed his chin to bring his eyes toward me. "Clayton, are you willing to do your part to get us out of here?"

He gave a tiny, feverish nod. Good enough. I pulled my Colt from my holster and pushed it into the furs of his chest. He stared at me with rheumy eyes. "In fifteen seconds," I said, "I want you to fire this gun twice, somewhere into the clearing. I don't give a plug nickel if you hit something. Just fire it! Fire it once. Wait for the sound to carry and fire it again. Got it?" He let out a small groan of pain, but I ignored it. "Count like in a game of hide-and-seek, with Mississippi's in between." One more nod from him, and then I was off. I hoped he had enough strength left in him to follow through. And that there were only two brothers.

I kept my body low and fast as I snaked between the trees, trying to keep my feet quiet. On my way, I moved my hefty battery torch out of my right fur pocket and into my hand—but I did not turn it on. The world had grown four shades darker with the moon behind the cover of the clouds, and I could feel my eyes working hard to adjust. I tried to time it right, but I got there a moment too soon. The shooter remained in the spot where he'd fired the gun. These boys hadn't gone to war, or they would have known better. But he was fast and turned his rifle toward me as I jumped over the final log that separated us. He would have got a shot off, but his finger fumbled as the sound of my Colt rang through the woods. Clayton came through.

Then I was on him. I swung the metal battery torch and slammed it into the side of his head. His body went limp, so I pulled his rifle from him and smashed him in the face with the butt. He fell unconscious or worse; there was not enough time to tell. I was still a target, even with him out of the combat and the moonlight dimming. These brothers would know each other's position.

I got low to the ground, turned, and looked into the clearing. The cloud had darkened the world, but it was easy to see the figure of Clayton as he staggered forward, back into the glade. He fired the Colt once and then once more into the trees beyond, like some sort of crazed lunatic, the gun pointed at random as if he was trying to kill the world itself. The muzzle flash from the other side of the clearing showed me where the second brother was, but I could not get a bead on him until he had fired his second shot, spinning Clayton to the ground. The spark from his gun made his face glow, and with a careful shot from his brother's Winchester, already cocked and loaded, I put him down into the cold earth, the bullet slicing through where I figured the right eye would be. Now, was there a third?

But I was stupid. I should have already known there

was.

****

She stood over me. Crouched as I was, I could only see her from the corner of my eye. She held her pistol in both hands, pointed at the back of my neck. I rotated my head, keeping the rest of my body still. She stood defiant, one leg on the log I had leaped over, her body still and steady. A petite woman. The black jacket tight, her dress billowing in the wind. I couldn't tell if she was pretty, for she had a scarf tied tight around her face and only darkness behind her. Besides, her prettiness wasn't the thing in question here. She had me dead to rights.

The forest took on an eerie silence. None of the three downed men were making a sound, and I wondered which of them had already shuffled their way off our mortal coil. My muscles tensed. I was not inclined to join them.

"Put down the rifle," she told me. Her voice came out strong without a shred of empathy. I considered what she might be to these men. A sister, cousin, lover? And which one she may be attached to. I prayed she felt something for the man at my feet.

"You wouldn't kill a man," I stated, but I heard her laugh, a strange sound that echoed through the trees. The thickening cloud now obscured the full face of the moon.

"It looks like I may have been the cause of three men's deaths today," she crowed. Could I turn the rifle quickly enough? My body was positioned wrong. I would have to pull the Winchester around my hips and then upward toward the center of her body. It would be clumsy and awkward. There wasn't a chance I could get a round off before she had put one in me. I let the rifle drop and raised my hands in the air, my only hope resting on the fact she had not shot me yet.

"If you care about these men, you must know they cannot survive out here in the open, in this cold, so far away from medicine." I put my hand by the brother's mouth and was relieved to feel some hot air blow against it. "He's still alive, but I'm the only chance he'll get the help he needs." I looked her over. "You couldn't carry him out alone."

I heard her sigh, the rifle now pointed at my forehead. "All my life, men telling me what I can and what I can't do. These two are idiots," she said as she glared at the man at my feet. "They should have held their fire until you both got closer." And then she cursed in a most unladylike manner.

There was silence until the wind began to howl, and the moon came away from the cloud. "So what's it going to be?" I asked her. "Everyone here is just getting colder."

"All right," she said, "but you can't get them out by yourself either?" Everything was going to work out. The gun was now at her side.

"I'll run back and return with a whole bunch of men and a doctor." I tried to smile at her. I figured she could see my white teeth in the remaining moonlight.

"And what then?" she asked. "It will be the long drop for both of them, I expect."

She may be right. Last year, they hung two men at Oakalla for much less. "I think your brother across the way is already dead. He took a shot to the face most don't survive from. But this man here is still breathing. And I can assure him a fair trial, not set as murder, for the only shot he fired was on poor Clayton, who may or may not himself be dead. It will depend on how fast I can bring either of them back."

She lifted her gun and pointed it at my chest. I am ashamed to say after all that action, I could no longer control my rising panic. It was an old enemy of mine, born in the fields of France, always ready to pounce when it felt I was at my weakest. I could feel my hands shake, the world twisted, and the sweat came to my brow despite the cold.

"Before anything else, you're going to check on the other two," and she made a motion with her rifle for me to move into the glade. I know she could see me shake as I rose from my crouch, but I followed her lead and walked straight across the clearing past the rock, her rifle pointed at my back the whole way. A handkerchief lay on top of the stone— a pretty thing. What was it about? Was it just part of the ghost story, designed to lure me into this ambush? There were more important things to think about.

Once across the clearing, I knelt in the snow to check the other brother's pulse. In life, I imagined him to be an ugly man. A bullet through the eye made him no more pleasant to look at and a lot more dead. I gave the girl a shake of my head and hoped he was not her favorite.

Could I run, pick a path through the trees, and take my chances? At this point, I was unsure if my unsteady legs could carry me. She motioned me to move toward Clayton, his body sprawled face down in the snow. I rolled the man over and put my head on his chest, but his thick furs prevented me from sensing anything. I leaned over and brought my ear toward his mouth, tiny amongst all that scruffy beard. For the first time, I was hoping for a noxious bout of bad breath. But I felt nothing. I shook my head once again.

"Are you sure?" she asked.

I wasn't. But I decided to stay mute. If Clayton were dead, she and her brother would be accessories to murder. If not, he could testify against them in a court of law—shooting at a Mountie was a serious crime. If only I could think!

I could not get enough air into my lungs. I tried to straighten my chest to release the pain in my muscles. My hands shook as I held them before me, and tears came to my eyes. If I begged for my life, would it make a difference?

Maybe she took pity on me. Or, she chose what was best for herself.

"What can you promise me?" she asked as I stared into the barrel of her gun.

"You don't need to be any part of this," I answered. There was too much emotion in my voice. "You can be a ghost," I insisted. "It was your brothers that ambushed me. The rule is a Mountie always gets his man, and I have two of them."

"A promise is a promise," she nodded, "and you just made one. Remember, this does not go both ways. I have made no promises because I may not be done with you yet." And with that, she walked off into the bush.

****

The thought of following her was fleeting. There was too much else to do. I rechecked Clayton for any signs of life but found nothing. Still, I moved his furs around to cover as much of his face as I could and tucked his gloved hands inside his coat. But was it enough? I snuck over to the dead Pickle brother and stole the scarf and hat from the corpse. His large woolen mitts, I found lying in the snow beside him. I used these to help cover Clayton and the unconscious Pickle brother further. With the temperature dropping, the risk of frostbite grew.

I still felt flustered. What about the weaponry? If the girl snuck back or the unconscious man awoke, they could ambush me again on my return. I rooted around but couldn't find the pistol I lent Clayton. Then I remembered the battery torch. I must have dropped it during the skirmish with the first brother. So I returned to the log and scrounged around on the forest floor until I could make out its shape, resting against a mossy stump. The poor thing was dented and sticky with blood. This was a favorite tool of mine, and I needed it for the trip back home. Fortunately, a few loud smacks on its backside made it light like new.

With its help, I found my gun, stuck barrel down in the dark shadows of a pine. Next, I gathered the brothers' rifles—two identical bolt-action Winchesters, almost brand new. They were better weapons than the Enfield I left at the detachment.

I looked around the clearing and paused to hear sounds caused by the girl's footsteps. Nothing. That same eerie silence. And then a wet drop on my nose. The first flake, a tiny herald, of what was to come. Little did I know what problems the coming storm would cause.

Then I hightailed it home. I ran as fast as I could, using the battery torch when needed to find our tracks. The adrenaline in me was dying, replaced by stumbling fatigue. The shame of my panic was still working its way through me. I could still see her spectral shape as she stood with one leg on the log. The cut of her dress resembled the cloak of the Grim Reaper, judging me, and I was so desperate to save myself, whatever the cost. I should not have let her get away. What other troubles would she make for me, and how would I explain what happened to everyone who would ask? This night was far from over.

****

The snow now came quicker. A blustery wind sent the freshly fallen flakes up from the ground and into my exposed flesh, my cheeks already red and painful. The cloud that once covered the moon now swept across the entire sky. I gripped hard on my dented battery torch, casting the light ahead in sweeping arcs as I tried to make out the best pathway through the bush. The temperature endangered both injured men, their bodies now in a state of shock. In the trenches, I saw countless men succumb, their nervous systems shutting down. Men who might have survived if they had received medical aid sooner.

I was out of breath when I arrived back in the old town by the river. With all the exertion, my body was now too warm, and a slick layer of sweat had formed beneath my coat. Stopping too long in town would create its own dangers. All the extra moisture I exuded could freeze on my return trip. And the comfort of being someplace safe could numb my desire to get this job done.

I emerged from the forest across from The Hole, its pale lights extinguished. I half-expected to find a welcoming party. Weren't they curious to know what happened? Certainly, there would be a few drunks still asleep at their tables, but no, the place was empty.

I knocked on the side door of the hospital first, hoping to wake Genevieve. She often told me about her sleeping problems. She would become supernaturally alert the moment her head hit the pillow. Another consequence of her time in a war zone. Sure enough, I pounded only twice before a light turned on. It was Genevieve in her nightgown, holding a lighted hurricane lamp out in front of her. She ushered me in through the door, the swirling snow falling over the threshold before me.

The shock of my being there was still in her eyes. She retreated a step as I closed the door behind me. Genevieve had been a nurse at both the Somme and Passchendaele. She and the doctor had settled here, hoping to begin a simpler, quieter life and forget all the relentless trauma of the battlefields in France. But it was that experience I wished to draw on now. Genevieve always handled matters with quiet efficiency.

The heat from the room welcomed me, but I knew I could not stay long. "How was he today?" I asked.

"He was a little lost," she replied. She was frustrated by the suspense. "What is it?"

"There's been a gunfight. One man dead and two others injured, about an hour into the bush." My nose caught a faint smell of citrus from the warmth of her body. I wondered how I must smell.

"You'll need to get some others to be stretcher-bearers," she said. That was the type of person she was. No questions. Her mind was already flashing to the task ahead. "I'll wake Kenneth, and we'll take him along, though I don't know what state he'll be in."

"Whatever you think is best." Dr. Moody, her husband, was over twenty years older than Genevieve and me. He sometimes became quite forgetful, his mind going places no one could follow. Fortunately, Genevieve could fill in for most things. I told her I would return to get them and then rushed back into the night.

****

The snow fell even faster now. If it didn't stop, the buildup would cause significant problems. There was much to do, and the minutes were ticking away. But I knew where I wanted to go first. Peter Stormcrow lived in the old sawmill by the river with his business partner Duffy Smalls. Peter was a good friend who helped me considerably in the short months I had been in Chambers. I knew he would have my back.

After the first knock, I heard his croaky voice respond from within. "Who's there?" he called, and I shouted my name back in response.

"Are you alone?"

The image of the three men lying in the snow flashed through my mind. "Peter!" I shouted, "Open the damn door. There's been a shootout."

The door latch released from the inside, and a narrow slit of intense yellow light broke through the darkness. Friend that he was, the squint in Peter's left eye suggested he was not interested in seeing me at this time of the evening.

"There's been a shootout, Peter," I repeated. There was panic in my voice. "I need your help."

He stood there for a few seconds—a cautious man. Finally, he opened the door farther to reveal himself and the room behind him. Peter had been awake. Despite the heat, a heavy wool blanket covered his shoulders, but his clothes underneath were not nighttime wear. Behind him, the chair still rocked. He must have left it to answer the door. He held an old Colt single-action revolver in his hands. I couldn't remember if I had ever seen him holding a weapon before.

"Are you expecting trouble?" I asked him.

He ignored my question. "What shootout? Are you hurt?"

I shook my head. "Not me. I've got some injured and some dead, and I need help to get them all back to the hospital."

Peter looked past me to the building storm. "You want Duffy too?" he asked. He pointed to a lumpy form in a bunk below the staircase. I nodded; the more, the merrier, as they say. Duffy wasn't the sharpest tool in the shed, but he did have his uses.

Peter did not appear convinced he should be involved. And I understood. Peter was a woodworker, and this wasn't his town. Besides, no one likes to trade a warm bed for a chill wind. But he had already been awake, and he was armed.

"Who's dead? Who's injured?" The words came out slowly as if he was testing out each syllable.

"Does it matter, Peter?"

But he only nodded.

We were losing time. I would need more men than Peter and Duffy, and I worried about the storm. The falling snow would make finding our way back to the injured men difficult.

"It's Clayton," I told him, "and a couple others."

"Clayton and who else?" He wasn't letting me off that easily.

"The Pickle brothers." He had some dealings with them back when he lived in Smithers. He would most likely close the door on me because of that fact. But he stayed there thinking, the door half open, like an unanswered question: *A frigid walk or a cozy sleep*?

"I don't know, Gus. Are the two of them still out there? I'm not going out in a storm just to get a bullet in me. "

I showed him the Winchesters—one on my back and one in my hand. I handed them both over to him. "Both men aren't armed. One's dead, and the other unconscious. They'll both be dead soon if we don't go get them." It wasn't my strongest argument, but it was the only one that came to my mind.

I stretched my arms out and glanced at the sky. "I could use your help here, Peter. I'll owe you one." But really, how could you pay someone back for such a thing?

"You're telling me you put down both Pickle brothers without getting yourself killed as well."

It wasn't as easy as all that, but I nodded.

Peter sighed. He rubbed the stubble on his chin as he spoke. "If you tell me it's safe, we'll give you a hand."

"It's safe, Peter," I assured him, but the truth was I thought there was no danger the last time I went into the woods. "Meet me at the hospital in fifteen minutes and see if you can get anyone else to come." I left before he had any more time to protest.

****

My next move was the telegraph. If this storm became a blizzard, it could disconnect the line; once it failed, it could be dead for days. The storm would halt the trains, and the railway would need to bring out special equipment to clear the rail and reset the cable. Before that, headquarters needed to learn about my gunfight in the woods. They would send me reinforcements to investigate the shootout, probably from the nearest detachment eight miles away in Plateau. For close to a decade, they posted two Mounties at the Chambers' detachment, but Taylor retired, and I was the only replacement for Sergeant Deacon. Still, I needed to try to get a message through.

Unfortunately, our train station was back near the detachment, so I needed to move through the old town, over the boardwalk, and then off down the tracks to the junction. My legs were heavy, and the cold was bone-deep, but there was no other way.

I found Mr. Benjamin awake, already at his post. When I pushed through the door at the station, I caught him glaring out the window at the storm; a stationmaster needed to be sensitive to any peculiar changes in weather that might affect the track's safety. Despite his faults, everyone I talked to agreed the man was a stickler for details.

"You're awake, Benjamin."

He turned. With the white light of the storm behind him, his shocked face looked ghostly.

"Albright! What? What are you doing here?"

"I need the telegraph. We need reinforcements."

"Reinforcements?"

"Yes, there's been an incident." I stamped my feet hard on his mat to get off the snow. "Speed is important, Benjamin. I need to get moving."

Benjamin moved to his desk and pulled out the tall wooden chair to sit on. "I've been trying for the last hour to get through to Prince Rupert, but they haven't replied."

"Prince George then?"

"No, nothing there as well. I think the line might already be down."

I stood before him, still huffing from all my exertion.

"Take down this message. You will send it out every

ten minutes. Understand?"

"Of course I understand." He pulled a pencil out from behind his ear, licked the tip, and set it on the paper.

Gunfight in woods near Chambers. Constable Albright ambushed but uninjured. At least one man dead, two injured. Need reinforcements. Please advise.

Benjamin coded out the message with blistering speed. I stood across from him, listening to the beats. Sharp and abrupt, much like the man. Staccato. Mr. Benjamin was a fussy little man, always well-coiffed, the lines of his meticulous mustache and beard drawn by his razor. He always wore a vest over his shirt, even in the summer heat, and frequently checked his timepiece even though there were never more than two trains a day.

My first position in the Royal Dragoons was as Batman to our company commander, Colonel Aimes. Among other valuable skills, I learned how to drive a motorized car, shine shoes, and operate a telegraph. My experience as a clerk during the war made me a confident message taker, but I could not match Benjamin's fluency. Of course, he sent multiple messages daily, including train orders, Western Union telegrams, and other news and social information.

After he sent the message, I returned to the window to watch the building storm. The light inside the station made it difficult to see, but I could make out the nearby trees tossing fitfully in the wind.

There was no response from the telegraph. Three minutes later, I asked Benjamin to try again. But still, there was no success, and I had two injured men out in the snow.

"I'm heading back out to the woods," I told him. "I want you to send this message out every ten minutes for the next two hours. Can you do that?"

Benjamin huffed. I once had hoped the two of us might be friends. We both were the last men at our post.

"If you get a response, accept any help they can give. I will be back to check on you."

Benjamin nodded, then took off his glasses. He opened his mouth to say something but decided against it. Good. The man's thoughts were of no interest to me. He needed to do the job I asked of him.

****

My quick detour over to the Grand Hotel in the new area of the town proved fruitless. I banged on the door and shouted as loud as I could, but neither brought the mayor, Tom Fox, to the door. The storm was becoming too fierce, the wind so intense its gusts drowned out all my efforts. Fox lived alone at the hotel, keeping only one staff member on his payroll. And guests were few and far between. Should I barge through the door? Fox needed to know what was going on. He could help me raise a posse and send someone to keep watch on Mr. Benjamin in the station house. But the wooden boardwalks were already buried with snow. And I did not have more time to try to rouse him.

I rushed back to the hospital to find a small crowd ready to depart. Genevieve and the doctor carried their medical bags, and the hospital's two stretchers lay in the snow. Peter Stormcrow stood beside Duffy, who appeared to be wearing every piece of clothing he had. He was so overstuffed. I doubted he could bring his arms to his sides.

Matti Larsen, the blacksmith, and his eldest son Anders were with them. Peter must have gone to find them. It was a ragtag bunch. It would have to be enough.

By blazes, Coot would have been an excellent choice! I should have called on him and his master Bernard in the stable yard when I returned to the station house. The storm would be too rough for the horses to carry us into the bush, but I could have used the extra men. And it would be fair play to rouse Bernard from his bed—so he could help finish what he had started.

We started walking at once, keeping a steady pace until the doctor grew tired. The man was confused. Genevieve didn't quite know what to tell him. To be walking in a storm in the middle of the night. Peter dropped back and helped Genevieve guide the poor soul. With his help, they could follow our tracks in the snow at their own speed. Larsen and his son took a stretcher each, and we plowed ahead, lanterns held high, as I did my best to keep us on course.

My original journey into the bush took forty minutes, but finding the clearing now took us over an hour. As we stepped into the clearing, I could see the bodies of the two Pickle brothers. But where was Clayton?

The man must have at least survived long enough to move himself. Clayton had crawled out of the clearing, leaving a pathway in the snow. He sat upright now with a trunk against his spine. I rushed over to see if I could find a pulse, but I felt no life between his dirty beard and the layers of his soiled furs. It was not until I heard him mutter a curse word under his breath that I knew the old rascal was still with us.

Duffy made motions to haul his body onto the stretcher, but I told him to wait for the doctor. Meanwhile, I went to find the injured Pickle brother. He lay right where I had left him, still unconscious under a quarter inch of snow. Thank the heavens I had the forethought to cover him so well, but the man needed a warm fire. Anders Larsen brought over the stretcher and shifted it so we could roll his body onto it. This Pickle brother was a large brute. It would take the efforts of more than one man to pull him over the sticky snow.

By then, the others arrived, and Dr. Moody and Genevieve gave the injured a quick examination before deciding we could do nothing for them while the storm raged around us. Supporting the men's heads, we tied and steadied their bodies on the stretchers. Genevieve then took Moody to examine the other brother, who confirmed the man was dead.

He wasn't the first person I had killed. The Royal Dragoons were already in France when I got around to enlisting. I was supposed to join a cavalry unit, but they had been dismounted and reformed as infantry. Since I was a late addition and had received little or no training, they loaned me out to different tasks, some of which kept me safe behind the lines, while others put me in the heart of the conflict. Ultimately, I became quite a useful soldier with a strong penchant for survival. My moments of panic came only in the war's last few months. Anybody who knew about them had kept silent or been silenced by the vagaries of war.

"What the hell is this, then?" someone shouted.

Larsen and his son were in the clearing. The handkerchief. Stupid. I should have remembered it was there.

"It must be the ghost girl's," said Matti Larsen.

Anders stamped his feet and took the lacy cloth from his father. "It looks old. Do you think the ghost brought the men here?"

I moved fast. "There's no ghost." I snatched the item and stuffed it in my pocket, then stared the two men down. I would have to get my story straight. There would be no mention of a ghost. Or a girl. If anyone like Millie got word of this, she would spin all sense right out of the story.

"You won't mention this. Any of it. You're here to help me get these men to safety. So stop lollygagging and get a move on."

Anders seemed diminished, but Matti scowled back in anger. Had I gone too far? Now they had something else to talk about. My poor reputation may take another hit, but by blazes, I was right. There were more important things to accomplish.

"Everything good?" Asked Peter, giving me the side-eye. "We'll take the Pickle brother if you two think you can lift Clayton."

Matti scoffed. "The Pickle brother weighs more. Clayton's yours to move. I never could stand the smell of the man."

****

The trek back was grim as we carried and dragged the men back through the bush. The storm let go for a few minutes, and we took advantage of the calm by upping our pace, only for it to return with even more ferocity. The snow had not been deep enough to warrant snowshoes, but now the heavy drifts caused extra exertion as we had to lift our legs high to get over them. Fortunately, Genevieve and Dr. Moody went before us, using our forward tracks to direct themselves. The rest of us took turns pulling and guiding the stretchers as best we could, sharing grunts and groans as communication. The trees were too thick at points, and we needed extra time to pull back their limbs and lift the heavy stretchers over or between the branches. It was hard work, and I was glad to have the help, but I felt for the injured men when we twisted the stretchers this way and that, hoping the straps would hold them tight and steady.

By the time we returned to the hospital, everyone was beyond tired. Genevieve had opened the ward and had rekindled the kerosene stove to give us warmth. The radiators in the wardroom crackled and snapped. She brought us a pot of coffee, which we guzzled before hoisting the two men off their stretchers and onto their beds.

Peter slumped on the end of a cot. "The next time you decide to shoot someone," he said, "you should do so closer to town." This attempt at humor received only a few tired grunts.

Then came the tricky part. Genevieve needed our help to remove the men's clothing. Duffy had found himself a cot by the door and had fallen back asleep while Larsen and his boy had disappeared, presumably back to their home. So I beseeched Peter to do me an extra favor. Lord knows how I would pay him back. With him on one side and me on the other, we took turns rolling Clayton's body back and forth while pulling at the sticky wet furs, which involved a great deal of tugging, turning, and even some tearing. We found underneath a skinny little man, reeking worse than the furs that wrapped him, and two bullet holes, one in the middle of the shoulder and one in his thigh. The third shot rested between the furs, a good thing, for it would have been a gut shot. That type of wound I knew was almost always fatal.

Through all this shuffling, Clayton's eyes remained

shut, his mouth mercifully closed. I didn't know the man could be quiet. And it only took being shot twice. Dr. Moody inspected him, pushing and prodding as he turned Clayton's scrawny body. "We'll have to wash him well," I heard Moody say, a job I would leave to the professionals.

But there, on Clayton's forehead, at odds with the rest of the grime on his face, lay two curved lines of pink. I touched it, and some color came away on my finger. I showed it to Genevieve, and we exchanged tired shrugs. Who knew what strange oddities they would find when they washed him?

The Pickle brother was as lifeless as Clayton, and I wondered if the pair of head thumps I had administered would be the end of him. At first, the blood on the pillow suggested an open wound, but Genevieve discovered it was only a lump of frozen blood melting out of his hair.

"Good news," said Genevieve after her investigation. "Neither man will need surgery." Both bullets that got through Clayton's fur went clean through his body. Someone must be looking out for the guy.

That was unlikely. Sure, Clayton was a survivor of sorts—the amount of liquid he took each night would drown most men. And the wounds would likely be infected. Who knew what matter of filth the bullets brought with them as they pierced through his furs? And once infection got into the bloodstream, there was little medical science could do.

"You need to rest, Gus," Genevieve said. "And, Peter, you too." I wasn't going to argue with her, but there was still something I needed to do.

Through the snow drifts, I marched the mile to the detachment. I checked on Benjamin quickly, only to receive a shake of the head. No replies from the telegraph. And therefore, no reinforcements.

Inside the detachment, I pulled two sets of handcuffs from their hooks on the back wall. Then, one more long walk before I locked the Pickle brother's hand to his bed rail in case he woke. I could not sleep if I knew Genevieve or Dr. Moody were in danger. The other pair of handcuffs I used on Clayton. While he was not guilty of any crime, I was confident he would get better treatment if we restrained him. The two men's beds were as far apart as the wardroom allowed. No matter how little I respected the man, Clayton did not deserve to be caught in the crossfire of a gunfight meant for me. I would do what I could to keep him safe.

Genevieve looked pensive as she watched the two men sleep.

"You okay?" I asked her.

She pursed her lips. "We can talk about this tomorrow, Gus. But I'm worried about you."

"Me, why?" Despite being tired, I was the only one who came out of the shootout, still standing on my feet.

"You know why?" she replied.

I had confided in her—one sleepless night when it was only the two of us. She didn't know everything about my nervous attacks, but she knew enough.

Duffy rolled and let out an enormous snore.

I passed Genevieve the key to the handcuffs. "I'll be back first thing in the morning. Sleep if you can."

She nodded, and I pushed on the door to the vestibule. Should I stay? I looked back and saw Duffy in his bed. Peter was in the cot beside him, also asleep. It would be fine. Genevieve gave me a nod, and I left.

When I got to my bed, I was too tired to remove

anything but my boots and winter gear. Lloyd George greeted me but not with his usual vigor. My head was still swirling, matched by the gusts of wind that rattled the walls and windows of the detachment. My mind kept returning to the girl in the woods and how she stood over me, how I panicked.

A girl as cold as that, to leave her brothers dead and dying like it was nothing? It gave me a lot to consider. Like, where would she go from here? There weren't many routes out of town. Should I keep to my word or make it known she was still a threat? Either way, there was regret at how I acted. With the promise I made.

I was too tired to knock the dog off the foot of my bed, its warm body resting across my feet. For a while, I struggled in and out of dreams, the night's panic mixed with the battlefield, clouded visions of men's faces, broken and shot through, and her shadowy figure lurking in the background. Waiting for me. Haunting. When I finally abandoned hopes of sleeping, my body settled, and I fell into a dark, dreamless slumber.

Chapter 2

Daniel's Deed

A hard crack woke me, the sound of metal dishware placed with assertion on the detachment's timeworn dining table. I'd left the door open in the night, and I struggled to my feet to peer out onto the lobby. Millie was there, her back turned toward me, as she fussed with our breakfast. Lloyd George stood nearby, watching her every move. I lifted my suspenders onto my shoulders, stepped out, and failed to suppress the sound of a tremendous yawn.

Our detachment was large for the number of people that lived there. It was built in 1917 in response to the rapid rise in population caused by the original silver find and the development of the mine. Its front facade faced north toward the waiting platform of the station house, the two buildings separated by the single-line railroad track that ran in between.

Inside, it was one large L-shaped room, with several smaller rooms taking space around the perimeter. From the front door, one could see the small sitting area, multipurpose dining table, two single-bedded jail cells, and the indoor privy entrance. Around the corner was the kitchen and larder, the door to the office, and a bedroom for the officer who would sleep there at night. Since there was only one constable present, these rooms became my own, as I was on call, day and night, for whatever problem arose in the town or surrounding ranches.

The job did not require much of me as yet. Sergeant Deacon ran the detachment since its opening, but he left the month before I came, leaving it unstaffed for a time. Deacon hoped to retire, still a Mountie in Chambers, or so Millie said. However, Command temporarily posted him in Prince Rupert because of his reputation as a strong man not to be trifled with. The mayor confided there was an unsavory element at the port that they hoped he'd eliminate.

Abandoned mining towns like Chambers were dotted all over British Columbia's interior. I understood my position here in Chambers was temporary and that headquarters would transfer me when the town lost the rest of its people or Sergeant Deacon returned. Whatever came first. Still, the population required general policing among all the other tasks I was assigned. Disagreements over land boundaries, mail delivery, gambling debts, and drunkenness were the central claims of my time.

"I didn't expect you to be here," I said to Millie as I leaned against the doorframe.

But still, Millie did not turn around to face me. "I can see that," she stated as she banged her wooden spoon on the side of the egg pan. "You must have had quite the night."

Ah! So that was it then. She imagined me on some sort of bender, carousing with the locals. I knew how far her imagination could travel.

She turned and gave me her coldest glare. "Can you eat?" she asked. "Or are you unsettled?"

I gave her my most impish smile and patted my belly. "All is good here," I said and sat at the table to await what she had prepared. I was, in fact, quite hungry from all the night's exertions. So I was pretty happy to find a whole mess of bacon, eggs, and toast placed before me, even if it came with a side order of feminine contempt. Lloyd George sat upright on the floor beside me. Someone must have taught the beast that part of its job was guarding me while I ate breakfast. I slipped him one tiny piece of bacon to keep him hopeful.

When I first met Millie, she had been a tall, spindly thing, but in our short time together, she had blossomed into a form some men may have called pretty. She had long brown hair of an unestimated length tied into a frizzy bun in the middle of her crown. Her expressive brown eyes worked with a pair of heavy brows to suggest all manners of shock, delight, and dismay. As a worker, she was punctual and meticulous in her cleaning. And she had a definite talent for cooking that gave her much pride and me a full belly. However, she was often distracted by conversations, even one-sided ones, where she would fill the roles of dramatic gossip and exuberant listener. It was understandable why one might create fantasies to relieve the boredom from the dull Canadian bush. But I preferred if she did so at home with her mother and brother. That said, her work greatly benefited the detachment, and I was optimistic she would continue to grow past her immature foibles and inconsistencies.

And in that buoyant spirit, I was going to ask for more eggs when the front door flew open with a bang, bringing with it blustery tendrils of snow and wind. In amongst them, clouded by the gusts, was the manful figure of the mayor, wrapped in his oilskin coat and elaborate camel hair scarf. He moved as fast as he could to close the door behind him. Finally achieving that end, he stamped his feet on our mat and began to de-layer—hanging his overlarge Stetson hat and cloak on the hooks by the door, all without a word or a glance.

Tom Fox had been elected mayor in the early days. He had come with the miners already with enough capital to build the hotel that stood as the only three-story building on the boardwalk—the centerpiece of what we all called the new town. According to Millie, his aggressive manner had irritated the bigwigs of the Grand Trunk Pacific railway, prompting them to build the town's station next to our detachment instead of across from his hotel and the town's other amenities. Since he had already purchased the land, he built the building on the boardwalk a full mile from the railroad platform. Still, his establishment had been a successful operation when the mine was booming, and he remained confident the town would flourish once again.

Now half-undressed, he took a long look around the detachment. "Millie," he exclaimed, "I'm surprised to see you here so early in the morning. And in the middle of a storm, no less. Shouldn't you be taking care of your mother?" The insinuation was obvious. Many of the townspeople had already put us two together—a young Mountie spending his time with a young lady of marriageable age. I wouldn't put it past Millie or her mother to fan those flames themselves.

"I'll have you know my mother was fine when I left her this morning. Besides, my brother Jeremy is with her." Her face had gone beet red, either with anger or embarrassment. "It takes a lot more than a little storm to stop a Norton woman," she continued before she turned on her heels and returned to the stovetop.

The mayor was all smiles as he came to sit across

from me at the table. He was a debonair fellow and loved to show off his trinkets. He often brushed his mustache only to show off his fancy new wristwatch.

"Well," he began, "it seems like we have a hero on our hands."

He shot me a coy look, one eyebrow raised as if I was some young scamp holding onto a secret. "I went by the hospital to visit our two unfortunate patients. Matti Larsen came by this morning and told me what had happened. That Pickle boy is in bad shape. You must have hit him hard." He leaned back in his chair, and for a moment, I thought he might put his feet on the table. Instead, he rubbed his hands together. "Okay, let's have it then." There was a real sense of excitement in his voice. "Give us the whole story."

I took a couple more bites as Millie refilled my coffee cup without offering one to the mayor. Then I wiped off my mouth and considered where I should begin. And end.

The mayor had always treated me as something of a rube, even though I was born in the city of Winnipeg and had traveled to England and France in the war. My posting in the small town of Chambers was the choice of headquarters, while his presence in the backwoods was of his own free will.

I opened my mouth to begin, then snapped it shut. How would the mayor react to certain events in my story? He was a smooth customer, but I knew some of his tells. He was drumming his fingers on the side of one leg. Nervous? I'm sure he knew much more about this town than I did. And possibly the Pickle brothers.

And he and Clayton were not exactly friends. Fox had thrown him out of his hotel's ballroom more than once, always for a good reason. But I had also seen the two men argue in the street. Fox had called him a *parasite* and a *reprobate* and made a move to hit the man. And yet, there was no change in the mayor's expression when I introduced Clayton as my story's central character. I wondered if Fox had already questioned Clayton at the hospital. I doubted that would have been a polite exchange of words. Poor Genevieve.

My retelling began with my neighbor Bernard's frantic knocking on my windows and door. I spent some time describing Clayton's conduct outside The Hole, and the men who held him back from going into the bush. From there, I narrated our walk in the woods, Clayton's entry into the glade, and the skirmish that followed.

Only then did I notice Millie. She stood over me, her mouth agape, the coffee pot clutched in her hand. I used my foot to nudge the chair at the end of the table and nodded for her to sit. She complied, still with a look of absolute shock on her face. I had to tap the top of my aluminum mug to get her to pour.

Here, I was a little more careful in my telling. A man had died, and two others were injured, and I didn't want either of my listeners to lose sight of that fact in favor of some conjured fantasy of heroism. I omitted the girl with the handkerchief. Instead, I skipped ahead to my return home and the search for help.

"I could find no hide or hair of you," I told the mayor. "I yelled and beat on your door till my fist was sore. Where were you last night?"

The mayor flashed one of his brighter smiles, mainly at Millie. "I am blessed to be a heavy sleeper. Perhaps it is because I have an easy conscience."

I doubted that for some reason.

"Please, continue, Constable."

I scanned his face, but he was resolute and eager to listen to the end of my tale, so I pushed on. I ended by explaining Genevieve's and the doctor's prognosis for the two injured men.

As I finished, the wind rose, and we all sat and listened to its howl against the detachment windows. Each in our thoughts. I took the moment to take the last bites of my breakfast, slipping one more bit of bacon to the dog. Even so, my stomach still felt empty inside.

The mayor spoke first. "So you stopped in at Benjamin's and sent off a telegraph?"

I nodded.

"Good boy! Though I doubt anything got through with the storm," he asserted.

Good boy? Really?

Fox leaned back in his chair and made a show of plunking one foot after the other on the table. I turned to Millie, who scowled back at me.

"It looks like we won't be needing any help, though." He then pinched and rubbed his chin. "No, Constable Albright," he continued, "I don't see any more coming of this. You did a fine job." His grin suggested he saw my actions as his success, as if I were his student or one of his progeny. If he could reach over and tousle my hair, he would have.

Millie grabbed my wrist. "You could have been killed, Gus," she said, the melodrama oozing from each syllable. Then she narrowed her eyes and swept one arm forward to admonish the mayor for his table manners. He yanked his legs back, losing his balance for a tricky moment before he caught himself.

"And what about the girl?" she asked. "Where is she

now?"

"Well, that's easy!" replied the mayor as he reached across the table to lift my cup of coffee to his lips. "She was just a distraction, Millie. A way of getting our poor constable out of the town so those boys could ambush him."

Millie shook her head. "But where is she? There's a blizzard outside. We need to find her. Unless you think she is…a ghost?"

All I went through, and Millie was still considering the fantastical. I cleared my throat, trying to take on the voice of authority. "I wondered the same, Millie. I too am worried about the possibility of this girl being out in the storm." I gave her my most challenging stare. "She's not a ghost, though. You can get that out of your mind. I'm expecting that when our sleeping Pickle brother awakens, he will give us some idea about her."

The thought of the mayor and Clayton together this morning filled me with unease. Why did he go to the hospital when he should have come to me first? I rubbed my thigh through my pant leg. If I was lucky, neither patient was awake when the mayor visited.

The mayor slapped his hands on the table to signify he was about to leave. As he stood, he reached forward and grabbed my shoulder, giving it a shake and then a series of pats. "When this storm blows over, we will have to have a celebration for our hero, Constable Augustus Albright." He walked to the door and began to dress. "Until then, there isn't much to do. We'll have to go dig that other body out of the snow of course. We'll get a group together to do it. And hopefully, the other brother will wake soon and tell us what brought them to us. When the trains get running, we can ship them off to the city to be tried." They would go to Prince Rupert, which had a full court and accompanying jail cells.

I met him at the door, ready to close it behind him to not let in the snow. "I'll be heading over to the hospital to check on Genevieve and Doctor Moody, and of course, I'll go by the station to see if Benjamin has received any response," I reported. I had other ideas of what to do, but I didn't think he needed to know all my possible actions.

As he stuck on his hat, I realized there were a couple more things I wanted to ask him.

"Did you know these Pickle brothers, Tom?

He pursed his lips and then shook his head. "I remember hearing something about them a while back. One of your boys killed their pappy, didn't they? Bad sorts, I would imagine."

"And how about Clayton?"

"How about him?"

"Do you have something against Clayton?"

He laughed. "Who doesn't? I don't think he has a single friend. You and he don't see eye to eye." That was true.

But there was something there underneath Fox's pomp. A guardedness. "What's your beef with him anyway?" I asked.

"Let's just say Clayton and I have a history. You know what he's like."

"A history? So you knew him before he came here."

Fox stepped back. "Only a bit. You don't need to know Clayton for long to know what type of man he is. I'll deal with him. We ought to get him to the hospital on the next train."

"I'll want to talk to him first. I need to ask him how

46

he knew it was the Pickle brothers."

The mayor grabbed my arm as he pulled open the door. "Take a rest, lad. Enjoy your time here." The insinuation was obvious and did not need the wink that followed it. Millie would be livid. But the mayor was gone, and I was the one left to hear her grumbling.

****

Redressed in a clean shirt and an ironed pair of pants, I ran across the short path to the station. Benjamin was still at his post. Say what you wanted about the man's haughtiness; he was committed to the job. Had he even slept? There were no visible signs of fatigue on his face.

He placed a book face down on his desk as I came in. By the fold in the spine, he was halfway through the novel. On the cover, there was a man in a coonskin cap dragging a woman behind him, his rifle resting on his shoulder.

"Any good?" I asked, tapping the top of the book with my finger. I was always looking for a good distraction. There were some nights at the detachment that felt endless.

"It's not bad," he said, turning it around to show me the cover. "I always like a good Western." He grinned. His mustache needed a trim. "You can borrow it when I'm done."

The station room was quieter than the detachment. Better windows, I would expect. The storm here was more remote, like I was just an observer, not inside the brunt of it. The building was almost new. I caught the scent of the wood stain and the liberal paint coatings. Millie came here occasionally to clean, though she, too, found the station master to be fussy.

Nevertheless, you could spot the pride she had taken in her work. Except for the slush I had pulled inside, the place was spotless. It helped there had only been a handful of visitors in the last few months.

"So it's all quiet? No word?" I asked.

He gave me a dismissive wave of his hand. He had begun reading as I looked away. The book's contents, I'm sure, were far more engrossing than anything I might have to say.

"Do you have any idea how long this is going to last?"

He peered over the front cover. "Well, I'd say this one caught them by surprise. Rain was reported at Prince Rupert. But it's always raining there. Usually, there's nothing left by the time it makes its way over the mountains. So I can't say…only that it was unexpected." He chewed his top lip, bringing the lower part of his mustache into his mouth.

"No trains are out there, though." I was looking out the windows at the tracks. I turned back in time to see an odd expression on the man's face. In the glow of his desk lamp, his features appeared frozen, his eyes vacuous.

"No," he finally said and shook his head. "There never is at night. Too dangerous. And, of course, they would have stopped all trains leaving this morning since the lines were down."

I ignored him and walked over to the window to look at the storm. To the east was the city of Prince George, three hundred miles past the ends of the mountain over rough and varied terrain. And then onward through Edmonton and back to my hometown of Winnipeg, a straight shot through an endless vista of uninterrupted prairie land. Between there and here, there were more than a thousand miles of track looked after by these station men. A whole system of rail joined our dying town with anywhere that mattered, east or south— the whole world at our doorsteps.

To the west lay the other half of the world. The track ran a hundred miles, adjacent to the Skeena River, a straight shot through the towering mountains to the other Prince—Prince Rupert. Built on an island on the edge of the Pacific, the dream was it would be British Columbia's next great port, rivaling Vancouver to the South—a gateway to the Orient and all its riches.

Two Princes, twins, both born less than fifteen years ago from the same now-deceased father, the Grand Trunk Pacific Railway. The port needed a railway to take the goods into the interior. And the prairie city needed the railway to take its grain to the Pacific. In the end, it proved an absolute folly. It didn't help that its visionary Charles Melville Hays had perished on the Titanic in 1912. Nor that the Great War devalued real estate prices and shifted demand. No, the truth was soon after its conception, it had already proven to be a misguided fantasy. Despite riots, cost overruns, and legal wranglings, they had forced the rail line through at enormous expense, an inconceivable sum of one hundred million dollars for the mountain section alone. By 1920, the venture was bankrupt, and the CNR took over the whole system. And with this failure, so too died the dream of a northern rail line and its promise to further connect Canada to the Alaskan panhandle, the Orient, and even the Panama Canal.

I shook my head, imagining it. All those men who had come through here to make it possible. The Grand Trunk had threatened to bring in fifty thousand Japanese to do the work, but in the end, they had to settle with the Irish and Italians. Often it was dangerous work, building bridges and blasting rock the whole length of the Skeena River from Prince Rupert to Hazleton. They brought in five steamboats to handle the construction. But the energy of it had vanished. The workers went to other jobs or the battlegrounds of France.

It was a wonder the mayor kept his faith. For him, this was all a brief intermission. He would double the track and have the ferries going in the winter. Of course, none of it mattered in a snowstorm. Everything was hunkered down and silent as if the world didn't even know we were here.

"Well…" I said, stifling a yawn. "I guess I will leave you to it. Let me know when you hear something."

"Will do," he answered.

Typically, part of Mr. Benjamin's job was to shovel the siding. The extra track beside the main rail that a train pulled into to let another one pass in the opposite direction. They built it here so the pit train from the mine could add its cars to an outgoing freight locomotive. Now it sat silent. It still had some importance as the last siding before Prince Rupert, but it was likely the plans for a siding in the neighboring timber town of Plateau would make Chambers redundant. I had seen him cleaning it from a smaller dump last week, but now he appeared determined to ignore it. I was glad he was so committed to my order to listen in on the telegraph. At last, the man was seeing me with respect. Still, he didn't acknowledge me when I tipped my hat and raised my fur coat to head out into the chill.

****

Back outside, the storm gave no indication it was on

its way past us. My coat's brown and gray color was soon lost by the whiteness inflicted on it as I returned past the fine buildings on the boardwalk to their older, more dilapidated cousins by the river. Not that I could see too far in any direction, but the whole place appeared deserted. Everyone else was smart enough to shelter inside until the storm blew over. I pictured people keeping themselves warm at their stoves, chimneys, or maybe even in their beds. Which is where I would have chosen to be.

The door was not locked when I entered the front door of the hospital building. I took time to stamp off the thick slush on my boots and then slapped my arms and legs with my hat and gloves so the snow wouldn't melt into my clothes. This process served a dual function as it often was the customary way of announcing your presence in the wintertime. Sure enough, Genevieve opened the inner door to invite me inside.

It took some time for me to get used to Dr. Moody's tiny hospital. Though it rarely had any patients, the layout of its only ward often brought back traumatic memories. Besides my time as a stretcher bearer in 1915, it reminded me of the three long months I had spent in Birmingham recovering from the Spanish flu before finally being shipped home in 1919. Three-and-a-half long years, too much of it in war-torn France, and I had escaped without illness or injury only to be brought to a sick bed in times of victory. My lungs were not yet fully recovered—one last souvenir from the war.

It's not like I liked hospitals much before that. It was my experience that nurses were the one good thing to find there. But I hadn't noticed the smell until that prolonged stay—a mixture of antiseptic, bodily fluids, and despair. I could feel my heart beating faster as I followed Genevieve past the empty bunks to where we had laid our two patients.

Genevieve did not look well, her face gray and haggard, and I stopped her before she could take the final steps to Clayton's bed. "You need some sleep."

"It's all right," she assured me. "Margaret has come, and she can take care of things so I can get some rest. Kenneth should be stirring soon as well." I pursed my lips and nodded. Genevieve had such sympathetic eyes—the kind a patient might like to see at his worst.

A strong friendship had developed between Genevieve, Kenneth, and me but as the doctor diminished, more often we became partners in his care. I made it a practice to visit at least once or twice a week for a game of cards in the living quarters attached to the hospital's westward face. And Genevieve often asked me for various favors when Dr. Moody was unwell. Twice, I found the man outside when he wandered off in one of his confused moments.

"I heard the mayor came by this morning," I said.

"It was quite the honor," Genevieve replied.

"So did he talk to either of them?"

"Only if he found them in their dreams. He wasn't here for more than a minute. The busy life of a mayor. I'm not quite sure how he does it."

Genevieve was a quiet woman, often saying words only when it mattered to do so. Though, like many who had been in the theater of war, she had developed a dry sense of humor that could catch you unaware. She was a kind and caring woman but also undeniably strong. What she had battled through, including Kenneth's recent infirmity, would have left me weak and whimpering.

"How are our patients?" I asked, surprised that Clayton was so quiet.

"Well," she huffed, "after you left, we had quite the time getting Clayton washed and bandaged. We are worried about his wounds becoming infected. He is not the cleanest of souls, as I'm sure you know." She pulled a curtain away to reveal the man lying asleep, his mouth round and open, a dark cavern set within his hairy face.

"But the real problem," continued Genevieve, stepping around the bed to inspect the man, "was that he woke as we were trying to dress the wounds. He was not happy being handcuffed or dressed in his gown. And he was in some considerable pain." She shook her head and then looked at me with wide eyes. "The things he said will not leave my memory too soon. Such profanity! And you know I lived in France!"

I smiled at her. I was all too familiar with Clayton's character. "But…he seems to be resting well right now," I stated, still surprised at how small his form was under the sheets.

"Yes, well. I convinced the doctor to give him a dose of morphine about an hour ago." She glanced at her watch. "Kenneth does not like the stuff. He keeps only a little of it around. He's had problems before, you know, with other patients getting addicted to it. But Clayton…" she paused for effect, gesticulating with her hands as she did so. "He needed a little help to calm himself."

I sighed. "I was hoping to interview the man. But it will have to wait." I looked back at her. My night was rough, but hers was no better. "I'll come back later. I would imagine the plan is to move him on to a bigger town for…" I didn't want to suggest that she and Dr. Moody weren't capable. But she was ahead of me.

"Yes, indeed," she concurred as she walked me over to our second patient. "Both of these men need more care than what we can offer." She stopped momentarily and took a deep breath before continuing to walk. I wondered if she was about to cry, but instead, she twisted on her feet to face me.

"I need to let you know that this poor soul may not recover." We stared at each other for a moment as the meaning sunk in. I may have killed two men last night, two brothers from the same family. I had not given myself a chance to think that through. There would probably be some sleepless nights ahead.

I caught the whiff of perfume, and Margaret came into the room smiling. She was young, not more than sixteen, with a cheerful disposition, which seemed quite out of place compared to the topic that Genevieve and I had been discussing. The smile on the girl's face and the bounce in her step were enough to break the spell.

Genevieve nodded. "I'm off to sleep, now then." But she did not move. Instead, she took my hand, her own so soft and small that it fit in my palm. "You be careful now. Don't go searching for that other body out in this storm." Those sympathetic eyes were wide, not blinking, and I could feel a lump form in my throat.

"I won't," I said before stuttering, "I mean...I will...I will be careful." We both heard Margaret giggle, and we broke away, Genevieve turning on her heel to leave.

For a moment, I stood there, my thoughts moving in a dozen different directions. Clayton gave off a loud sucking snore, and I turned to face him to find Margaret sitting in a chair beside him.

"Constable," she said with a smile stretched across

her face.

"Margaret," I returned the greeting.

"We are going to have to shave his beard, you know?"

I was confused.

"Clayton," she continued with a pretty scowl. "Dr. Moody says he has lice and all sorts of things in there. I thought we should do it while he slept, but the doctor said that was disrespectful…to shave another man's beard without asking him first. Though, the doctor won't give him any choice in the matter. He says it has to come off." She inspected it with her fingers, unbothered by its filthiness, a sign she could be a good nurse after all.

"Anyway," she sent me another ray of sunshine, "you should come back later. I expect we all might learn some new words." Her comment caught me off guard, and I couldn't help but give out a small chuckle.

Behind her, through the frosted window, I saw the snow moving sideways in deep gusts, and I considered picking a bed and having a mid-morning nap until Clayton finally woke. But there was no other way around it. I needed to jot down some thoughts for the report I would have to write. To figure out what details I should include for headquarters and what they might like to know.

But did I have all the pieces yet? Most assuredly, I did not. I turned to Margaret. "Did you find anything in their pockets?"

"We sure did!" Margaret flitted across the room. She returned from the shelf, holding a cardboard box out to me. I took the box and sat on the bed. But before I could examine the contents, Margaret perched herself on the edge of the bed and pulled out a folded sheet of paper.

"It's mostly Clayton's stuff," she said. "This was the only thing in the unconscious man's pocket."

She unfolded the note and passed it to me. I was surprised to find it was a signed will. Assuming he had not taken it from his brother, this man's name was Daniel A. Pickle. His signature was a messy scrawl, but his name was typed out underneath. The paper was crisp and white, and the typeset was neat and defined. It was notarized by Mr. Amadeo Ricci Esq. and signed last year in November in Prince Rupert.

"What is it?" asked Margaret

I ignored her as I scanned the paper front and back. Why would a man like Daniel Pickle possess such a meticulous document? Most of the paper was filled with legal jargon; however, there were critical details about the man's burial, his chosen inheritors, and his estate. The total value was two hundred sixty-four dollars, held in a safety deposit box at the Union Bank in New Hazelton. He named his brother Kaden M. Pickle and a woman, Catherine McGraw, as co-executors and the co-recipients of his estate. The woman's relationship was undefined, but the note listed an address in Prince Rupert. I never heard her name before. Could she be the mystery girl who held me at gunpoint?

"Is it a will?" Margaret whispered.

I nodded. "When I was in France, most soldiers carried around a will with them. There were empty pages in our Army Paybooks with instructions about how to make a legal statement. You were supposed to carry them around with you at all times because they used our paybooks to identify you if you were wounded or dead."

I didn't mention that you didn't do so when engaged in a trench run or another dangerous mission where your body was liable to be recovered by the enemy. In these cases, soldiers were to leave their paybooks behind, knowing that their superior officers would relay the information to their families if they didn't return.

"But I don't think these brothers went to war," I said. "So why would Daniel Pickle go to the expense of getting such an official letter with the signature of a proper notary?"

"That's a lot of money," said Margaret, pointing at the sum on the page. She was correct; two hundred forty-six dollars was substantial. It would pay for the man's funeral and still leave behind a handsome nest egg. The government would not release the funds if the inheritor were an accessory to a crime. Of course, if this Catherine McGraw were the girl in the woods, I would have to prove she was in on it.

I pushed my lips together and looked into Margaret's face to see if she had more to add. But she stared back at me, her eyes wide with delight. I set the opened paper on the bed and pulled the box toward me. In it were the contents of Clayton's many pockets: a pipe, some chaw, a pocket knife, a three-inch blade that may have once been a kitchen knife, three soiled handkerchiefs, a bottle top, an apple core (not sure why Margaret and Genevieve had decided to keep this), a piece of whittled wood, four quarters equaling a dollar, a broken whistle and a bit of flint rock. Plus, an oil-stained envelope with no words of origin. Just the printed name "Clayton."

"Well, are you going to open it?" Margaret asked. She was sitting now at the edge of the bed, gripping the belt of her dress in her fist. Poor girl—like myself, I'm sure she found the winter months in Chambers a dreadful bore. But I shook my head and placed the envelope back in the box.

"No," I said, "this is Clayton's business." If I needed to know more about him, I would ask him first. When or if he got out of the hospital, his cabin would be a short walk away. Besides, I did not need to know every secret of the man's life.

As for the rest of the objects, the dollar in coins was the only compelling item. Clayton didn't strike me as a saver. His thirst was too stubborn to be quenched. This cache would be a recent gain, then. Sometimes money pointed you in a direction, and sometimes it didn't.

Margaret stood while I placed everything back in the box. I was sure she had a thousand questions for me, but I didn't let her ask them. "You keep this safe," I told her. "I may be back for it. If you don't mind, write a list of what's there so no one can say that something's been stolen."

"Genevieve's already done that," she said smartly. You would have guessed we were at a carnival for the amount the girl smiled.

Genevieve's forethought didn't surprise me. I don't think I've ever met someone with more common sense.

I said goodbye to Margaret and promised to return in the afternoon; then, I went back into the anteroom to prepare my clothing for the freezing walk back to the detachment. Already, I could feel the cold from the openings around the doorframe. I decided to run the distance to the detachment. The warmth of my office and Millie's coffee—two good reasons to make the journey short.

****

After the first step, I knew my plan was impossible.

The wind was driving at me, lashing my face with sharp ice crystals. Each step was labored like I was wading through a rushing stream. I sucked the cold air deep into my delicate lungs, attempting to get a sustaining breath. It felt like I could freeze from the inside out.

Pushing onward, I saw a slender figure leaning against Peter Stormcrow's sawmill. The biting wind blew a screen of snow between us. Friend or foe, I could not tell. My pistol lay in my holster underneath my furs, and I pushed my hand between my buttons to find it. If it was her, I was unprepared. But as she stepped forward, I saw it was a familiar face. Bea Brannon. She waved me over.

"How's Peter?" I shouted over the wind.

"Asleep."

"Good." Even though I enjoyed Millie's breakfast, I regretted that she woke me with her preparations.

Bea took me by the arm. "C'mon," she said, "I'm buying you a drink." I wasn't sure if that was a good idea, but Bea was committed. She was tall for a woman, all arms and legs. She wore a gray coat covering her neck to feet, only revealing her long black hair and her weathered face. Bea spent most of her time outdoors, walking.

Like Peter and Duffy, Bea was a late arrival. She appeared at the detachment door in late summer, one of the few people disembarking at our station. It was a rarity to find a woman living as rough as she did, but this was the West, and no law said she needed a man or a place of lodging. That didn't stop me from worrying about her, though. Men were, on the whole, desperate for female attention, and Chambers was a desperate sort of town.

And yet, she did not report any troubles. Often, she

came to the detachment to ask me questions about the area. While I knew little history, I was pleased to show her the detachment's maps and find some information about the mine. For her part, Millie was delighted to impart her local knowledge, that is to say, *gossip*, and even in this, Beatrice was an eager listener. But I could never put my finger on why she was here. Perhaps she was writing a book—one of those romances ladies devoured. If so, I hoped I wouldn't be a character in it.

Otherwise, Peter was Bea's only friend. The two had a strange sort of relationship. They were close but not in a romantic way. Other than me and Duffy, they kept pretty much to themselves. So, it was not a peculiar sight to find her here leaning against the sawmill wall. She must have been waiting for me to pass by.

Bea hauled me over to the saloon on the edge of the boardwalk. It had never gained a name beyond *The Saloon*. The place should have been closed, but the door swung wide open when Bea pushed the handle. She pulled me over to a table in the corner and sat me on a cedar bench. I watched the storm out of the greasy window, blasts of snow washed against the pane with a rapping sound as if something was unhappy with me looking.

Bea went in the back to find someone to serve us. When that didn't work, she poured our drinks herself, two whiskeys, then left money on the bar top. I wondered if she would have helped herself for free if I wasn't with her.

"So what did Peter tell you?" I asked when she sat.

"Enough to know why you look like that," she replied. My reflection in the mirror did cast a less-than-crisp appearance.

"You boys were gone a long time," she continued. "If Peter woke me, I would have come with you."

The drink caught me in the back of the throat, and I coughed. Bea often stayed at Peter's place, sometimes for a week or more. It would be more of a scandal if we weren't all living in the bush. Millie was happy enough to talk with Bea when she came to the detachment, but I knew she was often shocked by Bea's chosen lifestyle. At one point, she even suggested that Bea might be one of those women who enjoyed the company of other ladies. I did my best to ignore the suggestion. I would wait for Bea to reveal her secrets when and if she pleased.

"How are you feeling?" she asked. She took a gentle sip of her whiskey. "It means a lot to shoot another man. Even more to kill one."

I nodded. "I can't figure it out yet. It all went so fast." I paused and considered the series of events. For now, it was all disjointed images. Flashes of panicked memory I didn't want to revisit. The bullet hitting the man's face, the sickening crunch of the rock, Clayton rushing the clearing. I shook my head and realized I was still wearing my warm winter hat. I took it off and drank some whiskey, allowing its warmth to gather in my throat.

"Last night was a blur. I'm not sure my brain has had time to work on it yet," I said finally.

Bea unbuttoned her coat. She was wearing a denim shirt underneath and, below that, a necklace. Her face wore a pinched expression. She wanted to tell me something. She took a breath. "Those Pickle brothers," said Bea, "I think I might have seen them beforehand."

I straightened in my seat. "All right," I said, waiting

for her to tell me more.

"Now, I can't be sure, but there were two men camping a couple miles north of here." She pointed off in the distance, beyond the rail line. "I kind of happened on them in the course of a walk. They were as shocked as I was when I broke through some brush and came upon their fire."

To the north, she said. What was in that direction? The pit rail, the mine, the Chambers Lodge, and behind them all, the grand curves of the mountains. Besides that, there were rocks, bushes, and trees for all I knew. And now lots of snow, of course. "What were you doing there?" I asked her.

"It's more like, what were they doing?" she responded. "That's an odd place to camp. It's not on the way to anywhere. And it's so close to town. Why wouldn't you get a place at the hotel? God knows it would be cheap. No one else is staying there." She pointed her thumb to the window, "There wasn't all this snow, but it was only a week ago, so it was cold."

I shrugged. What I knew of the Pickle brothers didn't make them sound too friendly. But I'd not heard they were hiding from something. They were ne'er-do-wells for sure, but to my knowledge, there were no outstanding warrants, and their dad's problems had died when the Mounties killed him in a shoot-out—the *sins of the Father* and all that. Still, I wish Bea had told me straight away. I would have been wary if I knew those men were in town.

"Were there just the two of them?" I prompted, thinking about my ghost girl.

"There were just the two. But they didn't invite me to stay, and I was quite sure I was leaving. They looked like a nasty pair. Rough and ragged. I believe they followed me for a bit, but I cut over to the rail line and was in town before them. If you like, I could go over to the hospital and identify them."

That was a good idea.

How long were the Pickle brothers camping there, and why didn't they show themselves in town? And if Bea came across them, did anyone else encounter these brutes?

"Why did you think the two men were the Pickle brothers?" I asked her.

"Do you want another one?" she replied, but my shot glass was still almost as full as when she poured it. I shook my head and gave her my best stare.

"I think I've come across them before."

"Go on," I prompted. Did I need to treat her like a suspect?

"I've been all around doing," she paused, "what I do. They like to gamble those two, and I may have taken some money off them at one point." There was pride in her smile. Gambling was illegal, but that was far down my list of concerns. Yet it did explain some of her caginess.

I took another sip of the whiskey. I should be getting back to start my report. "When are you going to tell me what your work is?" I asked her. I knew Peter and her had something cooking. I just hoped it was above board. For the first time, I wondered if it was some secret gambling ring. But I couldn't see Peter getting involved in something like that.

"It's nothing to do with this," she replied. "And it's private."

I nodded and finished my whiskey in one gulp. She

smiled at me like she was my mother and I was a good boy. I wasn't looking forward to going outside, but ever since she mentioned Peter's nap, I felt I deserved one.

But while I had her, there was more I needed to ask. "Where were you last night?"

"What do you mean?"

"I didn't see you at Peter's."

"I was there." She smiled. "I was sleeping upstairs. I was pretty sore at Peter and Duffy for not waking me. I would have gone out with you if they had asked."

I watched her finish her own whiskey before I asked. "Do you live at the sawmill now, Beatrice?"

She laughed, almost a giggle. More feminine than I expected. "Well, no, I have my own place. My things are at Morrison's lodge on the river."

I wasn't sure what that meant. I never heard anyone mention the name Morrison. He may have been a miner who had moved away or some other merchant or rancher who fled when the money stopped running into the town.

She must have seen the confused look on my face. "It isn't much," she said. "I would have to fix a few things to make it worth living there longer. But with everything going sideways around here, I don't expect I'll have to. This town is on its last legs, Gus. Soon, everybody will be searching for another place to live. That said, I'll have to invite you over sometime."

Was she flirting with me? I put that aside for now. The morning was getting long, and I would have to go and drag that body out of the woods. The thought of it made me shiver. As did the paperwork.

Both of us stood, and I thanked her for the drink. She mentioned going by the hospital again, and I told her I would drop into Peter's to find her in the afternoon.

But as we were leaving, Bea snuck behind the bar to put what was left of the bottle of whiskey back on the shelf. Then she took me by the arm to guide me outside. I took a quick peek over my shoulder to see if the money was still on the counter, just out of curiosity, but I couldn't quite make it out. Petty theft wasn't on my list of major concerns either.

We said our goodbyes in the swirling snow, and I watched her long form disappear toward the sawmill. And for a brief moment, I was alone in the world. I stood there in the cold, apart from anything and anyone. A cocoon of whiteness surrounded me, a slow whistling wind the only sound. The bliss of an empty mind came to me, but it did not last long.

Chapter 3

Stanley's Station

I lifted the collar of my coat and began my return walk to the detachment. As I stepped off the boardwalk of the new town, the visibility was such that I could not make out the stable yard, station, or detachment, which were clumped a full mile farther down the rail line. If I kept the river to my left and the tracks to the right, there was no possibility of getting lost.

I was about halfway between the town and the detachment when a strange sight confronted me. Something was moving beyond the station. The snow was so wild that I could not define its shape, but it was unconnected from the rail line. Its outline was at least twice my height, so it could not be a man. Could it see me? The threat of danger began to churn inside me, my chest heavy, as I tried to fill my lungs with air. There was a ragged furriness to it. A bear. But why would a bear be walking on its hind legs in a snowstorm?

Millie's stories came tumbling through my head—strange creatures of the forest—a bigfoot or yeti. She couldn't be right. Could she?

The figure moved closer, and I put my hand against my holster. My legs felt like lead, and the panic took me. I willed my legs to move, but they were frozen like the earth beneath me. My heart pumped madly against my ribs as a cold sweat ran from my armpits. Run, by blazes!

And then I got it. It was indeed a man. Riding forward, slow, on an immense horse. Cancel that. It was an immense man riding on a horse of proportionate size. He could see me now. He rode a few more paces forward and made a polished quarter turn, hailing me with a shout and the wave of his hand.

I could not make out his words, so I took a cautious step forward. What type of man would ride a horse through a blizzard?

"Who are you?" I yelled, my voice dying between the wafts of screaming wind.

The man crossed his legs and dismounted, still holding the horse's reins in his leather-gloved hands. That's when I knew what he was. The shape and fit of the gloves were too familiar.

"You're a Mountie," I shouted. The man was as tall as he was broad. He grabbed my outstretched hand and shook it, pointing off toward town.

"Where can I stable my horse?" he yelled into my ear, and I motioned for him to follow in the opposite direction.

I took him around the side of the detachment to the only other building across from the station, a low-lying stone structure that was the first property to be built in the region. The original family had moved away, and the Chambers family rebuilt it as a stable yard for the town. More than a half dozen horses lived inside, cared for by the two men employed there, Coot and his master, my late-night visitor Bernard.

I did not bother to rouse them. Instead, I lifted the large wooden bar that kept the main doors closed and then kept it open for the man to walk his horse inside.

Closing the door put us in a different world. Warm and cozy with the reassuring smell of horses and their simpler lives. This stable, so well kept, was my favorite place in Chambers. It reminded me of home, and Coot's quiet way added to its serenity.

As soon as I latched the door, the big man dismounted and offered me his hand. "Paul Stanley," he said, still merry despite his travels. "Constable Paul Stanley, that is. I almost forgot to say that."

I introduced myself, ignoring Coot for now, as he was already disassembling the large horse's saddle, patting and caressing it as he walked around the great beast.

"So obviously, my telegraph must have got through?" I asked.

"It did," said Stanley with a broad smile. He looked no worse for wear. I considered where he might have come from and how long it must have taken. "I was the one they could spare. I just arrived here two weeks ago at the Plateau detachment."

A recruit, then. The force was accepting a broad range of candidates as it tried to fill in its ranks. Constable Stanley must have been a recruiter's dream. There were men like him in the army—big men always with an entourage. Their followers hoped to borrow their strength as if they could be a safeguard from a bullet or machine gun. Most of these heavyweights accepted these roles as if they were ordained, their egos expanding with each fawning admirer. I understood the draw, but I always preferred being my own man. There were things out here that you had to learn by experience. Brute strength could not solve everything. I would be wary.

The irony was that the constable's size should have

kept him from becoming a Mountie. He was two inches taller and twenty pounds heavier than the regulations allowed. It was unhealthy for the horses to carry that extra weight. The recruiter must have looked the other way.

"How is Sergeant McClintock?" I asked. I met the officer on my way through. He seemed a gentle soul, but by Millie's reckoning, he was anathema to Sergeant Deacon. I don't know why. I always made it a point to hold nothing against a man until his actions justified my disapproval. Having never met Deacon, I couldn't say whether he held the same view.

Stanley smiled. "The man seems well. He sends his regards and was glad to hear that you were still in one piece. He and Constable Miller are trying to send telegrams to Hazleton, but this blasted storm overtook Plateau before I left."

I nodded. If the snow didn't diminish, the telegrams wouldn't help much. The fact that Stanley made it through was a stroke of good fortune. For the moment, at least, he looked like all the help Chambers would get.

"So there's three of you in Plateau now?" Command must have already decided that Plateau, not Chambers, would be the focus of growth inside the mountains. It made sense. Their sawmill operation had already put ours out of business. The timber trade was Plateau's, at least for now.

I could see by the look in Stanley's eyes that he was already trying to get the measure of me and his surroundings. There was a strange energy about him that was already beginning to irritate me. A playful sort of eagerness demonstrating his immaturity. He would need some grounding to help me through this mess.

"This is Coot," I told him. The boy had brought the horse to a stable and continued to groom him. "He and Bernard run the stable yards here. Your horse is in the best hands."

Stanley reached over the stall and shook Coot's hand. "They call her Pepper," he said as he nodded at the horse. "She has done good service this morning and deserves special treatment."

"Coot knows no other way," I said and saw the boy smile in his awkward way. From our first meeting, I felt a tenderness toward the boy. He was a mute, born with a harelip. He was quite a hummer, though, and often whispered in his horses' ears, though I was unsure if he used words or soothing sounds. Whichever, his temperament was well matched to his occupation.

"Follow me," I told Stanley. "We will get you some breakfast, and then we can talk," I said, moving us into the dwelling space attached to the stable yard. We walked through the messy kitchen and into a small sitting room where Bernard lay on the sofa he used for a bed. As I entered, he sighed, but when Constable Stanley strode through the doorway, his head inches from the room's wooden ceiling, Bernard sat up and became silent.

"Good to see you, Bernard," I said, though neither of us believed it. I never liked the way he treated Coot. In exchange for allowing the boy to work the stable yard, Mr. Bernard received a life of general leisure, lying in the back room for most of the day, sucking on cigars and drinking whiskey. There was nothing criminal in it, but it was clear the man was a parasite.

"This is Constable Stanley," I said, turning again to assess my colleague. "He is a new recruit," I decided to add, "and will be lodging a horse in the stable for a few days." I shrugged, "maybe more. Add it to the bill if you wouldn't mind." I was the only detachment member, but two detachment horses were stabled here, now three, counting Pepper. While the mine was running, the detail always retained either two or three men, each with their horse. But with Deacon busy in Prince Rupert and the mine closed, they neglected to fill the second human position but did not remove the horse.

"I'll add it," said Bernard, making no move to stand. "He's a big feller, ain't he?" he opined.

"Yes," said Stanley. "And he talks too." There was a brief silence. "It was nice to meet you, Mr. Bernard."

The man laughed. "What pretty manners," he smirked and opened the paper as a sign that the conversation was over. Leaving would have suited me fine. While the stable yard smelled of dried hay, wet wood, and horse manure, the odor in Bernard's lodging was more oppressive. And last night's rude awakening was still vexing me.

"Who told you to come find me last night?" I asked through the back pages of his newspaper.

He made a show of ruffling its sheets before giving me a cold stare. "That was Clayton. We were both at The Hole."

"Clayton?"

"Yes."

"Clayton asked you to go get me?"

"Well, maybe not Clayton; maybe it was some of the others who didn't want him to go off on his own."

I gave him a long stare. "Which is it then, Clayton or the others?"

Bernard's look was fierce. "I can't remember. I was

drunk then, and I'm hungover now."

He noisily shifted his weight on his sofa. "Why you, though?" I asked.

"Bah," blurted Bernard. "Leave me alone. Why ask me all these questions? I just wanted to be here sleeping in my bed, but I went to find you because Clayton was so shaken. You should be thanking me."

Did Bernard know about the shootout and the consequences of his actions? I noticed he did not mention the girl whose appearance had agitated Clayton. Would Bernard not have seen her if she was at The Hole? But this was not the time for those questions. I could feel the recruit Stanley peering over my shoulder, thinking, who knew what? So I nodded to the big man, and we worked our way back to the stable.

As he collected his things, I asked Stanley about his journey here. The man traveled light; a bedroll, rifle, small kit bag, and extra boots were the only things strapped to his mount.

"I left before the sun rose," he said. "As the weather was beginning to get rough. I was told to follow the train tracks, which was easy enough until the whiteout came." He shrugged, stepping back out into the stable yard. "Nevertheless, we made it here in one piece." He patted Pepper's neck as he passed by and thanked Coot, who was brushing the horse with a currycomb, entirely in his element.

"So you got our telegram?"

"Yes, something came through," replied Constable Stanley.

"What did the message say?" I asked.

"I don't know exactly. I didn't read it. McClintock told me to go, and I went."

"He didn't tell you there was a gunfight?"

"Yes, of course he mentioned that. Told me to be careful."

"Why didn't they send a message back?"

Stanley shrugged, "I think they did. Maybe it didn't make it through."

Did this all make sense? Mr. Benjamin said the telegraph failed when the snow first reached Chambers. He had tried to send a message to Prince Rupert to ask about weather conditions. Since the storm traveled eastward from the coast, it may have damaged the line in the direction of Prince Rupert early on. That means it would have been inoperable an hour or more before I returned to the detachment. Presumably, Benjamin was just trying to contact Prince Rupert before I made him send a message to Hazleton. And yet, there was no response. That said, I didn't wait long to hear one. Surely, Benjamin would have told me if he got a reply.

I realized we were both standing frozen at the door. I gave Stanley a long look. I was never good at telling if someone was lying, so I let it go. We both thanked Coot and walked back out into the snow.

****

When we got to the doorway of the detachment, I sensed what might happen next. I hoped to be pleasantly surprised.

I don't know how she knew, but she stood facing the doorway as the two of us blustered inside. As we removed our furry winter hats, I could tell she was drowning with excitement. Who, indeed, was this man that I brought with me through the door?

"This is Constable Paul Stanley," I told her flatly. I half expected her to give an elaborate curtsy. What we received instead was a barely contained giggle.

"Constable Stanley," I continued, "is a recruit." I let that part hang in the air for a moment. "He has just arrived from Plateau to reinforce us." Millie's eyes were so big I thought they might swallow the rest of her face. "Can you get the man something to eat?"

"All this way in a blizzard?" Mille gasped. I shook my head. Hadn't she chastised the mayor for suggesting the storm might impede her? Of how hardy Norton women were?

Stanley, to his credit, did not try to glamorize his actions. "Glad to be here," was all he said, and he removed his fur to reveal his red serge jacket underneath.

Lloyd George was on him now, sticking his nose where it didn't belong, readying himself to jump up and lick the man's face. I pushed him away with the sole of my boot. It was like these two had never seen a guest before.

"Millie," I tried again, "the man must be hungry. Do you have any breakfast to give him? Some eggs or oatmeal?"

She ignored me and took a step closer. "Will you be staying long, Constable Stanley?" she asked, her voice expectant.

He was not as broad now that his coat was off. I decided to keep mine on for a few moments longer. The Constable looked at me, but I didn't have an answer. "We'll find out," he told Millie and then added, "as long as you need me." It was clear Millie thought this was the perfect answer.

She began to speak again, but I interrupted. "Millie," I scolded her, "breakfast for the man, please." She shot me a sour look but finally shifted herself to the stove.

The two of us sat opposite, and I took a moment to consider the recruit. He had a full head of hair, all his teeth, a rock-hard jaw, but soft-looking eyes. There would be more than one woman in the town who would be interested in our new arrival. I would make sure this did not cause problems in getting the work done.

Millie came to the table and poured us both a cup of coffee, his cup first. "So," she started again, "where will you be having Constable Stanley sleep?"

"Either of the jail cells should work, I would think," I muttered, taking a long sip of coffee as I watched her reaction. She was, of course, appalled.

"No, Gus!" Millie always used my first name when she got angry. It was a bad habit she needed to correct. "You can't have him sleep there!" She looked around the room as if to find reinforcements for her argument.

I was about to further shock her by suggesting she could take him home, but Stanley answered before I said so.

"That would be fine with me," he said. "I've slept in worse places." I'm sure he had. At the very least, his training in Regina would have given him plenty of experience sleeping rough. But it made me consider how old he might be. And whether he had gone to war. There was already a division line between those who went over and those who never got the chance. The irony was that the former believed not going was a boon, while the latter often considered it a curse.

Millie stomped back to the stove. I was about to admonish her but instead took the high road, reminding myself of Millie's more useful features. Besides, adding Stanley to the detachment would mean more work for her, and with the shootout and the storm, I would need everyone's help.

Instead, I watched her as she fussed over the stove. I turned to Stanley, who was giving me the once-over. I lowered my brows to show him that a subordinate should not scrutinize a superior officer, but he did not shift his gaze.

"You had quite the night yesterday," Paul said. "Are you okay to talk about it?"

I shook my head. "We can talk about it later."

But Millie was having none of that and began to relate the events of the evening before I could stop her. Obviously, she would not get Paul's meal until she finished, but she was already exaggerating and adding incorrect details to my story. I directed her to stop and then began to relate the story's facts in an orderly manner, from one law officer to another.

Unfortunately, unlike the mayor, Paul did not know anything about Chambers. My retelling would make little sense without understanding the attitudes and relationships between the town's characters. And as I began filling in some of these more critical details, Millie took the opportunity to interject, offering details I missed. Or things I said she disagreed with. Or something I said she did agree with. Or exclamations to add excitement. All the while, she was serving and clearing Stanley's breakfast. When we got to the part where Constable Stanley arrived on the scene, it was getting close to my lunch.

Throughout this, Stanley listened with eager fascination, making all the right sounds and facial expressions to tell us that even the most minor facts were important. It was this eagerness that prompted Millie and I to keep explaining. I even learned some helpful tidbits from Millie's interjections, not vital facts but interesting bits of trivia she had stored somewhere in her head.

When Stanley took a little break, I helped Millie clean before collecting my notebook and pen from my desk. While the ideas were fresh, I decided to begin my report. Outside, the blizzard raged on and gave us little chance of returning to the woods to find and retrieve the body of the dead Pickle brother. Besides, Stanley needed some rest. I planned to introduce him to the mayor at the hotel before revisiting Clayton at the hospital.

Stanley, however, wanted to continue the conversation. He pulled over a chair and sat across from me at my desk.

"Chambers," he said. "Is the town named after William Chambers? The business tycoon?"

Lloyd George had chosen to sit by Stanley for the entire conversation. It was not surprising since the man was a little sloppy in his table manners. But now, with the food gone, he had fixed himself under the big man's chair as if that was always where he sat.

"Yes," I said, looking up from my writing. "He bought the mine with two other fellows, but he had the principal share. It's called the Chambers Mine, so it made sense to rename the place after him. It used to be called Preston, I believe. Right, Millie?"

Millie nodded. "Yes, but there were few people here. Most everybody came after nineteen-thirteen. And now most of them are gone." She was making some sandwiches: Ham and cheese.

"Chambers has a new claim near the border with the Yukon. His sons are now in the North." I added.

"I met Chambers in Toronto," he said. "I played ice hockey for St. Pat's for a year, and he was a part owner."

So Stanley was an Easterner. I wasn't surprised that a man his size might play sports and have the opportunity to move in larger circles than men like myself.

I watched Paul's face and saw his brow wrinkle. "He was what you might expect," he said, referring again to Chambers. "A proud man with a penchant for command. The type of man who couldn't be argued with. If he made a decision, he wouldn't concede even if it affected others in a negative way. A businessman through and through. He made out quite well during the war with his various enterprises. Did he ever come out here?"

"No," I said. "Not him. It was his three sons and another partner, Mr. Bryson, that ran the place."

"So, then the mine collapsed, and they all moved away."

"Not so quick as all that, but that's the essence of it. It was a major operation. At one point, they used an electric compressor to do some mechanized drilling. We have records here that show they were shipping about thirty thousand ounces of silver to the smelters in their heyday, but that amount plummeted in recent years. Finally, last year there was a flood, and the Chambers family expected it would be too expensive to fix the problem. So they all left, except for the one son, Philip, who still lives here at the lodge."

Millie turned and showed us her scrunched-up nose. "I never liked that one!" She brought the sandwich plate to the desk and stood behind my chair. "He was all swagger. Thought he could have any woman he wanted. And I heard he was rough with the workers, especially the Irish."

Then she stopped. She put a finger under her chin like she was trying hard to remember something. "But the accident changed him further. Not necessarily for the better, as Constable Albright here would know."

"Oh, yes?" queried Stanley. "You've had some dealings with him, have you?"

I leaned back in my chair and tried to remember the details. I met Philip Chambers only once, but it was recent. The excitement of the ambush made everything before it seem like a distant memory.

"Well, there was, as Millie mentioned, a bad accident at the mine," I said. "This was before my time here. What about two years ago?" I asked Millie.

"Yes, it was a bit more than two years. It was in the fall. I know because a cousin of mine had just got married in Prince George, and we finally got to take the train. It happened right after Mum, Jeremy, and I returned. I don't know the technical term, but it was a cave-in."

I remembered it as well. I was in Calgary, and the news made the paper. Mining accidents, unfortunately, were common, but this one injured twelve men, killing four of them. And one of the owner's sons had been wounded as well. Philip Chambers.

"He suffered several wounds," continued Millie as she walked over to the hooks where she took off her apron. "He broke his back, I heard. And anyway, did you know that his father did not even bother to come visit him? Fortunately for him, his brothers were here." She turned toward us, looking quite concerned. "And they were rich," she added, her eyes glowing.

Stanley helped himself to one of the sandwiches; a man his size would need to eat quite a bit to feed his muscles. "But he still lives here with everyone else moved on?" he asked.

"Well, not on his own," I interrupted. I didn't want Millie to get too carried away with speculation. "The man seems to have others living with him. I take it he never fully recovered from the accident and enjoys the scenery at the lodge. He has a couple of men who come into town to get his supplies from the train and the stores around here. An old foreman named Bunny Dix and some Yugoslavian fellow."

"A foreman of the mine," repeated Stanley, "now he comes into town to purchase groceries?"

"Well, not just groceries." I could see what he was getting at, and I admit it was strange. "Bunny seems a clever fellow, but the Yugoslavian bloke doesn't appear to know any English. In fact, I don't think anyone knows the man's name or even his history." I looked over to see Millie shrug.

Lloyd George came out from under the chair and moved his head so Stanley could scratch him. Did the dog have no shame?

"But they use the pit rail when it's clear. They have a handcar. Maybe they come in once or twice a week and get goods for the people living at the lodge.

"Anyway, all that to say, this man, Bunny Dix, got in a quarrel with Clayton at the General Store, and there was some sort of fight. Pushing and shoving, no broken bones but maybe some bruises. I imagine Clayton started it. He can be an absolute nuisance."

"This is the same Clayton as the one in the shootout?" Stanley asked.

"The one and only. It's been a pretty easy commission—boring, in fact—except for him."

"Oh, he's not that bad," Millie interrupted. I forgot she had a soft spot for the drunk.

"Anyway, the grocer didn't want to make trouble," I continued, "So he let it go, and Clayton refused to talk to me about it, but I figured maybe it was time for me to go take a visit."

"I told him he shouldn't go alone," said Millie. She walked forward to the side of the desk. "You could have taken Peter or even me."

I shrugged. "It's not far. There's about two miles of track that end at the mine, due north from here. You can't get lost even if you tried, and there wasn't any snow covering the tracks."

"You know that's not what I meant," said Millie, her arms crossed. "It was like last night. Why would you go out in the dark alone? You can see what trouble you can get into."

"I wasn't alone," I protested. "I had Clayton with me." Sometimes, it was too easy to tease her.

"Anyway, the Chambers Lodge is right across from the mine, inside the fences they've built there. The building and the barn are the only buildings there now. I'd seen pictures from before, and there were tents everywhere." Paul laid his knife and fork across his plate.

"I come walking, and I see Bunny Dix a little beyond the fence line chopping wood. So I hail him. Polite, like I'm meaning no harm. And he gives me a nod and I'm thinking that's enough to go in through the gate. But as I'm about to push it open, I hear a voice, and there, about ten feet away, is Philip Chambers. I'd never seen him coming."

"Isn't that weird?" asked Millie, shaking her head to answer her own question.

"So he says to me, 'You don't have my permission,

Constable.' He's leaning against a post on the other side of the fence, glaring at me."

"Tell him what he looked like," prompted Millie. "He was all sick and thin. Like he was close to death."

"He looked like a man who had come through an illness," I said. And it was true. His face was drawn, his eyes a pearly yellow, and his clothes were sloppy and loose. And he talked like he had trouble shaping his mouth to the words. Everything was pulled out extra long.

" 'This is Chambers' property,' he told me. 'And you have no reason for being here.' " I imitated Philip's face to show Stanley how he regarded me—like I was some sort of bug on his shoe.

"I told you, I never liked the look of him," said Millie.

"So I glare back at him and tell him that I'm here to speak to his man Bunny, but he just shrugs and tells me that Bunny has nothing to say. Then he points at the track and tells me to go back the way I came."

I was reading Stanley's face the whole time and realized there was nothing remarkable about my story—that I hadn't given the full effect.

"It was his manner," I explained, "it was downright menacing. I mean, I know he was in the right, but he was sort of threatening me. He wanted to make sure that I knew my place, and it wasn't there at his abandoned mine."

Stanley stroked his chin while I got out my cigarette case. I liked to have one after meals to settle myself. I offered them around, but they both declined. I knew Millie didn't like the smell.

"But it all worked out," I continued. "Bunny came

to visit me here two days afterward and told me he apologized to Clayton and that he paid Dvorak for the groceries. I checked with Dvorak, and he said the same thing. But as per usual I could not get a civil word from Clayton, only angry curses about me not doing my job."

I didn't add that his attitude irritated me beyond reason. I remembered raising my voice and wanting to hit the man. "At least I have a job!" I had yelled, but that too was answered with profanity.

I shook my head to bring my mind back in focus. "Anyway, it was all resolved," I smushed the cigarette into the ashtray on my desk. "I won't have to go back to the lodge anytime soon."

"Good," she said, waving her hand to blow away the remnants of the smoke.

"We should go say hello to the mayor," I said, though I had no mind to move yet.

"The girl," said Stanley. And I almost fell off my chair.

****

"I know," Millie gushed. She walked back and forth from the table, collecting things while talking fast, "That's just what I was saying! That girl! She's a real mystery, isn't she? I hope she's okay. How do you think she keeps disappearing? Do you think she is still out there? Some people think she's a spirit. Do you think that's possible, Constable Stanley? There's weird things in the forest. She might be Native or Oriental."

"Oriental," I muttered under my breath. I hadn't heard that one before. "What makes you think she could be Oriental?"

She stood with her hands on her hips. "Because of the other one, of course." She glared at me as if I had gone off my rocker. "Surely, you heard about that!"

I shook my head, and Millie pulled over a chair and sat at the side of the desk, all conspiratorial. "It was last fall, maybe six months before you arrived." She whispered now as if what she was saying was a deep secret. "I'm surprised Sergeant Deacon never mentioned it to you."

Sergeant Deacon had left little behind in the way of a report. Only a cursory review of the town with a brief history attached. There was also a handwritten note that suggested I ask the mayor if I had questions. I assumed he felt a population of four dozen people would be easy to handle. Until today, it was.

"It was an early freeze, and they found her in a stream." Millie was in her element now, her eyes wide as she took the two of us in.

"Drowned! Probably, farther upstream and moved to town by the current. They weren't quite sure where she went in, but her body surfaced across from old Oscar Lange's place. He was shocked when he found her." She looked at our reaction to see if we were as horrified as she was. For my part, I stayed as passive as I could.

"It was so awful," she continued. "She was so young. And pretty. I didn't see her, but that's what they said. They had no idea how she got there."

Stanley rubbed his unshaven chin. "An Oriental girl. That is unusual. I assume there were no Chinese or Japanese miners here. Women don't usually make it to the West."

He was right. Turn-of-the-century laws prevented Chinese or Japanese men from working in a mine or on a railroad. They couldn't even be employed to erect infrastructure like bridges and telegraph poles. And so there was little to bring them to a town like Chambers. As for their women, the country allowed only a few in each year. They didn't want the community to establish a foothold in the West. There were ten Chinese men for every woman in British Columbia.

Sook was Chinese, but he was the only one who lived in Chambers. He worked as a barkeep at The Hole and was a nice enough fellow. Lem, the Pole, let him live in the adjoining rooms. He couldn't work as a miner but was allowed to pour their beers.

"I've often wondered how she got here." There was a dreamy look in Millie's eyes. "She would have seen a lot more of the world than I have. "

"She was most likely a hired woman," I suggested. "The whole thing points to prostitution."

She ignored me and faced Paul as she spoke. "They buried her in the churchyard with no funeral or grave marker. Sometimes when I go by, I say a little prayer for her. I call her Arlene, since we never knew her name. Don't you think that's such a pretty name—Arlene?"

"Last spring, eh," I said. "Bring me her file, and let me have a look."

"Yes," said Millie as she jumped from the table, "Sergeant Deacon had me type something about her."

Stanley followed her over to the file cabinet. "Did Sergeant Deacon try to determine her origin?" he asked.

She shook her head, her fingers already flitting through the cabinet. It was a horrid-looking box. It was made by the retired Constable Taylor, who must have nailed it together in the dark. Millie had to yank hard on each drawer to get them to move. I would have asked Peter to build us a new one, but he was not on Command's list of approved sellers. If we wanted a new one, we would have to have one shipped in from Prince George.

"I don't think he had the time to find anything out," Millie muttered as she searched. "I mean, no one here knew anything about her, so he had nothing to go on." She pulled out a piece of paper from amongst the log jam, inspected it, and then fitted it back in the row, shaking her head. "I'm not sure where it is. But it must be here. It wasn't that long ago."

Stanley stood beside the cabinet as she worked. They looked a strange couple—him being so broad and tall.

"I imagine you would have to call Prince Rupert to see if they had any missing girls or knew about who might be smuggling foreign women into the interior," he said. "She must have come from that direction."

Millie shrugged. Her cheeks were turning red from frustration. She pulled on each drawer a second time and rechecked each file. "It's no use," she said. "It's got to be filed wrong, or it's squished between papers in there." Stanley was not helping—standing over her like that!

"Listen," I said. "You keep looking. It's not urgent. There's nothing we could do about it anyway. I'll take Stanley over to see the mayor, and then we'll go and see if Clayton is awake.

"We can question him," I said, turning to Stanley. He nodded, and we dressed to return in the swirling snow.

Chapter 4

Fox's Faith

The walk over to the hotel was miserable. The soft snow was gone, replaced by a biting slurry of hard, frozen rain, driving into one's face from all angles. By the time we had reached the building, a thick sheen of icy water had adhered to the surface of our fur coats and trousers. Both our faces were ravaged red. The boardwalk, once so pleasant to walk on, was now a perilous undertaking, and I had to use the building's facades to keep myself upright. Constable Stanley found the footing so tricky that I had to wait for him at the hotel's entrance. These Easterners often found our Western weather rough.

Stepping into the lobby, a welcoming warmth greeted us, and we heard the sound of voices lifted in debate. As we struggled to close the heavy doors against the wind, the conversation died away, and when we turned, we saw Mrs. Tuttle. She stood quiet and alone in the dining room entryway, her hands curled around a handkerchief she held at her waist. She looked even more nervous than usual.

"Mrs. Tuttle," I said as I removed my fur-lined hat. The lobby room we stood in was a testament to Tom Fox's vision. The place was appointed as if it were a fancy downtown resort rather than a traditional hunting lodge. A famous architect who worked on British Columbia's Parliament Buildings was paid to scrutinize his design. Fox shipped its heavy wood furniture with considerable expense from Toronto, the elaborate chandelier from Montreal, and the lobby desk from a bankrupt hotel in New York City. He enlisted stone masons from Winnipeg to build the grand fireplace, paying for their passage in both directions.

Mayor Fox told everyone these details. He wanted us all to accept his vision of Chambers, the next epicenter of the British Columbian boom. The first or last stop on the rail line before reaching Prince Rupert. A travel destination for those who want to see the mountains from the inside out. To hear him say it, he didn't mind that the mine had closed. It was just the first of many industries sure to come to Chambers. Mining, fishing, forestry, and rail, how could it fail?

Mrs. Tuttle returned my greeting with a slight nod of her head. She then peered back into the dining room for what I inferred to be further instructions. And soon at her side appeared Tom Fox, looking eager to receive us.

"Constable Gus Albright," he began. "What a wonderful surprise. And you've brought a guest," he said with a beaming smile, taking in the figure of my fellow constable. "We were all having a conversation about the snowstorm and your heroism. It would be wonderful for my guests to hear you retell what happened." He stretched out his arms to invite us into the dining room.

There was a reason why he was the town's first and only mayor, the same reason I supposed he did so well in business. The man was good. He had a way of putting you at your ease. As they say, his energy was infectious. But why then the heated conversation in the dining room?

Constable Stanley and I exchanged glances. We removed our furs to reveal our red serge uniforms underneath and then followed Mrs. Tuttle and Fox into the mayor's elegant dining room. I was curious to see who was there and whether guests stayed at the hotel. Surprisingly, there were only women present. Five other ladies from the town joined Mrs. Tuttle; all married: Mrs. Granderson, Mrs. Landers, Mrs. Saunders, Mrs. Poulson, and Mrs. Clack. All were immediately interested in my colleague, Constable Stanley. The looks that Mrs. Poulson and Mrs. Clack gave the man were embarrassing.

"Well, well," said Mr. Fox, rubbing his hands together as if eager to start the proceedings. "What's the word, Albright, and who is this rather large constable you've brought with you." He glanced around the room at all the ladies standing in silence. "Please speak plainly. These ladies are worried about the storm."

But he already said that the women were worried about the storm—was the repetition for them or us? His usual calm demeanor was ruffled. "This is Constable Stanley," I said. "He rode in from Plateau, in a blizzard no less, this morning after he received my telegraph."

These words produced a murmur of voices around the room. I decided to say nothing more. Something peculiar was going on, and I wanted to see who would take the initiative next.

It was the mayor who broke the silence. "Good one, chap!" He said to Stanley and bounced over to give the man a hearty slap on the bicep. "We are most glad to have your help." Stanley, to his credit, remained mute. He must have realized that I wished to take the lead. The recruit had some sense.

It was Mrs. Granderson who talked next. "We were just discussing the storm."

I nodded. That would be the third time it was mentioned.

But she continued. "We wanted to ensure there are enough provisions if the weather lasts and we are shut off from the city."

"Wouldn't Mr. Dvorak be the one to talk to about that?" I asked. He owned the larger of the two general stores in town.

Mrs. Granderson wet her lips with her tongue. "Yes," she said, "We planned to head over there next. But the storm is so violent, we decided to meet here first." So, how did these ladies come together in this way? Had they all come here alone, or was there an instigator who assembled them? I looked around the room to see if I could spot a leader. I eliminated Mrs. Tuttle for her timorous ways and Mrs. Clack and Poulson for their silliness. Did they come at the mayor's request? Or did he send his worker out to collect them? And why these five women in particular? Were their husbands not invited to join them?

"I talked to Mr. Benjamin at the station this morning," I told them. "He told me that the storm was a complete surprise and that he didn't receive any information for how long it might last. The telegraph is currently inoperative, but I know that they will get the trains running at the first possible opportunity. We should be fine."

My words appeared to have little impact in reducing the women's worries. Mrs. Clack and Poulson were holding hands while Mrs. Tuttle chewed on her lip, her face drawn.

Mr. Fox was all smiles, though. "Constable Albright, the ladies here would like to commend you for your heroism."

Mrs. Granderson cut in. "We are all so grateful that you were not hurt. And that you stopped two dangerous criminals sure to cause us many troubles. It will be a good day when men like that are locked away." I noticed she didn't mention that I had stopped one of the two by ending his life with a bullet to the head.

The women came forward as a group, affirming their gratitude and asking short questions: "Were you scared?" "How did you see them in the dark?" "Was I injured in any way?" They didn't ask about Clayton or the other wounded man. I was unsure of the exact details Fox had told them, so I tried to keep my answers short and vague.

The ladies offered cups of coffee and biscuits, which we accepted. Staying longer might help paint a better picture of what was happening here. So Stanley and I stood munching and sipping our refreshments while the women chatted. In Stanley's large hands, the teacups looked like playthings for a little girl, but I did not remark on it.

The conversation among them, however, was relatively light and somewhat stilted, as if they were manufacturing things to talk about. Nothing in it suggested another heated argument might begin anew. They had been discussing something they didn't want other people to hear— especially not us Mounties.

A couple of the women began questioning Stanley's origins. They probably hoped he would become a fixture in the town. Mrs. Landers, I knew, had a daughter that was soon to be of marriageable age. Not every mother wanted their daughter to marry a constable, but the pickings were slim here, and I had to admit Stanley was quite the specimen. That said, Mrs. Landers never thought of me as a possible suitor.

Besides, it was common knowledge that a Mountie was not allowed to marry in the first five years of his service. Marriage was considered an obstacle to movement. I knew some Mounties that had served at two dozen or more detachments in their first couple years of service, often dotted around the northern reaches of Alberta, Saskatchewan, and Manitoba. If a Mountie had a wife, she would likely be the only European woman for hundreds of miles and have to exist in harsh circumstances. Those men who wanted to get married early had to buy their way out of their service. The cost of that was a princely five hundred dollars. It would have to be quite the woman to prompt a man to pay such a handsome price. And that certainly was not Miss Landers.

Ultimately, the mayor walked to the door as the women dressed to go out into the cold. "I think we have nothing to worry about," said Fox as we fitted our feet into our boots. "This bit of snow will blow over, and everything will go back to normal." What normal did he mean? People were leaving the town in droves. And his hotel didn't have a lot of guests. He should consider *moving on* himself.

As the ladies departed, they all said their goodbyes. We warned them about the slippery surfaces outside, and they assured us they would help each other to their homes. Mrs. Tuttle was the last to leave. She wanted to say something to the mayor or us but could not find the courage. Mrs. Tuttle was a timid thing, unsuited to the rough life of a mining town or a Canadian winter. Seventeen years old and already with one child. Her husband, John, must have cared for the infant as she visited the hotel.

When she finally left, I turned to the mayor. "You probably shouldn't be telling everyone what happened last night. This is still an ongoing investigation."

The mayor nodded, but his grin told me he would do whatever he wished. We both knew this was the case. I wasn't going to arrest the town's mayor for talking.

"I thank you for your service once again, Constable." He said to me and then turned to Stanley, "You should watch this one. He's a real hero." I was unsure by his tone whether he was making fun of me.

"What were the women really here for Tom?" I asked. I wanted to catch him off guard.

But no luck. "You know women…" he quipped with the same leering smile he had used earlier with Millie. "They are always so worried about every little thing. This weather and your shooting have got them all in a twitter."

Not all of them. I knew a couple of good women who never twittered. And what did the weather have to do with my shooting?

"Well, we'll leave you to your guests," I asserted, hoping to knock the man for a moment off his perch. But he was unfazed, opening the door as if he were one of the servants and not the hotel's owner.

Stanley walked out first, but Fox pulled on my shoulder and closed the door as I was about to leave. I now found myself alone with the man.

"Just before you go, young man," he started. Young

man? He was no more than ten years my senior. "I wanted to let you know that I'm planning to write to your headquarters and demand that they give you some sort of commendation or even a promotion. This could mean big things for you, Augustus."

What in blazes was he getting at? I hated when he used my formal first name.

"This whole thing took everyone by complete surprise, and we, to your credit, are so glad that it was nipped in the bud. You deserve a break, my boy." He patted me on the shoulder. "I can tell that your Millie was quite worried about you. You should get her to cook you boys a nice meal."

So he wanted me to sit tight. Understood. But I would do whatever I wished. I was about to admonish him for calling her, My Millie, but thought better of it.

"I'll do that," I said and reached for the door handle. I didn't want Constable Stanley to think we were being conspiratorial.

But the mayor put his hand over my own. I noticed his breath was minty as he talked. "That's a good man," he said. I guess that was an improvement on *boy.*

As I stepped outside, the wind swept past me, and he began to close the door. But he had one more thing to say. "You're too important to us, Albright. We wouldn't want anything more to happen to you."

I turned around to reply, but the door was now closed.

****

The walk to the hospital was as miserable as the walk to the hotel. Our coats, frozen and then melted by the hotel's heat, became stiff on our exit and did little to keep out the cold gusts of blowing wind.

When we walked through the outer door into the vestibule, I was surprised to find Dr. Moody there, smoking a fat cigar. He took it out of his mouth and gave us a huge grin as we knocked the snow from our garments. Genevieve slipped through the inner doors and stood beside her husband. I could tell at once she was impressed by the bulk of my fellow constable, so I did the introductions, letting them know that he was in town to help me with my investigation.

"Well," said Dr. Moody in his gruffest of voices. "I have a bone to pick with you, my boy. It seems like you have given my wife and me some extra work. And I don't admire the patients you are selecting for us."

Was he joking? It was hard to know. He had fewer and fewer lucid moments. I looked over at Genevieve, and the doctor started to chuckle.

"Of course I am kidding, Gus," he said, then reached forward to hold my wrist as we stood. "The main thing is that you don't get yourself hurt. Genevieve and I have grown quite fond of you." His smile was genuine. "Now tell me, who is this friend you brought?"

Genevieve shook her head and guided her husband through the doorway and back to the infirmary as she explained our guest to him again. I watched Paul as they talked about him. He was unfazed, ready to get on with the questioning.

Clayton's voice lifted into his characteristic belligerence as we moved through the doors. Margaret was at the foot of the bed, her hands on her hips, her face as red as I had ever seen. Clayton must have been giving her the gears, but when we stepped inside, he shifted his focus to cast off his invectives in my direction.

His complaints were many, each one laced with a

liberal amount of cussing—words and sequences of words showing a depraved imagination along with a deep sense of victimization. Of course, he did have some issues that would cause any man grievance, namely the handcuffs, the two bullet wounds, and the lack of his familiar, though filthy clothes. But these were not the primary sources for his vehemence. Instead, he railed against the lack of alcohol or substitute, angry to be refused another dose of morphine. Also, Margaret had suggested he shave.

Genevieve discharged Margaret to attend to the doctor in the kitchen and then stood with us at the foot of Clayton's bed. Together, we watched his chest rise and fall with each fresh stream of invective.

There was no point questioning the man until he'd cooled, so instead, I turned my attention to Genevieve, asking her about the condition of the Pickle brother and her own health. Had she finally gotten some sleep?

She assured me she had rested. When I turned back to Clayton, I was surprised that the man was now leveling his complaints at my recruit. Clayton was sure that Stanley was the man to take him away to prison. His strategy was to threaten Stanley with profane commands, many of which were physical impossibilities. The constable, for his part, did not respond and kept his face passive as he observed the man's outbursts.

"Enough," I shouted over the top of Clayton, "Constable Stanley is not here to take you to prison! You're not going to prison, Clayton!" That got his attention, and in the silence, I moved a metal chair beside his bed and sat in it. "At least not yet."

"Clayton, you almost got us killed," I continued before the man could start again. "You should have listened to me."

He spluttered, "Almost had you killed, bah! I'm the one with two bullet holes, and you're sitting there no worse for wear."

I shook my head. "You have to tell us the whole story. How did you know the Pickle brothers were waiting for me?"

He pursed his lips. "That's nonsense. I never knew anybody would be there. I was expecting to see that ghost girl that we saw from the saloon."

"You told me who they were, Clayton," I said. He had identified them from across the clearing.

"Bah!" He shot back. "I figured they were the only outlaws. They had been in The Hole. They were carrying rifles and acting all superior and ready for a fight. Everybody was on their guard."

Beatrice and Clayton had seen these two men, and neither came to tell me. Nor did Bernard or the men in The Hole. Not one thought to mention them to me. Did they think so little of my abilities? That I couldn't do the job because I wasn't like Sergeant Deacon?

These Pickle brothers had a terrible reputation. And they were bound to have a grudge against the Mounties. I wouldn't have been able to arrest them because they had done nothing wrong, but I could have prepared myself or given them a warning. I stared at Clayton. The fact that he was adamant about following this mysterious woman into the woods never made much sense, less now that he knew two outlaws were about. I was sure there were things he was keeping from me.

The man grimaced. He was undoubtedly in lousy shape, but Genevieve told me he wasn't at risk as long his wounds remained uninfected. "Seems to me that I saved your life, Mountie." There were no curse words here, his eyes big and round. Did he think the puppy dog look would work on me?

"You should be treating me as a hero, not a criminal," he moaned, rattling the chain of his handcuffs for effect. "If I hadn't rushed the clearing, you wouldn't have been able to take the brothers out."

When I gave Clayton the gun, it did cross my mind that he might shoot me in the back with it. He had called me every name under the sun over the last few months. But there was no getting past the fact that without his help, I probably would not have survived the gunfight. Especially since I now knew there was an extra armed combatant—the girl.

"Clayton," I said. "Why did you run back into that clearing? You were supposed to just fire at them. You weren't supposed to put yourself back in harm's way."

He shrugged as I watched an expression of sorrow pass over his face. He looked for a moment like an elderly man. How old was Clayton anyway?

"It seemed like it was my time to do it," Clayton whispered.

For a moment, the inside of the infirmary was quiet. The wind buffeted against the boards of the building, and with it came the realization that we were still in the midst of the storm. I glanced at the unconscious Pickle brother; his curtain pushed to the side. There were too many unanswered questions—questions I didn't yet know how to ask. I looked back at Stanley. How might this all seem to him?

"Clayton," I said, "This isn't over yet. Constable Stanley and I are going to check out your story, and we will be back to question you." I pushed the chair aside as

I stood.

I expected another string of profanity, but Clayton was now deep in thought. I stepped away, ready to say my goodbyes to Genevieve when he spoke again.

"Did you see the girl?"

I felt a shiver run through me. A dark figure stood silhouetted by the moonlight—the barrel hole of the rifle pointed in my direction. A line of sweat broke out on my forehead, and my stomach seized. This girl wasn't going to go away.

"No," I replied, trying to keep all emotion out of my voice.

"I saw her," he whispered. "She was there. She was waiting for me."

I was speechless. My heart was beating too fast to form thoughts. I needed to sit—to collapse.

Clayton began shouting at Genevieve. "Get me something now!" He yelled, his curses making the sentence three times as long. "I'm in terrible pain!" He moaned, kicked the bed, and rattled the thin chain of the handcuffs.

Genevieve took me by the elbow and walked us away. "He wants more of the morphine, but I don't want to give it to him. He has a history of alcohol and addiction." She looked back at him. "But he is going to drive us all crazy."

What could we do about it? How were we supposed to help? I bent over at the waist and took long breaths as Genevieve put her hand on my back. What was Constable Stanley making of all this?

I straightened and ran my palm over my face. "We could bring him over to our jail? But I don't know if we could take care of him."

Thankfully, Genevieve shook her head. "No, we'll have to endure him. We might have to resort to giving him his blessed alcohol or something stronger to get him to sleep."

"Get us if you need us," I said. "Or Peter or Duffy. They are closer." Should I sleep in the infirmary? I needed to be out of here—to clear my head. To not have to think about this.

Genevieve sighed softly. "Margaret is staying the night, and Kenneth can still help." Dr. Moody may be more hindrance than help, but I did not want to argue.

Stanley and Genevieve talked as we got back into our gear. She was impressed that he arrived on horseback in the storm. Stanley was acquiring admirers wherever we went.

I felt a hand on my shoulder as I stepped through the door. I turned to see Genevieve. "Do be careful," she said.

I gave her a quick smile. "I'll do my best," I replied, and then we were out in the blizzard.

****

With a lean of my head, I told Stanley to follow me. Instead of returning to the detachment, I figured I would check Clayton's story while everything was fresh. Already, a lot had happened in a short time, but more than a few pieces were missing. Things were brewing in Chambers, and it was beginning to feel like people were trying to keep me in the dark.

The Hole was one of the oldest buildings in town. A turn-of-the-century log house whose original construction was shoddy at best. Later, injured miners repurposed the place, making a killing on spirits and late-night poker. British Columbia voted against prohibition, allowing the sale and consumption of beer and spirits, but I heard The Hole was famous for its rotgut moonshine. From the start, its ramshackle design attracted the unsavory. Now, the saloon on the boardwalk was its lone competition. Like most of its patrons, The Hole could be considered a survivor. But what's the purpose of survival if it leads to nothing more?

Its owner was a Pole named Lem, a large, ruddy fellow who was as unkempt as the business he ran. I was not surprised to see him stuck in his corner, a too-small undershirt, dirty and torn, revealing the final rolls of his fat belly. He didn't bat an eye when we entered; he just gave us a long stare as we passed the four clumsy tables and approached the bar.

Lem's customers were as derelict as his furniture. Three men, all of whom I knew to be drunks, were sitting, I assumed, in their customary spots, one with his head face down on the table, lending his snores to the room. Other than that, the only sound was our steps over the creaking floorboards.

I removed my hat and nodded at Lem, who made no move to greet us. I assumed he didn't consider us customers.

"Hello, Lem," I started. The man simply blinked. "I heard you had a couple of visitors from away last night." Still no response. I wondered if the man was sleeping with his eyes open. The whole place made me tired as well.

"The Pickle brothers," I said this louder for all three customers to hear, but it was as if my words had died in the air before reaching them. "Who can tell me about them?" I asked. I wondered if they had heard that I had killed one. It was a different world here, unconnected with the one I lived in. Lem shifted his weight and let out a sound which I will not describe, but I will say that its effect further added to the room's atmosphere.

The unexpected sound of Sook coming through the half doors of the kitchen was so loud it made me jump. He was talking fast and with a strong accent, repeating himself so I could understand him.

"Nothing to drink, Sook," I told him. "Were you here last night?"

"Yes, yes."

"Did you happen to see Clayton in here?" He nodded and pointed to the table where he must have sat. It checked out. The place did seem unbalanced without someone sitting there. Like it was one drunk short of its quota.

"And were there two other men here? Everyone calls them the Pickle brothers." I glanced at Lem to see if he would stop Sook from answering, but he didn't move a muscle. Impressive.

"Yes." He pointed over to where the Pickles had sat against the front window. There wasn't much happening there now, just Old Burke drooling as he snoozed the afternoon away.

"They drink a lot?" asked Stanley.

Sook had ignored my companion, but now he gazed into Stanely's face as if trying to find a squirrel at the top of the tree. He didn't make a noise as he held up four fingers.

"Each?" I asked, and he nodded, returning his eyes to my own.

If I had drunk that much, I couldn't shoot straight. That said, I had avoided such reckless behavior most of my life. Nothing in The Hole suggested I was missing out.

"Did Clayton talk to these men, the Pickle brothers?" I asked.

"No," Sook insisted, "The brothers had come in, drank for a couple of hours, and left."

"They didn't talk to anyone?"

"No, no, no talking from anyone. They come in, drink for thirty minutes, and leave straight away." His face was earnest, without a hint of a lie. It matched the general vibe of the place. It wasn't the spot I would choose for a conversation.

"What about the girl?" asked Stanley.

"Oh yes!" Sook began. He pushed past us and stood between the tables, pointing through the grimy window. "It was Mr. Clayton. He was sitting here, and then he saw something out the window, so he walked over here." Sook did his impression of the drunk. I enjoyed his attempt, but he didn't fully capture Clayton's character. It looked like something between a great ape spotting a predator and a mischievous child realizing he was about to get in trouble with his mom.

Clayton's seat was against the dirty glass across from where the Pickle brothers were sitting. A place of privilege, I supposed, for a frequent customer.

"Mr. Clayton was like this," Sook said, continuing the pantomime to show us Clayton's frozen shape.

"Then the ghost goes, and Mr. Clayton goes outside to find it."

How well could Clayton see the figure through the grime? The Hole, as always, would have been lit by just a few candles. But there was a full moon, and with its light reflected off the thin layer of ice, I expected he could have seen her. The tree line was around thirty feet away. Perhaps, like many townspeople, he was watching for the girl. God knows there was little else to look at in this place.

Sook was all energy now, bouncing on his toes. He continued to use his body to describe how Clayton had gone out to talk to her. The story was that the whole saloon had emptied after him, as they all tried to restrain him from following after the girl.

"Mr. Clayton was too drunk," said Sook, shaking his head. "He would have been lost going after that ghost. That is what the spirits do," he professed. "They make you follow them into the afterlife."

I presumed it would be a more liquid type of spirit that would carry Clayton to the hereafter, but I kept that thought to myself.

"Who sent for me then, Sook?"

He shrugged. "We were all concerned for Mr. Clayton."

Somehow, I doubted that. Lem, for example, wasn't jumping out of his seat to help Sook act through the details of the evening, and even Sook hadn't asked about Clayton's condition in the hospital.

"Who sent Bernard to find me then?" I asked.

Sook looked over at Lem, who gave no sign of interest. He showed little sign of life, for that matter. "Mr. Bernard told us to wait until you came," Sook stated.

I looked around to see if anyone else wanted to add to the conversation, but there were no takers.

"One more thing," I said. "Sergeant Deacon found a girl in the river last spring. "Do you know anything about her?"

"They never let me see her," he replied. He moved back behind the bar. "There are no Chinese women here, only in Prince Rupert." I felt terrible for the guy so far away from home, without a community, working in this dive. Even if he wanted to return home, he could not pay for the trip. I doubted he could pay for the trip to Prince Rupert.

"Do you have any idea where this girl might have been staying?" asked Stanley.

I watched Sook's Adam's apple bob as he gaped at Stanley. "No," he said, "This is no place for her."

"All right then." I turned to Stanley, "You must be tired. Let's head back." I took a final look around, memorized who was in there, and then took one last stare out Clayton's window. Without this blinding storm, the world would have appeared quite different twelve-odd hours ago. Everything had changed, and not for the better. Or was it me—not seeing the world for what it was?

****

The two of us trudged back through the houses of the old town toward the bridge. I was so lost in thought I didn't notice the woman standing in her doorway. Stanley grabbed my shoulder and turned me toward the house. It was the Tuttle home, the door open, Mrs. Tuttle silhouetted by the firelight behind her. We changed course and moved inside, squishing past her as she pulled the door behind us.

It was a simple cottage, one large room that served most of the family's needs. Mrs. Tuttle's infant child, Jane, stood in her crib, dressed in a gray-white gown.

But there was one member of the family missing.

"Where's Mr. Tuttle?" I asked.

Mrs. Tuttle crossed the floor to the infant, seized her, and settled her in the crook of her arm. She turned. Four large eyes stared ahead.

"He's not here," she said.

The little girl let loose a stream of babble, and her mother began to bounce on her toes, swaying side to side. I looked over at Stanley.

"Is there something you want to tell us, Mrs. Tuttle?" I remembered how anxious she was when we came into the hotel. She looked the same way now. Breathless.

She shook her head. "I don't know if it's anything, but this storm is so fierce, and Johnny, he went out to hunt with some others. And..." she broke off, spinning away momentarily with the baby.

"These others," I said, "they wouldn't happen to be the husbands of the women from the hotel."

She twisted back, now hopping from one foot to the other, the little girl cooing as she moved. "No," she insisted. "No, I don't know who he went with."

"What was he hunting?" asked Stanley. His voice was calm but somehow commanding.

Mrs. Tuttle brought the baby back to the crib and set it inside. She turned to face us full on, her eyes gone cold. "It's nothing," she said. "It's the storm. It's got me on edge. Johnny goes off sometimes. Hunting." She paused. There was something she was not telling us. "I'm sure they've found a place to hunker down."

She did not offer any tea or other refreshments. Nor did she invite us to enter the room further. So, we stood on the mat, silent, the snow from our clothing dripping messily on her floor.

"Is Mayor Fox threatening you with something,

Mrs. Tuttle?"

Her eyes went wide. The baby began to babble again behind her. She wanted to be lifted again, but Mrs. Tuttle ignored it. "I don't know what you mean. I'm just worried about John, out in the blizzard."

"Do you know which direction he went? Do you need us to go find him?" offered Stanley.

"No, no." She shook her head. "I don't know where he hunts. He'll come home just as he always does." She bit her lip, tears welling at the base of her eyes.

"It was nice of you to stop by," she croaked as she stepped toward us in the doorway. "When John returns, I'll let you know."

"Okay," I replied, my hand flat against the wooden door. "And if we hear anything, *we* will let you know."

We stepped into the snow and watched her shut the door behind us. She appeared frightened and small, like some sort of burrowing animal, trapped and unsure which way to turn. But how could we help her if she would not tell us what she needed? My head throbbed with the effort of guessing the meaning behind everyone's words and actions. I envied Constable Stanley for having no skin in the game. When the storm ended, he would be gone, and I would be left in this lonely town filled with sad secrets.

****

Back at the detachment, we found Millie amongst an explosion of papers. It looked like she had opened all the filing cabinets and then dumped the contents all over the room.

"What in blazes are you doing?" I spluttered as I began to shake off the snow. The wind from the door had sent some of the pages into the air, making Millie dash about to collect them.

"Close the door!" she shouted. We silently removed our outdoor wear as we watched her move about. Her ordinarily tight hair bun was now loose, and unfettered strands fell over her face as she bent and straightened herself.

"I can't find it! I know it must be here, but I can't find it! Where could it have gone?" She stared at me. Was she going to accuse me of taking it? Like that's what I did—wake in the middle of the night and nibble on some random paperwork.

My shrug only made her more exasperated. "Perhaps Deacon decided not to file it," I suggested, though it sounded wrong coming out of my mouth. "He was a busy man." I was thinking about the report that I had yet to write.

Millie shook her head. "No! I know he wrote something because I typed it."

"Well then," I suggested, "he would have passed it on to headquarters, and they would have a copy."

"Well, why don't you go to headquarters and bring one back?" It was insubordination!

Stanley put his hand on my shoulder. "Millie, why don't you and I take a look for it together? We can check each file as we put it back in the cabinet. Maybe one folder is inside the other."

"Fine," I pitched in. "But do the ones on my desk first. I have a new report to write."

Millie moved with me to my desk, pulled the documents off in a huff, and placed them on the floor. I stepped over them and slumped into my seat before retrieving my notebook from the top drawer. I must admit I found this type of writing difficult. There was a certain way they wanted you to phrase your words that sounded too mechanical. Plus, my poor spelling embarrassed me. Millie was kind enough to correct my mistakes when she transcribed them, but I hated that anyone would have to see them.

I waited for a moment before beginning. Stanley and Millie talked loudly about organizing the papers, and I couldn't figure out where to start. Writing it in formal English was more difficult than telling the story out loud. For one thing, I knew who might read it. Any officer discharging his weapon was a big deal, let alone killing someone. Something like this was likely to go all the way to the superintendent. It was essential to get all the details straight. The ones at least I was willing to write about.

Struggling to find the words I needed, I heard Millie say, "Thank you, Paul," as he passed her papers from the floor. And without thinking, still overcome with the momentous task ahead of me, I grumbled, "That's *Constable* Stanley."

Immediately, I raised my head and saw them staring back at me. I didn't know quite how to react. So I plunged back into my work.

For the next hour, as I threw one false start after another into the waste bin, I must have heard Millie say, "Thank you, *Constable* Stanley," about a dozen times, each time with her *serious* voice she put on to get under my skin. I was ashamed to guess what Constable Stanley could have thought of this. As a recruit, he was witnessing a shameful example of how a detachment should be run.

In the end, even with Constable Stanley's help, Millie still couldn't locate the paper, and we all had to conclude that it had been removed somehow. Whether by accident or on purpose, we could only guess, but both Millie and I were sure that Sergeant Deacon would expect it to be in our files. From what Millie told me, Sergeant Deacon was a stickler for details and expected everyone around him to comply with his directions. Whether he was here or not, Millie was still anxious that she may have made a mistake with his paperwork.

So over dinner, I let Millie know I did not blame her for the lost files. This eased some tension. Later, I did not get far in another attempt at my report. I think I was exhausted from the previous night's exertion. Ultimately, the three of us played cards before I walked Millie back to her home in the blistering winds. On my return, I considered dropping in on Genevieve or Mrs. Tuttle. Lights were on in both locations, but I was exhausted from the day's activities and the constant fight against the storm.

When I returned, I found that Stanley had readied himself for bed in one of the jail cells. I told him I was happy he was here, and we shook hands.

That night, I fell into a deep slumber but was woken by a loud, growling sound in the middle of the night. Between it and the howling wind, I could not determine what was happening. I reached for my holster at the foot of my bed, worried that some strange animal may have found shelter in our lodgings because of the storm. But a tiptoe walk out to the main room showed the main culprit to be Constable Paul Stanley. The man snored like a lumberjack's saw. I would have woken him, but I remembered his long ride to get here.

I found Lloyd George beside my bed when I returned to my room. The way he looked at me, I could tell Stanley's snoring had disturbed him as well. I closed my door, and for the second night in a row, the dog curled itself at the end of my bed. Thankfully, it didn't take long before I fell back asleep, a pillow clamped to my head.

Chapter 5

Kaden's Corpse
Day Two
Tuesday, February 22nd, 1923

When Stanley and I awoke in the morning, we had a brief discussion before Millie arrived in the still-blowing storm. I peeked outside and found that there had been several more inches of accumulation in the night. I was unfamiliar with this region, so I had yet to learn how unusual this storm was. Later, the newspapers called it a hundred-year storm, though I doubt the Plateau Times had records of more than twenty years. The native population may have known, but it was unlikely they were asked.

"Tell me about Sergeant Deacon," said Stanley. "When did he get his new posting in Prince Rupert?"

I watched Stanley as he began making us both a coffee. He assured me that he could do it.

"They moved Sergeant Deacon a full month before I got here," I replied. "I guess headquarters saw the writing on the wall when the mine closed. Plus, I heard that there were things happening in Prince Rupert that needed his type of leadership. They have him down at the port."

"What type of an officer is he?" Stanley asked.

I took a moment to consider this. I never met the

man but had heard enough stories to develop a feeling about him. Clearly, he was a strong man concerned with power and order. Millie was intimidated by him. She gave me the impression that he had worked her hard and had not suffered through her fanciful tales as I did.

Other than Millie, the townspeople quickly told me about his *heroic* deeds. To some, he was something of a legend. They marveled at his ability to keep the town in check during its boom. But Sergeant McClintock in Plateau did not like Deacon's methods. Sergeant Deacon often expelled workers and their families if he felt they were unsavory. Sometimes because of their conduct and sometimes because of their race. Many of these people settled in Plateau, which helped change McClintock's opinion about Deacon.

One story I heard from Mayor Fox and others was Deacon's dealings with the Kitsumkalum Indians who traveled the length of the Skeena River. The Grand Trunk Pacific maltreated this tribe. The rail line had been forced through a number of their graveyards. The band successfully sued for compensation but received little of the money owed. Instead of seeing them as victims, however, Deacon would have nothing to do with them. If a Kitsumkalum so much as stepped into Chambers, he would either intimidate them or form a gang of miners to oust them.

They told me these stories to make clear what shoes I was supposed to fill. To Fox and others, Sergeant Deacon was the epitome of Mountie bravado. The Wild West could only be tamed by an unwavering commitment to duty and discipline.

"He was effective." I asserted. While the man was not my hero, he still outranked me. And when Chambers was at its most populous, I'm sure the miners needed a heavy hand to guide them. Successful mining camps attracted all sorts—prostitutes, gamblers, thugs, quacks, and grifters all found work on the perimeter, more coming in on the weekends when the men needed to let off steam.

Stanley smiled at my remark. "So they needed that effectiveness farther west, eh?"

"Yes, though I believe he was planning to retire here. He worked ten years for the North West Mounted Police in the Yukon before the forces merged with the Dominion Police and became the RCMP. They gave him credit for all those years as well." I didn't know the man's exact age, but I got the impression he had only two or three years left.

Stanley handed me a cup of his coffee. I had to admit it wasn't too awful. But Millie wouldn't be too worried about losing her job if she tasted it.

"So I guess I'm wondering if he was the type of man to lose a report like that?" he asked. What was Stanley implying? That Deacon lost it on purpose? I couldn't imagine a man of Deacon's stature would do so. What would be the purpose?

Piles of paperwork still adorned most of our living space. They would have to rectify this—it wasn't a suitable look for a detachment.

The big man poured himself another cup of coffee. "It's probably not related anyway. Millie only mentioned the girl because of your ghost. Two strange women appearing where they had no right to be." He took a long sip of his coffee and stared at me over the rim. "It sounds like there has been a great deal of change here. It might be hard to know everything that has gone on."

"His former partner," I said, thinking aloud, "Constable Taylor had been transferred to Calgary to be with his sick mother. The death of this girl wouldn't be the only thing on Deacon's mind."

We let that sit between us. Most of the people that had shaped Chambers were long gone. Even those people I trusted in town: Peter, Genevieve, Dr. Moody—I still couldn't say I knew everything about them—the secrets from their past. I'd lived long enough to know that people could surprise you. One missing file was just the tip of a spear. We could only act on what we learned to be true.

Come to think of it, how well did I know Stanley himself? He blew in just yesterday, yet he was already so concerned about the comings and goings of everyone here. How shy and ineffectual I must have seemed when I first arrived. Stanley, by comparison, acted like an old hand, like he had been doing this for a decade.

****

After Millie arrived, I dashed across to the station. Mr. Benjamin was right where I had left him, sitting in his chair, the same Western novel pressed to his nose. His face reflected no pleasure in seeing me. Instead, he grunted, "No news," without laying his book on the counter.

There were other questions, though. The man sat at the epicenter between the town, the mine, and the rest of the world. He must know some of the town's secrets. I walked to the same cold window I had peered out of the day before. I knew the pit rail ran perpendicular to the station but could not see it under the snow. Still, I could guess where it was. They had disturbed the ground on each side so that no trees had yet grown there—a straight path to the foot of the mountains and the silver that had built this town.

"Mr. Benjamin, have you seen any hunting parties go by this way?"

I could hear the man huff. You would think he would want company after sitting alone. I turned toward him, and finally, with a sigh, he put his book in his lap and peered at me over the round glass of his spectacles.

"Hunting party?" He asked.

"Yes, maybe two days ago, maybe yesterday. A group of men."

"No hunting parties." He sounded bewildered. "No, anyone." He shifted in his seat, becoming rigid, his back straight.

"Aren't you bored sitting here?" I asked, but he made no move to talk, not even a twitch of that tidy mustache.

So I tried again. "Does anyone other than Bunny Dix and his mate ever use the pit trail?"

He shook his head. Why was everyone in this town so obstinate? I was beyond frustrated.

I took a deep breath and let my shoulders drop. "How often are you sending the telegraph?"

"About every half hour," he said. "I will let you know as soon as something comes through." He was pulling his book toward him so he could ignore me.

"What is this town hiding?" I shouted. He fumbled the novel, knocking it to the floor as he tried to catch it.

I strode over and grabbed the book, meeting his eyes the whole way. But the man was resolute. "Don't know what you mean, Constable," he said and accepted the book from my hand.

Snowstorm or not, we were going to retrieve that

body today. I was tired of all this evasiveness. I knew the dead Pickle brother wouldn't be able to answer my questions either, but it could reveal some important clues. Besides, the corpse should not be alone in the woods where someone or something else could get at it. I was done with surprises. I needed to take control.

****

I left the station without a goodbye and slammed the door behind me. My mood did not change on my short walk back to the detachment, so when I opened the door and glimpsed Stanley and Millie talking about who knew what, my temper leaped to the forefront.

"Stop mucking around!" I heard myself shout. "We have some serious work to do. This is not a social center for you two to get to know each other better. There's been a shooting; a man is dead." I felt the energy come out of me like a force, so strong I had to struggle to keep my balance. I would have taken a seat if not for Millie's crestfallen face. Instead, I rammed the door shut and lumbered back out in the swirling cold to wait for Stanley.

As I did so, I caught the shadowy figure of Mr. Benjamin walking away from the station. He held his wide-brimmed hat with one hand while he trudged through the deep banks of snow. He stomped north through the blizzard, not to town but down the snow-covered tracks of the pit rail, an inhospitable walk with one possible destination—Chambers Lodge. But why?

Stanley came out beside me, still buttoning his jacket in his haste to appease me. He must have followed my gaze. "Who's that man there?"

"The stationmaster, Mr. Benjamin," I said. "He must be going to visit Mr. Chambers, though I can't say why.

117

Maybe he feels it's his duty to check in on the lodge?" I shrugged and began walking. The quicker we were, the faster this all would be over. I could think of a few tasks less enjoyable than dragging a man's dead body out of a forest during a snowstorm.

I felt it gnawing away at me - the enormity of the fact that I had killed this man - removed him from this world. It was not until the last year of the war that I was put into the fight. Before that, I had done a whole series of tasks and been put in danger, but I had never been forced to kill until that final year. I hoped a quiet, out-of-the-way detachment would give me time to think—to make peace with what they made me do. But either not enough time had passed or no amount of time would ever make it right. Until time healed my wounds, I would have to steel myself and move forward through the onerous tasks ahead.

****

I marched us back to the hospital, but I decided to call on Peter Stormcrow first. He shouted at us through the door to enter. Inside, we found Bea Brannon and Peter sitting around the large oak table in the middle of their living space.

Peter was a status Indian, so he had difficulty holding title or land. In British Columbia, there had been a lot of heated arguments about Indian rights, bringing to light many prejudiced opinions. Any way you looked at it, it was a raw deal for Peter. His people were Cree from somewhere in the East. Technically, he should have been with them on a reserve out there, but he had decided to move west, taking on various jobs along the way.

It was his friendship with Duffy that had allowed him to purchase the business. It was all under Small's name, but Peter had done all the hard work. The sawmill had been in operation since the turn of the century. In the warmer seasons, they cut the timber and floated them to the ocean. Unfortunately, the more modern sawmill at Plateau had put Chambers' operation out of business. The town had put all its eggs in one basket. It was the mine or bust.

Indeed, the town should have been proud of what Peter had created in the last six months. It was about the only thing bringing in money from the outside. Peter was a marvel with anything wood, and the two had produced snowshoes, chairs, and other small furniture items. They shipped out the items by train to Hazleton and Prince George. Duffy's part was to handle the lifting and menial tasks. They also used his name when brokering deals with their clients.

As for Bea, I was unsure how she fit into their operation. Peter always laughed me off when I suggested they may have a romantic relationship. I had always wondered why. Were the divisions between their two cultures too broad, or was Bea simply not interested? Anyway, I learned not to ask too many questions. Peter tended to avoid certain subjects around me, and pushing didn't feel right.

I brought Stanley into the room's warmth, closing the door behind me. The place was always a mess. The smell of sawdust, varnish, and sweat permeated every inch of air. It was littered with sawhorses, tools, and half-made formulations mingled with dirty dishes, newspapers, and the detritus of casual living. I imagine it had some organization, but I could make no sense of it.

Duffy was carrying their finished works down the

ladder from the second floor, stacking them in a lopsided tower in one corner of their large workroom. When the trains got going again, they would most likely ask for my help to shift these pieces over to the station. It would be a small favor considering Peter's help the previous night. Better yet, I could offer Stanley's help. With his frame, he could probably split the time in half.

But now I had yet another favor to ask them. "We're going back out to fetch the body," I told them all.

Peter gazed out the window. "You sure," he said, "you could wait until this all blows over."

"No," I told him. "I wanted to get him out the night of the shootout. We just didn't have enough men or stretchers. And now I want to see what he had on him."

"Probably for the best," agreed Peter. "The wolves might find him, even if he is under all this snow." Or maybe the ghost girl would come back for him. Peter gave me a hard stare. "Gus?" he began. "Did the Pickle Brothers tell you why they were shooting at you?"

"No," I said. "I figured it was because I was a Mountie. On account of their Pa getting killed and all."

Peter's eyebrows raised as if to say he wasn't so sure of my reasoning.

"What?" I asked him, but he gave no reply.

"Give us a few minutes, and we'll come with you," said Bea. I didn't need her to come along. I hoped to borrow Peter and Duffy for the job, but I would take any help that was offered. Besides, with her agreement, Peter couldn't say *no,* could he?

Peter wasn't pleased, though. "It's a long walk, Albright, and I'm not sure how you could continue to pay me back."

Stanley was waiting behind me, and I saw Bea

giving him the once-over.

"So who's the big fellow?" she asked.

"Constable Paul Stanley at your service," he said before I had the chance. "I'm visiting from the Plateau detachment."

"Well, well," Bea said, a mischievous look on her face. "Millie must be pleased." Peter and Duffy chuckled, and the tension broke, though I was not pleased with the implication.

Still, I took the opportunity that was granted. "We are going to get a stretcher from the hospital," I stated. "We'll be leaving in ten minutes, and if you are willing, we would thank you for your help."

"And your companionship." I thought to add. Then, I turned and left with hopes that they'd come through.

****

At the hospital, I sent Stanley into the backroom to fetch the stretcher. While he was gone, I asked Genevieve about our patients. She told me that Dr. Moody had agreed to give Clayton another shot of morphine, which silenced him long enough for her to rest. The symptoms of fatigue had made her face drawn and colorless. I felt sorry for her. I decided to visit the hospital later in the evening to give her some respite.

"And the other one. Has he gained consciousness yet?"

Genevieve shook her head. That wasn't good news. I thumped him hard but did not expect him to be out for so long.

"You never know with an injury to the head. I know you, Gus. You meant to do no harm."

I wasn't so sure. I had acted fast, my instincts overpowering any conscious thought. The truth was, in the war, I showed time and time again that I would do pretty much anything when survival was on the line. I had made it through that last year by transforming myself into a killer. And now, in the bush where I imagined I could live a more peaceful life, the violence had found me again.

It was then that I remembered that I had something to ask her. "Why didn't you tell me about the Oriental girl?"

Genevieve stepped away from me, her face shocked. "What do you mean?"

"You don't know about the girl found dead in the river last spring?"

Genevieve's eyes squinted, and I felt myself step backward as well. "Of course I know." She sounded hurt like I was accusing her of something, but that was not my intent. I backed farther away, lifting my hands to show her I meant no harm.

"What do you want to know?" she asked. There was still some irritation in her voice.

"Well, first, why did nobody tell me about her? A dead body in the river is not a tiny thing."

"No, it's absolutely not," she agreed and then took a deep breath. "I'm sorry, but I assumed that Sergeant Deacon would have filled you in on it."

I shook my head and watched a frown form across her brow. "That man! Kenneth and I were called to the riverbank when they found the body. It was clear that the girl had been dead for several hours, the poor thing. She must have been no more than thirteen or fourteen years old."

"Kenneth wanted to do an autopsy, but Deacon wouldn't allow it. He claimed that he didn't trust him to do it. This was when Kenneth was starting to take a turn for the worse, but still, the two of us together could have handled it. Instead, Deacon had her buried in the churchyard. He told us that he would request a coroner from Prince Rupert to come and take the body away, but I assume the girl is still buried there."

"That spring, Kenneth and I wrote three letters to the coast informing them of what happened, but there was no reply, and still no one came. So we had to assume that no one was interested. I hate to say it, but if you are female and foreign in British Columbia, you might as well be invisible. Even here in Chambers, the story seems to have disappeared."

"These letters," I asked her, "they would have gone out by train, I would suppose?"

Genevieve shrugged, her lips tight.

The letters would have been given to Deacon, Taylor, or Benjamin to be put on the outgoing train. Interesting. I would tell Stanley about this later and see what he thought. Along with Millie's missing file, it was all becoming quite suspicious. Was it just callousness on the part of Deacon not to care about the girl, or was there more to it?

Stanley appeared with the stretcher, and I gave him a nod to take it outside.

I turned back to Genevieve. Her arms were crossed, her hands clutching her elbows. "Listen," I told her, "if this had been during my time here, I would have handled this differently. I would have let you examine the body and made sure that your letter got a response."

Genevieve closed her eyes. When she opened them again, she breathed deeply, and the muscles in her face relaxed. "All right," she said and tapped me on the arm.

"Good luck out there. We will be waiting for you."

I watched her as she moved back into her living quarters. Sometimes, it didn't pay to have so much empathy. She needed some weight off her shoulders. I felt my body sigh. It was time to get this done.

****

I was happy to find Bea, Duffy, and Peter outside dressed for the storm. Bea was eager to get going. She made Peter show me the rope they had brought to tie the body to the stretcher and a ball of blue string, which she said she would use to mark our path. She also had her hunting rifle across her back and a rusted shovel tossed over one shoulder. And Duffy had brought us pairs of well-crafted snowshoes to help us from sinking into the snow. I had not considered the need for any of these things, though I know I should have.

However, once we started, we realized that finding the spot where the shootout occurred would prove difficult. We should have marked the trail when we first returned, but it was dark, and the storm was in its infancy. I had just wanted the night to end.

Nevertheless, we used our memories of the path to pick our way forward. On the night of the shooting, there had been full moonlight and fresh tracks in the shallow snow to follow. With the cloud cover and blowing snow, our visibility was obscured. At times, we saw the world only in patches, our scarves wrapped as close to our eyes as possible to avoid the stinging snow.

I was surprised, but Bea was an excellent tracker, and even though she had not been on the original journey, she found as many traces of our previous progress as we three men put together. Ultimately, we had her go ahead of us, Stanley walking a step or two behind, asking her questions about her findings. Whenever she came across some clue, Peter would stop and tie a blue ribbon around a nearby branch so we would not have to guess our way back. I was glad that I had stopped and asked the three of them to come.

Reaching our destination took much longer than my previous journeys. About halfway there, I broke my silence to ask Peter some questions. As part of his westward travel, Peter had spent some time in the foothills. Because he was so good with his hands, he knew men throughout the north. Between these skilled laborers, it was often a small world, and men gathered a reputation as hard-working or lazy, reliable or untrustworthy.

"You lived near Smithers once, didn't you? Have you ever run into these Pickle boys?"

Peter chuckled, "Not if I could help it. They were like rabid dogs, those two. It's a good thing you put them down, Gus. They were the type of men that would keep doing evil until they were stopped." We let the thought rest as our feet crunched through the snow.

"But still," I began again, shouting over a gust of wind, "you know a bit about them."

"Sure," said Peter, "I think most people who lived around there did." He pulled some branches back to get by and didn't let go until I was past. "What do you want to know, Gus?"

"Well, first, how many brothers were there?"

"Just the two," he replied.

"Just the two and their father, right?"

Peter nodded. "The mother died in childbirth with the younger one. Their pa never remarried. Mostly because he was a nasty piece of work." He stopped and turned toward me. His breath in the air made a long plume of smoke. "Now, there's only one left. I could never tell which one was which. They were both just as mean. Can't say if I care if that one you put in the hospital bed ever wakes."

I moved beside him so we could face each other as we talked. Then I put out my arm to stop him from moving forward. "That one, I believe, would be Daniel. Do you remember the other one's name?"

"The one you left under the snow. That would have to be Kaden, then." He began to move again, the wind too cold to keep his body still.

I tried to picture them alive and how they might have lived. Peter was a calm man, never a drinker, and not one to become enraged. They must have been bad business if he had problems with these boys. But I knew at least one person willing to deal with them.

"How about Bea?" I asked.

"How about her?" His eyes were paying attention to the other's footprints.

"She told me she came across them."

"Makes sense," he said, still focused on the tracks. "She comes across a lot."

I nodded. Bea seemed to get around. "She wouldn't take up with them, though?"

That gave me Peter's eyes. "You know her," he asserted. "She wouldn't give those boys the time of day. And if she did, they would lose in that bargain."

But Bea admitted to me that she had spoken to them—probably more than once. There were reasons to suspect Bea, but her shape didn't match that mysterious girl I encountered in the woods. Besides, why would Bea want to hurt me? There was no motive. She sought me out yesterday morning and then volunteered everyone for this little trek the next day. Is she trying to stay close to my investigation out of a guilty conscience? Or to keep tabs on me? Or was it simply friendliness? I always wondered if she took a shine to me.

"Any more kin, Peter?" I asked. He looked confused. "The Pickle Brothers…you think there will be others that will come to settle the score?"

"No," he replied. "You're safe there, Gus. No other kin. At least not around here. And I can't see anyone else caring, either. They were loners and layabouts."

He grabbed my arm as my snowshoe caught against a shrub, allowing me to recover my balance. "No sisters, aunts. No women folk either?"

Peter shook his head. "No. Just the two of them after their Pa was shot. Bad business that. You think this ghost girl was consorting with them, don't you?" He sucked in breath through his nose as he considered this. "No, I don't know any womenfolk who would want to be around them." So, Peter wouldn't know about the woman listed in Daniel Pickle's will.

I changed the subject. "Before, you wondered if they had given a reason for shooting me. Maybe you feel that their Pa's death wasn't reason enough."

Peter shrugged. "It seems a little random. They weren't on the best terms with their pa. I always imagined they were happier with him dead. And it was a while ago". He sniffed. The wind blew softer now. "And why you? You weren't the first Mountie they would have come across. They didn't even know you."

"Maybe I was an easy target?" I offered.

Peter chuckled. "Well, they sure gambled wrong on that one, eh?"

I lessened my pace, letting Peter stamp ahead. It was easier to walk in single file as the young birch grew close together here.

So there was no sister. And yet, she had suggested that was who she was. Or was that my doing? Perhaps a sister by another marriage or union. Someone who a stranger like Peter wouldn't necessarily know about. Or maybe she was a wife instead, a sister-in-law to one of the brothers. When the storm had stopped, I would have to telegraph my colleagues in Smithers. Gather some more information. Until then, I hoped to get some clues from the corpse in the woods.

I struggled to draw even with Peter again. "Did you know that Bea saw the Pickle brothers right before the shootout?"

"Yes, I was aware." Peter did not turn to face me or slow his pace.

"Why didn't you tell me then?" I asked, "Didn't you feel I should know if they were about? You told me yourself how dangerous they are."

Peter stopped and motioned for me to stop beside him.

"I know you consider us friends," he said. "And we are." He spent a moment searching for the words. "But there are things about my past that I would rather keep to myself."

I cocked my head, encouraging him to continue.

"Let's just say that we didn't think the Pickle brothers being here had anything to do with you. If we knew that they had plans to shoot you, we would have alerted you. We thought they were here for another reason."

"What reason?" I prompted.

"That's what I'm saying. For a matter that does not pertain to you and which I'm unwilling to discuss. Regardless, we were wrong, and I'm sorry."

Peter started walking, but I wasn't willing to quit. I seized him by his shoulder and tried to turn him. "Peter," was all that came out before he shrugged me off.

"What else are you not telling me?" I asked, unable to keep the irritation out of my voice. But he did not answer, and for now, I didn't press my luck. He was attempting to clean the mess that I had started, and I was grateful for that, but still, I didn't like that I could not fully trust his motives.

****

We came across the fated clearing after two hours of slow progress. It appeared smaller than in my memory. Before we entered, I had my party stop, and for some moments, I stood and stared, trying to recognize the different places my body had moved, piecing the action out bit by bit. I looked at Stanley.

"I've got to act it out," I told him. "You be Clayton." I brought him forward, narrating as I went, showing him the point when Clayton was first hit, where we must have lain, talking, devising my foolhardy plan. And then I took him with me as I tried to trace my brief run through the trees. Snapped branches showed that it wouldn't have been soundless.

Finally, we came to the spot where I hit the now-unconscious brother. I mimed my way through it, the strike with the battery torch, the rifle twist, the butt smashing against the man's forehead, the shot itself. And then nothing.

"About there," I said, pointing through the trees to the other side of the clearing. "I imagine that's where the body is."

I realized that Stanley had been observing me. He was testing out my story in his mind, trying to find any inconsistencies or impossibilities in my narration.

I called out to Bea, Duffy, and Peter to meet us on the other side of the clearing, and we all moved forward into the space between the trees.

The snow fell even gentler now, and the wind slowed to a soft breeze. I stopped and gazed up, receiving a face full of large wet flakes. Stanley inspected the rock in the middle of the clearing. It had grown a tall cylinder of snow like a white stovepipe hat.

"Is this where our ghost girl was supposed to have disappeared from?" Stanley asked.

"Yes," I replied, "Clayton told me the tracks ran to the stone and then stopped. I never had the chance to investigate it, though."

Stanley removed the tall pillar of snow, using his broad forearm to knock it to the ground. When he was done, the rock sat naked and inert. I remembered the handkerchief still lodged in the left-hand pocket of my fur. I neglected to mention it to Paul, Millie, and Mayor Fox. I put my hand in my pocket to pull it out but thought better of it and pushed it down farther.

But its presence on the rock led to some interesting questions. Was it part of the ruse, the effort to ambush me in this clearing? Such a feminine object. Did the Pickle Brothers formulate this scheme on their own? They were described as being lowbred and crude. So it was more likely to be the girl's idea. But why? Did she feel that the narrative of the ghost story needed a physical article to make her appear more real? Martin Blood showed me the one he had collected. I figured it was a loose end to a strange story. Now I would probably need to visit him to compare the two.

Peters's voice brought me out of my reverie. The others were speculating without me. "Weird thing that," I heard Peter say. "How was it done?"

Stanley shrugged. "Most likely a board," he said, then looked around to see if we had the same idea.

"She wouldn't have carried it with her," he continued. "She probably had the place marked out and left the board against a tree." He rotated on his feet, pointing behind him at the opening to the clearing. "Then she walked in here, laid one end of the board on the rock and the other in the crook of a branch." He rotated again, this time to the other side of the clearing. "There's deciduous trees here. She would have picked one of them." As he walked over to them, he pretended to balance. "She would climb in the trees for a while before she jumped. Somewhere out there, her footsteps would have begun again, but even without the snowstorm, they would have been hard to find. Now, it would be impossible, I would suppose." He looked over at Bea.

She agreed. "But if there was a board or rope, it might still be here or some damage on the branches." She eyed some likely trees.

The girl would have had to have exceptional balance. The board must also be quite long—twelve feet at least. So strange. And again, why? What did it mean? A chill came over me. Our sweat was beginning to freeze, but that was not it. I got the feeling someone was watching us. I peered through the branches but could see no one. I could not let paranoia take hold.

"The Pickle Brothers must have come from a different direction to avoid making tracks," Stanley mused. "Several people saw them leave The Hole before Clayton saw the ghost girl. The Brothers, therefore, were probably already positioned in the bush like a couple of hunters. But they must have been working with this woman. It would be interesting to know if she was around to see the gunfight or had already scampered away. Anyway, that's one way it could have been done. There's got to be other ways if you thought long enough. Obviously, it's not impossible because we know it happened."

Stanley's imaginative response demonstrated he was thinking this all through. He must have been trying to put all the pieces together. I didn't want to be out here anymore. And I didn't want to speculate anymore about this girl.

"So she's not a ghost, then?" Asked Duffy. My gods, I could have hit the man!

"No," Stanley replied. "I don't think any of this is the work of ghosts."

"But, it's a possibility," he asserted. There was a look of absolute befuddlement on his face like the ideas were bubbling up before he could catch them. "Maybe it was just a phantom trying to lead Gus and Clayton to their deaths."

"Let's have that shovel, Bea," I said. Then, before anyone could say more, I passed the tool to Duffy, pointing at the snow on the other side of the clearing where I believed the body was lying.

"Be careful to not dig too deep and hit the body."

Duffy was delighted to be given a task. He trotted over and began to take scoops of snow from the surface and fling them into the woods. The rest of us used our arms to help him, reaching in so as not to stand where I imagined the corpse would be lying. It was a strange sight, a type of morbid mining.

Ultimately, I had to take Duffy's shovel away from him. I was anxious that his overzealous digging would leave grotesque gouges in the corpse. I didn't have to worry. Kaden Pickle's body was six feet farther on than I had estimated. I became fearful for a few desperate minutes. Had the body been moved? Or had I imagined the whole thing? Maybe that bullet hadn't pierced his eye. Could he have disappeared like the girl was supposed to have? Vanishing into a single white handkerchief. I feared listening to Millie's musings was making me daft.

But that was not the case. Peter found a boot, and we soon uncovered the frozen corpse. It was a horrible sight. The force of the bullet that had pierced Kaden's eye had knocked him over into a fetal position, his right arm extended above him as if he was reaching for the heavens. From Peter's description of the man, I doubt he got there.

His left eye was wide open. I hadn't thought to close it when I checked his breathing or pulse. Nor did I think ahead and stretch the man out, allowing the corpse to be tied more effectively on a straight stretcher. At the time, I was only thinking about how to put the conflict behind me. I was surprised at the force needed to get the poor man off the ground. We used the leverage from the shovel and a stick to pry him up, the ice cracking around him as we lifted. Underneath, we found little blood. His heart had stopped pumping when the bullet hit the brain, and what liquid did come out froze in an unsettling lump.

I had seen more than my share of dead bodies in the war. For a time, I was a stretcher bearer and, before that, an ambulance driver, first with horse and then with automobile. And I can tell you that there is no dignified way to die. I'd seen it all: mangled, burned, eviscerated, rotting, dismembered, shattered, and severed in half. But there would always be something new, like the mustard gas deaths of Ypres, bodies still standing on their feet tangled in barbed wire.

When it didn't get to you, you knew you had a problem. While working, you gather the resolve to push it away, to do the dirty jobs because they matter. But it always comes back. In your dreams. Or in a quiet moment when your mind had a chance to churn. No matter how hard I tried to forget, to vanquish my darkest thoughts, they always returned.

When we placed the frozen body on the sled, nausea passed through me like a wave. The sound of it, like two boards scraping. Two inanimate objects. The others must have seen my face, but it spoke well that they said nothing to me. I was glad that they were there. And I was glad there was silence.

Peter tied the corpse tight to the sled; its awkward shape would have fallen off otherwise. But I regretted that we did not bring a blanket. Peter, Duffy, and Stanley took turns pulling the sled. Often, the trees would be too tight together, and they had to lift and angle the stretchers to make it through. Stanley's large body, which had difficulty negotiating between the trees on the way in, now had even more problems as he twisted and stretched, the branches poking and slapping him as he went. More than a few times, they lifted the corpse off the ground and carried him like a palanquin as if he were some great conqueror on his way to a glorified funeral.

I did not take a turn. Instead, I walked behind it in

case the body slid off the stretcher. Bea walked with me. Silent.

By the time we returned to the hospital, it was past midday. The snow was still falling, but the wind was not as rough. Could it be a sign that the tides had turned? That the storm was waning like the moon?

We brought the body in through the side entrance to avoid bothering the two patients. I did not want Daniel to see his dead brother if he was awake. Margaret held the door open for us and then ran to get Genevieve. Together, we negotiated the corners and placed the body in the examination room to thaw.

Kaden Pickle's was the first death in Chambers since the undertaker had left. The funeral parlor was right behind the hotel in the new section. While the mine was in operation, he would have a steady trade, but even death is not a growth industry in a dying town.

We would have to ship Kaden's body to Prince Rupert or Prince George. The bill would likely come from the man's estate if money were in the Hazleton bank. I couldn't imagine the town of Smithers wanting to pay his bill.

Genevieve was unperturbed, ignoring the body and asking small questions about our journey. She already knew that it was successful and, from our wearied faces, an ordeal. She offered us tea, but we declined. It was time to get back to the detachment to rest.

Before leaving, I asked Margaret to fetch me Clayton's letter. I was in no shape to interview Clayton a second time.

Margaret brought it back with her regular enthusiasm. "I thought you said that was Clayton's business," she trilled, bouncing on her toes.

"I changed my mind," I said. Margaret was curious about what was in there, but I was not in the practice of sharing other people's secrets, especially with one so young. Instead, Stanley and I thanked Peter, Duffy, and Bea for their help and made the toilsome walk back to the detachment.

Chapter 6

Millie's Mission

Thankfully, a wonderful bowl of venison stew, hot off the stove, greeted us on arrival. The meat was so soft it melted in your mouth. Millie initially gave me the cold shoulder, but after a few complimentary remarks about her cooking, I was back in her good books. Besides, I had an ace up my sleeve. Something I was sure would make amends.

Both Stanley and I helped by clearing the dishes, and once done, I asked Millie for the favor I knew she couldn't resist.

"Mrs. Tuttle," I told her. "I want you to go over there and see if her husband, John, is back from his hunting trip. If you want, you could tell her that I am concerned about his absence. Or you could treat it as a social visit. I don't know how well you know her, but she could probably use the distraction.

Millie was all smiles. "You want me to do some investigation work for you?"

"Sure," I replied. "And if you can, try to find out who John went with or any other details you can discover. I'll check them against what she told me."

"I get it," she said. She grew serious. "I can be shrewd when I need to be. She won't even know why I'm asking. I'll tell her I wanted to visit Jane."

"That's good," I said, "and after, if you still have time, maybe you could go visit Mrs. Granderson or Mrs. Landers and see what they have to say. But not both of them mind. They would get suspicious. Just pick one of them." I had left the younger wives out of it—Mrs. Poulson and Mrs. Clack. I heard through the grapevine that they snubbed Milie for being unmarried.

She went to the sink and pinned her hair back in place. "Don't worry; they won't have any idea why I'm there. I can be quite the conversationalist."

I let the comment go. Why did I not think of this before? Most people underestimated Millie. She was more clever than she appeared.

"Okay," I told her. "After you clean up here, you can head on over."

I glanced at Stanley. "I'm going to take a little nap. But not a long one," I assured him. "Afterward, we can talk about our next steps."

Stanley peered around the detachment. "If you both don't mind, I would like to have another try with your files. Millie has shown me her system, and I hope she knows I will keep things organized."

I looked at Millie, and she beamed. "All right, by me," she said.

Well, we were now a team. That suited me fine because I needed that nap.

In the army, you learn to sleep whenever and wherever you can. I had perfected the process and could wake myself on cue after five, ten, twenty, or thirty minutes. Today, I decided to treat myself to a restorative thirty-minute session. I removed my jacket and indoor slippers and lay down on my back; my fingers interlaced across my chest, and I got what I wanted—thirty minutes of dark, dreamless sleep, back to back to back. I woke a full hour and a half later, startled and annoyed. Too much sleep in the middle of the day disorientates me, and it took some time to get myself to a sitting position, my head in my hands as I tried to breathe out the fogginess. What would Stanley think, me sleeping the day away as he worked alone in the lobby? I could hear his feet shuffling on the other side of the door.

As I put my hands on my knees to rise, I remembered something. Clayton's letter from the box in the hospital. What difference could an extra few seconds of solitude make? I lifted it from my jacket and examined the word "Clayton" marked on its front. This invasion of privacy was probably unnecessary, but I wanted to know more about the man hiding behind the drink, the furs, and the rough exterior.

I notched my finger under the flap and wiggled it open, trying to do as little damage as possible. Inside was a folded note. A single piece of once bright white paper imprinted with pale purple flowers I believed must be lilacs. Pretty.

The note looked fresh, the paper clean, the fold lines stiff. I unfolded it to reveal four words written in a jagged scrawl.

Your debt is paid.

That was it. I flipped the page over to see what was on the other side—nothing. The envelope was empty as well. What did it tell me? That Clayton owed someone money, which he repaid, was the most obvious answer. But who? There was no signature, nothing to indicate the nature of the transaction. Could this be the reason why he was getting pushed around by the mayor or Bunny Dix? He did have those four quarters in his pocket. Had he come into a windfall somehow?

He could have carried the note for days, months, or even years. Where did Clayton come from anyway? Whenever I questioned him, I always received a filthy diatribe in return. Honestly, I barely listened to the man. I assumed he was a fixture in the town, but I heard he only arrived in Chambers a few months before the mine closed. I rubbed my legs, trying to get some feeling back into them. Who would know more about Clayton? There had to be someone who would give me some straight answers.

Of course, the note was unlikely to connect to the shootout. You don't ambush or shoot a man *after* he has paid a debt. I stood and stretched, fitting my feet back into my slippers. Outside, the afternoon light was already fading. Should I go back to bed and hope everything would work out? It was tempting. But the noise of Stanley's work was beginning to irritate me through guilt. I folded the letter and put it in my pocket—time to write that damn report.

****

When I stepped out into the lobby's warmer air, I was shocked by the mess of papers that littered the room. My two assistants had found a common interest: building paper piles in places where they did not belong.

"This is all so interesting," Stanley told me. He had removed his jacket and was working with his sleeves rolled past his elbows. Even his forearms were muscular, his big paws an amusing juxtaposition to the feminine office task that engaged him.

"What is?" I asked him. "How to take apart my detachment?"

He stood and, with manic energy, began to walk the

room, pointing and slapping at things as he talked. "This here," he said, "are files from the beginning of the detachment, from before the railroad—1910-1913. Sergeant Deacon was already here, but he had partners before Taylor. He ran through them pretty fast. And he did most of the writing himself. Most are land disputes, some stealing, drunk and disorderly conduct, fistfights, that sort of thing." He shrugged his shoulders. "It's pretty much what you expect from a growing mining town. Look at the size of it!"

I did. It was a sizable mess.

Stanley shifted. He walked over to point at the top of the ill-made file cabinet and Millie's stovetop. Files also lay on the floor by the furniture's feet. "These are the files after the railroad began between 1913 and 1920," he explained. "Things become much more technical. "There were three Mounties or Dominion officers here at one point. Taylor comes near the end after other men transfer in and out. It's still the regular stuff, but it's getting louder, more heated, more of everything, as you can see." And indeed, the pile was much larger than the first one. "I want to go through it to see if anything connects to what we've discovered in the last couple of days and how much of it is written by Deacon."

What was he suggesting?

"Now," he said, walking to my writing desk, "this is from the period before you arrived, February 1920 to May 1922. Notice something?"

"There's hardly any files," I murmured. Indeed, a standard-issue wastebasket could hold the lot with room to spare.

"I don't need to go through these because I already

have," Stanley continued. These are all minor infringements, and they are all done by Taylor. I haven't found a single file by Deacon during this time."

He now strutted over to the doorway of *his* jail cell, where he pointed at his cot. "This here is all the files that you have written since you got here." I glanced back and forth from my desk to the cot. I was proud that my pile was taller than the previous one. "And remember," said Stanley, reading my thoughts, "those papers on your desk, the ones from 1920 to 1922, were from when the mine was still open. There were close to a thousand people here then. Now, what do you have? Forty people in the town and a few more on the outskirts."

I nodded. That was about right. "Why didn't Millie notice this?" I asked.

"Well, she did. At least she did yesterday when she took the files out. Remember, she said that she had typed the report about the missing girl. I believe some of the files were made and then destroyed. Others were padded with extra papers to make them appear larger. That's what gave me the idea that more than one file may have been tampered with."

"Tampered with?" It was too big of a word for such a small town like Chambers. "But why?"

Paul was standing right in the middle of the disorder, hands on his hips, his eyes darting back and forth between the piles. I got the sleep, but he looked as fresh as a daisy.

"I can't say yet because we don't know what's missing, but it seems like there were some fishy things going on with your Sergeant. He is the common link in all of this."

Deacon would not be too pleased with the mess

Stanley was making or his conjectures. Constable Stanley was too young to know the consequences of this type of insubordination. The RCMP had a hierarchy of command just like any other police service.

And yet, there was something there. Whether it connected to anything else that was happening around town was unclear. We were stuck in this snowstorm without much more to do, so Stanley might as well continue his project if he felt it was necessary.

I glanced around at the mess. It wasn't a job for two men. "I'm thinking of going over to Clayton's cabin to take a look around. I found a note in Clayton's pocket that suggested at one point he had some debts to pay." I took the note out of my pocket and passed it to him.

Stanley held it to the light of the lamp. "Interesting," he said, his eyebrows raised.

"What?"

"It's messy, but my guess would be it's from a woman's hand."

"A woman?" I asked. "I don't think so." I took the note from him and reviewed the four words again. "It's too sloppy," I concluded. "Not flowery in the slightest."

"Was the envelope it came in opened or sealed?" he asked.

"Sealed," I replied. "Why would it matter?"

"Well, then Clayton might not have known what was inside it."

That was a good point. Why did Clayton not feel the need to open it? "Or maybe he already knew what was in it," I said. "Perhaps he was going to use it as proof to somebody else that he had already paid the debt."

Stanley shrugged. Those eyebrows of his, still hovering high on his forehead.

"Okay, you stay here and work on these papers. Can you make the place appear like it hasn't been overrun by squirrels and raccoons? I'll see if there's anything in Clayton's cabin that suggests the reason behind this note."

Once again, I put on my things. As I checked that my pistol was in its holster, I saw Lloyd George looking at me. I realized the creature had not been outside for longer than to do its business. I could take him with me, but he would be a hassle in the snow. His sorrowful eyes made me relent. I would make it a short trip.

****

The cursed storm was worsening yet again. The snowfall was not heavy, but violent gusts of winds made fierce cyclones out of the surface snow. I pulled my scarf tight and jogged over to the station to see if Mr. Benjamin had returned, the dog keeping pace beside me. This time, I decided I wouldn't leave until Benjamin answered my questions succinctly.

But he wasn't there. Had he not returned since I last saw him walking the pit line? His book was lying face down, opened to somewhere in the middle. So he must mean to return. But when? I took some moments to poke around. His outdoor things were missing, but had he taken anything else? I commanded Lloyd George to lie down, and he complied, his eyes giving me his most doleful expression. I ignored him. I wanted to check out Benjamin's private quarters and did not need the dog between my legs.

There were two small sets of rooms in the station, one for the stationmaster and one for the postmaster. Since Mr. Benjamin fulfilled both roles, the other bedroom was empty except for the furniture it came with.

A small kitchen between the bedrooms held nothing but the articles one would expect.

The second bedroom, Mr. Benjamin's, looked identical to the postmaster's. The room was as tidy as the man himself. If not for the heavy smell of pipe tobacco, the place felt unlived in, like a hotel room after it had been reset for the next guest. Now, where would a man like Mr. Benjamin keep his things? I opened the desk drawer but found nothing more than blank stationery supplies. Benjamin had locked one drawer, but I felt cracking it open was beyond my authority. So I searched the closet and underneath his tidy bed. The contents of each suggested he had not packed for a journey. He would want to return by nightfall to change his clothes and read that book.

Under his bed, I found a small valise, similar to a doctor's bag. I released the catch and looked inside, unsure if I should do so. The bag was empty. I hoped there would be clues to help interpret what type of man Mr. Benjamin truly was. His room was so barren of personal items that it made me think he must be hiding something.

On a whim, I poked into the postmaster's room. All I remembered of the man was the stretch of his uniform over his expansive belly. He was here for the first week of my arrival and then was gone. I assumed he had been granted the same position elsewhere on one of Grand Trunk's other lines. His room was as clean as Benjamin's, but instead of a pipe, the aroma was fruity and delicate. There were no clothes in the dresser or the small wardrobe in the corner. I was about to leave when I spotted some cloth tucked in between the wall and a bedpost. I kneeled and pulled out a long black stocking.

Its size and the delicacy of the fabric made it unlikely to belong to either of the men who had lived here. It was a female garment. I racked my brain but could not remember any involvement between Benjamin and any member of the fairer sex. Not a surprise; the man's fustiness probably drove them away. I trailed the stocking through my fingers. And yet there was this.

I balled up the fabric and shoved it into my coat pocket. It would be important to remember it was there before Millie found it. I could only guess what she might infer from it.

It was then that I remembered the handkerchief from the woods. I pulled it out and peeled it away from the sticky stocking. I sat on the postmaster's old bed and unwrapped it until it was a smoothed-out square. It was a pretty thing, off-white with embroidered edges. The one bit of color was a dark blue *M* in a full serif font, hand-sewn into one corner. Blood's handkerchief was said to have the same monograph. Curious. Why would they leave it on the stump? And in Blood's clearing? Why leave anything at all? Surely, the idea of the ghost girl was strange enough.

The whole thing was frustrating. I squeezed both garments together and rammed them back into my pocket. Where the hell was Benjamin anyway? He should have been here all day, trying to get through to Hazleton or Prince Rupert.

Lloyd George trotted over to me as I came from the room, and I gave it a little pat as my mind turned. If Mr. Benjamin was not sending out my messages, he might have ignored all my previous orders. And yet, the telegram that brought Stanley here must have gone through. I could feel my cheeks turn hot with irritation.

Lloyd George barked, and I shushed him.

I had some practice with telegraph machines, but it had been some time since I used one. I sat and, using the poster of the code tacked to the wall, beat out a quick message. *Please respond, Chambers* was all I typed for now. Then I put my feet on the desk to wait a while. I opened Benjamin's Western novel and read the first few pages. Already, I was hooked. The man knew how to write.

So did I. I grabbed a pen out of the drawer and scribbled a quick note on a piece of paper. Since Mr. Benjamin had no qualms about leaving his post, I told him to come to the detachment and report when he returned. I left the note on the now-closed copy of the book. I made no mark to indicate the page the man had been on. A piece of nuisance that I hoped would communicate my frustration.

****

My walk to Clayton's cottage included a pass by Mrs. Tuttle's. Was Millie making headway with the poor woman? There was a light on inside, but the curtains were closed. Lloyd George was slowing my progress. While its legs were long, it had difficulty making its way over the tall snow drifts that sat in waves before us. More than once, it gave me pleading looks. If the animal could talk, it would have asked me to carry it. I ignored it as best I could.

As we crossed the bridge over the rushing river, I became curious about the body they found last spring. The river was too swift to freeze, though floes of ice sometimes floated amidst it, and its banks often developed a thin crust. The water would have been frigid when they found the girl in late spring, but no heavy ice would exist. I walked the river bank toward Oscar Lange's home to see where they discovered the body. There was no obstruction to block the passage, but sticks could have become lodged against the rocks to catch the corpse. I looked upriver. The girl either entered here or upstream. Both possibilities seemed unlikely. Mr. Lange was an old man. I couldn't see him hiding a runaway or running a criminal operation from his home. Nor did he associate with any ne'er do wells. And yet upstream, there was nothing, from here to Plateau and then again to Hazleton, just a few unmanned utility sheds erected by the railway. Otherwise, North or South, the mountains would seriously impede movement. The thought of anyone climbing through them untrained and unequipped made my head shake. So what would an Oriental girl be doing here? Dead or not.

I was alone for the first time since Constable Stanley arrived, except for the dog. I felt vulnerable, almost naked. Standing beside the mountains' enormity and the rushing river's merciless force, I was small and powerless. Strange emotions poured over me, ones I could not name. A sense of deep loss and loneliness.

In the war, it was clear that one's life was not one's own. You were a plaything in the hands of fate. There was no rhyme nor reason to it, no moral compass or central theme to guide your actions. The longer you searched for one, the more bitter you became. The only plausible action was to live in the moments between the horror. To surrender to the absurdity and continue forward. Not forward, just continue.

It had been four years since I left Europe and its war behind—four years of reckoning and trying to forget. The relative serenity of the natural world had helped to soothe me. Being here in Chambers sometimes felt like I had traveled to a different space and time, where only the news spoke in distant echoes to the places I once knew. And there was some comfort from the people here as well. Those few I had come to know as friends.

As for the confrontation in the woods, it needed further reflection. The cold wind had brought tears to my eyes, and I decided to let them come. The dog would not think less of me, I decided, and so I took some moments to weep, to push some of the pain in my chest out to the mountains. They could take it. They could handle anything.

I wiped my face.

As I passed the church, I remembered the girl's unmarked grave was in its cemetery. What could it possibly show me? Probably nothing, but it could help to make the girl feel more real. Besides, as odious as he was, Pastor Stevens was one of the few people who had been here from the beginning. As the town devolved, all the other clerical leaders left, leaving Stevens as the solitary man of faith. He still held services, but few attended.

The church stood on a small hillock beside the river, the tallest building in town, minus the mayor's Grand Hotel. I read 1908 on its foundation stone, but the church walls showed signs of critical decay; the spire bent to the left as the foundation sank into the soft loam of the river bank. The lack of footprints in the garden suggested that no one had entered or exited the building for at least the day. Girding myself for the upcoming conversation, I scrambled up the steps and opened the creaking main door.

The building was dark and shockingly cold, without

a single candle or lantern lighted either in the main room or the vestibule. Millie's gossip suggested that a ghost haunted the church, and while that was utter nonsense, I understood how being in this space could lead to macabre thoughts. For one thing, the pastor refused help from his parishioners to clean the place, nor did he lift a finger to put the church in order himself.

I left Lloyd George tied in the vestibule and walked the length of the nave, ignoring the cobwebs interlacing the back pews. Their weavers would thank the almighty god when they reawakened in the spring and found their creations undisturbed.

As I opened the door to the church's small vestry, a tremendous heat emanated from the room's open fireplace. The door was so thick, and the room so crammed full of trinkets and papers that the air had little space to move, resulting in a tight, constricted den fit for a cave troll or a demon. Pastor Stevens, dressed in pale pink underwear, sat in repose, his legs stretched open, straddling the room—unwashed, I'm sure, for quite some time.

The man greeted me with one lifted eyebrow and then swished his hand to indicate that the door behind me should remain closed. I complied, knowing that my overcoat and other winter furnishing would soon be a torment.

"I haven't seen you at service," croaked the Pastor, refusing to shift his body to allow more space inside the chamber.

"I've been working on my faith at home," I replied. "I just came to ask…"

"You know that our Heavenly Father can see everything." He pulled his arm back to reach through the jumble behind him. "It is your duty as our sheriff to impose the laws of good government on the people here. The good Christian laws that bind the society as a community under God." He pulled to his mouth what looked like a half-eaten cigar.

I ignored the bit about the sheriff, unwilling to take the time to correct my rank and position. "That is why I'm here," I started again. "There's things happening in this town that only God seems to know about. Maybe you would be good enough to get on the horn and see what he's willing to divulge."

Stevens placed the tip of his cigar into the fire behind him. When he turned back, I noticed the gap in his long johns lay open. I averted my eyes. Could the situation become even more uncomfortable? He waved the cigar in front of him as he spoke. "Ask on," he said. "And revel at the Lord's teachings." He sounded like a psychic at a country fair.

"The Oriental girl that was buried here?"

He sliced the foul-smelling stogie through the air to cut me off. "She was not a Christian."

"How do you know?" I asked, beginning to choke.

A cruel expression passed over his face. "In the spring, I'm going exhume that body and stick it back in the river where it belongs." Even for him, the invective was overdrawn. He shifted himself, his face inches from my own. "We weren't meant to mix, you know. That's what God says on the matter."

And so, I got my answer. The room could become more uncomfortable—bigotry and bad breath. My right arm flailed behind me, hunting for the door knob. "So you can't tell me anything about her then."

He laughed, brown spit sprayed from his mouth. "I

151

have lots of things to say about all sorts of heathens. But it's not her who you should be asking questions about."

I knew that it was my duty to ask. The man, after all, still had a congregation, small as it was. Some people still listened to his caustic lectures, having nowhere else to go. "Who then?"

He chuckled before placing his cigar in an oil can filled with ash. "I see who you hang about with. That native, his idiot friend, and that strumpet. The tramp at the hospital. The reprobate who calls himself the mayor."

I took a deep breath and closed my eyes for a moment to not have the man in my sight. My left hand curled around the doorknob, the right clenched in a fist. "The mayor?" I tried but failed to keep my voice flat and expressionless.

"The mayor," he repeated. He was scratching himself now, down below. "He's no mayor, just a pompous jackal. He has sold himself to the devil. Where does his money come from? You would ask if you weren't in his pocket yourself." He spat at my feet. Was the man so desperate to get a stiff punch to the face?

I breathed out again and let my emotions churn through anger and frustration. The pastor was small, a rodent, a rat in a dying cage with nowhere else to go. As miserable as they come. I had already wondered about the mayor and the state of his finances. Who was paying his bills now that most customers had left town? But I couldn't take this much longer. I could feel my underarms pouring out sweat.

"Who then?" I asked. "Who's the mayor's devil? It's easy enough to say, but do you have any real answers?"

The man sat back, grabbed the soggy cigar, and

returned it to his mouth. I took a moment to imagine the crumbling church falling on top of him, his charred corpse sitting in his chair, an evil grin on his skeleton's face.

"It's everyone," he said, his voice a plaintive croak. "Everyone is the devil."

I turned the knob and stumbled out of the room, enclosing the heat, the man, and his vitriol inside. Never had I enjoyed the chill of the church more than at that moment. I couldn't help but let out a shudder. It was hard to believe he was in there now, sitting, waiting to treat his next visitors with his poisonous words. Even after France, I didn't contend that everyone was the devil. The dignity of man always made itself evident—sometimes where you least expected it. But if I had to draw the devil's face, using Pastor Stevens as a model was a good start. Fortunately, that was not my task.

I collected Lloyd George's leash and pulled him back into the white world. "We'll head back home soon," I told him to reassure myself.

****

I broke into Clayton's cabin with ease. Presumably, he had not latched the door, and it now stood a whole hand's width ajar. The only work needed was to brush away the snow with my boot. I pulled the door wide to reveal the dark, cavernous space beyond. I turned on my dented battery torch and, with a sweep of my hand, gave the contents of the mean cabin my full regard.

The place smelled of whiskey, smoke, rotting food, and stale body odor. A tonic that spelled out all my cumulative experiences with its owner. Regarding articles of furniture, Clayton had an old chest, a wooden desk and chair, and a low flat box that I assume he used as his bed. Beyond that, the place was an absolute mess. It looked as if the squirrels and raccoons that had made their way into Stanley's paperwork had found this place last, held a party, and then made it their home. Everywhere I pointed my light, there were dirty rags, broken glass and pottery, splintered wood, and bits of paper.

I made ready to leave when my flashlight shone on the face of a drawer. It was lying at an odd angle perched atop the debris, and I realized this was not this cabin's normal state. I had let my prejudice see the room as I wanted it. The place had been ransacked with a ferocity that suggested deep emotional anger. Whoever did this wanted Clayton never to return *home*. Did they mean to destroy, or did their passion overtake them? Were they too searching for a missing piece of a story? Or did they take the opportunity of Clayton's hospitalization to rifle through his things? Either way, it was doubtful I would find anything of use.

I poked around the cabin, handling random bits and tossing them into the pile. There were slices of paper that may have been once part of more letters, but they were now so shredded they were impossible to decipher. Lloyd George, for his part, was content to sit in one corner, unsure, I assume, what the jumble before him meant.

There was no lack of people that Clayton had irritated. The whole town was tired of his antics. But I could think of no one who would make it their plan to harm him. He already seemed to be doing a good enough job of it by himself.

And yet the room's violent disorder suggested he did have an enemy. There was someone who wanted to destroy his home. Was I not the Pickle brothers' target? I pictured Clayton stepping out into the clearing, the moonlight on his open face as he looked back at me. The shots that had come were immediate and from both directions. Clayton was wearing nothing like a Mountie's coat, and they would have seen him earlier in the Hole. Why did they fire, then? They were only giving themselves away.

The girl was displeased. What did she say? "It looks like I might have killed three men tonight." Was she their kin then? Or was that all me—my assumption? "Three men," she said. I'm not sure it all made sense.

I had been an idiot. Someone was out to kill Clayton. Someone who I knew was still on the run. It must have been her who made this mess. I was not thinking of Clayton but Genevieve, Margaret, and Dr. Moody.

I ran as much as a man could in the wind. Clayton's door was not unlatched; it was broken, and I couldn't let anything else happen.

****

My eventual stumble into the hospital lobby made such a sound that it brought Genevieve out to see what was happening. It took a while to catch my breath, so I could not speak at first. She put her hands on my shoulders and commanded me to take a moment to calm myself. Lloyd George's whine came moments afterward, and thankfully, Genevieve opened the door to let the poor creature inside as well.

"Is everyone okay?" I gasped. My lungs were on fire.

"Yes, well, we had a bit of excitement, but nothing now to worry about," she replied, her brown eyes round with concern. "What's happened?"

I guided her through the lobby doors to take a look. There was no movement except for the rattle of Clayton's chain as he tried to sit forward to see who had entered. He called out, "What's that? Who *in the blazes* is there?" Except he had substituted *in the blazes* with other words.

"It's fine, Clayton," Genevieve shouted back and guided me through the doors of their living space. She closed the door and faced me with a severe expression. "Tell me what's going on! I just got Clayton settled. It may have been a mistake, but I gave the man a bit of alcohol to…"

I interrupted her. "I think he is in danger. Someone is out to get him, and I imagine they might come here to finish the job, which puts you in danger as well. All of you" I held her hand in mine.

"You mean kill him? Murder him?" she asked.

"Yes." There was no reason to be evasive. I watched as she considered this, chewing her bottom lip with her teeth.

"But why?"

"I don't know, but he probably does." She let go of my hand as I began to pace. "I will talk to him, but I believe the danger remains regardless of the answer."

"I never would have guessed," she said as I turned back toward her. I had made puddles on the floor, and I couldn't help but notice the water was seeping into her shoes. "Well…what do we do?"

"Well, first, I need to talk to him." I was still considering all the possibilities as I spoke. "And the Pickle Brother. If he is not conscious, then I must examine the dead brother and see if he was carrying anything to help us." I took in her face. "And I must sleep here tonight."

"In the infirmary," I added. "I will get Peter or Duffy to take my place over supper so that I can talk to Millie and Constable Stanley."

"Millie was here," Genevieve reported.

"Here at the hospital," my brain was speeding ahead. "Why? Is she all right?" I could not think of why she would be here. Was something wrong with her? Some feminine issue she could not confide in me?

"Yes, yes," she reassured me once again. "She was here with Dorothy Tuttle and her child, Jane. The baby had a rash, and they worried she might have a fever to go with it. But everything is fine." It was a curious fact, but I let it go. There were more important matters to contend with.

"Let me go talk to Clayton," I said. I was eager to hear what he would have to say. I tied Lloyd George's leash to the inside handle of the door. If someone entered this way, at least the dog would make some noise as he tried to lick them.

"Is the doctor about?" I asked.

"He's resting but should be waking soon." She reached out and held my hand. We stood like that for some moments until I let go and pushed on the door to return to the infirmary.

Clayton called out as soon as he heard the door close behind me. He demanded answers about my frantic arrival. The bold smells of the hospital filled my nose, and as I walked toward Clayton, I drove away the flashes of memory that played about my head.

Where to start? I dragged a chair over to Clayton's bed and sat. I slowly inhaled as I listened to him rail, not concentrating on his words. Then, as he cooled, I slipped my hand into the pocket of my serge jacket and pulled out the envelope. Clayton went silent, confusion all about his face.

"We found this in your pocket," I said.

"What is it?"

"I thought you would tell me." I pulled out the single sheet of paper and unfolded it before I passed it to him. He looked at it dumbstruck, his uncuffed hand shaking as he read the words.

"What is it?" he asked again.

"It was in your pocket," I repeated. "Who did you owe money to Clayton?"

"None of your goddamn business." His voice was a whisper, and he crumpled the paper before dropping it onto his lap. Then he closed his eyes and turned his head away from me. It was strange to hear the room quiet after so much histrionics.

"Clayton," I continued. "I went by your cabin."

He turned back toward me and opened his eyes. I was surprised to see them full of tears. "Well…yes…" he stuttered. "Sometimes, when I get too drunk, I go off my head." I waited for him to see if he would continue to speak.

"Sometimes," he continued, "When I get drunk, I do horrible things. Horrible things. But I can't stop it. I can't stop any of it. It's a terrible thing that I can never make it right." He was a different man now, small and tremulous; the bluster burned away. "You know what I'm like."

So he knew that his cabin was in disarray. I didn't believe for a second that it was his doing. Therefore, it must have happened before the shooting.

"Who took apart your cabin, Clayton?" I asked. I did

my best to make my voice soft and slow. I wanted to keep this version of him talking.

But it was the wrong question. Immediately, the anger returned to Clayton's voice. "Did what? I did it. It was me. When I was drunk." He would not catch my eye now. "You don't want to know."

"I do," I told him. "But there's a lot you're not telling me. And I think you're still in danger. Was it the Pickle brothers? Or was it the girl?"

"What girl?" he shot back. It was a stupid thing to say. Of course, he knew what girl. There was only one girl that had lured him into the woods. He had given himself away.

"So, it was the girl," I said. He shook his head, but I was on him now. "What does she have to do with you Clayton?"

His face turned red, his eyes fiery, and the old Clayton returned with a new string of hateful invectives, loud and awful. They filled the room so loud that the doctor rushed in, Genevieve not far behind. They tried to calm him, but Clayton still moaned and cursed. A list of torments spilled out of him, directed at everyone around him. He was in too much pain; he was being harassed, he needed his booze, he required more painkillers. He was being punished like a criminal, a litany of complaints without even a suggestion of a pause to continue the conversation. He was having none of it.

I stood and joined Dr. Moody and Genevieve. Genevieve ushered us all out. "When a child has a temper tantrum," she advised, "it is best to ignore them." She was right. Clayton wasn't going anywhere.

We all left the infirmary, but I took the extra steps into the examination room, where the body lay. It had been about three hours. Not enough time to thaw out, but I could check out the corpse's clothing. I tried my best to ignore the grotesque positioning of the body and edged my hand into each of the corpse's pockets: four in the trousers, one in the shirt, and two in the jacket. I struck out until the final pant's pocket, back right against the floor. It was another envelope.

I brought it over to the lamp on the windowsill. I took a deep breath, willing it to be something good, a much-needed clue. But it was the same Will and Testament found in Daniel's pocket. I walked with it still open in my hand and found Margaret sitting in the hospital kitchen with Dr. Moody. Presumably, Genevieve had gone back into the ward. I could hear some cursing still, though not as loud. At least it told me that Clayton wasn't in any immediate danger.

"Margaret, can you get me the will that was found in Daniel's pocket?"

She grabbed the shoebox from the shelf, rummaged through it, and then brought over the note. I unfolded it and placed both papers side by side on the table. The three of us, Dr. Moody, Margaret, and me, stared at the two wills without saying a word. The papers looked almost identical. I flipped them over and then back again.

The same notary signed this document—on the same date as well. Maybe both brothers were thinking of a dangerous task they might have to undertake, though the November date wasn't relevant to our little shoot-out. Could it be that the brothers were just considering their mortality, or maybe this Mr. Ricci was offering a two-for-one special?

Kaden's estate was to be shared in equal parts by Daniel, a woman named Olivia Morris, and a child named Rose Morris—perhaps the lady's daughter, though it did not name her as Kaden's child. Again, an address was given, this time in my hometown of Winnipeg, though it was a street I wasn't familiar with. So the two hundred ninety-six dollars was to be shared three ways minus funeral costs. The woman and her child would gain the entire amount if Daniel didn't make it.

"Why would they both have a will?" chirped Margaret.

I shrugged. "I guess they felt they owed these ladies something." That satisfied Margaret, but it didn't explain everything. When I saw the woman's name on Daniel's will, I figured she might be the ghost girl, but there were two other female names.

Dr. Moody, however, was still staring at the two papers. "I know this man here," he said and pointed at the notary's signature: Amadeo Ricci. "He used to be a lawyer in Prince Rupert. A real shyster. I remember he worked for the railroad, weaseling money out of workers who tried to get just compensation for their injuries. The man would sue the bone out of a dog's mouth. A real piece of work. I heard he got caught doing something fraudulent. "

"When was this?" I asked, but the doctor looked bewildered. "You know bad stuff goes on in Prince Rupert," he said.

I did know that. *Bad stuff* goes on everywhere.

"I can't picture the man's face." He pulled off his glasses and rubbed his eyes. "You're not going to bring us any more patients, are you, Gus? That one in the examination room appears quite unwell."

"I'll try my best," I said and folded the two wills together. I would bring them back to the detachment for

161

safekeeping, maybe show them to Stanley and Millie since they were obsessed with shifting papers around.

I returned to the infirmary and stood at the end of Clayton's bed. He was pretending to sleep. I guessed that his throat was sore and he needed a break. That suited me fine, but I still had something to say.

"I'm not going to stop Clayton. I'll keep asking until you tell me what you know. I just hope it's before you get shot to death." I saw one eye open for a moment.

I moved across the aisle and sat on the bed. There was so much to think about, but the soft bed gave me another idea. I stretched out and stared at the ceiling, my hands behind my head. Back and forth I went, trying to piece all the events together. Only more time would tell which ones were important and which ones weren't. I closed my eyes for a moment and willed the storm to stop. Under all this snow, I wondered, was there an answer?

****

I knew if I didn't return to the detachment for supper, Millie would be upset. But I made good on my promise to go by Peter's and ask him or Duffy to take a turn being a guard at the hospital. I left Lloyd George behind but didn't feel confident in the dog's ability as a lone sentry.

Peter was alone at the table when I got there, chewing through a dinner of beef and beans. I could hear Duffy creaking around on the floorboard upstairs. Peter didn't say a word as I sat across from him at the table. He didn't offer me any supper, which was all for the good, as I would have had to decline. Millie had a sixth sense for knowing when I had filled my stomach with something other than her meals.

I let the silence linger before I asked him where Bea was. He shrugged as he concentrated on his stew. I figured he must be tired from everything I had asked of him since the storm started.

So I changed my tack. "These Pickle brothers," I began, "how did they make their living?"

Peter pulled a bread crust over his plate, mopping up the remnants of his meal. "How did they make their money? Hmm…" he said, looking at me. "I'd say any way they could, but most especially if it didn't take too much work."

"Lazy," I said.

"No, I wouldn't say lazy," he replied, "more like they were always looking for an easier way to make a buck. Moonshine, I'm sure, maybe other things like that, and people probably hired them as muscle. They were also both gamblers. Which, as you know, is the source of many peoples' trouble. Of course, they had more than their share of problems, being cheaters and obvious ones at that."

He paused. "They went away for a time." He was remembering something. "Some thought railroad work, but I expect that wasn't it. I think they went to the coast."

"Prince Rupert?" I asked.

"Could have been," he said with another shrug. "They weren't the type of men who spent their time talking. They were gone and forgotten. When they came back, it was to most people's regret."

"And they never went overseas to fight?" I asked.

"Bah! Those two? No, I expect if they were conscripted, they would have run farther into the bush. I figure they weren't too interested in fighting for your king." He sat back. Peter hadn't gone over either. I knew some Indians that did, but many didn't feel our war was their fight. I didn't blame him. Having gone over myself, I would say it was an intelligent choice. And Peter was quite clever. He felt that Status Indians who went over had not been treated well on their return, so it didn't make him have second thoughts.

In truth, Peter was the second native man I had befriended. During the last stages of the war, I had the misfortune of being paired with a sniper named Lou Kenosha. It was not the man that troubled me but the task itself. Most snipers worked in pairs. Each one took turns to spot the other one. However, I was just the live body, filling in for Kenosha's partner, who had perished after stepping on an artillery shell. And since I was not an excellent shot, my job was only to spot, to get a clear sight of the enemy, and make sure that there were no dangers so that we could escape. Always, we would have a long slow visual of the German officer that we would assassinate together. I have not forgotten one, so seared they are upon my consciousness.

But I digress. Kenosha was a good man. Despite his task as an executioner, he was a gentleman. Often, when we weren't on assignment, we would sit and pass the time, forming rich discussions on all manner of topics. Unfortunately, I lost touch with the man after being transferred back to the Dragoons and my subsequent sickness the following year.

Peter reminded me of Kenosha, and not just because of their ancient heritage. They were both thoughtful men, aware of their place in the world but hoping for much more. Wanderers, unsure of where they were headed, trying to find peace in a rough world.

I leaned on Peter for his wisdom. The man had lived

and worked in every province and territory but Prince Edward Island. He had avoided being recruited by keeping on the move. He had no interest in fighting for the King because he had no illusion of what Britain and Canada represented for his people. Each man should have a right to decide what they fight for. Conscription was an evil, and I hoped it would not be supported again, though my greatest hope was that the Great War would be the last one. It had to be. It was doubtful humanity would survive another like it.

"Okay," I said, deciding Peter had given me all he knew about the Pickle Brothers. So I took the plunge and asked him yet another favor. In the end, he sent Duffy over to the hospital. Duffy was only too happy to do it. The man was interested in Margaret, though he was too old for her. I was pretty sure Genevieve already had her eye on it and that Margaret would not tease the poor man too much.

****

Of course, I quickly peeked into the station on the way back, but it was still the same. I was beginning to get worried about Mr. Benjamin, even beyond my annoyance at the man. Could he have become lost in the snow? The sky was already as dark as it would get. I had not seen him carry a lantern or torch on his departure, but that didn't mean he didn't have one.

When I entered the detachment, I was surprised to find Stanley was there by himself with his shirt sleeves unbuttoned pouring over the files in fewer and neater piles. He nodded at me, then returned to reading as I put my winter gear away.

"Where's Millie?" I asked him.

"She hasn't come back yet," he said, but he didn't

sound concerned. I couldn't remember the last time Millie had forgotten to prepare something for my dinner. I went to the stove to see if she had left something.

"I think I've found some things of interest." Stanley stared at me. He was excited to tell me his findings.

"Oh yeah," I said, distracted by Millie's absence. Could she have left a cold plate in the icebox? "Anything about the Pickle Brothers?" I asked.

"A bit." That piqued my interest. I approached the table as he pulled over a file he had set aside. "They got into a little trouble when they worked here."

"Really? They worked here."

"I believe so. They were both detained twice. Once in December 1918 and once in March 1919. They were put in these very cells." He pointed at the two empty cages behind him. "Drunk and disorderly for both the first time, and then both on assault."

From what I remember, Tom Pickle, their father, was gunned down in 1919. He'd been thieving homes and cattle. They had cornered him, but he came out shooting. Fortunately, Tom Pickle was the only casualty. I did not remember the exact date, though.

"Now, here's the thing," said Stanley. "They weren't listed as miners. They were listed as *hired men*."

"*Hired men?* What the blazes does that mean?"

"I guess it could mean anything. But it probably doesn't mean miner."

"No," I said, "It probably means that they were used to keep the other men in line. Peter told me all about this. Often, when you signed on to a work crew as a section hand or as a miner, it would cost the company money to ship you to a remote town like Chambers. The companies would then employ heavies to make sure those workers stayed in place. Quite often, they were in competition with other mines that would try to draw men away by offering higher pay or better working conditions. I wonder if the Pickle Brothers were hired to keep the order."

"Or to work something else." I wasn't sure what Stanley was getting at.

"And do you want to know who else was listed as a *hired man*?'" Stanley asked, emphasizing the peculiarity of the title.

The word "Yes" came out of my mouth when the door opened with a gust of cold wind. It was Millie looking quite out of breath.

"Oh, there you are," I said without thinking as she struggled to close the door. "I wondered where you were. Are you aware of the time? Where is our dinner?"

She was working fast at getting off her winter garments, but there was a deep scowl on her face. She was not one for holding her tongue, and when she let it loose, she gave me the longest dressing down I had received since basic training. Amongst other things, she insulted my manners, my gender, my ingratitude, and my general character, all in front of Constable Stanley. Even in the moment, I knew that she was right, but the shame of it was hard to bear. I was about to respond in kind when Stanley spoke as if nothing at all was the matter.

"Millie," he said, "I'm keen to know what you learned. Did you get to talk to Mrs. Tuttle? I have some things to share as well." He was holding a piece of paper to demonstrate his initiative.

"Yes, Constable Stanley," she replied, annunciating each syllable to its fullest. "I did more than that and found some interesting information." She moved to the icebox, avoiding my eyes. "Dorothy was actually delighted to see me. Her baby is sick, and she didn't quite know what to do." She pulled out a container of soup she had previously made and lit the burner on the stove. I enjoyed that soup, one of Millie's specialties, made with generous amounts of potatoes, onions, and cream. It was always filling on a cold day.

"So I was able to help out, and we got to talking." She retrieved a can of ham from our small larder and began to open it. "She eventually let it slip that her husband, John, was not on a hunting trip. And that he left by train five days ago."

I had some questions but recognized that it would be as yet imprudent. Instead, Stanley asked for details about John's departure.

"He caught the afternoon train on Friday morning," she glared at me before she returned to cutting slices off the loaf she had brought out. "She said he was sent to retrieve something and that he was supposed to be back on Monday. The day of the shooting."

"So he wasn't hunting. Did she say who it was that he did this for? Or what he was supposed to retrieve?" asked Stanley.

Millie paused as she buttered the bread out to its edges. "She didn't know what it was, but she presumed it was the mayor that sent him out." Evidently, she was pleased with herself for retrieving so much information.

"But that's not all. Mrs. Granderson also came calling. Kyle Granderson's wife." She was cutting cheese now for the sandwiches as I sat with a lump in my throat. "That's why I was so late. I didn't want to make it seem like I was prying. I wanted them to think that they had introduced the topic of discussion." She stopped her work and stared at me. "And because I was patient, I got two other tidbits."

Millie walked over to the table with a bowl of heated soup for Stanley before she retrieved mine. I grabbed her wrist as she set it on the table. I had forgotten that we had already had a disagreeable moment in the morning. I stared at her and saw a pair of stern eyes with two tiny reflections of myself.

"Millie," I said, swallowing hard, "I want to apologize. I had no right to talk to you like that."

She gave me a half-smile in return. "I accept your apology."

I could tell this was not enough.

"I don't think you should." The aroma of the soup wafted toward my nose; my stomach twisted in my gut. "I have been irritable lately. I don't know why, but it is inexcusable."

She stood for a moment with me still holding her wrist. She put her hand on top of my own. The warmth of it made my arm tingle. "Two nights ago, you shot a man," she said. Her voice had changed now. "You will let me accept your apology, and we will forget about it." She patted my hand, and I looked over at Stanley. The expression on his face was all business.

"Come sit with us then," I said, turning back to Millie, and she nodded. We waited to begin as she brought her bowl and spoons to the table and then returned to get the ham and bread. We said a quick prayer and then began to eat. It was simple fare but to my liking.

"So continue," I said to Millie. "You were talking about Mrs Granderson." There was a stillness to the room now as if the floorboards had absorbed all the energy of our previous exchange.

"Yes, her husband also left on the Friday train with John Tuttle." Millie began, moving stray hairs from her face as she talked. "There were other men that went with them. Maybe five or six in total. She knows they all left in the morning, but both Mrs. Tuttle and Mrs. Granderson were asked not to come to the station."

"Strange. Why would you need five or six men to retrieve something?" I asked aloud.

"Exactly," said Millie. I could tell she was pleased with herself. "And why the secrecy?"

"Did she say what time in the morning they left?" Stanley asked her.

"Ten-thirteen," I interrupted. "There is only one Friday train, and it always comes at ten-thirteen on its way to Prince Rupert." Initially, the Grand Trunk had assured British Columbians that the rail line would handle fourteen daily trains. But it was easy to remember the schedule as a train only passed through our station eight times every week.

Stanley's eyebrows lifted. "And can I ask where you were at that time?"

"Who, me?" I replied.

"Both of you." Stanley looked serious.

"We were right here. That was the time that Bunny Dix came to sort things out. You remember that, don't you, Millie?"

She nodded back. "Yes, he came around ten in the morning." Since it didn't happen so long ago, I could remember the details of it. The man had stayed for a good hour. After his apology, he got on the subject of hunting and regaled us with an overlong anecdote about a moose he once shot. I had planned to get information about the Chambers Lodge but never got a word in edgewise. Who knew the man could talk so?

"You mean Brian Dix," said Stanley. I looked over at Millie, but she was as confused as me. He pulled some papers toward him. "That's Bunny's real name, I think. And you know what? Just like the Pickle Brothers, the job roles list him as a *hired man*. I don't believe he was a foreman at all. I expect he works for the Chambers family."

He was a bull of a man with a bald head, large hands, and hard, piercing eyes. A laborer, one might think, but his clothes were too fine, and his back was too straight. There was power in the way he held himself. That's why I assumed he must be a foreman.

"His name is mentioned a couple times in the files," said Stanley.

He then began to show Millie the paperwork he had shown me earlier. At first, she was unsure, but once he got going, they became engrossed. For some time, I sat by myself, eating my soup as the two asked questions of each other. Like at the hospital, I tried to place everything in its time and place. I ran things backward and forward in my mind to see if I could find any pattern in the events. There were connections, but nothing holding them all together. The evidence pointed to a few things happening at once, each containing its own set of mysteries.

"Hey," I interrupted their cozy conversation, "Is there any mention of a Mr. Amadeo Ricci in there?"

Stanley froze and then laughed. "Yes, he's all over the files. He's on pretty much everything that the mine has touched, from the title for the property to its dissolution. He's the company lawyer. Everything, big or small, has his signature."

"That's interesting," I said, retrieving the wills from my coat pocket. I then unfolded them on the table side by side. "I found these in the Pickles' pockets."

Stanley and Millie came over to look. I could feel their hot breaths over my shoulders as they read through the contents. When done with the first side, I flipped them over and pointed out the signature on the back.

After he had finished, Stanley took a big breath of air and started pacing the room, leaving Millie alone beside me.

"Now why would his name be on these?" I asked.

"I'm sure it's a coincidence. I mean, some lawyer has to notarize them, right?" Mille replied. Millie must have seen the look of surprise on my face. I didn't expect her to know anything about the law. "My father had a will made when he got sick," she explained. I nodded. It made sense that she would know that, at least. Her family had gone through a lot in the last few years.

I shifted my eyes back to the paper. "No, I don't believe it's just a coincidence. The brothers may have met this man Ricci when they worked here at the mine in 1918, 1919." It was Millie's turn to look surprised.

"Stanley found that in the files," I explained.

"I suppose I don't know what they look like, but I never heard their names," she said, a puzzled expression in her voice. Millie prided herself on knowing everyone in the town and how they were connected. But single men living at the Chambers Lodge when she was still a teenager may have been a little out of her scope.

"Oh my! Do you think this person, Mr. Ricci, may have contracted them to kill you?" she asked, her eyes open wide.

"Perhaps," I said, though I was beginning to think

this was more about Clayton than myself. "But I doubt it. This is a lawyer. He makes things go away by using legal tricks. He may be working for someone who did, though, and if so, he might be covering their tracks."

Stanley, all this time, had been pacing. He stopped momentarily, stared at the two of us, and started again. He was so deep in thought I could see the tension working in his jaw.

"I've got Duffy over at the hospital, keeping watch," I said. "Clayton's cabin was vandalized, and I have reason to believe that someone is trying to do him harm. So, Stanley, I'm going to sleep on one of the hospital beds tonight. Lloyd George is already over there. So the place is all yours to do whatever you want with all these..." I waved my hand around the room, "with all Millie's files."

He stopped and looked at me. I wasn't sure he was registering what I was saying.

"Oh! Wait!" exclaimed Millie. "There's one more thing that I forgot to tell you. Mrs Granderson is angry with the mayor. I'd say she's furious. And so when she was over there this morning, she was snooping around a bit." She took a breath before launching into speech again. "And anyway, she heard from Gayle Pippens, who works there as a maid, that the Grand Hotel has had little business. Like almost none. Because who would come to stay there?" She paused to build the tension.

"But they did have one visitor at the end of last week," and now she stopped talking, her eyes as wide as I had ever seen. She was almost standing on tiptoes, waiting for me to ask her what she had found.

Finally, Stanley put her out of her misery. "Who, Millie, who?" he asked. It was the closest I ever saw him come to irritation.

"A young woman," she said.

The room was silent. You could just about hear the mice snoring in the floorboards.

"A young woman," I repeated but without the same level of enthusiasm. In fact, it was lacking any enthusiasm at all.

"Don't you get it!" she cried. "A young woman. By herself. And there is a young woman appearing over and over on the outskirts of town."

"So you think this young woman is staying at the hotel?" I asked. "That would make her much easier to find."

"No, she left after staying one night." Millie looked crestfallen that we weren't accepting her theory. "But maybe she found another place to stay. Or she's staying out in the woods. There's plenty of unused cabins and houses around."

That part was true, but matching this new visitor with the woman from the woods was a stretch. Why would an out-of-towner who could afford a train ride and a stay in a fancy hotel start meandering around in the woods? That didn't make any sense. But it reminded me of something—the stocking I had found in the station house.

"If Mr. Benjamin was here, we could ask if she left on the train the next day. There's so few people stopping here you would think he would remember everyone's coming and going. Come to think of it, he would have seen John Tuttle and those other men leave. He might know where they are going."

"But he's not back yet?" questioned Stanley.

"Still gone. I still can't figure out why he'd leave or

where he was going. We could go looking for him at the Chambers Lodge. It's where he was heading, but I don't think night is the right time for that. Maybe that can be our task for the morning."

Stanley nodded.

"Check the station before going to bed. Maybe, see if the telegraph is working yet."

Stanley thought it was a good idea. He was also eager to get back to sifting through the papers now that he had more to go on. Millie began preparing to leave, and I packed a small bag. I decided to sleep in my pants rather than change into a nightshirt, but I brought my pistol, rifle, and battery torch along. I also added the draft of my report to finish while I was in the infirmary.

Just as we left, I imagined Constable Stanley sleeping in the jail cell. The beds in there were small, even for the average man. All his life, Stanley must have either slept with his feet over the end of the bed or curled up like a child.

"Constable Stanley, feel free to use my bed tonight. The room is warmer, and the bed is larger." He appeared pleased and gave me a nod. Little things can sometimes make a difference.

****

The snow was falling softer as Millie and I stepped out into the night. I still felt ashamed of my previous behavior and made another awkward attempt to apologize. Millie dismissed me, though. She was enthused by all the secrets we had shared and prattled on about the different possible interpretations of events, none of which I found plausible. She did say she would ask her mother about the names we read in the Pickles' wills, though. Her mother had been the town gossip before her, so I agreed with that plan.

As we were nearing the hospital, I asked her about her visit there with Mrs. Tuttle.

"She was distraught," said Millie, "and was unsure what to do about the girl's rash. I do hope John comes back soon. I think she needs his steadying hand."

I agreed with her. Mrs. Tuttle was younger than either Millie or Stanley, and she moved here with her husband only three weeks before the mine closed. Millie suspected they probably didn't have enough money to pay their fare back on the train. John did odd jobs for people around the town but, like many, had no steady income.

"I saw Genevieve," Millie said, changing the conversation. I did not need to face her to know she was staring at me.

"Oh, yeah," I said, "that makes sense."

"She looked drawn," Millie breathed. "She needs some sun, I think, for her skin."

"Well, she has been busy as of late."

"Yes," Millie agreed. "I think she has too much on her plate. Her skin is so pale. I imagine all those years in France have aged her. Plus, it probably doesn't help that she is married to a much older man. "

"I think she looks fine," I told her, though, of course, the events of the last couple of days would affect anyone. Millie was perceptive. She could judge social situations as well as anyone. She came by it naturally, which gave me an idea.

"I should say hello to your mother." It was out of my mouth before I could stuff it back inside.

A look of excitement passed across Millie's face, and she sped ahead. "One second," she said, opening the cabin's door, leaving me on the other side.

"Mother!" She yelled.

I should be returning to the hospital. How could I safeguard it from here? I could sneak away and deal with the consequences tomorrow. I didn't expect her to accept my offer so quickly.

The door opened with a rush of warm air. Millie was in the doorway, all smiles. "You can come in now," she announced.

I removed my hat and then moved inside, letting Millie take my fur coat to hang on the hook.

Their home was large and quite comfortable, built in the old town across the river and near the mill. Gavin, her father, had been an engineer at the mine, relied upon to ensure the structural integrity of the underground structure. From what I heard, he was not responsible for the cave-in as he had been quite sick for several months beforehand. Dr. Moody diagnosed silver poisoning as the likely cause. Millie told me that before he died, her father's skin turned gray as smoke from head to toe. A horrible way to pass, I'm sure.

Millie guided me by the elbow into the sitting room where her mother lay on the settee. I hoped Jeremy was around, but the boy was nowhere in sight, leaving me with the two ladies. By the look on Esther's face when I entered the room, I realized this was unlikely to be a short visit.

"Constable Albright," she clapped. "Well, what an extraordinary surprise. I am so delighted that you have come. Millie has told me all about your latest daring adventure."

And with that, I was regaled with the entire story of my gunfight in the woods and subsequent investigation, up to and somehow including Millie's recent conversations with Mrs. Tuttle and Mrs. Granderson. It was pretty dramatic and heavy on the details, most of which were exaggerated too far beyond the truth for my liking. But to get a word in edgewise was beyond my ability. Every time I tried to open my mouth, her excitement reached a higher pitch, and I was left gaping, waiting for the next possible break where I might insert myself.

Millie was no help at all. She sat there the whole time, perched on her chair like a bird, hands folded in her lap, legs crossed at the ankles, never once glancing toward me.

Finally, Esther joined us in the present and told her daughter to fetch me a refreshment.

"No, no," I insisted, "Millie served a delicious tea after dinner. I smiled in her direction, hoping she would help me get the conversation back on track, forgetting that she did not know my reason for intruding on her mother.

I cleared my throat and turned to Esther, "I have a question for you."

"You do?" Esther straightened, clearly fascinated. The poor lady suffered from arthritic hips, knees, and ankles. She confined herself to almost permanent bed rest but, at this moment, was unperturbed by her pain.

"Go on," she continued, and I felt a lump rise in my throat. I looked back at Millie, realizing what this might look like. Though Millie often invited me to drop in, I always declined, knowing how long her mother could talk. But here I was after all these months.

I cleared my throat, but my gorge did not descend. "Um," I started. "Well, the thing is." Both women's eyes were on me, so I examined the floorboards.

"I wonder if Millie could get me some water," I coughed. It was good to have one less woman staring at me, but as soon as Millie rushed from her seat, I realized I was now alone with Esther.

It was best to keep talking while I had the floor. "What I want to know... Esther is..." Esther was leaning forward now, her face open and alert. I heard Millie rummage around in the kitchen. "When did you all come to town?"

Esther's eyebrows shot up. "Come to town. Well Gavin brought us here in 1913. It was a well-paid position. Millie's father was well regarded, you know. A brilliant man from good stock and a good father. We were able to raise both Jeremy and Millie off his salary. He was a Christian man and saved his money, never spending it on vices or trivial luxuries. I still collect his pension. And we aren't destitute as you see."

A wealth of little trinkets and paperbacks filled the copious shelves in their living room.

I nodded. "Um, yes, so you were here when the Grand Hotel was built." Esther looked confused. I doubt she guessed this was the road I wanted to go down.

"Yes, we were here for all of that. We watched all the new buildings be built on the boardwalk. It was an exciting time. We thought Chambers was going to be quite the destination. And it looked that way for a long time before the mine went bust. You know, we would have moved away a long time ago if it wasn't Millie's job at your detachment. She is quite consistent in her desire to work with you. For you. She speaks highly of you, Augustus, if I might call you that."

"That's fine," I told her before I launched into my

next question. "Is it possible that Clayton was here before? Do you remember hearing something about him?" The mayor had given me the idea when he told me that he had a longer history with the man.

"Clayton... the man you followed into the woods..." She looked bewildered, her face pinched, and then her eyes twinkled. "No, no, no, it can't be the same man."

"Who?"

"There was a Clayton here, but he left early on just after the Great War started, in the spring of 1915, I would think."

"Did you meet him? Would you recognize him?"

"I would, " she said. "But you know I've never met the Clayton that lives here now. He has a beard, doesn't he?"

"He does. Was your man bearded?"

"No, he was well-shaven. From what Millie tells me, the poor fellow in the hospital is a slovenly sort. The Clayton who was here in 1913, was a man of means. This poor arthritis of mine doesn't allow me to get around much. Most of the news I get is through Millie or Jeremy. The way they described Clayton, I never thought there could be a connection."

"So the Clayton from 1913 wasn't a malodorous drunk?" I asked.

"No, the man was a drinker, but I would call him dashing. Something of a lady's man. From what I remember, he was a partner of Fox's. The two of them got a large loan to build the hotel and the boardwalk together."

"Clayton?" I asked.

"Yes, Fox's business partner was called Clayton.

Clayton Cole, if memory serves me correctly."

I felt a warmth behind me and turned to find Millie, a glass of water in her hand. She must have been listening the whole time. She was transfixed as she passed me the glass and then went to the settee to sit with her mother.

"So why did he leave?" I asked.

"Well, now, a lot has passed since, so give me some time to think and get this right." She leaned back, and Millie took her hand. The two women sitting so close together were, for the first time, both quiet and I realized how comfortable a room like this might be.

Esther stuttered, stopped, looked at her daughter, shook her head, and then turned back to me. "Well, both the men, Fox and this Clayton Cole, had women. Women, not wives, you understand. Fox, if I remember, changed his frequently." She shook her head as if she couldn't imagine why a man would do so.

"But I believe Clayton's was a married lady from Calgary who had come West away from her husband and met Clayton on the journey. They were a couple, the two of them. This Clayton Cole was not unattractive, from what I remember, and possessed the money to go along with his looks. He was no Mr. Norton, but I could see why some frivolous women might find him interesting."

Handsome and wealthy checked neither of the boxes for the Clayton, handcuffed to Genevieve's hospital bed.

"Anyway, and this is the part I'm having trouble remembering. This woman of Clayton's died in mysterious circumstances." Esther paused there and took the time to gaze into each of our faces before continuing what she determined to be a most sordid tale.

"Now this lady of his, her body was found trapped and tangled amongst some broken branches in the spring rush of the Skeena River. Somehow, the poor soul fell in, and her heavy dress dragged her under and held her there!" Esther was in her element now; bent forward, she squeezed her daughter's hand. "As we all know, the river becomes a powerful force as the snow melts off the mountains. There was more than one soul that lost their life to it over the years. But, of course, there was quite a bit of speculation about how exactly she got there. Some believed it was an accident. But you know how people are. Some folks love to spin a tale out large and add whatever is their fancy."

It was challenging to maintain a blank expression, but I did so.

"*Was she pushed*, some asked?" She considered this as if she was a jury member before she answered her own question. "Or was she murdered beforehand, and then her body put there to make it look like an accident? There was no end of speculation, I tell you. There were even some that said Fox did it. That he didn't get along with the lady. But in the end, no one knew. Clayton Cole left town within a month and was pretty well forgotten. I can't remember hearing his name again in the years since. Until now."

"So, this man just left."

"That's how I remember it - heartbroken. My memory is not what it used to be. It's awful to think that a man with such promise could be brought so low. The man at the hospital sounds like quite the reprobate. I hate to think Mr. Cole could be so depraved."

"Oh, Momma, he's not that bad," Millie interrupted. "He's quite sweet if you get to talking with him."

"If you say so, darling," said Esther, wrinkling her nose. She sat back, silent, considering. "But you know what?" She was patting Millie's hand now. "We could look through my old diaries. Couldn't we, Millie? Millie would be happy to do it."

"Of course, Mom." Both women were smiling at me now, and I became anxious. I should have been at the hospital by now.

"One more question," I said. The mention of this woman drowning in the Skeena made me think of the Oriental girl. *Arlene,* as Millie called her. Two drownings, and I hadn't heard of either of them before my gunfight.

"Back in 1915, was it Sergeant Deacon who was in charge of the investigation into this woman's drowning death?" I asked.

"I suppose so," said Esther. "He was in charge of just about everything. But all this happened before my Millie got her important job working for you boys. She would have been no more than twelve and pretty as an apple."

This information was fascinating, but I decided it was time to leave.

"Well, I should go," I said as I rose. "Thanks for the water," and I turned to leave.

Esther called after me from the settee. "Oh, you could stay longer."

"Millie, go after him," I heard her whisper as I moved out of the room to the coat hooks. "You could bring out the cake."

I shrugged on my coat and awkwardly twisted my body to retrieve my hat from where I had fumbled it. Finally, standing, I found Millie had sneaked behind me.

"Sorry," she whispered. "She's here by herself all day and needs someone to talk to now and then. I didn't tell her that… that there was anything… I've never…."

"It's okay, Millie," I reassured her. "I have a mother too. She might think the same thing if I brought you home." I regretted it the moment I said it. My cheeks were as hot as Millie's were red as I stumbled out the door.

Chapter 7

Genevieve's Grace

As I moved through town toward the hospital, my mind was racing, not just with the possible implications of Clayton being at one time a town bigwig but with the general tone of the conversation. I hoped Millie's mother did not assume my visit was anything other than collecting needed information for my investigation. But hope is usually what it is—just hope. I shook my head, unsure what would be more uncomfortable, a second conversation with Pastor Stevens or Esther Norton.

Consumed by these thoughts, I almost missed the dark figure rushing away from the hospital. I was confident that the person had been spying through the lighted window of the wardroom, and my body sprung into action. My arms dropped my kitbag and rifle, and my legs churned through the snow.

This was no ghost. Though cloaked, the size and shape resembled the girl who had ambushed me in the woods. If it was the girl, she had seen me, for she bounded as fast as she could through the heavy snow. My heart pounded hard against my chest; the cold air sucked into my lungs as I gasped for breath. The girl's small form was an advantage in this kind of race, and I soon realized that the distance was too great to catch her. But still, I tried.

She took us around the two houses to the east of the hospital and soon vanished into the woods beyond. Darkness came early at this latitude; it had already been three hours since the unseen sun had set. The snowy clouds did make the world lighter, but as I came to the edge of the forest, I knew there would be little chance of finding her. She could have stopped behind a tree twenty yards away, and I would not see her. I could follow her tracks, but she had the uncanny ability to make even those disappear. Besides, I was exhausted. And so instead, I stopped, hands on knees, hoping my stomach would not discard Millie's simple supper.

My battery torch was inside my kitbag, dropped back before the hospital. I could return and get it, pull Stanley and Peter out to hunt the girl through the dark forest. It all seemed fruitless. The blizzard could become stronger without a moment's notice. The tracks could lead us to where she was hiding, but if she was smart, which I knew she was, she could double back through the town and disguise her tracks with those made throughout the day. Even though Chambers appeared quiet, there was evidence that lots of people were moving about, more than you would expect: the mayor, the wives, Bea, Mr. Benjamin even Millie. Maybe many more that I didn't know.

I retrieved my kit bag and rifle, which were already covered with a thin layer of snow. From the tracks outside the building, the figure did not appear to have tried to get inside. The footsteps came from the west and paused beside the window. The deeper impression in the snow suggested she may have stood against the window for several minutes. From there, one could see both men's beds inside the infirmary. If only the snow could give an impression of what the girl thought as she stood there.

I ached to talk to her, but that was just more hope. My choice to stay the night at the hospital was now a necessity. Even though I doubted her return, I remained vigilant. Whatever she was about, she was not working alone. Numbers—it always came down to numbers.

****

I entered the hospital through Moody's lodgings and found the doctor in the kitchen. I was unsure whether he had moved since I last saw him. He faced away from me, so I could not see his expression. He was staring at the blank wall before him. I decided not to disturb his reverie with a greeting.

As I entered the infirmary, I almost tripped over Duffy, who was having an enthusiastic conversation with Lloyd George as he scratched the dog's belly. Genevieve was getting a kick out of watching the two play. But they all stopped when they saw me. I thanked Duffy and asked him if he had any plans tomorrow.

"Not if the storm is still happening," he told me. That was good; I may need him if Stanley and I were to investigate more. I wished I could pay him and Peter, but I had no discretionary spending. Duffy would not be bothered, but I was worried I was stepping on Peter's good graces.

The infirmary was, for the moment, quiet. I hated to disturb the silence, but I knew I would have to ask Clayton these questions at some point. I walked over to his bed and dragged a chair to sit beside him. His eyes were cold as he watched me put my rifle and kit bag on the bed beside his.

"Clayton." I watched the lines on the man's

forehead and the corners of his eyes. "Clayton Cole."

He made no sound, no movement, just the same cold stare back.

"That's you, isn't it? Not Clayton Caufield, Clayton Cole." Of course, I wasn't sure, but I made my voice sound like I was.

There was still no sign he was even listening.

I sat back in my chair. Unsure what this all meant. "So, you and the mayor were business partners, and now you're back. Maybe you wanted some payback. Did the mayor kill your girl Clayton?"

I'd never seen the man so quiet. The silence meant something, and yet the silence told me nothing as well. The frustration was building inside me—a hard lump in the center of my chest. Somebody was going to have to talk!

"Clayton!" I shouted. "You are in danger!" I swept my arm around the room. "And you are putting the rest of us in danger, damn you! I could have been killed! They could be back for you. They will shoot you in your bed! Answer me!"

With great effort, Clayton shifted his body so he could peer into my face. I saw his lips working inside his beard, teeth grinding behind them. He gave out a little "Humph" and then turned his back to me. My frustration took hold of me. I moved to tear the man back toward me, but I felt a firm hand on my shoulder holding me back.

It was Genevieve. She shook her head. "Not now," she said. "It's not the right time yet. Let him rest."

I wanted to argue, but it was no use. I was plenty tired of it all. I retrieved my things and found a bed in the middle of the room.

****

I lay on my back for the rest of the evening, scribbling away at my report. My fatigue made it difficult to find the right words, but I pushed on regardless. Ever so often, my mind turned away from my writing to consider the two patients. Would I ever get the truth from either man?

At about nine o'clock, Clayton woke from his stupor. I could see the man was suffering. His skin was clammy and hot, and soon he began to moan, an awful sound coming from deep inside his chest. I called out for Genevieve, and she scrambled to his bedside. She took his temperature and pulse, all without exchanging a word. I watched her as she worked. Cool-headed but caring. She looked at me momentarily and then nodded as if she concluded her examination.

I wanted to ask her what she was thinking. Instead, I let her stride past me into the waiting room. She came back with a bottle of medicine and a spoon. She sat beside Clayton, cradled his head, and served the man his dose before gently releasing his head back into the pillow.

For several minutes, she watched over him, holding his hand, until his body relaxed and he fell into a less conflicted sleep. She came to my bedside after she sneaked away from Clayton. "Morphine," she whispered. "I think his fever is from the pain and withdrawal rather than an infection. At least, I hope so. The wounds seem clean."

I nodded.

"I should look in on Kenneth," she told me but stayed to talk with me for several minutes more about the storm and when it would pass. I noticed she had not asked Dr. Moody's opinion on her use of morphine, but I did not say anything.

After she left, I got to work on my report in earnest. I put aside my worry over who might read the document and was able to put a broad sketch of the recent events on paper. I knew that headquarters would be most interested in the cold, hard facts and not my conjecture, yet it was difficult not to make certain assumptions while describing the events.

The writing allowed me to reconsider all the details. The missing pieces remained more intriguing than the facts I knew. It was enervating to be lying across from the man who might hold the clue to what was happening in this town. I couldn't help feeling that all I saw were the dead branches, not the living roots beneath the frost.

I was readying myself for sleep when I heard the hard slap of the hospital's outside door. Lloyd George, who had been dozing on the floor between the beds, came awake and lifted himself to standing, sending me a worried look before beginning a guarded walk toward the doorway.

Facing the door, I sat on the edge of the bed. I eyed my rifle. My pistol hung by its belt around the footpost of the opposite bed, whereas my long gun leaned against the hospital wall. The heavy bang of boots in the vestibule brought me to standing. I grabbed my holster, pulled it around my waist, and unclipped the button. Lloyd George, still sheepish, took a few more reluctant steps toward the door.

I saw the wave of his long green oil slick before I saw the man, Mayor Fox. He made the turn and stopped, as surprised as I was at our meeting.

"Constable," he said as a greeting, then made a show

of removing his gloves before lodging them in his coat's spacious pockets. He peered down at Lloyd George as the dog sniffed around his legs.

"I didn't expect to see you here." His voice betrayed his irritation.

I nodded my head, inviting him to continue. Instead, he paused and made a show of restoring the lines of his mustache with his long fingers. I watched him as he stepped into the aisle and examined the sleeping forms of the ward's two patients, first the Pickle Brother and then Clayton.

"They are both asleep," he said, a fact I didn't think needed further comment. Clayton had been as inert as his bunkmate the last hour. Besides Clayton's occasional suck of breath, both men seemed lifeless.

"So this is where you're sleeping tonight, Augustus," Fox snorted. He turned as he spoke, casting his glare over the various articles I had brought with me. There was no point denying it. I had already put quite a wrinkle in the blankets.

I was about to give the man a sarcastic reply when Genevieve saved me. She had entered the ward through the kitchen without us sensing her. I expect she could feel the tension in the room, much like Lloyd George, who had crawled between my legs and under the bed.

"Mayor," she said, looking at my face as she tried to read me. "To what do we owe this honor?"

"I was going to ask that myself," I said.

But two against one was never a test for the mayor when it came to words. Instead, he choked out a dry laugh. "It's my duty to help those in need. I'm checking in on our two patients to see if there have been any developments."

I wondered what developments he was hoping for.

"I heard you went out to find the other brother's body," he continued. "You should have called on me. I would have lent a hand."

I nodded, not sure what he was getting at.

"I came this morning and found Miss Brannon waiting here with Genevieve." He paused, letting the thought sink in. Why had Genevieve not mentioned it? Why did it matter?

"She isn't to be trusted." Fox's voice had changed. I'd marveled before at how fast the man could alter his disposition. Instead of his usual slickness, there was a commanding presence. "That woman is working to tear this town apart."

I glanced over at Genevieve, but she appeared confused as well.

"Bea Brannon?" I asked. "How? This town seems to be falling apart all on its own accord."

Fox moved closer now, so we stood in an almost perfect triangle. "On the contrary, Constable. Everything will be just fine. There are better people than us, working to ensure this town not only survives but thrives. We don't need people like her coming in here and gumming up the works."

I tried to speak, to protest, but he silenced me. "She is working for the enemy Albright. She's here to salt the land. To make sure nothing grows. She cares about no one but herself." He paused. "She's probably a part of whatever this is as well," he added, pointing his finger at Clayton.

I still wasn't sure exactly what he was implying, but Bea's curiosity was peculiar.

"How?" I repeated. Our triangle was thinning as

Genevieve moved to my side. "Give me specifics, Tom. I don't understand."

Fox looked over again at the two patients. He had expended all his energy and was ready to leave. "The only specific thing you need to know, Constable, is that she shouldn't be trusted."

The room now became silent. The mayor pulled his fine gloves out of his pockets and made another little show of putting them on. Genevieve and I exchanged glances but no words.

"Enjoy your night." The sneering smile that formed on his lips gave clear intent that he wished to embarrass us both. His implication that I was some type of ladies' man was shared by no one else I'd ever met.

I let him walk to the doorway before I spoke.

"Clayton Cole," was all I needed to say to make him pivot. His eyebrows were high on his forehead, and his jaw pushed out toward me. But he didn't speak.

"Clayton Cole," I said again. "He was your business partner, wasn't he."

The mayor smiled, "I wouldn't say that."

"He was part owner of your hotel from what I understand."

"Well, then you *misunderstand*," replied the mayor, but his grin was beginning to turn menacing.

I pointed over toward the sleeping Clayton. "This man here," I said. "This is Clayton Cole, isn't it? That's why you have such a vendetta against him."

"Vendetta," he scoffed. "You're mad, Albright. Clayton is a useless drunk. You're seeing things that aren't there."

"Like that ghost?" I asked. "The one those brothers used to lure us out into the woods. What are you hiding,

Mayor? Are you a player in all this?"

He looked mortified, his hand clutching at his heart—the picture of innocence. I turned to Genevieve to see if she believed his act, but she only looked confused.

"I'm leaving," said the mayor. He sent his eyes about the room before meeting mine once more. "You need to get some sleep, Albright."

"I won't be sleeping, I told him," and stepped after him as he moved to the door. I aimed to press farther. "These benevolent people of yours. Who might they be?" I waited to see if he would turn again to face me, but instead, he shouldered the door, stepping through it into the vestibule, now wet with the snow he had brought along with him.

I held the swinging door open with my hand as he pressed on through the outside door. "Philip Chambers?" I asked, "William Chambers? Amadeo Ricci?" It was the last name that made the man turn. I caught a quick glimpse of his shocked face as the door sprung back to closing. Interesting.

I stood in the doorway momentarily, wondering if I had overplayed my hand. But it felt good. Real good. I stepped back and felt Genevieve's soft body behind me. I didn't realize she was so close. I grabbed her arm, shifting my feet so she could regain her balance.

"What in the blazes was all that about?" I said, still holding her arm. Genevieve's blue eyes reflected the harsh light of the lantern in the wall bracket beyond us.

She shook her head, not stepping back, not stepping forward. "That's the fourth time he's been in here since your shootout."

"When else was he here?"

"Both mornings and both evenings. But he doesn't

stay long. He just asks about their conditions and then leaves."

"Has he talked to Clayton?" I asked. She looked down at my hand, and I released the grasp on her forearm.

"No," she shook her head again, letting me walk past her. "But I think Clayton has only pretended to be asleep in the morning."

I looked out the window to see if anyone was staring in. No one was there, but I closed the curtains on all four windows. Typically, it was so dark in the early evening that there was no reason to shut them, but now they made me feel vulnerable.

I examined Clayton as I passed by. He wasn't pretending to sleep now. He was fully unconscious.

"What happened when the mayor came and found Bea here?" I asked Genevieve. "Did they exchange words or something?"

"No, just cold stares from both of them. I could tell they were surprised that the other one was here," Genevieve added. "But it didn't come to more than that. Are you really not going to sleep tonight?"

"Let's lock all the outside doors," I told her, "but keep the door open between the ward and your lodgings in case we need each other." That sounded wrong, but I knew she knew what I meant.

"I should check on Kenneth," she said. "Unless you want to take turns on guard duty."

"No," I decided. "I did this all the time in the war. Besides, I'm sure nothing will happen. You should get some sleep." Her face looked drawn, her shoulders hunched forward. I didn't like to see her like that.

"You'll call me if you need me, right?" she asked

"Yes, if Clayton or the Pickle Brother wake, I'll knock or call out."

She nodded and then slipped out the door to the lodgings.

After I extinguished all the lights but one, I moved my belongings to the bed opposite the vestibule doors, which also put me across from Daniel Pickle and in the same line of four beds with Clayton. I unholstered my weapon, placed the pistol on the night table within easy reach of the bed, and then stretched out with my rifle beside me. Lloyd George took his place at the foot of the bed, a habit I would have to break later. He was soon asleep, but I was too anxious to go there myself. I would have to use the sound of the wind as company. I'd done it before, and I would do it again.

****

I was out of practice. Clayton's shouts brought me panicked out of a dreamless sleep. A frantic glance across the wardroom, the light too dim to make out what was happening. I grabbed my pistol but lost my balance as my legs tangled in the sheets, and my chin hit the floor as I toppled out of my bunk. I scrambled up, still searching for my weapon, and kicked it underneath the bed. The screaming hit a higher pitch, and I ducked under and pulled the pistol to my hip before I launched myself into the aisle separating the eight beds.

I felt a wetness on my chin as I crept toward Clayton's bunk. His body thrashed about as he dreamt, and I felt myself calm. There was no one else here. I placed the pistol on the bunk beside him and snuck closer. He was talking in his dream. I couldn't tell what he was saying; he mumbled like a drunkard. Was it someone's name? An essential piece of the story? I put my ear to his mouth, the hot stench of his breath on my cheek. One word, was it a name?

Clayton grabbed me, his arms flew out, and sharp nails pierced the flesh of my shoulders. We wrestled. I pushed down on him as he brought me forward. His strength was incredible; hate filled his eyes. I pressed into his wounded shoulder, and he screamed, letting go, and I fell back onto the hard floor.

"Haven't you punished me enough?" he shouted, rolled over in the bed, and grimaced at me, his teeth jagged points. "Haven't I suffered enough!" He was wild, still not released from his dream. His whole body twisted on the bed in his hallucination. Footsteps. Genevieve charged into the room, the skirt of her nightdress flowing, and I was breathing hard, trying to suck the air into my lungs as I crawled backward into the wall. Genevieve touched me, but I felt my body flinch.

She knelt between us, me on the floor and Clayton on the bed, and all had turned quiet. Clayton's throes weakened. Genevieve shushed us both, like Coot with his horses. There were hot tears on my cheeks before I knew I had been crying. Genevieve grabbed me, and, this time, I did not shy away. We held one another on the hospital floor, my breathing, my heartbeat slowing, settling. I nodded my head and tried to speak, but she quieted me. It was uncomely to show such weakness. I yearned to be alone but did not want to leave this spot or her embrace.

I felt a tickle on my wrist and saw Lloyd George's nose push itself between Genevieve and myself. The dog must have hidden somewhere while we fought.

Genevieve released me and helped me to my feet. She escorted me to my bed, and I lay on its rumpled covers. In the pale light, I saw a hideous streak of blood across Genevieve's face and hair. I tried to talk, but she shushed me. I felt the exhaustion burn through me from head to toe. Lloyd George jumped up and began to lick my chin, but Genevieve pushed the beast away then went to the next room to get some bandages.

"You cut your chin somehow," Genevieve whispered. Her face was close. Her eyes squinted in the bare light as she dabbed at my face with a warm cloth, wiping my tears, my blood, my panicked sweat. Lloyd George jumped back on the bed and lay across my feet. The warmth of its body was a welcome comfort.

"You sleep," she told me, and I watched as she stretched out on the bed beside my own, positioning the pillows behind her head. My eyes were too heavy not to close, and I gave into the relief of sleep.

Chapter 8

Gus' Gamble
Day Three
Wednesday, February 23rd, 1923

I was awakened at dawn by Genevieve's hand on my chest.

She shook me, calling my name away from my dreams: the Pickle brothers, lost soldiers, and venison stew mixed with Clayton's vile ministrations of pain. Genevieve was not a dream, however; not this time and not last night.

"Someone's knocking on the door," she said. "I thought you should get it."

The light was dim, but I could see her silhouette; her hair was loose, flowing over her shoulders and parts of her face. What must it be like to be woken by a woman each morning? But her request was urgent. I stood and grabbed my holster before I realized I had left the pistol on the other bed in the middle of the night. I slid over in my stocking feet and holstered, leaving the clip unlatched. Clayton and Daniel Pickle, still asleep, were unmoved by the repeated pounding on the door outside.

I worked my way through the beds to the vestibule, the sound of Genevieve's soft feet padding behind me. As we passed Lloyd George, he lumbered to his feet and followed us.

"Be careful," she whispered as I set myself ready. My hand hovered over my holster, my left foot before me, ready to turn or move forward.

"Who is it?" I croaked.

"It's me, Stanley. The girl has been sighted." His voice was clear and insistent. I opened the door. Behind him, a thin light shone through purple clouds and a curtain of soft snow.

Stanley's expression was earnest. "I was woken by a man this morning who told me the girl has appeared again. She was spotted near Ronald Smith's place," he told me.

Smith's place was a short walk by the river, a little farther down from the church. I whispered back. "If we're going to follow her, we should go soon, before any tracks are covered and the trail is still hot." I neglected to tell him about my encounter with the girl the previous evening.

I let him in, ran past Genevieve, and grabbed my coat, hat, and rifle. Genevieve lit a hurricane lamp and stood in the aisle close to my bed as I collected my things. "Don't worry about making the bed," she said in a husky whisper. She reminded me of a choir girl or an angel, her nightdress covering all but her ten little toes.

"I will get someone to come by as protection," I told her, but she shook her head. She didn't want it, but she must have known I would make it happen anyway.

I told Stanley to wait while I ran the fifty yards to Peter's mill. It was easier to move now as there was no wind. The air did not feel as cold, all signs to show that this storm might be in its last hours.

It took some moments to get Peter to the door. There was a sleepy look on his face, but he came to alert when

I told him what had happened. To my surprise, Bea Brannon sat at their table with a cup of coffee in her hand. She suggested that she and Duffy could come with us, but instead, I asked her to help Genevieve at the hospital. Genevieve would not want Duffy to see her in her nightdress.

Peter went to outfit himself. I didn't even have to ask him to come this time. I wasn't going to look that gift horse in the mouth. He was already upstairs rousing Duffy.

While I waited, I took a moment to sit across from Bea. Her raised eyebrow told me that she knew I had questions. And I did. Plenty. But not a lot of time. So I said it straight.

"I don't know how far I can trust you, Bea. But I do need help. There are good people in this town who I don't want to get hurt."

Bea tried to talk, but I raised my hand and went on. "This girl who keeps appearing at the edge of town. I think she is quite the trickster and a dangerous one at that. Making us go out to find her could be another trap to get us away from the hospital." I was thinking aloud now, but I could tell Bea was following me. "If I leave you behind, will you promise me that you will protect the people at the hospital until we get back?"

"Of course," she started to say, but I raised my hand again.

"And by people, I mean Dr. Moody, Margaret, and Genevieve most of all. If someone comes looking for the patients, tell them to leave, and if they don't, get everyone else to safety. Even if that means leaving Clayton and this Pickle man behind." I scanned the sawmill. "Bring them back here and lock the door. And then wait until we get back."

Bea reached across the oak table and put her hand on my arm. "You can trust me, Gus. They're my friends, too." I looked her in the eyes. I couldn't believe that she was working to hurt the town.

Heavy footsteps clattered down the stairs. It was Duffy, not the most agile of men. We could move faster without him. "Duffy, good man. Go with Bea over to the hospital." If Genevieve didn't want people to see her in her nightdress, she was out of luck.

We all walked as a unit to the hospital, where we met Stanley.

"So who woke you?" Bea asked.

"A man named Birch," Stanley replied.

I knew the gentleman. He was not the friendliest of characters, but he was respectable. Honestly, I was glad to hear it wasn't Bernard. His participation during the night of the shootout still seemed suspect.

Genevieve joined us, Moody's fur coat buttoned up over her nightdress, boots on her feet, her wild hair still untied. She had made thermoses of coffee for us to take and packages of oat biscuits. A simple breakfast, but I was glad for it. Birch came along next with Per Larsen, Matti Larsen's youngest son. All of them carried rifles. Birch also brought his scruffy dog, an animal no one had a name for. Part wolf, I would guess, and maybe some hound in there as well. The creature was undoubtedly more accustomed to the snow than my pampered terrier. Lloyd George, I would leave behind in the warmth of the hospital. Lucky animal.

We had a little posse now. With any luck, we could work together to capture this girl and solve a significant part of this mystery. I was not without worry. The last time we followed her, she led us into an ambush. And what would she tell Stanley about the shootout if we caught up to her? I would need to be at my best.

Equipped with snowshoes and our heavy weather gear, our party walked down the bank of the river, skirting west through the acreage of several properties. The chimney smoke rising from some but not others showed which owners had pulled stakes and left town over the last year. There were more hangers-on than I would have guessed. Nevertheless, there were sure to be fewer next winter.

****

We approached Ronald Smith's lodge and saw the man standing on his slanted porch dressed in a tatty pair of long overalls, a matted fur coat, and a hunter's cap with mismatched ear flaps. He waved us over, and we walked close to hear what he had to say.

Smith was a man from the Deep South of America. Before coming to Chambers at the height of the silver boom, he lived in Alaska and the Yukon. Even after all that travel, Smith still talked with a slow Confederate drawl. Rumor was that he had suffered an injury to his knee that made it difficult to move without pain, and he survived on the money his two sons sent back from Vancouver.

"She went that way," he barked, indicating the forest behind his meager cottage.

"How did you see her?" I asked. The porch was facing the opposite way.

The man spat into the snow, a viscous brown mess that burned into the whiteness. "I rise early to check my traps," he droned, making the sentence about five times longer than needed. I looked at my companions, but no one doubted this explanation.

I shrugged, and the five of us walked to the woods, where we spotted the tracks. Whoever stood here pressed their feet deep into the snow. The footprints were too muddled, but those that led off appeared to be the footprints of a small woman, the front of the boot curved into a point just like before.

The tracks led off in two directions, one to the southeast and one from the west. Should I split the party and send a couple of us off west? It would be interesting to see where she came from. There were only a few plots in that direction before one was out of Chambers and into the bush. Of course, her path could have veered north over the railroad tracks and to one of the ranches. Mitch Blood's ranch was in that direction—the man who had seen the girl early on. I would have liked to know his take on things.

I pointed southeast. There was no time to lose; I wanted a good-sized posse if the trail led us into another trap. Since we had come together as a group, we shared few words, and the silence continued as we moved through ever denser brush, using our arms and fingers to point out the trail when needed. After half an hour, we had formed into three separate groups, Birch and Larsen with their hound in the lead, Peter and I behind, and Stanley about twenty steps behind that. The constable was having considerable trouble moving his big body through the tangle of vegetation.

Birch and his hound kept us at a steady pace. Per Larsen, his young companion kept turning his head to ensure we were following. As a young boy, I'm sure my recent activities intrigued him. The young often enjoyed stories of derring-do.

I caught his eye when we stopped to wait for Constable Stanley. "Is there something you want to ask me?"

The boy's face went red. "Is that the rifle that you used to kill the Pickles with?"

So he was attracted to the thought of violence like most boys his age. "I shot only the one brother," I said, "and it was with the other brother's rifle." I remembered leaving both rifles at Peter's place. I should have retrieved them and brought them over to the detachment. We might need them as evidence of their crimes.

He stared back at me, his eyes wild. "I heard it was quite a shot, though. Right through the eye. You hit him in the dark."

I offered no reply.

After a half-hour of walking, we stopped for a more extended break—Stanley now lagged a few minutes behind us. At first, I figured it was the forest that had impeded him, but his actions had been strange since he found me at the hospital. Was he trying to avoid me? Had I done something to lower myself in his estimation? Perhaps all the awkwardness with Millie had left a bad taste in his mouth? Or worse, he suspected I was part of whatever criminal activities the Pickle Brothers had brought to Chambers. We would have to find a time to talk this through. It was becoming more and more apparent that I needed his help.

But once again, it was Stanley who took the initiative. When he finally reached us, he pulled me away from the others. "Do you see where we're heading?" he asked.

I took my bearings. The trail had twisted and turned. "Southeast," I said, though I was far from confident.

He nodded and shifted his back to shield us from the other men. "I think we're heading to the same clearing as before." He opened his fist to show me a blue piece of string. The same type of string Bea and Peter had tied to the trees when we went out to fetch the bodies. "This is a wild-goose-chase Albright. We are being led this way for a reason."

"What are you getting at?" I could see no reason the girl would return to the ambush clearing.

Stanley's face was flush. "They are wanting us out of town, just like before. There's something going on that they don't want you or me to see."

"Who? Who wants us out of town?"

"I don't know," said Stanley. "But I don't think we will find the answer out here."

I considered this. Why would someone want to move Stanley and me so far away from town? We would be at the detachment with Millie if we weren't here. "Do you believe it has something to do with the detachment or the railroad?" I asked.

"Perhaps both." Other than the stable yards, those buildings stood alone from the rest of town.

"But there's no trains running. And there are other people there." Like Millie, Bernard, Coot, and Mr. Benjamin if he had returned.

His eyes were piercing. "I think the snowstorm and your heroics have changed the game."

"What game?" I asked, my voice a whisper. I shifted my eyes to Birch, Larsen, and Peter. The three were staring at us. They would be wondering what we were discussing.

"I'm not sure," said Stanley, "but it's something big. Something that has been going on for quite a while. And it's time to figure out what it's all about."

"Okay," I said. I could see the resolve in the constable's eyes. He was on to something.

"I'm not even sure there is a girl at all," he said. "And if there is, she's a small part of this."

So he hadn't figured out the girl. I felt guilty that I had not told him what I knew. Since the previous evening, I had decided that Stanley was trustworthy. Yes, he appeared too polished and composed for one so young. And his arrival in the middle of the storm was suspicious. But it was that damned paperwork. I could not imagine anyone having the will to uncover what he found unless they were committed to the task. The revelations that he had deduced with the help of Millie were substantial and pointed to something nefarious.

Yes, I decided to trust him.

"We head back to town. Straight as the crow flies." Stanley pointed off through the woods. "And we catch them at it now. They've been leading us around, and now it's our turn to fight back."

I nodded, then walked over to where the other three were standing. "We're stopping this pursuit and heading back," I said, my voice as cool as the wind.

Birch looked astonished, while the boy appeared confused. "But," said Birch, "we're so close. We can get to the bottom of this."

I shook my head. "No, we're through." I didn't give them any more time to argue. I patted Stanley on his bicep and started walking south through the forest.

"Well…" Birch stumbled, "We're going to keep going. But you know this is not our responsibility. It's what you Mounties are supposed to do! There's a goddamn missing girl out there, and she's connected to your shooting."

I didn't look back. I wasn't sure if Birch was in on this thing. I felt something on my right and saw Peter pushing himself past me.

"What the hell, Gus? Do you want me to come with you guys or to follow them?" he asked. I felt a rush of guilt. We should have included him in our thinking. I mean, he was out here doing us a favor.

"Follow them for a bit if you don't mind, but be careful," I said. Both Birch and young Larsen carried rifles. No one had a reason to put a bullet into Peter; he was sensible enough not to walk into trouble. But I still had to say something. "Be careful with those two. Remember, last time this brought me into an ambush."

Peter nodded, "I can handle myself. I'll meet you back in town."

I hurried on. Stanley was already struggling through the branches. The man meant business. I joined him, not worrying about the noise we made in our quick retreat. We were on a mission now. As the man said, it was about time.

****

My heart beat fast as we plodded through the untouched snow. We loosened the buttons on our coats and let the falling flakes melt on our faces and tunics. It was a good sign that things were getting warmer. If the temperature rose above freezing, the railroad could get the necessary equipment running to clear the tracks. By tomorrow, trains could bring more recruits, and others would be tasked to solve our mysteries.

We exited the woods closer to the mill than we expected. As we crossed the bridge, I scanned the town before us. The snow on the boardwalk lay undisturbed, and when we peered into the windows of the Grand Hotel, all that greeted us were our dark reflections.

But beyond the boardwalk to the west, piles of churned snow sat in ragged heaps. As we moved closer, we could see it was the work of horses—a herd of them. The tracks stopped at the boardwalk's edge and returned west toward the detachment. What in blazes were they doing?

There was only one place in town to get so many horses. I gazed westward. There, a half-mile distance, a fallen figure lay against the wall of the stable yard. Without a word to Stanley, I started to run. My lungs heaved in the cold as I tried to find the breath to carry me the distance. I struggled forward, trying all the while to will the figure to its feet, the body slumped, the head at a precarious angle. The last few steps, I slid, letting the slipperiness of the snow bring me to Coot's side.

His hot breath made fog in the wind as his eyes turned toward me. Oh, thank heavens, the boy was alive—injured but alive. Whatever this was about, it was not worth killing this boy over. He must have fought them when he realized they were taking the horses. Of course, he fought for them. He loved those horses.

I put my arm around him, pulled his head to my chest, and watched Stanley stumble the last bit of distance. I felt a sickening bump in the boy's hair. Whoever hit him gave him a swollen eye and cut lip as well.

"Oh, Coot," I panted. "Who did this to you?"

But the boy did not answer.

"Stanley, help him to his feet, and let's get him inside. He's not dressed for the weather."

The big man held his knees as he worked to regain

his breath. "Who did this?"

Who indeed? What type of man or men would injure a helpless boy and then leave him outside in the cold? And where the hell was Bernard?

We took Coot by the arms and walked him as best we could to the open doors of the stable.

Once inside, Constable Stanley latched the door to seal the door behind us, and I helped the boy to a bench. Then I took stock. One horse and one pony were still in their stalls. That meant they took ten, including Pepper and my own horse Fitch. I motioned to Stanley to stay with the boy and went off to see if Bernard had suffered a worse fate.

I moved through the doorway, walked the eight steps through the kitchen, and found Bernard reclining on his bed, smoking a cigarette.

By God, I wanted to thrash the man on the spot. He lay there as Coot, his charge, had been assaulted and left in the snow for dead! I struck out against the wall, hurting my hand in the process, then gave the man a piece of my mind, my pitch rising as he shrugged off my expostulations. When this was over, I would find a way to throw him out of his easy living. His duty did not end with feeding the boy that did all his work. I knew he was lazy, but I was unaware of how utterly callous the man was. Getting no response, not even an excuse, I was too livid to share his space any longer and marched back to the stables.

Stanley held a ball of snow wrapped in a handkerchief against Coot's head. He was talking to him about his love of horses. A tender scene, to be sure and at just the right time. Here was a man who could have bullied others but had the kindness of a lamb. Perhaps not all was wrong in the world. I took some deep breaths and turned back around into the house.

On my second try, Bernard gave me some answers. A group of five men came to take the horses. When Bernard came out to confront them, they pushed him to the ground, and he wrenched his knee. He said it had been a struggle to get back to his bed. His excuse did not soften my anger, but I put my complaints aside to get the names of the intruders.

Mayor Tom Fox, Matti Larsen, his eldest son Anders, Alexandr Dvorak, and the now mysterious Mitch Blood. Five men for ten horses. The extra ones might be to carry supplies, or maybe they took them so we could not follow.

They must have brought the horses back to the boardwalk to load their supplies before moving westward. Of course, they could be meeting with other men somewhere. Either way, it would be a large contingent. If they were heading west, they would encounter more snow closer to the coast. But where did they hope to get to? There was no settlement between Chambers and Port Rupert.

When I came back to the barn, Stanley and Coot were still together, now on their feet, as they examined the one remaining horse. "We should get this boy to the hospital," said Stanley. "It's a nasty bump on his head, and someone should watch to make sure it doesn't get worse." Stanley was right. I didn't want to leave him with Bernard. I trusted Margaret, Genevieve, and even Dr. Moody to take better care of him.

"There's more bad news," said Stanley. He pointed to the remaining horse. "This one was already injured. Bum knee. Maybe arthritis? I assume that's why they left it. It won't carry anyone too far."

"Which leaves us with one pony if we want to go after them." I couldn't help but chuckle as I pictured us riding double on such a small mount.

Paul nodded. "We should go now to the hospital if Coot can walk. There is something I want to ask your doctor."

He must have seen my raised eyebrows. Dr. Moody was the last person I expected to be part of this. "Don't worry, he said, I'll be kind."

I nodded back. I was beginning to get the full measure of the man.

****

We were about to make the move when a thought hit me. How long had we been out in the woods? My watch read nine o'clock, a full hour past Millie's usual start time. Most likely, she would have returned home when neither of us arrived.

"Did you leave a note telling Millie where we were going?" I asked Stanley.

"No, should I have?"

"Probably." I didn't intend my voice to sound so hard. How was Paul supposed to know how long we would be or when Millie got in to work?

I patted him on the shoulder. "You go ahead, Paul. I think I should check in on Millie. I don't want to think she might have run into these characters."

"You want me to come with you?"

Coot let out a small groan—poor kid.

"No, go ahead. I'll check out the detachment and then come and meet you at the hospital. We'll have to figure out what to do next."

After Paul left, I ensured the remaining animals

were safe in the stable yard and the outside crossbar was in place. Then I moved to the front of the detachment. My heart dropped into my gut as I stepped onto the porch. The front door was unlatched. It bounced against the frame in the wind. Should I call Paul? They were already back near the boardwalk. Too many footprints here. I unbuttoned my holster and raised my pistol. My breathing came unstuck as my familiar panic arose inside me. If something had happened to her, I would never forgive myself.

I cursed myself under my breath. I could not get my feet to move. I wiped my forehead with the back of my left hand. Should I run and find Paul? Was this another ambush? Was someone waiting inside the door, ready to gun me down? The ghost girl, Bunny Dix, or some other hooligan?

I needed to get myself together. I forced my arm to move and pushed the gun's tip between the jamb and the door to stop it from rattling. "Millie," I cried. My voice cracked, "Millie! Are you in there?"

"Gus! Gus!" Her voice held a mixture of excitement and relief. I waited to hear her footsteps, but there was nothing. Could it be a trap?

"Come to the door Millie?" I shouted. I could feel every muscle in my body tense. If I went in low and fast, I could surprise anyone inside. Get a quick shot off like I did in the woods.

"I can't," Millie cried. "I'm locked in the jail cell."

"Are you alone?"

"Yes, I'm alone Gus! Get me out of here!"

I took a moment to survey the surroundings. No movement, not in the station or through the snow. A mass of horse prints ran from the stable yard and alongside the track to the west; that and a single pair of fresh boot prints skirted the corner of the station house and joined the jumble of tracks on the porch.

"Gus!" Millie shouted again. She was past frustrated now as she pleaded with me. Would she sound that way if someone was in there with her?

You can do this. I took a deep breath and shoved my arm forward as I pulled back on the door.

There was nothing but the cold wind whispering around the cabin. I peeked around the corner. The detachment was dark, but there was enough light to see Millie's shape. She stood rigid in the jail cell as her fingers gripped the bars.

Still nothing—I stepped into the center of the doorway and moved into the room. Millie shot me a plaintive look, but before I went to her, I closed the door behind me and checked the indoor latrine and my bedroom, still with the gun in my hand. Someone had disturbed things for sure, but we were alone. I grabbed the keys from my desk and rushed to the lock.

Only then did I notice Millie bleeding from a wound on her temple. The rage I felt with Bernard built back inside me. Whoever did this was going to pay.

Millie rushed out as the door swung open. She grabbed me under my arms and squeezed her whole body against me. I lost my balance but held onto the bars and kept myself erect. She embraced me for several moments until, finally, I guided her forehead back with my hand. The cut was small but angry; the blood dried in a line down her cheek.

"Who did this?" I whispered.

"Oh, Gus, it was horrible." Her eyes filled with tears. "He was so angry, I didn't know what to do! I thought he might kill me!" She buried her head into my chest and started to blubber. I could tell she was not ready to give me the answers I wanted, so I put my hand in her hair and let her cry.

Finally, her body settled, and I stepped back. Her dark brown eyes were the opposite of Genevieve's crystal blue. "Let's get you some coffee." The pot rested on the stove, which meant the coffee was fresh. She must have made it before whoever came assaulted her.

I guided her to a chair by the table and removed my winter gear before pouring two cups. Millie sat curled over the mug and breathed in the aroma.

"I think we should take you to the hospital." I pulled around a chair to sit beside her.

"I'm fine. It was a horrible shock. I never would have expected him…."

"Who did this?" I couldn't keep the anger out of my voice. "It was Fox, wasn't it." That cad! Hopefully, her blood had ruined his fancy gloves.

"It was Sergeant Deacon!" Her eyes went wide. "He came back."

"Deacon? But he. But he's in Prince Rupert. Why? What was he doing here? Why would he? Why did he hit you?"

"I finished brewing the coffee and was making Paul's bed. Your bed. I didn't know where either of you got to, but that's me, faithful Millie, doing her work. And I came out of Paul's room. Your room. And he was standing there not two feet from this table looking at me like I was the one who had intruded on him."

"I shouldn't say this, but I never liked the man," she continued. " It was always Constable Taylor who would give me the time of day. He'd say things like 'How are you, Millie?' and 'How's your mother, Millie?' but never Sergeant Deacon." She put her hand on my wrist and gave it a squeeze. "He would only say something if it was an order as if he had no other way of being."

She looked off into the corner of the room and became quiet.

"What did he do to you?"

When she turned back, a fierce look was in her eye. One I had never seen a hint of. "He slapped me. Hard. There was no warning even. He just stretched out and hit me. And then he pulled me into the cell. I should have done something but I was so startled. He locked the door before I had time to think."

"I'm sorry," she breathed and squeezed my wrist once more.

"What in blazes do you have to be sorry about? He's going to be sorry, I'll tell you that." Without thinking, I slammed my fist on the table, and Millie jumped. "Why?" I asked her. "Why would he do such a thing?"

"I don't know," Millie cried. "He went over there and pulled out a box. I think he came to collect something. He also took one of the rifles."

There was indeed one missing piece off the wall. And a small metal box turned over on its side. It was smaller than a breadbox with a hook for a lock. But now it was open and empty. I moved over and kicked it hard with my foot. The sound it made as it clattered against the wall gave me a slight feeling of relief.

"Where did he get it from?" I asked Millie. She pointed over to the corner where a potted plant always stood. Deacon had moved it away from the wall, revealing an open cache.

"It was a bunch of papers I think. Maybe money,"

Millie said. She was wringing her hands as if she was the one to blame.

I shook my head. "I'm taking you to the hospital where you'll be safe. No arguing."

She stared at me.

"Millie, you did nothing wrong." I stepped toward her, and she moved into my arms, hugging me around my waist. I let her settle there a minute until I finally told her to get her coat.

The two of us dressed, and I locked the detachment door. It wasn't much of a precaution if Deacon had a key, but I suspected the man had traveled off with Fox.

As we stepped off the porch, an idea came to me. "Millie," I turned to her. "Is Sergeant Deacon a large man?"

She huffed. "He's about your size, Gus, but doesn't have your shape. His figure isn't as nice as yours."

I ignored her last comment and moved into the snow near the station house. There I inspected the single line of footprints around the corner of the building. It was clear now that they were coming from the direction of Chambers Lodge.

I motioned Millie over, then used the sweep of my hands to ensure Millie would not walk in the footprints. "Was he wearing his government-issued boots?"

"Well, I don't know," she said.

I placed my foot in the snow so it lined up with the boot print. It fit perfectly.

"It looks like Sergeant Deacon had a visit with Mr. Chambers." His tracks ran parallel to the pit line.

So when I tried to talk with Bunny Dix at Chambers Lodge, could Deacon have been lurking in the lodge? Chambers did not welcome my visit. Was this connected to the ambush in the woods? And the girl? Whatever was happening sure had a lot of people involved. The attacks on Millie and Coot were simultaneous. Deacon must have left with the others. But why?

Paul would have an idea. I let Millie take my arm on the way to the hospital. She needed my comfort, but I would not let this anger go. I needed it to dull my panic. Deacon and all those others; what they did to Coot and Millie. They needed to be caught and punished. And soon.

****

On our walk to the hospital, Millie was mum. It was the shock of what happened. The whole way, she stayed close with her arm hooked in mine. But as we crossed the bridge into the old town, something must have jogged her memory.

"Momma found out the name of Clayton Cole's lover," she announced.

The words Clayton and lover still sounded farfetched to me.

"It was Matilda," she said before I could reply. "Matilda Withers. And she was right. The lady had left her husband to follow Clayton out here."

"By definition, I don't think a *lady* could do such a thing," I couldn't help but say, but Millie was in full swing.

"She died in April of 1915. The sixteenth. That was a Tuesday. And she was buried here in town at the church. Supposedly, the husband did not want the body coming back home to Calgary. There was a daughter involved as well and the father didn't want her either. He said she wasn't his."

I stopped. The wind had subsided, and the snow in

the air was delicate and soft. I pulled the handkerchief out of my pocket before realizing the black stocking was attached to it. In my embarrassment, I dropped both into the snow.

I stooped over to grab them and quickly returned to standing, only to find Millie laughing.

"Well, Constable, that's quite the collection of finery you have in your pocket. It makes a girl wonder what's in the other one."

At first, I was shocked and angry at her response, but as she kept giggling, I remembered what had only just happened. The cut on her forehead was beginning to bruise.

"It's all part of my investigation," I told her in my gruffest voice. "We Mounties can't leave any stone unturned."

She hooked her arm on mine again and then took some time to inspect the articles I held out to her.

"The stocking, I found in the old postmaster's room, scrunched in a ball underneath the bed."

"That's weird." She looked concerned. "My cleaning is always thorough."

"This was difficult to see. Did you know if the postmaster had a lady friend?"

"A *lady friend*," she laughed again. Now, it was her turn to put on her gruffest voice. "I think, by definition, a *lady* wouldn't be leaving their stocking in a postmaster's bedroom." Of course, she was right.

"But no," she said in her normal voice. "I can't imagine either he or Mr. Benjamin having a clandestine relationship." Millie loved putting the word *clandestine* in as many stories as possible. I'm sure the word appeared in all her mother's pulp fiction paperbacks.

"That's not what I wanted to show you," I told her, separating the handkerchief from the stocking. "This was left at the crime scene. At the ambush. On the rock in the middle of the clearing." I pointed at the letter *M.* "Could that be for Matilda?"

Millie's other hand flew to her open mouth. She looked like she might faint. "So it's true," she stammered. "She's come back to haunt Clayton! Something horrible must have happened, and she is back to get her revenge! I can't believe it's true!"

It took several shakes of my head before I could even speak. "No, Millie," I pronounced. "There's a better explanation." And I started to move toward the hospital.

"What, Gus? Tell me!" Millie implored.

But I shushed her. "Give me a minute to think," I told her. "Clayton was not shot by a ghost." She looked annoyed, but I quickened our pace. Millie's information was another piece of a rather complicated puzzle, and I knew I needed Stanley to help me figure it all out.

****

When we entered the hospital, no one came out to meet us. Unsure what to expect, I stepped in front of Millie and swung through the inner doors. Dr. Moody stood alone in the aisle between the hospital's eight beds. Clayton was sitting up with a peculiar look on his face, made stranger by the jarring quietude that filled the room. Clayton wasn't made to be quiet.

I walked forward and curled my arm around Dr. Moody's shoulders. He looked at me, not shocked but surprised that someone was there. His hands were at his waist, and I saw that he was twisting his fist around the fingers of his other hand.

"That man has died," he said, his eyes blinking. I

glanced at Daniel Pickle's bed and then at Clayton, who nodded back. "Just now," said Moody. "I think. Poor man. I expect there wasn't anything that I could do. It happens sometimes."

Millie shouted through the living quarters, and Genevieve, Bea, and Stanley soon appeared. Genevieve must have sensed what had happened because she immediately went to Daniel's body and checked his pulse. We watched as she gave him the sign of the cross before pulling the blanket over his head.

"Should we send for the pastor?" asked Bea, but no one answered her.

Instead, Genevieve moved to her husband and directed me to sit Dr. Moody on one of the beds. I did so, still holding him by the shoulder even as we sat. He was never a large man, but lately, his body had lost significant weight.

Only a nurse could move so quickly between the dead and the living. She had noticed the gash on Millie's face and took her into the examination room to treat her.

Stanley sat on the opposite bed in front of Dr. Moody and me, the bed making a mighty creak from his weight. He looked at me as if to ask permission, and I shrugged.

"Doctor?" asked Stanley.

Moody's head rose to face us, but the expression on his face was dull and lifeless. "Dr. Moody," I tried. "It's me, Constable Albright. Gus. This is my friend Constable Stanley."

There was light in his eyes as if I had given a spark to a flame. "I've got a bone to pick with you, young one." His smile was mischievous. "You've been giving Genevieve and me some extra work. And I don't admire the patients you've been selecting."

"What did he say?" shouted Clayton across the way, but we ignored him, knowing that any attention would worsen his interruptions.

I nodded over at Stanley, curious about what he was about to ask.

"Dr. Moody," he began. "Your wife told us that you don't like to give your patients morphine."

Moody nodded. "Yes, a double-edged sword is that drug. I believe it's caused as much harm as it's helped." His eyes were shining now; his memory returned. "I knew a doctor who prescribed it to pregnant women during their labor. Can you imagine that? I remember hearing that there were women who would pretend they were in labor so they could get a dose." Moody shook his head. "The problem is you don't know how each body will handle it. Whether it will get into your head. That's the difficulty with it. It is… terrible stuff for some."

"I could use some of it right now," shouted Clayton from the other bed. "Or at least a good strong drink." His fever of the previous day appeared to have vanished, and he was back to his usual self. God save us all. He started rattling his handcuffs. Bea stood near his bed but did not give him her eyes.

We should be having this conversation somewhere else, but I could tell Stanley did not want to lose the moment, nor did I.

"Doctor," Stanley started again, his eyes glued to the older man's face. "Can you tell us what patients you gave morphine to here in Chambers?"

The doctor shook his head. "Oh, no, no, no. I could not do that. That's against my ethics as a doctor. Sorry, but no."

"But it's important," I told him, unsure where Stanley was going with this. "People are getting hurt! Millie and Coot!"

Still, the doctor shook his head. "I cannot do that, boys, I'm sorry."

Stanley smiled at him. "Let's do it this way then. There was a mining accident here a couple of years ago. Constable Albright told me about it. There were a number of injured men. Did any of them require morphine?"

"Yes," said Moody. His memories were coming back to him. "Some of those men were wounded. They were in a lot of pain."

"Okay then," continued Paul, not rushing the man, trying to keep him in that space and time. "And did any of those men have issues with it? Have trouble coming off it?"

"Yes," asserted Dr. Moody. His hands were picking at the coarse blanket on which we sat. It had pilled from overuse. How many miners had laid in these beds?

"There may have been one or two that had troubles with the drug. But I would never give them more," the doctor assured us. "I learned when you should stop. There is a certain look to a man when their wants grow into a need."

"Did any of them ask you for more doctor? Did anyone steal some?"

"No," he barked. "Genevieve and I are meticulous, and I do not allow much on the premises. Only for emergencies. Anyone that's too injured, we have to send them away anyway." The doctor glared over at Clayton. "That man should be moved. He needs more help."

"Speak for yourself!" yelled Clayton, then offered

us a slew of profanity. He began attacking the doctor, his parentage, and his mental disposition. "The man's gone crazy," he yelled. "He shouldn't even be practicing anymore." But things went off the rails when Clayton started going on about Genevieve, calling her a shrew and other epithets.

At that point, the doctor sprang to his feet and shouted back at Clayton, moving toward him with the power of his invective. I'd never seen the doctor angry and would not have guessed he could match Clayton with cruel words and curses, but he did.

The noise brought Genevieve back into the room, and it took the two of us to guide the doctor out of the infirmary and to his tidy bedroom, where he slept by himself. He was winded now. Genevieve sent me dirty looks as she worked to calm him. She must have felt that we had violated her trust. I did not try to defend myself. It wasn't worth stressing the doctor out further.

Finally, after Moody calmed himself, I left the couple to themselves. I found Coot bandaged in the observation room next door. He sat on a chair, humming to himself. "We'll get those horses back," I told him as I passed, and I saw him smile back at me.

In the infirmary, Stanley stood beside Clayton's bed, stretched to his full height, the constable towering over the skinny man. Clayton was quiet. Did Stanley use words, or did his physical presence subdue the man? Bea would know. She sat off to one side with an excellent view of all the proceedings.

Stanley stepped away, and we entered the vestibule, finding privacy between the outer and inner doors.

"Is Clayton willing to talk now?" I asked Stanley.

He shook his head. "I don't believe he has anything

to give us. He's not a part of this. I expect they used him because they knew he was a pariah. That no one would care if he vanished or died."

"I think he is part of this," I assured him, but I didn't elaborate.

"What happened to Millie's head?"

"Millie was attacked by Sergeant Deacon. He slapped her in the face and locked her in the jail cell."

The young constable looked shocked. "Sergeant Deacon? That's awful," he said. "It was good that you went back to check on her. I should have gone with you."

"The footprints indicated that Deacon came from the North," I told him, "and the only thing out there is the mine and Chambers Lodge. That's where Mr. Benjamin went as well. What in blazes does it all mean?"

"I don't know," Stanley said. "We need more information. And I think we have a big decision to make."

"You believe Philip Chambers had something to do with this, don't you?" I asked. He was the only reason Stanley would have asked about the mine accident and the morphine. I remembered my meeting with Philip. His gaunt and sallow face. The unfocused eyes. His whole bearing. They were all signs that he had never recovered from the accident."

"I think he is a key participant in all this," Stanley said. "The pit rail ends right at his lodge. I think the people here are smuggling something using the rail track. I don't know what or why, but I expect the answers may be found at Chambers Lodge."

I didn't see how Stanley got to the idea of smuggling. If I told him all I knew, could he connect the pieces? I should have told him about the girl in the woods long ago.

"I've failed Stanley." Saying the words aloud, my chest and shoulders tightened as a wash of guilt passed through me. "I couldn't protect them: Millie, Coot, Clayton, all of them. I should have seen this coming. They put me here because they considered me weak. And they were right." I backed into the wall behind me.

"You're a good man, Albright," Stanley said. "We already know that a dozen men are involved in this scheme, maybe more. You're only one person. We just have to think this through."

"Two," I said. "We're two men now."

Stanley nodded. "We've got some choices to make."

"Go on"

"Well, going to Chambers Lodge is an option. It would catch them off guard, I think."

"It's something we are going to have to do at some point," I said. "Or we could follow those men downriver and see where they are going. I don't understand why they would take off into the wilderness. They must be desperate to escape."

"Or they are off to find something," Stanley added. "In which case, a third option would be to sit here and wait for them to come back."

"I'm ruling out that option. It's too passive, and we'd be working in the dark," I said. "It's either the lodge or going after the men on horseback." We let the silence filter into the small space of the vestibule, each of us willing the other to speak first.

Finally, I broke. "Those men that stole the horses probably believe that they have us fooled. Your gambit in the forest paid off in spades. Without it, we would still be out in the woods, Coot would be freezing in the cold, and Millie would be locked in a jail cell. I say let's do what they are not expecting and check out the lodge. We wouldn't be able to catch the men on horses anyway."

"Agreed," Stanley said, "But it's dangerous. They may be armed."

"That's true, and we don't know how many people will be there."

"We need more men," Stanley stressed.

"Yes," I replied. "But we left Peter out in the woods. And I wouldn't trust Duffy with a gun. He'd probably shoot off his own foot."

The doorway creaked as Bea pushed into the tiny vestibule. Lloyd George was caught between her legs. "You two are up to something, aren't you?" she asked. "What the hell is going on?"

Paul spoke first. "We're thinking of going to see Philip Chambers."

"That's a good idea," she replied, but before she could finish the thought, the doors to the outside were pulled open, and a gust of chill wind filled our space. It was Peter, red in the face from the cold. He stepped inside as Stanley, and I yanked the doors closed behind him.

Peter was out of breath, so we let him settle.

"Did you find anything?" I asked finally.

"Not even a handkerchief this time," Peter grumbled. He shook his head. "Just tracks that wrapped around and back into town. Birch and the Larsen kid went home. Birch was furious about it."

"I'm glad you checked it out, though, Peter." I shook his hand, and he nodded back at me.

That's when we told them about Coot, Millie, and the riders.

"We're heading over to Philip Chambers Lodge to get to the bottom of this," said Bea.

I didn't remember telling Bea she could come along for the ride. I was about to nix the idea when Genevieve opened the door and found us all squished like a dozen clowns in a telephone booth. We were all so embarrassed that we filed back into the ward. Somehow, Genevieve had worked her magic to calm Clayton, and he now faced away from us like he was sulking. My questions for him would have to wait a bit longer.

"We're coming with you," Peter proclaimed. The two had been talking since we came back into the room. "Bea's got her mind set on it."

I faced Bea. "I think you should stay here. Genevieve and the doctor need you."

Bea shook her head, "Duffy can stay." I glanced over and saw that the man had entered the room and was now eating an apple on one of the hospital beds. Out of all of us, he was the one who needed a rest or a snack the least.

"I'm coming," she asserted.

"I know her," said Peter. "Once she's decided a thing, she doesn't back down." He was gazing at her with a curious grin like he was proud of her. "She'll just follow us."

"Besides, I have two things to offer." She lifted one finger. "I have met Philip Chambers before when I lived in Toronto. I know how to talk with men like him."

I didn't bother to contain my surprise. "You know him? How? Are you and he friends?"

"No, of course not. He may or may not remember me. We are acquaintances who have some common interests. I know people in his circle." I wanted to know

228

more, but she raised a second finger. "I also know a path through the woods that connects to the back of Chambers Lodge. That could be useful to us."

I shook my head in disbelief. Stanley said what I was thinking. "How do you know about this path, Bea? What have you been doing at Chambers Lodge?"

We watched as she considered her answer. She looked at Peter. "I've been prospecting."

"Prospecting?" I let out. "Prospecting for what? Silver? Gold?"

"For land," she said, "speculating." I still didn't understand. "I am interested in purchasing the property."

What followed was a long, uncomfortable silence. Bea stood unruffled, staring at the two of us as we passed looks back and forth.

I scanned the hospital ward. Everything was in chaos. People dead and injured. I knew I couldn't fully trust Bea, but I didn't believe Peter and her would shoot us in the back. No doubt about it, we needed help.

"All right," I said slowly. "But if we do this, we will have to do it right. You will do what we say. You will not do anything dangerous or put yourself in harm's way." I watched as Peter, and she nodded their consent.

"I'm making you two Special Constables," I announced. The force had Special Constables throughout the North, often in remote places where we had to count on natives and frontiersmen to keep what order could be maintained. I probably didn't have the authority to grant the title, but no one was here to stop me.

"You as well, Genevieve." I turned to see her expression. "And as a Special Constable, I task you to get in touch with Plateau and get help as soon as the lines are operational. Bea and Peter, I'm having you act as officers. You will carry guns, but you must only shoot in self-defense and then must stop when given the order to do so."

"No," said Peter, "I will not be a Special Constable." He stared at me unnervingly. "I will help you out, but I don't want to be any part of your organization."

"Okay," I said. I wasn't sure what he was getting at. "We can call you whatever you want Peter, as long as you follow our orders and keep safe."

Peter shrugged, and there was an uncomfortable silence.

"So that's what we're doing then," I said. Everyone nodded, but I could tell that no one, even Bea, was excited by the prospect. Good, it would be dangerous work.

I told Bea and Peter to get something to eat before meeting us over at the detachment.

Then I sent Stanley ahead to prepare our things. Me, I was going to make one last try at Clayton.

In all the exchange, I failed to notice that Millie was now sitting on the chair beside Clayton's bed, holding his hand. Genevieve had tied a tight white bandage around her head.

Walking with Millie to the hospital, I already decided what words might get Clayton to talk—an angry diatribe focusing on his selfishness. But for some reason, when I saw the two of them together, both looking so pathetic, the energy of my rant dissolved.

I plodded over to them and took a quiet perch on the end of Clayton's bed. I should have asked Millie's opinion when we planned our latest operation, but it was hard to even look at her bandage without feeling considerable guilt. I needed to put that aside.

"I know you're Clayton Cole," I said, just above a whisper. "And I know you think as Millie does that the woman you saw in the woods was Matilda coming back from her grave. But it wasn't."

Clayton started to speak and then stopped himself.

"I think the woman you saw outside The Hole was Matilda's daughter," I continued, my voice calm and measured. "I don't know her name. I think they used her to get you and me out of town so they could ambush us."

Clayton nodded, tears in his eyes as Millie squeezed his hand. "I asked the mayor to look for her," he croaked.

"Why? Why did you come back to town, Clayton?"

He spoke to Millie instead of me. "To put things right," he told her. "To pay my debts and get what was owing." His voice lacked anger, just a deep sense of sadness and loss.

"Emily, Matilda's daughter, that was her name. *Is* her name. I helped raise her, those three years I was with Matilda. I spoiled her." Millie patted him on his arm, and he continued, "But when the accident happened, it was too much. I should have taken her with me or made sure she was kept safe, but I didn't. I couldn't. I wanted to kill myself. I don't know why I didn't. Matilda shouldn't have died. It was me that should have died."

So that's why he rushed the clearing. He still blamed himself for Matilda's death. It was the longest I had ever heard him talk without profanity.

"What happened to Matilda, Clayton?" Millie asked.

"You want to know if I murdered her?" he asked. His eyes were on me now. Cold and dark. "I might as well have. Truth is, I don't remember. I didn't even remember the next morning. It's the...." He was about to curse, but Millie squeezed his hand. "It's always been the drink."

He closed his eyes, his head pushed into the pillow. "Matilda…" he said, his eyes still shut. "We both enjoyed the drink. That night, she fell into the river, I suppose. I woke on the floor of my cabin with no idea in my head. Didn't know she was even gone until someone came to fetch me."

The tears ran into his beard as his breath came in heaves. For the first time, I saw the man he might have been. He was still in that moment ten years ago. Millie rubbed his arm now, looking at me as if to warn me off. But this was too important.

"Clayton," I asked. "What did you mean by 'getting what you were owed?' What is the mayor's scheme? He's hiding something and hurting people in the bargain. Isn't he?"

Clayton lurched forward, hands in fists, a string of profanity popping ready on his lips, the drool already collecting in the corners of his mouth. I braced myself for the onslaught. He went from a pitiable wreck to a rabid dog in a moment. "The mayor owes me!" He exclaimed.

But Millie eased him backward, shushed him, and put her hands on his chest. I wouldn't have believed it if I didn't see it myself. It was like Coot with his horses all over again. I should have used Millie on Clayton ages ago. I might have had a civil conversation with the man.

"I am as much an owner of that hotel as he is." Millie nodded as he talked. She kept her face close so he couldn't see my own. "He made thousands on it, Millie, thousands! And not one cent came into my hands. Not one."

"But it's worthless now," I couldn't help but say.

"That devil has a different plan," Clayton continued. "He told me to wait. That there was new money coming in. That if I was patient, I'd have my share. But I know he's got his money hidden. That he just wanted me out of the way. There's your reasons for the Pickle Brothers constable."

"A new plan," I said, still considering this new information. "Do you know what it is?"

"Well, how the hell would I know? Haven't you been listening, Albright! The man wants me dead. He had me shot. And now you're telling me he had my own daughter out to get me...." And so began a string of curses. Millie tried to calm him, but the man was resolute, spit flying across the bed sheets in my direction.

That brought Genevieve back, with Coot trailing not far behind. I saw now that he wore the same head bandage as Millie.

I stood and patted Genevieve on the shoulder. "I'm sorry," I told her. "I had to know what we might be walking into."

Millie stood now and pushed her way between us. "You shouldn't go, Gus! These men are dangerous. The mayor, Sergeant Deacon, Philip Chambers, they are all a bunch of scoundrels." Her face was bright red, a crease forming on her forehead. Genevieve nodded along, her own face a mask of concern, as Clayton continued his rant in the background.

"It's my job," I told them as I walked toward the vestibule. "I'm not letting anyone else get hurt. Don't come back to the detachment Millie. Stay here. Lock the doors and don't let anyone inside." I did not look back.

Instead, I pushed through the lobby doors letting them slap closed behind me.

Chapter 9

Philip's Folly

Together at the detachment, we readied ourselves with a firm silence. We were taking charge of things, but I felt vulnerable and powerless. My wish to get something concrete out of Clayton yielded only partial results. I worked through the pieces, and one thing became clear. Stanley's inferences we're always ahead of my own. I was going to have to confide in the man. He was able to think faster and to connect things that I didn't realize were related. If we put our heads together, we could stop whatever treachery was afoot.

Peter and Bea remembered to bring the two Winchesters captured from the ambush in the woods; however, they declined to use them. Bea preferred her Springfield rifle because she didn't want to use a gun she had never fired. Peter, for his part, elected not to carry a weapon.

"In The Dominion of Canada, bad things happen to Indians who carry guns," he said. He seemed committed to the idea, so I let it go.

As we left, the snow fell in large, delicate shapes that floated on the gentle wind. In the distance, their mass still formed a clouded curtain, but up close, the visibility was clear. The four of us kept our eyes on the near ground, searching for signs of movement, but even the squirrels and birds that had withdrawn with the storm were not yet ready to venture out. Besides that, there were no new tracks in the snow. I could barely make out Mr. Benjamin's footprints, their shapes covered with the constant accumulation of snow. But Deacon's footsteps were visible by all, a straight line over the buried pit rail from the direction of Chambers Lodge.

The walk should take half an hour, but we were encumbered by our guns and packs and forced to walk on the alert. My legs, already sore from all their extra work, complained at the weight of the heavy snow despite the help of our snowshoes.

I waited for Bea and Peter to fall a few paces behind, then matched my pace with Constable Stanley. We needed to talk. I started by asking what he and Clayton discussed when I was in the back with Dr. Moody.

Stanley looked at me sideways. "I asked him about the girl, Gus." It was the first time he had used my given name, and I could feel the hairs on my arms rise under my jacket. "He told me that he was cursed. And that she had come to destroy him. He told me he knew her, Gus. I know there is something you're not telling me." He didn't sound angry. Instead, there was a measure of concern in his voice.

I took a few steps and listened to the crunch of our snowshoes in the snow. "I spoke to her, Paul," I finally said. He turned to face me, but I continued to stare ahead down the length of the rail line. "She got the jump on me, and I panicked. I couldn't even move. She could have shot me just like that."

I came to a halt. "Ever since the war," I continued, "I've had these moments where I can't act. Where things are too much for me. I know I should have told you, but

I made a promise to her and to myself."

"What promise?" he asked.

"The rest was as I told it, but in the end, she had me dead to rights, and I hate to say it, but I was full of fear. I promised if she let me go, I wouldn't chase her. That I wouldn't tell anyone about her." I closed my eyes and tried to picture her form against the dark cloud behind her. "I let her go."

Paul grunted, and I opened my eyes. "Sounds to me like you did what you had to," he said. "You had already beaten the odds. She could not have expected you to take out both brothers. It was a heroic thing you did to get there. There's no shame in that." He looked me in the eyes. "You were a soldier, Gus. You know what men will do when facing death. I might just have run."

It was nice of him to say, but I doubt he would have run. At this very moment, he was walking into a situation of potential danger.

So, I told him about all the other details I had collected. "I think she's the daughter," I said. Stanley's forehead wrinkled, his brows dropped, and the muscles in his jaw began to work. He was thinking things through, trying to find patterns as he considered all the possible alternatives. I still felt guilty about not coming clean to him in the beginning. I worried he might have found information in all that paperwork if he knew all the details.

"Did you see Clayton's name in those files of yours," I asked.

"I don't think he was involved in the mine," Stanley said. "So I wasn't looking for his name."

How much was missed because I didn't come clean beforehand? I could do nothing about the past. It was time to focus on the present and figure out this mystery with Stanley. Whatever the secret was, it was terrible enough that they would have killed a Mountie. From what he asked the doctor, Stanley must have thought it was about morphine and the railroad. But I still wasn't sure. It didn't seem possible in a town as small as Chambers.

I looked over at Paul. If we were going to get to the bottom of this, I would have to trust him. He noticed me staring and gave me a nod: Paul, Peter, Bea, and I. I just hoped it would be enough. Damn thing! It's always about the numbers.

****

After twenty-five minutes of walking, I stopped us, and we huddled close in the snow beside a grove of trees. If we were to find out what was happening, we would need to challenge whoever still lived at Chambers Lodge. But we had several disadvantages. Other than Bea, none of us had an understanding of the surroundings. From what I remembered, the lodge faced the mine opening, its back to the forest. I knew the building was a large, two-storied cabin made out of wood and windows, but beyond that, I had no real idea of its contents. Or how many armed men might be inside?

Our main advantage was our surprise. We assumed that the people inside wouldn't know about our new plan. Deacon's footprints were the only fresh tracks, and considering the accumulation of snow, it was doubtful that anyone would use a different route through the woods.

And yet, Deacon coordinated his attack with the horse riders. How did he know of the mayor's plan to steal the horses?

"I think Benjamin brought a message to Deacon at the lodge," I told the others. "If that is the case, he would have told the others here about my investigation—and Stanley."

"But from what you tell me, Benjamin knows only part of the story," said Stanley. "He wouldn't know anything we found out about Clayton or the Pickle brothers. And he wouldn't know that the second brother had died."

I considered this. "They will still be wary," I decided. "But there can't be many people there: Bunny Dix, the Yugoslavian, Philip Chambers, and Benjamin. Probably other thugs as well."

Everyone was silent, so I went through the plan. We would pair off into two groups. Constable Stanley and Bea would use Bea's path to move in from behind the lodge and investigate from the rear.

Peter and I would wait a few minutes and then approach the main pathway—the covered railway line. If no one saw us, Peter would take a position on the side of the building while I moved to the front entrance. Even though we all were armed except for Peter, we would try to investigate without firing a shot. We would take a look and then meet back in the woods and discuss what we saw. It would be a reconnaissance mission. Best case scenario, we could figure out how many were inside. We could ask to parlay with Chambers or one of his men.

Of course, they could get spooked and start shooting. There were real dangers here, like not knowing each other's whereabouts and hitting each other in a crossfire. If anyone got wounded, we would be a long way from help.

"If in doubt," I told them, "get out of there fast." It

was unlikely they would chase us, as that would surrender a secure position—unless more were in there than expected. Numbers, always numbers; if only we could know how many combatants we faced.

Stanley and Bea left first, using the path to slip into the woods to the east. Peter and I crept along the rail track before we crawled through the underbrush to the fence surrounding the encampment. From here, we would sneak to the side of the lodge.

As we got to the barrier, I scanned the fence line and saw their wide-open main gate. Because of the snow, we could not see the rail line, but I assumed it ran another three hundred yards to the large oak barn west of the main building. That's where the Chambers must have stored their old pit train.

The lodge itself was an imposing sight. Two high-ceilinged floors with a peaked roof made to appear like some European chalet. The front facade held generous windows that peered out on the workyard, but there were no signs of life except a weak line of chimney smoke wavering in the wind. I looked behind me and caught a glimpse of Peter's leather coat as he started to work his way through the trees to where he would climb the fence to my right.

We took turns bumbling over the fence without hearing any alarm. The place remained silent. My muscles ached from the tension. Our actions were rash, but I did not falter. Instead, I snuck the fifty feet across the yard to the side of the lodge and put my back flat against the timbers. I had decided not to hold my rifle or to remove my pistol from my holster. If someone was watching us, I didn't want them to think we were coming to challenge them. And yet, what else could they think?

Fortunately, there was only one window on this side. And no indications that anyone had spotted us. I prayed that Bea and Stanley weren't doing anything foolhardy.

Peter came next. He kept his body low as he ran and crossed the distance without alarm. I gripped Peter's bicep and gave him a nod. He would stay here while I moved onto the front porch to take a careful look through the large front windows. I kept my head low as I moved around the corner of the lodge. With a final glance back at Peter, I grabbed the porch rail and hoisted myself under it to remain concealed. Then, I pressed my body against the facade and walked sideways to the edge of the long front window.

I could see the stairs of the front porch were unshovelled. Broad snow drifts had settled on the veranda, yet the boards still creaked as I moved my weight forward. I turned my body and peeked through the dirty glass to see a large open room and the central stairwell. There were still no signs of life, so I breathed in and took a gamble. I hurried past the window and came to a standstill at the lodge's front door.

Everything remained quiet. What now? Should I move forward to look in the window on the other side of the door or try the handle? A crow cried out, and I could feel a bead of sweat break out along the center of my spine. Nerves don't fail me now. Then a whole chorus of crows and the first shot sounded.

The bullets came quickly. They sounded like firecrackers from where I stood. Men's voices called out, the sound of breaking glass, and I shouldered the door, pushed down on the latch, and forced my weight against it. I tumbled through it as the latch released but regained my balance and brought my pistol out of my holster to the level of my eyes. Ahead was a staircase—to the right and left, large rooms and messy floors. No one.

Another round of shots rang out, coming from the back. Stanley and Bea—were they pinned down? Why did they not retreat into the forest?

I wiped a line of sweat out of my eyes and gulped the air. I pushed off from my ankles, ignoring the staircase to the left; I dashed through the corridor in front of me. Into a kitchen, the first step through and I tripped. I tumbled into a man—our bodies tangled—the wind knocked out of me. I tried to breathe, but it caught in my throat, and I felt the other man's feet scrabble against me. Reaching out, clawing, I found the man's head; only instincts now. I grabbed the hair and banged the forehand hard against the floorboards and then again. Another man running toward me from a side corridor. I realized I'd dropped my pistol and saw its shape on the floorboards. The man below me screamed in anguish— a round red blood mark on the floor. I saw his face now; the tiny glasses crooked over his nose and a tidy, well-coiffed beard. I knew this face. Mr. Benjamin.

The threat persisted. This other man was now upon us. A shot whizzed through a broken window and into the wall with a splash of plaster. I needed to make a decision. My gun lay three feet away. Should I grab it or reach out to trip the man approaching? I reached out, my knee cracking against Benjamin's nose. I wrapped my arms around the runner's waist and used my weight to tackle him. We crashed against the floorboards, a painful jumble of knees and elbows. I raised my fist. The arc of my arm poised well. Blazes! It was Peter. Of course. He'd come through the door from the side of the lodge. And I resisted my urge to strike him.

The confused face of Mr. Benjamin stared at us, blood pouring from his nose as he squirmed to one side. I grabbed the gun, stumbled to my feet, and ran into the opposite wall with my shoulder, looking back to survey the scene. We were in some kind of kitchen, but there was garbage everywhere. Peter eyed me with a passive face, showing little concern.

"Take care of him," I screamed at Peter, too loud for the room. A new round of shots rang out, and I yelled, "Stay down." For a moment, I marveled at my beating heart as it thumped in my chest. I knew if I stopped and thought beyond that, I would panic. So I didn't.

Instead, I rushed to the back door that led out of the kitchen; a bullet broke through the glass inches from my hip. There was a window in it, but it disintegrated from the shot—fragments all over the floor. I flicked a piece of glass off my coat and pulled my body flat against the wall, my hand on the knob. In a breath of silence, I yanked open the door. A small landing lay in front. I moved through and saw two men crouched in the snow, using a large oil drum as cover. They shot one at a time. One reloaded as the other shot. They did not sense me.

I waited to the count of three and tried to time it to a moment when they were both distracted. I moved out, and a bullet from the forest blew right over my shoulder, crashing into the door behind me.

"It's Albright," I shouted, flapping one hand. The two men turned and saw me; my pistol pointed toward them as I moved forward. I descended the stairs, hoping Bea and Stanley had finished taking shots. All the while, I watched the men's eyes. They had a decision here. Would they make a wise choice? Bunny Dix just shot while the Yugoslavian reloaded. It was his choice. To turn, to run away, to lay down his arms. I shuffled toward them, testing out the shapes on my periphery. Were there other enemies about, tucked away amongst the jumble of snow, rusting metal, and encroaching forest? The man laid his rifle into the snow. And for the moment, it was over.

Stanley and Bea came out of the woods once they saw my hand outstretched. I forced the assailants to retreat and then moved forward to collect their rifles. I then threw them behind me into a snow bank.

"Are you alone?" I asked them. They didn't reply.

I did not relax. The situation was still fraught with peril. I paced around to the other side of the oil drum, holding the two brutes frozen with my pistol. I aimed to put them between me and anyone firing from the house. I waved to Stanley and Bea, who came out from hiding. So far, so good. Other than Mr. Benjamin's well-deserved thumping, no one was injured.

I don't know what my foot hit in the snow. It was long and thin, like a pipe or a rake. Whatever it was, my toes got underneath it, and I went bum-over-tea-kettle into the snow, my face scraping on the sharp crust. Within moments the Yugoslavian was on me, his knee in my back. He punched me in the back of my head, using his weight to push me farther into the snow so I could not breathe. My pistol hand was caught under me, and I felt him grab for it. I knew I was a dead man if he got his fingers on it, but I could not move. I tried to push up against him. But it was no use. There was no leverage, and I sank farther, panicking. A desperate situation.

And then I felt him lift away. I twisted out of the snow in enough time to see the man fly above me. Stanley had him by the neck and leg, and though the

Yugoslavian was not a tiny man, he threw the rogue head-first into the oil drum. I scrambled to my knees, my face on fire from the cold, and saw that Bea had Bunny at the end of her rifle. She shouted at him to sit back in the snow.

Stanley gave the Yugoslavian two hard fists to the face even though the man still hadn't recovered from the shock of being lifted and thrown. He could not even raise his arms to defend himself. I remembered how I used my rifle butt on Daniel Pickle. I wanted to tell Stanley to stop, but my voice wouldn't come. He had the man by the scruff of the neck once more and, hooked his arm between the Yugoslavian's legs, lifted him sideways, turning his massive body to get momentum.

This time, he threw the man head-first into a small bank of snow with such force his head was buried to his neck. Then, for good measure, Stanley placed his boot flat on the man's bottom and pushed hard, sinking him even farther, past his shoulders. Bunny finally sat. Surrendering to an overwhelming force is what they call it in the military. Stanley now reached in and pulled the Yugoslavian back out. There was no fight left in him as well.

"You all right?" Paul asked me.

I stood as I brushed the wet snow off my coat and pants. My face was still raw, but I had suffered no other damage except, of course, to my pride. I surveyed the scene. Both men appeared broken, and there were no other threats, at least for now.

I surveyed the damage to the lodge. Stanley and Bea had hit every place where the men weren't. There wasn't a bullet hole in the oil drum the men had used for cover, just a Yugoslavian-sized dent.

"What happened?" I asked as I picked a hunk of snow out of my collar. "You weren't supposed to exchange gunfire?"

Bea laughed. "Your man here got caught running into a hedge as he tried to retreat. I had to fire cover-shot so he could untangle himself."

Stanley did not seem amused. "They started firing from nowhere, and so I turned and ran. As was our plan. Except the hedge was there. My boot got caught, and I couldn't get out of the darn thing."

I looked at his feet. They were the length of a loaf of bread. Bea and I should have used the back trail instead.

We handcuffed the men to each other. I shouted to Peter that we were coming inside and he appeared at the broken window.

"All good in here," said Peter. "Except I heard some noise upstairs."

Stanley and I pushed our captives through the door. Inside, Mr. Benjamin crouched against the kitchen's back wall, a paisley handkerchief pressed to his nose. He was far removed from the prim and proper Mr. Benjamin of the station house.

I had a bunch of burning questions, but I wanted to secure the place before having what was sure to be an enlightening conversation. We used two handcuffs to lock the two goons' wrists in a circle around a table leg in the messy kitchen. There was so much rubbish on the floor that we had to kick and clean away the debris before they could sit on the floor.

"What type of noises did you hear, Peter?" I asked.

"I don't know," shrugged Peter. "Some banging, maybe some voices."

"Okay, you and Bea stay here while we check

upstairs. If you hear more gunshots, take Benjamin out the back door into the woods. You can leave these two in their restraints," I said, pointing to the two goons.

****

As soon as I said it, we heard thumping footsteps, and through the corridor, I saw a tall, skinny shape rush down the steps and out the front door. There was no doubt it was Philip Chambers. My feet moved before thinking. If it was a trap and other men were on the stairs, they would have shot me in the back of the head. But there were no other men. And so, I was out in the heavy snow again, my lungs and legs wanting no more of the exercise.

Philip Chambers was no doubt fast. Probably faster than me. But the fool had rushed outside without a coat, hat, or even proper footwear, a pair of bedraggled bedroom slippers on his feet. I'm sure that was good for the first few steps, but the cold would be fierce. His shirt was ragged with large holes that showed his skin, and his pants weren't much better.

He ran in a panic. He sped at first toward the gate, then for the mine opening, and last toward the large barn to the west. All this non-decision allowed me to catch him as I kept a steady course. When he sensed I was onto him, he turned one hundred eighty degrees and twisted past me. He must have imagined he could return to the lodge, but Constable Stanley's sizeable outstretched arm flattened him out in the snow.

We dragged him back inside, a constable on each side, the man limp as a drowned cat. "My back, my back," the man moaned as we lifted him onto the porch and through the front door.

Stanley pulled a sun-ravaged Chesterfield from one

of the front rooms over to the base of the stairs while I used the wall's surface to keep the man erect. Then the two of us poured him into the settee. I would have gladly sat as well, but there was more work to do.

"Philip Chambers," I panted. "We are going to move to the second floor. Tell us what we will find there. More men with guns?"

"No." He shuddered. The man had gone quite pale, beads of perspiration dotting his face. "Just the girls," he croaked. "No guns."

I looked at Stanley in shock. "I'm going. If this one runs again, give him a hard tackle. Or let him freeze to death down the mine."

I dashed up the stairs. The second floor held an open space facing the mine entrance. Perfect for any employer wanting to keep a perpetual eye on his workers. When the mine was working, temporary shelters would fill the space between the lodge and the mine, opening between spring and fall. In the dead of winter, the company would lay off most of the workers, who would go back home or into the city to spend their income. Some miners built permanent, more insulated shelters in Chambers. They would spend their winters working in the town or doing odd jobs at the mine site. Now all I saw was a clean blanket of snow with the footprints from our latest chase.

This great room must have once held the Chambers' accomplishments, a physical manifestation of their success. Now the only items of substance that remained were the over-large oak dining table and four matching chairs. Discarded garments, wrappers, and odd bits of instrumentation covered the floor. But this was unlike the vandalism of Clayton's cabin. It would have taken weeks or months to create the mess. I moved to the table to further investigate the pieces lying on its surface, but there was a noise to my right, and I remembered what Philip Chambers had said about *the girls*.

I peeked my head into the first room across from the exit to the stairs. A large four-poster bed stood incongruously amongst another jumble of castaway items. The bed was unmade, the sheets bunched and pulled in such a way to describe either a tortured evening or a sordid one.

In the next room, I found the five women huddled in a corner, frightened by the sudden impact of our arrival. All were Oriental, and all were young. None of them spoke, staring at me with wide eyes. How could they know what to make of us? I shouted downstairs to Stanley.

"The second floor is safe, but we need Bea here now."

Surely, I had a right to be angry. To think all of this was going on right under my nose. I could not help myself. I left the room before Bea was on the stairs. Bounding down it, I grabbed Philip Chambers by his shirt and dragged him off his comfortable couch. If it weren't for Stanley, I would have punched the cretin in his face.

"In the kitchen!" I shouted and grabbed Chambers by the armpit. I made him walk before me ignoring his moans and lurching gait. I deposited him in a chair at the kitchen table and then began pacing the room, trying to release some anger inside me. My fury could not be contained. My voice, when it came, was a loud growl.

"Who's going to talk? Which one of you is going to talk?"

I glared at each one of them until I found the weakest

link. He was the only one not to look at me, blood still dripping from his nose. "Mr. Benjamin," I said, "Fancy seeing you here. In this den of iniquity. Can you explain yourself?"

I squatted on the floor to hear his mumbling until I could take no more.

"Speak up! Louder! I don't care about your sniveling!"

"I wasn't really part of it!" He protested. It was a child's voice, a pathetic squeal, which contradicted all his posturing as an honorable gentleman. "All I was asked to do was to keep silent."

"Then do so," came a voice. It was Philip Chambers, sitting upright now, his tongue rolling over his blackened teeth. "None of us here will talk, until we see a lawyer." So that's how he thought he would get away with it. Get Daddy to solve all his problems. And yet it was Daddy who had left him in the middle of nowhere with a crew of miscreants and a broken back. Plus, me and my anger.

Chapter 10

Bea's Betrayal

"Did someone call for a lawyer?" Bea said, as she entered the kitchen with five young women tailing behind her. "I am a lawyer. Osgoode Hall, Toronto, class of 1915."

I looked at Peter, and he nodded his head.

"But I wouldn't take your case," she continued, "and I pity the lawyer who would. These constables have the right to be here. The Opium Laws of 1919 state that police officers have the right to search locations presumed to import, hold, manufacture, or sell opium for non-medical uses. Either of these is a serious criminal offense, with a minimum sentencing of imprisonment for seven years."

Philip Chambers looked stunned, and then his face fell. "I know you," he muttered. He turned to me and swore. "Her family has a vendetta against us. She wants to ruin everything we have created here."

Bea ignored him. "Further to that, they are sure to lay charges against all of you for human trafficking, kidnapping, forced confinement, assault, multiple counts of attempted murder, and multiple counts of attempted murder of federal law officers. British Columbia has the death penalty, and if I was your prosecutor, I would ask it for all of you."

I wished I owned one of those new cameras, the type I read about where an everyday bloke could take a picture and develop it for themselves. If I had, you would see a picture of the four most depressing faces possible, none more so than Mr. Benjamin. He was still the weakest link.

I moved toward him, fists at my side, but his eyes weren't on me. They were peering around my legs toward Bunny Dix and his Yugoslavian friend. I cast my eyes the same way and saw both men look away. They were not only trying to silence Benjamin but Philip Chambers as well. Maybe these men didn't work for Chambers. This man, Amadeo Ricci, a lawyer himself, must mean they were all part of something bigger. Bunny and his friend were the ones in charge. They were only using Chambers for his lodge, rail, and addictive personality.

But we needed someone to start talking, and I didn't want Benjamin worried about some heavy in Prince Rupert. I wanted him to worry about me.

I turned to Peter and Stanley. "Let's move these two outside. I don't even want to look at them."

That's when the Yugoslavian decided he could speak English, an accented form with a heavy emphasis on curse words and menacing threats. He tried to stand, but the effect was comical since the handcuffs were still attached to Bunny. He wasn't going to get loose, but he was putting on quite the show of strength, so I took two steps toward him and gave him a knee to his stomach. Well, not quite his stomach. As Bea had stated, I had rights under the Opium law to take decisive actions when faced with exceptional circumstances. The important thing was he stopped speaking.

Stanley and I unlocked the handcuffs and brought the two back to the yard with whatever force we deemed necessary. We locked them to a metal pipe on the side of the building. Peter watched from the porch step as we did so.

"Make sure they don't move," I told him.

The two of us stepped past him back into the kitchen. Bea had taken the girls over to the table on the other side of the room. I could hear Bea trying to converse with them by making her sentences short and her words loud.

"Ask them about the dead girl!" I called over to her, and Bea looked back at me, confused. "Last spring, they found a drowned girl in the Skeena near Oscar Lange's place. See if they know anything about it."

Bea didn't look any less perplexed, but I turned away, pulling off my hat to run my hand through my hair.

All I needed was one word with a pointed finger to get Benjamin started. "You!"

"Oh, ah, this has nothing to do with me. I was intimidated. They said they would hurt me, and they threatened they would take my job away. I never took any of their money. They just told me when the train was coming and to be quiet about it."

"What train? Be quiet about what?" I asked.

"The pit train, of course." His expression was incredulous like I should have figured it out months ago. "They've been smuggling with it." He said the word "smuggling" as if it was the worst of their crimes. "I didn't know it was opium, though. Filthy stuff." He scanned the room to see if he had any supporters.

"You would have known it when you came here," said Stanley, "and yet you didn't come back and report it." It was a good point.

"I told you," said Benjamin, "those two were threatening me." He was pointing where Dix and the Yugoslavian fellow once sat. "They wouldn't let me leave."

"Wait," Bea called over, "if they are smuggling stuff using the pit rail, then why did they leave on horseback."

You could see the lights go on around the room. "The snowstorm." We all said it at about the same time.

"You weren't expecting the snowstorm, were you?" I said, turning to Chambers. "And now your precious shipment is out there, on the rail tracks between here and Prince Rupert."

"Including the men on it," Stanley added.

That meant that everyone in the town was in on the scheme. They had shifted businesses from mining to smuggling. And smuggling not only opium but also people. I looked at the five women sitting in the room's far corner. I didn't want to think of how they got here, in the middle of the Canadian bush. Their journey was far from over. The government would most likely deport them.

But Stanley was right. There were men trapped in the snowstorm squeezed between the mountains. Whether their actions were illegal or not, they needed help. They had been stranded downriver for three days.

The enormity of their scheme was disorienting. And it didn't fit together yet. I turned back to Benjamin. "How many times have they done this? Used the pit train to smuggle people and drugs?"

Mr. Benjamin hung his head. "I count three times over the last six months. The first time was when there was no Mountie at the detachment. After Sergeant

Deacon had left but before you came." I felt the anger build inside me again. I kicked some debris across the floor and pounded my fist on the counter before glaring at Chambers.

"Six months," I seethed. "Six months, under my nose." How could Stanley remain so calm? Maybe because he wasn't taking this personally. The kitchen was hot and stale and smelled of tobacco, decomposing food, and sweat. It was stifling.

"So you've done this at least twice before?" I tried to make my voice soft, but it came out hard. "Three times. How? How did I not know about it?"

"Wait," I realized something. "Were you lying to me? Does the telegraph actually work?"

Mr. Benjamin gulped. "It was working the first time you came, though I thought it was already dead. That first message must have gone through somehow because that's the only time I sent it." Otherwise, Stanley wouldn't have arrived. I was beginning to realize Constable Stanley was a bit of a game-changer. I wouldn't be standing here now if it wasn't for his help.

"But why then was there no return message?" I asked.

"I kept my finger on the transmission key until you left. Then I cut the wire and stitched it back together so there was no connection in case you tried yourself." I stepped toward him. "I'm sorry, I'm sorry," he yelled. "You don't know what pressure I was under."

"You idiot," I yelled. "The men on the train could have been trying to send you a distress signal!"

"It doesn't matter," said Chambers. "Deacon will find the train, I have no doubt. Now there is a real man."

****

Chambers was smiling now, his grin showing the rot in his mouth. "It was easy. You were so gullible. So willing to assume that everyone was decent. That we were all powerless people who couldn't do anything but let the town die."

So Chambers had an ego that he couldn't help showing off. I could use this.

"But how?" I asked. "How did you do it the second time? The station was right across from the detachment?"

"It was easy." He sat back. "We moved you around like a pawn. We always operated during the full moon so we could see the tracks after we made sure you were out of the town."

Yes, there were times when I was away, staying over on someone's ranch after an excursion for one reason or another. Cattle poaching, fishing trips, or a simple invitation. How was I to know?

"But this time, you got a girl to do your dirty work for you." I was thinking of Bunny now. He didn't strike me as the type to shy away from violence. So why and how did the girl get involved?

"Haha! The latest ploy was serendipity rearing its ugly head." He went on, "The girl had money and wanted a man dead. The Pickles owed us a favor. The whole thing would have you looking the other way. When you started nosing around, coming down the tracks to snoop, we knew we needed something bigger to distract you. You just got lucky."

Or they underestimated me.

If the plan was to kill Clayton, they wanted me there as a witness. There would be a manhunt to catch the Pickle brothers, and they would lead us northeast to

Plateau and beyond, maybe even into the mountains. I assume they believed they would be able to escape. They had me outnumbered, outgunned, and picked the ambush spot. With Clayton shot, they imagined I would be stuck there helping the injured man. I must admit there was a certain amount of pride that I had beaten the odds.

But it didn't make sense. "Wouldn't that mean Command would place a more prominent Mountie presence here, especially if I had been injured or killed?" I said

"You still don't get it, do you?" He was laughing now. "So stupid," he jeered. It took everything I had not to smack him across his patronizing face. "You're a little puppy dog who doesn't even know who his master is."

"Sergeant Deacon," stated Stanley. "Deacon was on his way back to take over the detachment. He would lead a manhunt if there needed to be one. And he would lead it in the opposite direction to Chambers Lodge."

"There wouldn't be a body anyways," he continued. "No one would even know there was a shootout. After a day or so, they would wonder where you were, and they would assume that you and Clayton went out to the forest at night to look for the ghost girl and got lost. Or maybe you had been taken by a spirit."

That's at least what Millie would believe.

"There'd be a search, but your body would be buried somewhere else. You and Clayton would be two more victims of all this wilderness. It may have worked."

"It damn well would of," Chambers snarled.

Stanley glared at Chambers now. I could tell Chambers didn't know quite what to make of Paul. He must have known he was young, but his size was intimidating. "Why come here to the lodge at all? Why not use the pit train to take it farther to Prince George?"

Mr. Benjamin broke in. "We are the first manned station east of Prince Rupert. If they went farther, they would have to threaten even more stationmasters. Believe me, if I had known it was opium…"

Chambers interrupted him, his voice mocking. "It wasn't that at all. The opium came here in its raw form. It is only an ingredient, powerful as it is. The girls and I had a way to prepare it and package it so it could be shipped out in small quantities."

That explained the mess of ingredients and cookware upstairs. It didn't excuse the chaos down here, though. These were filthy men in every meaning of the word.

"Where did you get the girls?" I asked, my voice low so they wouldn't overhear.

"Why are you interested?" he asked. So I took a step forward and slapped him hard. When he turned his head back, there was a look of absolute shock on his face, his hand against his bloody lip. "How dare you? Do you know who you're dealing with," he shouted. "You'll pay for that! You puffed up backwaters peacock! I'll get a real lawyer and sue the lot of you."

I gripped my right hand into a fist and shifted my weight forward to show him that the next slap would be a punch, and he wriggled in his chair, looking all the more terrified. "How many women have been here?" I asked, thinking of the dead girl in the churchyard that Millie had named Arlene.

"Only them," Philip stuttered, but I could tell he knew his lie wouldn't fool anyone.

"Sometimes," he said but didn't continue. His back was arching now, and he seized, rolling onto the floor, grimacing and making the most pitiful moaning sounds. I couldn't tell whether it was an act or not, but I did know the discussion, for now, wouldn't continue.

Of course, there was so much more I wanted to know, but I kept imagining those men who might be in the mountains. John Tuttle and Kyle Granderson. I turned and faced the still-cowering Mr. Benjamin.

"So, let me get this straight. The engine would need a trained crew to run it," I said, thinking aloud. "There's no one like that in Chambers."

"The team came in a fortnight ago from Prince Rupert and drove the locomotive out that night under the half-moon,"

Once a week, I had to deliver uncollected mail to some of the cabins and lodges that were farther out. It let me visit with people that didn't come by the detachment. One night on one of these patrols, I stayed over at Mitch Blood's place after helping the man build a fence; the nerve of these people, asking me to do favors for them as they were committing these heinous criminal acts.

I realized the anger was beginning to seep back into my words, but I didn't care. The whole thing was beyond shameful. Lies built on lies. "And then what?" I barked.

Benjamin jumped. I expect he was worried that I might hit him. "Then they have a place to hide the locomotive and load it, close to Prince Rupert. An abandoned cannery, I believe, or one that's being built."

That would mean there must be many people in Prince Rupert who were also in on it. This cannery would have to have a siding for the train to turn around. And the objects or people, like the girls upstairs, would have to be smuggled in from the docks at Prince Rupert. No wonder they needed someone like Deacon to make it run.

It was no fly-by-night operation.

"But what did they need our townspeople for?" John Tuttle and the other young men had no special skills.

Benjamin shrugged. "I'm sure they had them load the stuff. The cannery would be nowhere near the docks. It was insurance, also," he continued, "so that everyone would keep quiet. If we all had a part in this, we all would be culpable if someone squealed."

I wondered why no one had ever approached me to take on a role. Fox and Chambers must have known I would have nothing to do with it. Or because they believed I had nothing to offer. Did Deacon want to use me to take the blame if something went wrong?

"So the night of the shootout, they were to come back. But they didn't?" I asked

Benjamin nodded. "They didn't make it through."

"How did you know they even left then?" asked Stanley. It was a good question.

"They sent me a telegraph when they left to tell me they were on the way. They should have arrived back at the Chambers' mine before you got back to the station."

I laughed. "They sent you a telegraph saying that the illegal opium was ready to be shipped."

"We had agreed on a coded message."

"Which was?"

Benjamin's eyes dropped as he spoke. "Skies all clear. The message was '*Skies all clear.*' "

I couldn't help to shake my head.

I motioned for Stanley, and we went back outside, passing Peter on the porch. Bunny and the Yugoslavian man appeared sullen. I didn't have much leverage on them, but they might talk if I appealed to their professional pride.

"You two are quite the lackeys, following Chambers's orders, getting him groceries, doing his dirty work." I saw Bunny's face flush. The Yugoslavian opened his mouth to talk, but Bunny made a growling sound that silenced him. I had heard about gangs like this. They protected each other. Chambers wasn't one of them. They used him for his pit rail. That must have been galling for them to care after a lesser man, a morphine addict to boot, deep in the bush.

"Did you two do something wrong to get this gig?" I asked. "Stuck way out here. Looking after a rich man's spoiled son?" Neither man would give me their eyes. Stanley stepped forward, reminding them of his strength.

I squatted and scowled into Bunny's face. "Tell me about the girl. Tell me why you couldn't do the job yourself." I watched the anger wash over his face, his jaw and lips quivering with the strain, before mumbling out an epithet comparing the mystery girl to a female dog.

"And the Pickle brothers, too," I went on. "They're such rubes. I took them down easy. Though you two aren't the best shots either." I could tell the man was ready to blow, but the Yugoslavian grabbed his shoulder, and Bunny spat, though he missed my face.

I would have to question these men separately, but not now.

I returned to the kitchen and took the stairs to the second floor. The setup was clear now that I knew what I was looking for. Across the table and on the floor were metal drums and tubes, which they would use to soak the opium. I had heard about such procedures in our training. The object was to macerate the larger sheets of opium to produce a product addicts could smoke with a pipe.

The newspapers were predisposed to suggest that

workers from the Orient brought the practice of opium smoking with them when they came to help build the railroads. But opium has been used for decades in Europe and North America. Doctors and soldiers used it on the battlefields in France to stem pain and counter shell shock. It was common for soldiers to be addicted to it. Some veterans turned to crime on their return to Canada because of their craving for the stuff.

For their part, the Chinese in Canada were often forced to live and work in deplorable conditions. They were thousands of miles from home in a strange land. Politicians and journalists often referred to them as if they were a plague. I could understand how some might succumb to opium smoking as an escape.

Whoever was at fault, it was now a medical epidemic. I read in a leading Canadian magazine that in Canada, one in every thousand men was addicted to the drug. It was a habit that the RCMP was now putting their best efforts into defeating, with new laws and penalties for the perpetrators. Bea was right. Philip Chambers would have to answer for this. He should expect many years behind bars.

Continuing my search, I was surprised to find a long table with four Singer sewing machines in one of the larger bedrooms. The machines appeared to be brand new, though there was some wear on their foot pedals. Long floor-to-ceiling cabinets filled the opposite side of the room. I opened a random door and found neat stacks of cotton shirts and dungarees. The quantity was the only exceptional thing about them. I picked out a pair of trousers and inspected them. Neither the women nor the men here were wearing garments like these. Strange— did they have a cottage industry selling poorly made workwear? There were no extra rolls of fabric about. The amount of clothing here would require reams of cotton and wool. But there were only scraps. Was this something else they were bringing in on their train?

I opened a few more cupboards to reveal some plaid shirts made from heavy cloth and tucked a pile under my arm. Then I went back out into the main room.

In the clutter, I found funnels, pipes, and fittings I assumed were all parts of an opium still. It didn't look like it was ready for a new shipment. Was Chambers job to refine the opium, or was he the host and frequent sampler? Either way, he was a guilty man.

Pillows lined the wall in one corner of the room. Their shape suggested that someone had been lying on them. I rooted around and found three instruments made with metal and glass—pipes, well made and decorated with intricate Oriental designs.

Crammed between the cushions, I discovered a purple pouch filled with tiny pea-sized spheres. I rolled one of these balls in my fingers—such a little thing to mean so much to so many people. I wasn't familiar with the smell, but the muskiness had an exotic quality. I put the pouch in my pocket and selected the smallest pipe to fit in my satchel. Once reinforced, we could come back here and search the place further.

As I descended the stairs, I found Peter, Bea, and Stanley talking in whispers at the house's back door. They nodded at me as I showed them the shirts, pipe, and pouch.

"We should be getting back," I said, passing the shirts to Bea to give to the young women. They were better than what they were currently wearing. Getting everyone to the detachment would take time and careful thinking.

Clearly, they had kept the women captive by depriving them of winter weather gear. The clothes they wore were thin and worn through. Stanley and I would share our furs as we wore our regimental tunics underneath. Between those, the clothes upstairs, and the winter gear of our four prisoners, the girls would be warm enough for a walk to the detachment. Bea and Peter helped the girls wrap fabric around their bare feet. The best we could do for now. Equipping them all with snowshoes would be too awkward with such a large group.

As for the men, comfort was not my priority. Bunny or the Yugoslavian would have to wear their handcuffs. That would stop them from running. We tied Mr. Benjamin's hands behind his back using some string we found upstairs. As for Philip Chambers, he acted like he couldn't walk. His attempt to escape had expended all his strength. Peter and Stanley created an improvised toboggan from a piece of tarp and some rope. It would have to do.

As we made our exit, Stanley asked. "This train. It's a pit train, right? How would it have the steam to climb these mountains?"

I laughed. It was a common mistake if you did not know the actual geography of the place, and Stanley was, of course, an Easterner. He must have misunderstood where he was when he came to Plateau. Standing here in the shadows of the mountains, you might think them impassable, but the truth was that the Skeena River never made it beyond three hundred meters above sea level. Over millions of years, the force of its water had worn the perfect trail in the mountains. The railroad ran northside along its flattened banks, sometimes passing over its offshoots by a bridge. It didn't need to climb because the engineers worked on the land until it was flat.

"It's a 4-6-2 G1 Class Locomotive from Montreal," I told him.

Stanley gave me a curious look, but I ignored it. "Your old pal William Chambers is quite an astute businessman. He didn't own any shares of the Grand Trunk Pacific Railway but was an investor. Instead of losing his shirt, he was able to make them pay him off first. And as part of his compensation, he took one of their locomotives."

My father was a train enthusiast. He dreamed of being an engineer, but his nearsightedness disqualified him. Instead, he was a produce manager in Oak Bluff, outside of Winnipeg. He shipped wheat, fruits, and vegetables in and out of Manitoba. On the weekends, he took me and my two sisters to see the trains and filled our heads with facts and details. Paul looked impressed, so I continued.

"They used the pit train to bring the ore to the sidetrack. From there, they would hitch the cars to a passing locomotive. The engine's strong enough, though, to run to either of the two Princes carrying cars on its own." I heard William Chambers' plan was to ship the engine to the Klondike in the spring. For now, they kept it stored in the barn on site.

The way back to town seemed to take forever. The members of our column moved like an accordion, as we were always waiting for some group, whether they be the reluctant thugs, Philip moaning on his stretcher, or the crowd of young women who walked huddled in a pack as if they were soon to be attacked.

****

Somewhere along there, I found Bea lost in thought. I cleared my throat, and she smiled over at me.

"So a lawyer," I said, "I wasn't expecting that."

"No, few people are," she replied. I could see the confidence in her stride; she was gazing past me to the mountains beside us. "I was the seventh woman to graduate from Osgoode Hall."

"And now you're here," I said. Why would a lawyer be out in the bush? And a female one at that? Lawyers spent most of their time at their desks or in court, making people's lives miserable.

"And now I'm here," she repeated. The woman liked to be a puzzle.

I gave her my glare, and she relented. "We worked long and hard to get the vote," she explained, "And we now have our first parliamentarian. What's the point of all that if you still expect us to stay home and wait on you men? There's still work to be done, and I have the mind to do it."

Bea wouldn't like me to say it, but Canadian women should have been happy with their recent gains. Getting the vote was a hard-fought battle that even many women disagreed with. It wasn't wise to push the agenda further. It was probably not a good idea to argue with a lawyer— too tricky. Even now, she was playing a trick on me, trying to change the subject. It was what her type called obfuscation.

"I need more from you, Bea," I said. I didn't remove the frustration from my voice. I was tired of people trying to keep me ignorant. "I need to know that you aren't a part of this—you and Peter."

Bea stopped walking, and we let the others pass us. When there was some distance, she spoke. "Can you keep a secret?"

I shrugged. "Most likely. Just tell me, Bea."

She sighed. "I'm working for someone in Vancouver. I can't tell you who it is. There is attorney-client privilege. I shouldn't be telling you any of this. He's asked me to be secret, but I think this is a pretty odd circumstance, and now you're telling me that I'm getting in the way of an ongoing criminal investigation, right?"

"Right," I told her.

She nodded, and we started walking again, keeping our distance from the miserable-looking pack in front of us.

"Well, this man I'm working for, he's trying to buy as much land here as possible—on the cheap. So I'm visiting properties and then purchasing them."

"So your client wants to take over Chambers and reopen the mine."

"God no," said Bea, shaking her head. "My client wants to take over Chambers and kill it outright."

"What?" I couldn't believe what I was hearing. "How does that work?"

"There is a considerable number of people in Vancouver who feel that we already have too much competition from the American ports on the Pacific. They do not want the dreams for Prince Rupert and its railway to come to fruition. These last few years have gone well for my clients."

"So that's what the mayor meant about salting the earth. You're here to make sure Chambers doesn't come back from the dead."

"Yes," Bea said. "But it seems like you have done

much of the work for me and my client. This affair will put the final nail in this town's coffin. My client will be thrilled."

I shook my head. They were like wolves tearing out each other's throats.

"And Philip Chambers recognized you."

A sly smile broke out on Miss Brannon's lips, "I went on a few dates with his older brother Francis while I was in Toronto working on my degree. My family, even then, were interested in the Chambers' rapid accumulation of wealth. It never went past a few dates. Francis probably couldn't even recall my first name. They were all so sure of themselves. I guess you have to be, to bully others."

"So you're a Brannon," I murmured. "Part of the family from Vancouver." I knew they were well off. They owned a couple of newspapers and a chunk of Canadian Pacific Rail. I never thought of attaching that family to Bea, though. The surprises kept coming.

"It's your father, isn't it?" I asked. "You're working for him."

"I cannot say," Beatrice answered.

I'm sure the look on my face showed how displeased I was about this new information. Nothing was illegal about it, but it went against my oath to serve and protect this town.

"I believe William Chambers recognized long ago that this wasn't going to work." Bea continued, "That's why he pulled out of here so fast. I suspect he flooded the mine on purpose so he could spend his time and his money on something more lucrative."

I wasn't sure how that made things any better.

"And that's why you were interested in coming to

see the Chambers Lodge?"

"Yes, I received a pretty brusk reception last time I went round. And my investor was interested in acquiring the property. Now, it just might go for a song. I would imagine William Chambers would want to unload it, especially if there was any suspicion that he knew what was happening here."

"And Peter, what has he to do with all this?"

"Well, that's another secret," Bea replied and then turned to look at me. "I assume he hasn't told you he's my brother."

He hadn't.

"He came this way to find me after our mother died, and he's been helping me out."

"But..." I stammered, "you're not..."

"Indian?" she spoke. "I am half Indian, less because Peter is not full either. Our common great-grandfather was a French missionary priest. It's complicated. We have different fathers. I don't know who mine is, and I don't care. I was lucky enough to be adopted. It's a fact that my family doesn't want me to divulge. And technically, by law, I can't call myself Indian. People with native heritage have to forfeit their status and culture to become lawyers."

"So is part of the reason you came here to find your people?" I suggested.

"Ha! My people live in Port Grey. West Vancouver. You know that Peter's not from here either. Our mother was Cree from Northern Ontario."

I nodded. It was a stupid question. While I didn't know much about Peter's family, I did know he was from the East. I assumed he liked to be alone, and that's why he was not with his people. There was a lot more to his story than I had thought to ask.

"The Cree don't share much with the tribes out here," Bea continued. "Peter found out I had been adopted and then contacted me. He was moving from job to job, and I told him to come to Chambers. We're still getting to know each other, but he's been instrumental in figuring this all out."

"Half the town think you two are...lovers."

Bea laughed. "Yes, Peter knows my family wants to keep my native heritage a secret. Plus, Peter doesn't feel welcome in Chambers. I get the feeling that he has never felt welcome anywhere." We walked silently for a moment as we let that thought sink in.

"Besides," she continued, "our secret doesn't seem so salacious compared to what's been going on in Chambers. And honestly, I don't care what people think." She just might if she heard what Millie had said about her.

"This girl. The one that keeps appearing at the edge of town. Do you have any idea of who she might be or where she could be staying?"

I could see Bea think through the options. "No one comes to mind. As for staying somewhere, there are too many places to choose from. There are lots of abandoned houses and hunting lodges. If you wanted to stay out of sight, it wouldn't be hard, especially if you were getting help."

I nodded. That all made sense. "What about this Amadeo Ricci fellow? Did you ever come across him?"

She made a sucking sound with her lips. "Oh yes," she said. "I've never met him, but he is well known. Everything north of Vancouver is his territory. And he doesn't mind getting into bed with all types."

"All types?"

"As a lawyer, you can refuse clients if you're not comfortable with them. He seems to be comfortable with everyone. He's connected to all sorts of shady people from Chicago, New York, and Alaska. That doesn't mean he's a criminal, mind you. Even bad people deserve a good lawyer."

I agreed to that on principle, but right now, I would have locked up Philip Chambers, Bunny Dix, and the Yugoslavian and thrown away the key. I'd seen enough. They didn't need a trial.

"I know Ricci used to be a lawyer for the Grand Trunk Railroad," Bea went on. "I believe he made a name for himself when he helped to prosecute the miners in Prince Rupert who took part in the Battle of Kelly's Cut back in 1911. His career seems to be built on procuring settlements favorable to the company and not the worker."

Interesting. "Wait a second. When you saw those Pickle brothers before the shooting, you didn't tell me because you believed they were there for you."

Bea nodded. "The mayor had suggested that things would get bad for me if I didn't leave."

"He was right," I said. "I mean, you were messing with some powerful men."

"I wasn't worried. I made sure the mayor knew what family I was connected to. I was certain they were only trying to scare me off. There's no doubt that these are nasty people, but hurting or killing a lone woman connected to a powerful Vancouver family. I don't think so. There's an honor code. Besides, I can take care of myself."

"And you had Peter and Duffy," I added. She gave

me a quick nod. They probably took turns on guard duty while the Pickle brothers came into town. That explained all of Peter's caginess that night. And his Colt revolver.

Beyond that, I wasn't so sure about Beatrice's assumption that her family would protect her. The Pickle brothers weren't the honorable type. They had ambushed a Mountie, for heaven's sake.

"So, are we good?" asked Bea. "Are you okay with me being a lawyer?"

"Well…" I let my voice drag out just for fun. "So far, you're the only lawyer I've met who isn't as nasty as a shark." I smiled at her. "But I thought you didn't care what other people thought?"

Bea stopped walking. "You're different, Albright," she said. "Of course I care what you think." And there was something in her expression that suggested that Millie might not quite have her number. I wondered how Peter would react if his sister got together with his friend, the Mountie. For some reason, the idea tickled my funny bone.

"You know," said Bea, pointing ahead, "you should talk to those women. They're Chinese. The tallest one can speak some English. She said her name is Tai Lee."

What could I possibly do for them? Women were foreign to me—and these girls were from a culture I knew nothing about. "What did they tell you?" I asked.

"Pretty much what you might expect. They helped to cook the opium. To turn it into little balls that could be smoked, called Chan Du. She said the men wanted it like that because then it could be transported much easier. The balls they were making were no bigger than the size of a pea."

"Like these ones?" I asked, pulling the small pouch

out of my pocket and pouring the beads into my palm.

Bea shrugged. "I don't know much about it, but they look about right."

Here, where no one was watching, the girls could convert the opium to a more saleable form, and it would be free from inspection moving west. They only checked for drugs at the port city. They would bring the drugs from Asia on ships, then hide them in the wharves of Prince Rupert. After, their little ghost train would transport it here for processing. A smart plan—but not smart enough to outwit a well-timed snowstorm. And two Mounties who wouldn't leave well enough alone. Maybe I should talk to the girls.

"They told me they were ordered to sew opium pellets into shirts and trousers. I assume that's how they moved surreptitiously down the line."

So that's why there was no extra fabric. The gang must have bought cheap clothing and made the girls use the machines to nip and tuck the drug into the seams. It was quite an operation. Most customs officials were looking for alcohol smuggling, not opium, and I doubt anyone would think of examining a poorly made pair of dungarees for an illegal drug.

"Did she mention the one who died?" I asked

"Yes and no," said Beatrice, her face drawn and serious. "They told me there were at least a dozen girls who came through. They moved most of them on. Those five have been together at the lodge for at least six months. The others would disappear. By train or foot, they didn't know, but it was always frightening to them, for those that left and those that stayed. Most of the new ones were not there for more than a few days. She expected one of them maybe escaped out of desperation.

They all knew what would become of them."

She paused. "I expect if they trust us more, they might tell us what the men had them do." I sucked in a long breath of cold air, trying to chill my heart and my anger. I let this happen. I should have been more forceful in my dealings with Mayor Fox and Philip Chambers. Beatrice must have been reading my mind.

"You couldn't have guessed," she told me, her hand on my arm. We both stopped, staring past each other, me to the deep woods and she to the mountain. "These are evil people. We don't think like them."

But I should have. I knew what evil could do. I got more than my fill of it in the war. How did I expect it to be different here?

"What will become of them?" I asked.

"That's for me to figure out," she stated. "They're my responsibility now. Women like these don't get a voice unless someone else trumpets them." There was passion in her voice. "I'm pretty sure they will want to deport them. Some members of our government are working on laws to put a head tax on the Chinese so they can deport them as *undesirables*. Opinion seems to be against them."

"Still, I will make sure that they are taken care of. My family has some influence. If they want to stay, I will fight for them. If they don't, we'll make sure they get back home with something in their pockets. The way I figure it, this country of ours is still being fashioned, and us in the right have to make sure it moves in the proper direction."

I nodded, but I wanted to hug her. Those reflections were so much better than my own. We started walking once more, fitting our boots to the footprints we made coming in and the new ones we were making moving out. The snow was still falling, and there was no sign that it would stop.

Chapter 11

The Ghost's Grief

By the time we reached the station, it was already noon. Despite my order to stay at the hospital, Millie swung the door wide as we came toward the detachment. And she was not alone; Mrs. Tuttle and Mrs. Granderson were also waiting, both quite anxious to talk with us. They were sure that their husbands were now in dire straits. But I waved them both off. There were too many people to contend with.

I asked Peter and Bea to take Philip Chambers to the hospital. We had gone about a quarter mile before he complained the dragging was worse than the walking, so Stanley had assisted him the rest of the way. Chambers could take the bed that Daniel Pickle had vacated. And the handcuffs as well. When Millie discovered the five Chinese women with us, she offered to take them home to her mother, but Bea demanded that they be taken to the hospital first. I sent them off with a message for Genevieve that we were all safe and sound, at least for now.

Stanley and I then locked Bunny and the Yugoslavian into our two jail cells. Neither of them was talking now, which was fine by me. There were other people to straighten out first. Millie offered lunch, but I sent her off to fetch her brother Jeremy, instead.

Mrs. Tuttle and Mrs. Granderson decided to try again, beseeching Paul and me to tell them what we knew about their husbands. But I was too angry to talk, remembering Mrs. Tuttle's evasiveness. I let them shed some tears and then told them to sit and wait. There were too many other important things to do, and I needed to keep a clear head.

After Millie returned, I marched her brother and Mr. Benjamin across the track to the station house. Jeremy and I watched the stationmaster as he fixed the wire and replugged in the set, then sent off the first telegraph. The message was a plea for immediate recruits either by train or foot.

Send recruits. Second shooting. Armed gang. Men and train stuck on track.

"You are to send this off every ten minutes," I told Benjamin. "Jeremy, you will stay and make sure he does this. If there is a response, bring it immediately to Bea and Peter at the detachment. If you get tired, get someone else to spell you off. Understand?

"Yes," said Jeremy. The thought of a fifteen-year-old boy supervising Mr. Benjamin gave me pleasure.

But as I stood there, looking at this fool, I realized he might have more to offer. The girl in the woods, if she had come to town by train, then he would certainly remember her. The station was not teeming with travelers, and Mr. Benjamin, for all his faults, was a professional who strived to maintain order as a stationmaster should.

"About a week ago, a woman came to town," I said, "I assume she came by train. We know that she stayed at the mayor's hotel, and I am sure you remember her."

Benjamin raised a single eyebrow and then nodded.

"She was our only visitor last week." His bloodied nose made his voice even more peevish than usual. "She came from Prince Rupert and paid her way to Chambers and not beyond. If she had a chaperone on the train then they didn't exit along with her. She did not ask for a return ticket and made no introduction. Instead, she just walked off in the direction of the boardwalk." He stopped, and there was silence. Finally, he shrugged as if to say that was all he had to offer me.

"Describe her!" I did not try to mitigate the sharpness of my voice.

"I make it a practice not to notice the details of a lady's appearance nor to describe them. I believe it is indelicate to do so and would speak ill of me as a custodian of this service. People would complain if they deduced I was ogling the passengers."

I made my outward breath large and noisy to show my frustration over the man's hypocrisy. Then, since I was still irritated, I banged my fist on his table and made Jeremy and the man flinch. "I'm not asking you to ogle your passengers, you nitwit! I want to know what she looked like. You mentioned a chaperon, so I'm assuming you thought she was young."

Mr. Benjamin looked abashed. He took off his glasses and cleaned them as he talked. "Yes, I suppose she was young." I'm sure he could see the frustration still evident on my face. "She was short but thin with long brown hair, no more than a hundred pounds. She carried a black carpet bag and was wearing a long brown coat that looked like a cloak." He finished and took a seat at the table.

"Did she leave on an outgoing train?"

Mr. Benjamin shook his head as Jeremy stared at

him, still with the wide-eyed expression he had worn since entering the station.

"And you don't know where if she stayed after the hotel or where she might have gone afterward?"

Mr. Benjamin again shook his head. There were many places that the girl could have hidden, but I remembered the fruity smell of the postmaster's bedroom.

"So all this time, you knew who this mysterious woman was, and yet you said nothing!"

I reached into my pocket and pulled out the silk stocking. "I found this under one of the beds here. It looks like you have been taking advantage of the situation here."

Benjamin's face went round with shock, and he mumbled a few words neither Jeremy nor I could understand. I grabbed him by the shoulders and shook him until he began to splutter.

"It wasn't me. I had nothing to do with it." Each sentence was coming out in a gasping sob. "It was those filthy engineers. The men they brought in to drive the train. They entertained some of the women here. But I was gone. I stayed over at the hotel. I wanted nothing to do with it."

His little speech did nothing to calm my anger and frustration. Still, I pushed the man harder than I should have, and he landed hard on the floor, still wallowing.

"I'm going to get to the bottom of this! No stone will be left unturned!" I hollered at him, though he wasn't looking me in the eyes. "If I find you have been lying to me, I will personally make sure you are punished for it. For every last thing you did." I threw the stocking at him, and it bounced off his chest.

I took one last glance at Jeremy, who looked as terrified as the stationmaster. I wasn't sure if he was frightened of me or of being left alone with such a wretch. Either way, I did not have the energy left to console him. At least there was some victory in knowing that my earlier judgments about the man were warranted. But I knew I wouldn't be satisfied until I saw the scoundrel get his just desserts.

****

After I settled myself with a quick walk in the wind, I returned to the detachment. It was time for Stanley and me to have a conversation and a spot of lunch. Since two men were in the cells, we went into my bedroom and closed the door. Millie warmed our soup and toasted us some beautiful cheese sandwiches. We were both ravenous after all the tension and the work.

"So those men out there in the snow," I began. "It seems like we have another choice to make. A big one, and I don't think we can wait until we hear from Command."

Stanley nodded. I was sure he knew where I was going. "Those men could be anywhere along that line stranded in the cold without the proper gear to help them survive. Do we go to help them?"

Stanley raised his bowl to his lips and drained his remaining soup in one gulp, his prominent Adam's apple bobbing. Then he wiped off his lips and stared at me.

"I don't feel we have a choice," he said. "We got to help if we can. We might not know the train's precise location, but we know they are on the rail line. Even I can track a rail line." I smiled, remembering Stanley's bumbling about in the snow. And the mighty figure he had struck when he first scared me on his horse. It was hard to believe he had only been here a few days. Then I shook my head.

"That's not all there is to it," I responded. "First of all, it means we won't be here to protect the town. Yes, we can leave Peter and the others in charge, but there's still so many loose ends. We don't know where our mystery woman is and who else in this town is working with Philip Chambers."

"I think we've come across a lot of people we can trust," countered Stanley. "Bea can stay at the hospital and help look after things there. Peter, Duffy, and Millie can stay here. I imagine a lot of the women will pitch in if we're off to find their husbands."

I didn't like it. "I could see us making the problem worse. Neither of us has much experience tracking fugitives through the snow. And now that the weather is getting warmer, there are risks of snow slides or even avalanches."

I could see Stanley hadn't considered that.

"This train was supposed to come through while you were out in that forest," Stanley said. "How long do you think you were out there? An hour and a half? Two hours in and out? Trains travel fast. They should have been close if it didn't start snowing until you were already in the clearing. The train might be just a few miles away." I nodded along. He had a point.

"But then, why haven't they arrived in the last couple of days?" I asked. "You were able to ride in the snow from Plateau, a full ten miles. You think if they were close, they would have found their way back by now."

"Maybe the snowstorm was too fierce," Stanley replied. "Maybe they got caught in one of your avalanches or got lost in the blizzard. Maybe the cold was too much for them. Who knows? Except they are in trouble. And there's two more things you're not considering."

"What's that?" I couldn't help but ask.

"The opium and the girls"

The opium. From what we know, it could cause a whole mess of trouble.

"If they have time, they will hide it. They'll say it was Philip Chambers that smuggled it. They'll say that they went after missing townspeople while we were rooting around in the woods. And then they or someone else will go back for it. This stuff is as precious to them as the silver they pulled from the mine."

That silver. That mine. This railroad. It had all cost men their lives. But this opium was supposed to be worse. A contagion threatening to infect the body of our faltering society.

"The women, too," added Stanley. "Who knows who they had aboard that train? This is not just about opium. They have a side business in trafficking as well. And you saw how they treated those ladies at the lodge."

I took a deep breath. I could tell Stanley was determined, but as the officer with the most seniority, this was my detachment and my decision. "You would have us travel the length of the Skeena River, eh?" Stanley was a big man. I pictured him as I first saw him, larger than life, like a yeti or ferocious bear, covered in a cloak of snow. He was made for this, but I was unsure of my own strength.

I stepped past the man, opened the bedroom door, and found Peter back from the hospital talking to Millie. I called over to them, and they squeezed themselves into my tiny room. With the door shut, it was close quarters, an intimate space. "We're thinking of traveling the line to get those men."

I was expecting both of them to argue. To show us some resistance, but instead, they were silent—Millie silent.

"I'll want you two to stay and look after things here. That will mean sleeping here, Peter. I'd like you to get Duffy too. Both of you need to check on Mr. Benjamin, though I've put the fear of God in him. And you will want to keep in touch with the hospital. Millie, maybe later you can go by and get some women to help at both places. We're hoping that the rail line will be open soon and more reinforcements will come."

Neither of them said a thing. I had to ask, "Can you do this?"

They both assured me yes, and with that, Stanley and I were now an expedition team.

I pulled Peter back as we were about to head out of the room. He looked confused, and honestly, I didn't know quite what to say to him. But I was in command, and commanders sometimes engaged in difficult conversations.

"I talked to Bea. I got to say I don't know what to think about all this. You and she were working to destroy the town, it seems."

Peter nodded his head but otherwise made no move to speak.

"I can't say why I feel this way, but it seems like it was also an attack on me. My job, Peter, is to serve and protect this town and its inhabitants, and you were going behind my back with Bea and buying properties to tear the whole place down."

"Or to put it back the way it was." Peter's eyes were fierce now, his hands on both hips. "Your duty should also be to protect this land. This railway of yours hasn't caused anything but destruction."

"Where were the Mounties when your companies took the Lheidli T'enneh reserve to make Prince George? Or when the Metlakatla people were removed from their land to build Prince Rupert? Or when their brothers, the Kitsumkalam people, fought to protect the graves of their ancestors? When you blasted and built your railroad straight through their territory? For thousands of years, this land has lived without Chambers. And it will live long after. It doesn't need your town."

"My railway! My town!" I couldn't believe he was lumping me in with the plutocrats who had created all this. "I'm just a Mountie, Peter. I didn't even choose to come here."

"Like you didn't choose to be in the war?" Peter shook his head. "Are you just a pawn, Gus?"

It all felt like a punch in the gut. But I was smart enough to take a breath and think. I never considered things from Peter's position. The RCMP had come west to bring law, order, and civilization to the land, but at what cost? Were we protecting the right people? No one could suggest that the Grand Trunk Pacific had brought anything but failure to the region. And yet, I still felt betrayed.

"Well, if I'm a pawn, Peter, then what are you?" The words left my mouth before I could draw them back.

But Peter had spent his rage. His voice was a whisper. "Something less. Another ghost like that woman in the trees."

I could not be angry with the man. He had been

nothing but helpful to me these last few days. "You're nothing like the girl," I told him. "And you're no ghost. I'm glad you were with us today, and I still need your help if you are willing."

He gave me a nod, and we shook hands, but it still felt wrong.

"Are we okay here, Peter?"

"Yeah, we're okay." He gave me a tiny smile. "We'll make sure there's still a piece of Chambers here for you to return to."

I let him go. I would have to think more about what he said, but now wasn't the time. Instead, I made myself busy fixing my bunk and tidying up, putting the things I could back in their intended order.

****

Time was now our problem. Mayor Fox and his little gang rode out an hour after sunrise, and now we were at the crest of the day. The snow made the world brighter, but we would not want to travel too late into the evening since the storm appeared to be rising yet again. These circumstances left us several hours behind with still much to prepare.

The detachment was equipped with cold-weather gear, a large tent, and heavy sleeping bags. Otherwise, we would want to travel light. Coot would not like it, but I knew we must use the stable yard's last healthy occupant to carry our gear. This modest beast belonged to Mr. Balderson, who had left the pony behind when he left Chambers. I figured Coot would not mind us using the animal to help bring back the other horses, but I decided it was better to tell him our plans, which meant yet another trip to the hospital. Besides, I wanted to ensure Genevieve was okay with everything before I left.

I came out of my bedroom to find Millie fussing over our food, unsure how long we would be gone and how much weight we could carry. I told her she should pack enough for an eight or nine-day journey. Our missing men and women may have eaten through their supply. These details flustered her more as she was sure there was not enough food in the detachment, what with Paul being such a sizeable fellow.

Alexandr Dvorak, the greengrocer, backed these men. He fought with Clayton and rode with the opium gang. "Take Mrs. Granderson and go over to Dvorak's. Take whatever you feel you need. The man surrendered his rights when he threw in with the mayor." The idea calmed Millie somewhat. It was a lot to ask of her, but I had faith she could do it.

We dressed together and stepped out into the blowing snow. I could feel my body stiffen. None of this was going to be easy. At the bridge, we parted ways as I pushed forward through the wind into the old town.

As I entered through the lobby doors, the hospital was a hive of activity. Chambers was in the bed across from Clayton at the far end of the room, looking pale as a ghost. Otherwise, the Chinese women were busy chattering in the aisle, some standing, some sitting on the ends of the beds, each with a mug of tea. Duffy was amongst them doing an ugly job of mopping the floors. And so was Margaret, overjoyed by the random accumulation of humanity that had newly arrived in her sphere.

Genevieve and the doctor must have been back in their lodgings, so I asked Margaret where Coot was and learned the boy was already back at the stable. A wasted trip, but I decided to treat myself to one last conversation with Clayton to get a more detailed account of what he knew and what he didn't. But the old grump was fast asleep despite the general din. I put my hand on his shoulder, ready to shake him awake, but my conscience got the better of me. It would be unfair to leave Genevieve with a frenzied Clayton. It was a result of my actions that there were so many people now populating her ward.

Should I interrogate Philip Chambers? He, too, was asleep, his gaunt face green and yellow. I guessed that his next few days would not be pleasant—not with the doctor refusing to give him his precious opium, handcuffed to the bed with no means of escape. For the first time, I felt some sympathy for the man. But I pushed it away where it belonged.

Time was running out, but I did not move, still reflecting on the gargantuan task ahead of me. I headed toward the living quarters, but before I got there, Genevieve stepped in front of me, grabbed my coat sleeve, and pulled me over to the lobby doors.

"You are not going out there!" she insisted. "Bea told me what happened. You have tempted fate far enough, Gus. A second shooting in as many days. You are lucky that you weren't killed or wounded. Peter, Bea, and Constable Stanley as well."

I tried to speak but could not get a word out. Instead, Genevieve pushed me through the lobby doors and began again. "What's happening here is way larger than you, Gus. These are evil, desperate men who don't care about your uniform. They won't let you get in the way of their plans. And you don't need to be a hero." She was poking me now with her finger. "You've given enough!"

"Can I talk?" I asked. "I don't have a choice, Gen.

There are men out there. And maybe women, too, like the girls we brought back from the lodge. They didn't have anyone to protect them. Someone needs to put a stop to this!"

Genevieve moved closer, wrapped her arms around my fur coat, and pressed her face into my chest. "But not you," I heard her murmur. "But not you." We stood there for several seconds before I realized my coat must be cold and wet. I pushed her backward and saw that she was crying, two lines of tears on her reddened face, and a different type of sympathy rose inside me.

I held her shoulders and cleared my throat. "Gen, I…We've decided that we need to do this. If we are in danger from the snow, we will turn back. If we are in danger from the men, we will retreat. But this has to be stopped, and we are the only ones who can do it. Soon, reinforcements will come, but for now, it's just us."

She did not look convinced. "Look," I began again. "Keep everyone here. The girls, Margaret, Duffy, Bea. Keep Clayton sedated and Chambers too for that matter. And lock the doors at night. Everyone who was a part of this is here, gone, or captured."

"Except the girl from the forest," stated Genevieve.

"Except our mysterious girl," I agreed. "But I don't expect she will come alone with so many people here." And then, without a backward glance, I turned and left. I should have said goodbye, but something in me didn't want to.

****

As I stepped outside, it was clear from the swirling snow that this storm was far from over. Its message was crystal clear, stay indoors. But just like with Genevieve, I decided to ignore the warning. Even my body yearned to retreat as I felt it stiffen from the punishing wind. Or the punishing world.

I teetered through the heavy banks of snow, consumed by thoughts so dense I didn't realize I was passing John Tuttle's meager home, and almost gouged myself on its southeastern corner. I was glad to find it. I ran my hand against its length as a guide to where the bridge across the river must be.

A chilling wind caught me in the face, and instinctively, I raised my arm to protect my eyes. When I brought it down again, she was there, a dark, angry shadow, skirts blowing behind her in the wind. She was not two yards distant, an insistent pistol pointing at my face.

"Inside," I heard her growl, and I stepped back. Could I disarm her? The raging wind, the cold, and the absence of her face tucked deep within a shell of a brown cloak made me stutter, and I found myself walking backward as she came forward.

"Inside," she growled again, and I got the point. I pushed against the Tuttle's door to reveal the stillness inside.

Carefully, she shifted herself around the doorway, and with her gun, pointed me towards the rocking chair in the center of the room, the one I had seen Mrs. Tuttle use with her daughter Jane. It wasn't until I was seated, the heavy fabric of my coat squishing me on both sides, that she finally took a moment to close the door behind her.

"Your gun," she said. "You are going to put your hands on the chair's arms and leave them there where I can see them." I did so and watched as she walked around me, her pistol focused on me the whole way.

Finally, I felt her squat and unhook the button on my holster. Was it time now to act—to use our strange geometry as a way to overcome her? But I decided against it for the same reason as when we were out in the forest. If she wanted me dead, she would have shot me by now.

She came back in front of me before she chucked my gun into the corner of the room. The silence mounted, both of us waiting while the snow from our coats turned to water and dripped to the floor. My body came to rest. It surprised me. There was no panic in my breath nor tightness in my chest. This moment did not feel as dangerous as the ones that preceded it, or maybe my body was too tired to make a fuss.

She pulled off the scarf around her neck, her hood flapping back to reveal a soft face, pretty but with scowling hot eyes. "You made a promise," she said. "I'm here to make sure you keep it."

"You must be the daughter then," I answered and then forced myself to smile. "It's Emily, isn't it? Clayton was looking for you to make amends."

"That miserable piece of vermin. He won't be forgiven. You told me he was dead."

"I presumed he was." I shook my head. "But it's my job now to make sure no more killing happens."

"That's going to be hard if you're dead yourself." She shook the gun, and for a second, I worried she might kill me by accident. A strange look came into her eyes, and she reached inside her cloak with the other hand, pulled out a piece of creased paper, and threw it on my lap.

As she stepped back, I peeled off my gloves and opened the parchment, the yellowing paper cracking in its creases.

"It's worthless now, I expect. It's all worthless." Her countenance was that of a sulking child.

It was dark in the room without a fire or a candle, but I could still make out the words on the page, The Grand Hotel, spelled out in intricate cursive. Three people signed the deed, not two: Thomas Fox, Clayton Cole, and Matilda Withers.

"Matilda," I said. "Your mother. She was part owner as well. And when she died that would have given the hotel to Clayton and Fox, unless of course she had a next of kin to claim it. I was right. You are Matilda's daughter, then."

"And I've come back to get what I am owed."

"Clayton was trying to find you. He wanted to make things right. To pay his debt for his part in this."

"No!" She screamed, her pitch so shrill that it pushed me back in my chair. "No!" She yelled again, and once more, I worried about her careless grip on her gun. "Clayton killed her. He got to go on living, and my mother was dead. And no one. No one did a single thing for me. They shipped me off. They sent me off..." Something caught in her throat, and I could see her body begin to break; tears began to spill onto her cheeks, but I could tell she was still holding the worst of it back. That if I wasn't there. If she didn't have me at gunpoint, then that hurt inside her might find its way out.

Instead, she sucked in the air and pushed the gun straight before her. "No," she said, her voice gaining its control. And now I could feel a chill more resounding than the winter winds beyond us; her manner became rigid, solid, deep frothing anger mounting inside her. "No, you wouldn't know what unspeakable things happened to me when they sent me away. My father was a coward. He killed himself, so they told me that I was going to go live with my uncle. Only he didn't have space for me. Instead, I became a ward of the state. They institutionalized me. And I was powerless. Powerless to stop them…"

There was silence again, and I realized I didn't know how all this would play out. I was thinking of the men on the mountain, of Paul, Millie, and Genevieve. And of all the townspeople who had worked to worsen this horrible situation.

I decided to break the silence. "We all have misfortunes," I started, but the dark look on her face stopped me in my tracks.

"Sodomy," she said. "Is that a misfortune that has been placed on you?"

The lump in my throat made it hard to breathe, and I sensed my old friend panic knocking at the door. How she looked at me now told me I should have been silent. I wasn't so sure now that she could control her anger.

A whistling wind rattled the thin window frames of the Tuttles' cottage as I shifted my weight in the uncomfortable chair. I changed the subject. "Why Clayton? Why not Fox? He's the one that benefitted the most from your mother's death. He must have made a mint off the hotel. Things were rolling here for ages."

The girl's laugh was absent of any mirth. "Fox! Ha! The idiot. Every dollar he made, he sank back into the mine, back into the town. He was so sure it would work, that he sold his soul to the Italians. This whole mad scheme was his way of still turning a profit so he could pay them back. So he could pay me back as well."

"So that's why you went along with it? The whole

ghost thing. The ambush. You thought Fox would pay you out?"

"He wanted Clayton dead as well. That bastard was blackmailing him. He'd found out about his scheme."

All those things Clayton told me in his stupor. The fights he kept having with the other townspeople. I was so sure it was his natural belligerence that I didn't listen.

"I figure I'm owed something for what they all put me through. This was the first chance I got of any type of life."

I couldn't help to shake my head. "How did you know that Clayton would follow you? What would happen if he just ignored you and went on drinking? Then neither of us would be in the woods."

A vicious smirk twisted her lips. "I haunted him all week. The ambush wasn't my first visit. I'd already drawn him out the night before. He followed me from his cabin, too drunk to walk in a straight line. I took him into the woods until I was sure he was lost. I could have left him there, but that wasn't part of the deal. They wanted you gone as well, and I was glad to oblige. So I let him follow me back to town.

"That's how I knew the man was guilty. The handkerchiefs, these clothes—he wanted to believe that I was her. My Mama...her death...it didn't take much to drag him along. He killed her."

"I don't think that argument would hold out in a court of law," I told her. "So you brought him out, and the others made sure I'd go with him?"

"Fox made sure you understood that it was your duty to solve my little mystery. He played with your ego. He knew you wanted to prove yourself, that you could be a big strong Mountie like that bastard Deacon."

Everything she said, and the way she said it, she wanted to hurt me. She wanted someone else to feel her pain.

"So what now? Are you going to shoot me and then go to the hospital and murder Clayton as well? You ought to know it's filled with people now. Girls that we found at the Chambers Lodge. And a guard as well. That's a lot of innocent people you will be putting in danger. Women like you, who have come through misfortune."

"Misfortune!" She snorted. "You sure are naive to call it that. No, I am not made to shoot people, though I would fire this gun in an instant to save my own skin. There's only one true killer in this room, and it's you. I saw what you did in the woods. Quick to violence is an understatement."

I let that thought lie.

"No, I've got you dead to rights again. So it's time for another promise. I got away from those who imprisoned me, and I'm not letting any man hold me again. My role in this is too small to matter. And so you are going to let me go with my promise that I won't make an attempt on Clayton's life again. I just hope I've hurt him enough. Regardless, it's time for me to skedaddle. In return, you won't track me, and you will find a way to punish Clayton for his crimes. And Fox, too, for that matter."

"No," I heard myself say. A voice steady and solid. It surprised me, but I let it continue. "I won't make those promises. In fact, I rescind my former promise on the grounds that I was under duress." There was a surprise on her face now. Not anger. Not fear. But timidness—a vision of the girl she once was. I went on. "I will promise you this, though. If you do anything to hurt anyone in this town, I will hunt and find you wherever you are hiding. I will make you pay. For now, I can't be bothered with you. There are people down the river that need my help. And I've wasted too much time talking to you already." I threw the deed on the ground between us. "Either shoot me now or let me go."

I stared at her, ignoring the dark hole of the gun barrel. Honestly, I couldn't be sure what she would do, but my lack of panic buoyed me towards a strange sort of bravery. I knew she could see the commitment in my eyes.

She shuffled back and opened the door with the gun still on me. The wind rattled around her in the doorway as I studied her.

"How did you do it?" I asked. "In the woods. Did you use a plank, a rope, or a tree branch?"

"Yes," she said, then slipped into the wind as the door slapped behind her.

****

Back out in the snow, I found the girl's northward tracks. I suspected that they would lead me back into the new part of the town, but I could find no motivation to follow them. No matter where she hid, she was stuck here for now, a loose end I supposed I could untangle later.

At the detachment, I found Stanley moving our gear out to the porch. It looked like he was eager to leave. I pushed past him and found Peter awaiting his instructions. He was never to be alone in the detachment with the two prisoners. Bea, Millie, Benjamin; it didn't matter who, but another person needed to be present. They could take turns using my bunk throughout the night. Millie would see to their needs.

On top of that, neither of the men were to leave their cells for any reason. When the prisoners needed to use the washroom, they could pass them a bucket through the small door in the lock bars. I left notes on my desk along with the papers appointing Genevieve, Bea, and now Duffy as Special Constables. The hope was that they wouldn't be long without some Mountie reinforcements.

As we were about to leave, Millie blew back in the door, accompanied by Mrs. Tuttle and Mrs. Granderson. I remembered I was supposed to speak to them.

Both were quite frazzled and looked disgusted at the two men behind bars. "We need to talk to you, Constable," Mrs. Granderson breathed. Her hands shook. If only they had told me where their husbands were before, we could have been searching for them.

"We know your husbands are on the missing train," I said. There was no point sugarcoating it. "The fact that none of them have returned means they might be in serious trouble."

Mrs. Tuttle began to weep, and Millie held her hand. They were like three schoolgirls in trouble with their headmaster.

"I know the mayor has gone to find them, but I don't trust the man," said Mrs. Granderson. "We don't know what Kyle and John have got themselves into, but it was Tom Fox and his cronies that made them do this."

I shook my head. "Why didn't you tell us this before?"

Mrs. Granderson looked at the other two women. "We were scared," she stated. "We didn't want to get our men in trouble."

"Well, they are," I said. Mrs. Granderson's chin

shook, and Mrs. Tuttle let out a sob.

I softened. "Whatever choices were made have already been acted upon. Now, we have to focus on getting your husbands back. We will do everything we can to bring them home."

But that wasn't enough to calm these women. I breathed in and started again, softening my tone further. "John and Kyle are good men. I will make sure their part of the story is heard." That was as far as I could go. Their men might be dead or wounded. Fortunately, my words placated the women enough for them to stop pestering me.

Millie came forward as the two women sat at our table, consoling each other. She was carrying something under her arm.

"Constable Albright," she declared. "I have made something for you." And she began to produce a set of matching gloves, scarf, and hat, all of stitched furs. Rabbit, I believe. "The scarf is still a little short, but all of them will keep you warmer than your regular wear." There was no hint that I could refuse them; honestly, I was glad to have them. Who knew what warmth we would need as we approached Prince Rupert? While we had been issued winter wear as part of our dress, we could substitute items in case of severe cold.

"Thank you, Millie," I said and saw a bright sparkle in her eyes. "They are an excellent gift." I was glad my words delighted her.

I stepped outside and went through Paul's parcels to double-check we had everything we needed. All was in order, but something was niggling at me.

I opened the door of the detachment and came inside, standing on the doormat, making no effort to remove any of my things. From this position, I could see the two men in their separate cells and Peter drinking a cup of tea at the table with the two wives.

"Millie," I called and saw her dash around the corner. She must have been at the stovetop. She came toward me. There was something not quite right about her eyes. They were foggy and unfocused.

"This other woman," I began. "The one you told me about at the hotel. You were right. She was the same woman as the one in the woods." Millie nodded. "I just came across her again." Millie's mouth formed a perfect "O" as Paul stepped into the detachment, closing the door behind him.

"She's a slick one." I continued, looking at the different faces around me, "She ambushed me, and we had a little talk."

"Gus!" Millie said, her hand pressed against her breast. Everyone looked alarmed except for Peter, who took another swig of his coffee.

"Her name is Emily Withers, and her intention was to have Clayton murdered. Beyond that, I don't think she is dangerous. I don't even think that she wishes to fulfill that aim anymore. But she is armed, and no one is to go near her. When reinforcements arrive, they are to look for her and not let her steal onto the train. Got it?"

There wasn't a sound in the room, all of us standing like statues. The promise of danger still lingered in the air.

"You want me to ask the other ladies and maybe examine the visitors' books at the hotel?" Millie asked as she walked toward me.

"No," I said strongly. Looking her in the eye was difficult with her so close, but I wanted to clarify my directions. "I want you to hold here, to not go anywhere but here and your home." I talked around her to everyone else in the room. "The important thing is for everyone to stay safe until help arrives. Stay together and no silliness."

I turned back to look at Millie, who gave me a tiny nod, her eyes still glassy.

I pushed past Stanley and opened the door, letting the chill pour into the room.

"Good luck out there," Millie said. "We'll be here waiting for you."

And that was the last time I ever stood in the Chambers' detachment.

****

As expected, we found Coot in the stable yard, but he was not alone. Bernard lolled in the opposite doorway, watching us enter. He wore nothing but a yellowing undershirt and a pair of dirty trousers. Nothing even on his feet, blackened toenails exposed.

"Were you in on this as well?" I called over to him.

"In on what?"

I ignored him while telling Coot our plans for Mr. Balderson's pony. I could feel the old letch stare at me. Finally, he made a grumbling sound in his throat. "No sense in changing things," he called.

Bernard woke me the night Clayton brought me out to the forest. The same man who had trouble getting out of bed in the middle of the day, banging on my doors and windows as if hell had come for a visit.

"You best get ready for change," I told him. Despite what I said to Coot, those men wouldn't need a stable to house their horses. If the horses did come back, it was likely not to be with the men who owned them. They would all be locked away if I had anything to do with it.

Bernard spat into the straw. "You young ones. You always think the world will get better. You gotta take what you can and do everything to keep it."

I doubted Bernard had ever done more than the least amount possible. I turned to Coot and waited for him to stop his final brushing.

"Whatever happens, Coot, there are people here that will help you. You don't have to stay with this man if you don't want to. Do you understand?"

He nodded, and I stretched my hand forward to shake his. I gave Bernard one more shot of the evil eye and walked the laden pony outside. There was quite a crowd there to see us go. Everyone I cared about except those at the hospital. I still wasn't convinced this was the best course of action, but we were prepared. I didn't look back until the last moment—just before the turn of the rail track, the tall pines on either side. There was still a little crowd there watching us to the end. I hoped they would be there to watch us when we returned.

We got underway three hours after noon. The wind slowed, and the temperature rose to produce thick, wet snowflakes. If luck was on our side, we might catch the opium gang before they found the train. I hoped it would all be moot. The storm would stop, the snow plows would come out to clear the tracks, and the reinforcements requested through Mr. Benjamin's telegraphs would speed ahead and do the dirty work for us. The blizzard had to end at some point.

The Rocky Mountains rose to over 7500 feet, but the Skeena River had been carved through them by the sheer force of nature, providing a natural pass-through to build the railway. Throughout the trail, we marveled at the sheer ingenuity and perseverance needed to carve out the rail line we followed. Charles Hays, its grand conceiver, declared that he wanted the entire line to be as level as the prairies. When the cost proved impossible, he settled for the same gradient as the Grand Trunk's line from Montreal to Toronto. Even so, it required an enormous amount of blasting and engineering. A triumph of the human will, as misguided as it was.

We did not make much distance on that first day of our trek. As the air cooled, the winds off the steep cliffs pushed mini snow cyclones into our faces. But as tired as our legs and lungs were, we remained committed. The tracks of our quarry filled with snow, but we were not worried that as long as we kept the Skeena River to our right, we would stay on course. It was a wide river with a heavy current. We were happy to see that the mayor and his little gang had given the river a wide berth when possible, no doubt worried about the thin ice that would be frozen close to its shore. Even this close to Chambers, falling into ice at this temperature could be a fatal misstep.

We walked a few hours with lanterns before the way ahead became too dangerous. Here we came to a narrow bridge over an offshoot of the river, too perilous to even think about crossing in the dark. The river was rushing fast, at least sixty feet beneath us. After deliberating over the location of our campsite, we retraced our steps and found a spot under a cliff face that kept us sheltered from the wind. Not worried about being chased ourselves, we were able to build a small fire with our tinder, kerosene, and the kindling we had been wise enough to bring. While there were abundant trees, we could not collect their fallen branches as snow covered the ground.

Chapter 12

Deacon's Dare
Day Four
Thursday, February 24th, 1923

That night, we decided to sleep in two shifts of five hours to protect ourselves from hypothermia, wolves, and the possible arrival of those we pursued. Paul took the first shift, and even though my mind was fretful, I was soon fast asleep, Millie's fur hat snug on my head as the rest of my body stayed cozy and warm in my sleeping blanket. Strange as it sounds, I missed the weight of Lloyd George on my legs and wondered if the dog had tried to crawl in with Clayton, Dr. Moody, or even Genevieve.

Paul woke me at the appointed time with nothing to report, and I spent the next five hours stoking the fire and staring off into the darkness. Stanley's snoring, loud enough to scare off any bear, also served as the perfect antidote to my continued sleepiness, so I took the time to ruminate.

Off in the distance, far past the bend of the river, Chambers stood. I imagined it as a miniature world of its own, the people inside suspended in time and space. The world outside it knew nothing about the town, its history, and the myriad ambitions of the people who lived there. Would it matter if it disappeared? Wiped from the face of the earth? Who was I to care so much about it when the rest of the planet did not even consider it?

So why were we even out here chasing these desperate and violent men through the center of a winter storm? Was it my sense of duty, my responsibility to the uniform that drove me on, or something else? A desire to make the world right? To repair the damage that Sergeant Deacon and Mayor Fox had caused? Or to make myself right? To repair the damage that continued to hurt me?

A strange feeling came over me. I felt unmoored. It was the wind. I hadn't noticed, but it had spent itself out, finally dissipating into an otherwordly silence, the heavy snowflakes drifting down now with only the force of gravity to guide them.

In my war years, I found the silence to be where true terror sunk. The tension would coil like a spring as you waited for something, for anything, to happen. Men would often go mad if it stretched out too long. They would get brash, childish, punch drunk, or even, at times, suicidal, launching themselves at the enemy in the darkness. When the shells came and the shooting started, my fear evaporated, and the all-encompassing work of survival began. It did not take long before you forgot "silence" was even a thing for the living. Until your ears and eyes became all that you were.

Later, when I returned to Canada, I found the silence difficult. That caustic tension was still working on my nerves; my brain's obsession with persuading me my survival was still and always would be in question. I hoped if I joined the police force, my military brain would settle into duty. And at first, during my training, it worked. The companionship of men was like liniment for my spirit. But it did not prepare me for the loneliness of a northern detachment; too much time to let my mind torment me.

A few hours in, Stanley rolled, and his echoing snore vanished, leaving me with the crackle of the fire as the only sound to focus my mind upon. In falling snow, the world gains a serenity. No crow or raven caw. No howl of the wolf. Even the tiny forest creatures had found a place to curl away. And I realized that I felt no terror.

I opened my eyes wide. The moon still hid behind the clouds, but the falling snow gave my world a soft, milky glow. Beyond my circle, I could convince myself that there was nothing, that I had passed through this life, not to death but to another better place where no bad things occurred. Where nothing had happened and nothing ever would. Just this still moment, finally without terror. My only wish to share it.

The rise of the sun broke through my reverie. The dull light bloomed in a line above the trees, a soft purple glow with frosted bands of pink. Somewhere off in the distance, there was Chambers, and for the first time, it felt something like home.

But was it? My understanding of the place had been wrong from the beginning; my poor assumptions guided me away from what I should have discovered long ago. And yet, at its essence were Millie, Bea, and Genevieve, Coot, and Dr. Moody. There were good people there that needed our protection. Was this my failure? Or was failure baked into all of us? Maybe Peter was right. Was it the failure of the white man who never saw the land for what it was? The landscape was beautiful enough without the need for an iron rail.

And then Paul snored.

****

I shook Paul awake and then tempted him with morning coffee to get him to his considerable feet. I could tell he was not impressed with my version of the drink; tepid water and floating coffee grounds. But we drank to the bottom of our cups before we packed and continued our trek.

The bridge was indeed treacherous. The railings on either side were weathered and worn. They gave no comfort. The gang's tracks had melted and froze, forming icy crenellations. Our pony, which I had named Old Balderson after its original owner, balked at the crossing, and we had to prod it and pull it, careful of our footing. When we made it across, I glanced at the rushing river and was surprised that the drop was not as far as I expected. Still, even falling into the raging river from this height could result in death by either drowning or freezing.

Ironically, after ten minutes of walking past the bridge, we came around a bend to find three large buildings facing the water. I did not want to wonder whether our fugitives stayed there for the night. If so, we could have discovered them with a brief walk the night before.

We strode forward, concerned that they might still occupy the buildings, but it soon became apparent that we were alone. We determined that the ruins were an abandoned sawmill. Before the war, over two dozen sawmills were scattered along the Skeena River from Prince Rupert to Hazelton. Now, there was one working factory, the new timber mill at Plateau that put the Chambers' sawmill out of business.

While the building was derelict, it would have been

an excellent site for our opium gang to make camp. They could have fit their horses in the main building and slept in the attached wood lodge. And yet, there was no evidence that they spent their time here. They may have been lucky enough to find a similar site farther west, but I doubted it.

It would have been a more comfortable place for Stanley and me to spend the evening. While the fire and sleeping bags had helped, there was already a deep chill in our bones that we hungered to get rid of. And so, we pushed on.

For a brief time, it stopped snowing, and a strange light appeared in the sky. The clouds had parted, and a hint of the sun breathed over us. I could not explain the elation I felt at the sight, and for a while I marveled at the sublime beauty that surrounded us. I could see God's mighty fingerprints everywhere I looked. It let me forget our dangerous journey and the evils we had left behind.

Alas, this did not last. An hour before noon, we came across a gruesome sight. We saw it at a distance as a single unexplained dot of darkened green. As we came forward, I guessed its form but prayed I was mistaken. The body was prone, buried from feet to waist in ice and snow. The upper half was on a slight rise; the face turned away from the track as if the person had fallen asleep, though even from the back, we knew no life was there.

I recognized the coat but circled to the other side to make sure. It was John Tuttle, his eyes closed, cheek pressed to the snow.

"It looks like they tried to dig him out," said Stanley. Indeed it was true. The packed snow around the body showed that the men had taken some time to try to release the body. With time, they must have seen the fruitlessness of the task, the lower body too encased with heavy ice. Perhaps they had chosen to return this way, hoping for a thaw to do the work for them.

"The poor man was injured," I told Stanley, crouching in the snow. His face bore a heavy bruise on the upward side, and his shoulder appeared dislodged. I checked the one open pocket I could reach but found nothing inside. He carried no tools to help him in his walk.

Paul squatted on the other side of the body, leaning over to see the man's face. "Do you think he died from his injury or from the cold?"

"We still have no idea how far he walked," I replied, considering how much farther it was to Chambers. "It could have been both, I suppose. The injury became too much. He laid down to rest. And then, because of the cold, he never woke."

"Let's think about this," said Stanley. "We know there were four or five men that left Chambers on the train." I nodded. That's what Dorothy Tuttle told us. "And we believe that they left to go load the pit train and bring it back during the night of the shootout. So I feel it's safe to assume that John Tuttle wasn't the only one on the train."

"Yes," I said. There was nothing new to what Paul said.

"So, where are they?" Paul asked. "Could they all be buried under the snow?"

I shook my head. The idea was absurd—that a whole group of men would freeze together; surely, someone would either be behind or ahead. And besides, we would have seen signs of them. "It's possible one of them made it back and told Tom Fox what had happened." I dismissed the idea as soon as I said it. We would still have seen some sign of their eastward tracks if they had arrived yesterday.

"I think one of the wives would have found out and told Millie," Stanley said. It was a good point. They would have been upset that one husband had returned and not the others. However, they had kept quiet before. I was finding it hard to think through all the possibilities.

"I think there was some kind of accident," Paul continued. "This man here was wounded, and this is as far as he got. So based on that, we could speculate that a non-injured man would have made it farther, perhaps all the way back to Chambers."

"That makes sense," I said. The train might have overturned, for example. Steep slopes, wide turns, and cliff walls, all in the dark, with only the train's lights to guide it. And a snowstorm in an area where mudslides and avalanches were always a danger. Who knows how fast or with what ferocity the blizzard had arrived? I imagine the men feared nothing when they first started.

"Or…" I was thinking aloud. "This man could have been injured by the others. He wanted out; there was an argument, and he escaped. John Tuttle was a gentle man. Certainly, he would have been considering his wife and daughter. I imagine he was coerced into this thing, but then had a change of heart."

"Sounds like a good theory," said Paul, standing. "I wonder what your mayor and his men felt. They traveled past him." He looked at the path ahead, the sun glowing behind him. "We may make some time on them now. This can't help their morale. Big groups move slower because they have more people to satisfy. And all those extra horses—more mouths to feed, more legs to tire."

I said a few Christian words before we left John Tuttle in the snow. We had an extra blanket that I pulled over his head and torso, and we stuck a branch in the ground to mark the spot in case the falling snow buried him farther. We could only hope that a hungry animal wouldn't find the corpse before our reinforcements did. It would be a small mercy for his wife.

****

As we continued, I considered Constable Paul Stanley's deportment and attitude over the last four days. He certainly was strong and intelligent enough not to be regarded as a green recruit. At times, I had to admit he had been the key to our progress.

"All of this does not appear to affect you," I told him.

Paul looked over at me, his eyes squinting against the light of the snow. "I assume you have seen worse," he replied. It was true. I had seen much worse. "My grandmother always told us that the weary carry on. There's not much else you can do." His steps were larger than my own, and sometimes I felt like a child walking with a parent.

"That didn't work for John Tuttle, though."

Paul shrugged. "She never said it worked. She just said they did it." He had me there.

How had I survived through all those hopeless years I had spent abroad? How did anyone? I used to believe the effects of mental trauma were not visible, but I could see them plainer than any wound, both in myself and those I encountered. Men like Paul were the best answer to it all, men unexhausted from the drama of death.

The man was astute.

"I'm having trouble believing that Sergeant Deacon

was in on all this," I told him.

He looked at me, confused. "You believe that he had nothing to do with it?"

"No," I corrected him. "That's not what I mean at all. I can see that the man is corrupt. I just don't see how any Mountie could go so far astray."

Stanley nodded, and for a moment, there was a profound silence.

"You know," he said. "Deacon wasn't a Mountie until the Royal Northwest Mounted Police were amalgamated. Maybe he never wanted to be. Maybe he was always corrupt. Some men look for the easy path even if that means stepping on the throats of others."

I wasn't going to debate that point, but it hurt me to think that my so-called superior, a man I was supposed to admire, had deserted to the other side. He sent someone to kill me, for gosh sakes.

But there was something even deeper, something scratching at my soul. The thought burned so hot that I couldn't help but mutter it aloud. "He played me like a patsy."

Stanley stopped and held me with his eyes. "He tried," he said, his voice deep and resonant. "He tried, Albright, but we'll get the better of him."

"We will," I agreed, still not feeling so good about the whole thing.

"That's what it's all about. Us against them. And our strength is not letting them break the rest of us apart."

Wise words, indeed. This man would go much farther than me. And what's more, it didn't bother me a bit.

****

"In the war," I said, "I was lucky enough to go over

the top twice. For many men, it only took once to not return. This one time, the second time. I got turned around and found myself alone." I stared at Paul's back as he pulled the pony beside him.

"There was a shell, and I was knocked prone. I was frightened, and instead of moving forward, I found a crater to crawl in." There was a tightness in my chest that I could not release. "There was a man in there already. Another Canadian from Galt, in Ontario. His name was Walter Evans, no middle initial. A private." I swallowed. "The man's legs were gone and he was in considerable pain. He was shouting and crying, calling for his mother and father to help him. I did what I could to calm him, but I'm not sure if he even knew I was there."

"At one point," I continued, "I was sure we would be found. I considered killing the man to put him out of his misery. Stabbing my bayonet into his heart." The blasted snow started falling again, the morning's pink glow gone.

"I couldn't do it," I said. "And in the end, the man became calm. He told me about his home and who was waiting for him and then he died. In the middle of a sentence, his life ran out." My voice cracked as the icy wind placed a tear on my cheek.

We each listened to our heavy, plodding footsteps in the snow for a while. I could tell Stanley didn't know what to say.

"How did you get out?" he finally asked.

"Daylight came," I said, "and I found I was no more than fifty feet from our trenches. I waited there all day with Walter's body and then slipped back into our trench when it was dark. I don't know if they ever retrieved his body. Either way, he's buried now, hopefully at peace, somewhere in France."

"The weary carry on," Paul said as he stared ahead through the mountains. I nodded behind him.

****

At one point, as we walked in silence, one behind the other, Paul began to whistle, and I joined in, watching the frosted tops of the mountain pines swaying in the wind.

Another half hour and we found their camp. It was a welcome sight, for it proved that we were now but a few hours behind them. They had, like us, been forced to bed without shelter, though their party of ten horses and six men meant a broader camp with less protection from the wind. We did not know what gear they had taken, but they had a chance to plan, so we guessed they outfitted themselves well.

We rooted around to see if they had left anything behind, but they had been careful. By this time, my legs began to cramp, and my calves became angry, painful lumps that groaned at every step. Our snow shoes helped a bit, but with each step, we raised our feet out of the snow, and while a gradual increase in temperature felt good on the face, it added weight to the top layer of melted snow. What would Paul think if I stretched my body over the back of Old Balderson and let him do my work? But still, we kept marching.

As we rounded a bend, I took stock of the mountain peaks around us. The heads of five frosty giants surrounded us, and I became overwhelmed by the thought of an untouched world. The Kitimat people had lived here for thousands of years, but had they ascended to the many peaks that gave grandeur to the British Columbian coast? How had we been so reckless to believe we could tame this all? With each step, I was now farther west than ever, never once taking the train to Prince Rupert myself.

"You know she admires you a great deal," Paul said. Not a word had passed between us for more than an hour.

"Who?" I asked.

"Millie Norton, of course."

This statement surprised me. What was Paul getting at? "Well, I admire her," I replied. "She is a diligent worker. I admire her as a colleague, and that's it."

I expected to leave it there.

"Oh," chuckled Paul. "I didn't mean to insinuate anything further." But his inference was clear. And that made me angry.

I turned to him with his meaty hands and his broad jaw-boned face. "Well, she admires you a great deal as well."

Paul let the silence of the glacier cold fill the air between us. Then he said—a twinkle in his eyes—"Well, I admire her." Pause. "But only as a colleague."

I don't know how he did it, but my anger twisted, and I snickered, which turned into a chortle, and before you knew it, we were both laughing up a storm. We got so loud I worried an avalanche would take us out. By the time we finished, Paul had to take hold of my shoulder to regain his balance, and that got us going again like two schoolboys on their way home from school. It was somehow freeing.

And from that moment on, I believed Constable Paul Stanley to be amongst the best of men, except for his snoring.

For the rest of that day, we saw only the natural beauty of the mountains: no more bodies or man-made objects. Mayor Fox's opium gang must have eaten while they traveled, for there was no second rest camp. In the afternoon, the sun came out again but then disappeared; soon enough, it began to snow again. A steady attack of hard, icy pellets made the grade slick and uncomfortable to walk upon. And still, we trudged on, Stanley's relentless footsteps the rhythm that pushed us forward.

As the dusk grew, we were lucky enough to come upon an unmanned station. It consisted of a signal light, a small boardwalk, and a tiny hut. The Grand Trunk Railroad had planted buildings here and there to assert its dominance over the region with the grand hope that several small towns and even cities would flourish along the entire length of track. While it was a solitary building, built of knotty wood and no insulation, it was as welcoming a sight as a mansion. Paul suggested that we wait and watch before approaching, and though it pained me to do so, I had to admit that this made sense. Soon enough, we would see a fire if the men had stopped there.

In the end, the hut was ours. The gang before us must have had quite a discussion before moving on. It was too small of a structure to house them all, but it had to be a temptation. We fed the pony well and tied it to the signal post, then spread our blankets on the floor and ate dinner by the light of our lantern.

Day Five

Friday, February 21st, 1923

That night, the storm was fierce. We kept watch and repeatedly poked our heads out to check on Old Balderson. Finally, as strange as it might sound, we decided the poor pony would fare much better in the hut with us. The animal provided extra warmth as we could not start a fire in the shed as it held no chimney or stove. And so one of us tried to sleep while the other leaned against the pony to prevent it from stomping on our bedrolls. When it was Stanley's turn to take his rest, the noise of his snoring upset Old Balderson to the point I had to kick Stanley twice to get him to roll over. As bad as that sounds, we hoped the smugglers were even more miserable.

When it was my turn to try to sleep, it would not come. What might I be doing if I were in Chambers and none of these strange events had occurred. Tonight was a Wednesday, so I would be at the hospital. At least twice a week, I would go over after dinner and play a game of cards with Genevieve and Dr. Moody.

What we played depended on how Kenneth was feeling. A year ago, we started with Whist. If Millie or someone else joined us, we tried Bridge. Though lately, all we played were variations of Gin, sometimes only with Dr. Moody watching. Either way, Genevieve maintained it was good for Dr. Moody's mind to keep it thinking here in the present. Often, even during the games, his mind would wander, and he would become confused about where and when he was. Genevieve called him her time traveler.

She knew he was slipping away, but abandoning a patient was not in her nature. It was beautiful to watch, to see how she would dote on him. She told me that he would do the same for her. It was a thought I did not want to divest her of, but in my experience, you could never infer what someone would or wouldn't do in stressful situations. The reality was often heartbreaking.

Genevieve tried to keep her troubles to herself, but I could see through her. Her heart was too large not to suffer cracks. She had spent so much of her life giving to others that she forgot about her own needs. I tried to help her when I could, but she often refused my offers of support. As Dr. Moody's condition worsened, I feared it would become too much for her. Everyone has a breaking point.

Finally, in the early morning hours, the storm abated. It was the final fever that burned the last of the infection. As we departed from the cabin, we were greeted by a bold blue sky. It was like the world had been created anew. Oh, how I wished that was the case.

We pulled Old Balderson out and started moving. With the sun out and the snow and ice melting, we felt this was our day. Sure enough, after only two hours, we came across markings that suggested a campsite. The poor fools had traded our relative shelter for two hours of extra walking and a brace of trees that only protected them from the north. From there, we found their movement frenetic. They must have chosen to plow on while the storm was still raging, their visibility still poor. They were gambling a better place of shelter was ahead. If so, it was unlikely they found one.

We discovered more evidence of their chaotic night thirty minutes later. Two of the town's horses were walking toward us. This pair must have panicked and got separated from the herd. Only one carried a pack and saddle. This presented a new problem. We could not leave them be. Their domesticity would make them prey for wild creatures; worse, they could be dangerous to the trains once they started moving.

"Well," said Stanley, "we're supposed to be mounted." I liked his way of thinking. I let him take the saddle, and for the next two hours, we traveled on the backs of these magnificent beasts, a welcome load off my aching calves.

Soon after, we found the gang's second campsite, more protected by the rock's natural features. The horse's pack held only foodstuffs. Here, a variety of items littered the snow, a sleeping bag, a broken lantern, a fur hat, and a length of rope. They were getting sloppy. It was good to see.

We rounded a steady curve at two hours past noon, and our newfound horses became excited. Either they caught the scent of a wild animal or their tame stablemates. We tied the three animals together and sneaked forward until the view was unobstructed.

The track here did not run beside the river. Instead, the water twisted through rocky cliffs that must have been too difficult to blast through. But as we completed a turn, a wide-open panorama came into view. The cliffs had come apart here to create a small sloping plateau about a quarter of a mile wide. We could make out a wooden bridge at the horizon's edge, though not the crevice it spanned.

We brought the horses through a jumble of heavy rocks and boulders that lined the valley's floor. Stanley believed he could see some of the other stolen horses ahead. After we rewarded them with apples, we tied Old Balderson and the two horses to a tree behind a rocky outcrop. Then we sneaked forward using the boulders as cover.

****

Before coming to the bridge, we skirted out wide and crept to the edge of the crevice. Here we found a deep gulch. At the bottom, the rushing river moved in a southwestern direction. But this was not what held our attention. For there, in the water, smashed from the force of its descent, was a diesel locomotive, and the remains of the rail car still hitched behind it.

We slunk forward now, knowing this was the end goal for those we were following. They could not have been here long. Two or three hours at the most. So this is what John Tuttle had escaped from and why no men had straggled back. It was a wonder that the man had survived. The only reasonable possibility was he had jumped before the train veered off its track. The bridge ahead was undamaged. The pit train must have skidded as it rounded the turn and then jumped the track into the gorge. No one could survive that fall. Hopefully, others leaped from the train car before it went over.

We moved north, skirting the chasm's edge, eyes scanning to find evidence of the mayor's little gang. After all, the train contents were what they had come for. Hiding the mess below would be impossible, but they might try to salvage or hide the opium. Of course, they had no idea that we had already stormed the Chambers Lodge and were on to their smuggling. Their strategy now was a desperate one. How could they explain the train being here? Its markings identified it as the Chambers' pit train. And there were most likely dead bodies below. Just what our world needed right now, more weeping widows.

We made our way over to the bridge. Looking into the gulch, we saw the engine, long since gone cold, lying on its side under a layer of snow. Behind it, its single cargo car lay bent against the rock where it came to rest. Two men were clambering on top of it. They had removed snow from its upper surface and peeled back the door. A third man was inside. You could make out his hands as he hoisted a box out of the dark space of the cargo hold.

By how he held his body, I could tell that one of the men was Alexandr Dvorak. I guessed the second to be Anders Larsen, but the man in the boxcar was unclear.

Their descent must have been difficult. Two ropes still hung on the near end of the bridge, but there were few natural rock ledges on the cliff face. Did they plan to use these ropes to pull the boxes up, or would they aim to hide the contraband below?

"Where are the others?" asked Stanley, and a bullet pierced my shoulder before I even heard the shot. We broke. Stanley to the left and I to the right, trying to find cover. Men above us on the incline were moving now, firing, their bullets making trails in the snow. My body lost its rhythm, and I fell as a second bullet missed me. I tripped and tumbled in pain as I slid toward the chasm. I could see them now—three men with rifles positioned behind cover. Stanley found safety behind a boulder. I willed myself to move and scrambled to the side, the men above reloading. Three more frantic steps, and I lost my footing again, just making it behind an icy crag before shots rang out again.

"Are you hit bad?" shouted Stanley, his back pressed hard against a rock. I inspected the damage. The bullet had passed clean through, missing any major artery. I had never been shot before, but I knew the agony it could cause, especially if infection set in. But that, of course, was not the worry of the moment.

"There's three of them," I called back, holding that many fingers before me as another shot rang out. "Fox, Landers and Blood," I yelled with confidence. In winter, you could know a man by his coat as well as you could by his face. Fox's was a green oilskin of the highest quality, a statement piece that showed him off as the town's bigwig. Larsen wore a Hudson Bay Company coat down to his ankles, much worn but still warm. Blood I knew from his large whiskers but also the cracked leather jacket and Stetson that he wore as a mark of a frontiersman.

Stanley took the information in. "That's six then," he shouted over. Six men had taken the horses, Bernard had said. I hoped his count was accurate and that no one joined their group on their way out of Chambers.

So three above us and three below, though the ones in the gulch were not a threat for now. It would take a lot of effort and time for the men to climb those ropes, and it would put them in the line of fire.

Stanley removed his pack and set it between his knees. Smart thinking. My pack fell off in the tumble and lay between us, impossible to get without substantial risk. Stanley was removing his rifle from his ties right now. Good man. It was unlikely we would get out of this without a fight. I peeked around my block of ice and rock and saw the three men above us still in position. They weren't coming forward yet.

"Do you need medicine?" Stanley half whispered at me. The men above were sure to know they'd hit me if only by the way I moved, but there was no use giving them more information. For the moment, I was fine. There was not a lot of blood as yet. The tightness of my shirt and coat was helping to put pressure on the wound.

"Do you have a mirror in your pack?" I croaked back and saw Stanley's confused face before he began rummaging around in his belongings.

"We have you, Albright!" It was the mayor's voice,

loud and proud. "Blood got you good! You may as well both come out now."

Stanley found his cigarette case, a thin compact the size of his palm. He motioned to me and then threw it over, using the crisp snow to glide the distance—a perfect pass. I gave him a nod back to show him thanks. I opened it, and sure enough, a mirror was underneath its lid.

"C'mon Albright!" The mayor shouted again. "You're outnumbered and injured, and you're going to get plenty cold sitting in that snow!"

He was wrong, at least for now. The sun was refreshing, an old friend that had returned in our moment of need. Fortunately, it was positioned more or less straight above us, letting me use the mirror without casting a reflection. I could see them now, farther than a pistol shot but easy reach from a rifle.

Stanley was sitting, his back still against the rock, his rifle pointed in the air beside him. He was watching me as I worked the mirror around. I nodded over to him and gave the sign for three again. If there was a skulker, he was well hidden.

"What's the plan?" I mouthed to Stanley. And I saw the big man smile and then shrug.

"They have the high ground," he called back, not so loud. They would know we were talking but might not know what we said. "They have more men, and they are probably better shots. At least better shots than me." He sounded unperturbed.

When the mayor called out again, I decided to go for it. I charted it out in my mind, how my body would have to move with the increasing pain in my shoulder. I knew I was stiffening. I could feel beads of sweat break out on my forehead.

"Now, Albright, be reasonable," said the mayor, and I ran. Well, I stumbled forward, willing myself onward. I saw the men's rifles resting at their sides through the mirror. They were so sure they had us. They failed to send a single shot before I got to Stanley's rock. Where I collapsed, winded, and in pain.

Stanley was shocked by my risky maneuver, but he soon recovered and took the time to inspect my wound through my coat. He nodded as I got the mirror ready.

"We don't want to have to kill you, Albright. But we will. For the survival of the town." I could see Paul ready to reply, but I put my fingers to my lips to hold him off.

"The way I see it," said Paul. "We are going to be just fine."

"How do you figure?" I said. I moved the mirror around the rock's edge to find a better angle. There was no movement for now.

"Well," Paul explained. "We have something they don't, barring the injury to that arm of yours."

"What's that?"

"Time." He was watching a soft white cloud hovering in the sky. "They're going to open that rail line, and then what will they do? We've split them in two. The ones on the bottom can't communicate with the ones on top. How are they going to hide the opium?" He let that sink in. "Also, they need us dead. If we get out of here, they know we will talk. They've got to come for us eventually."

"Well, that's reassuring." My arm started to throb. Would I be offered morphine if we got out of this mess? "So we wait them out?"

"I figure they will only start moving when they feel

we've dropped our guard, and then they'll make their way toward us. They'll have to come out in the open, and that's when we attack."

"So we wait," I said. The plan had some obvious problems: their numbers, the high ground, my wound, and Blood's ability to shoot.

"Not just wait." And he gave me one of those Paul Stanley grins. "You need to give me a shooting lesson."

Was he being serious? I remembered the shootout at Chambers Lodge. His misses were so off-target they could have cost me my life.

"Well," I began but stopped. I remembered all the times I had to fire my weapon in the war. About my sniper friend Lou Kenosha. And the Pickle brother I shot through the eye. "It's the simplest thing to shoot a gun, but shooting a man is something else entirely." I watched Paul nod. "The problem is that you have to want to shoot him, which means causing them pain or maybe ending their life. Which is pain for all those left behind." I took some moments to breathe.

"You have to want to shoot them, Paul, and I don't think you do. You're not the type of man who wants to create more pain in this world."

"Okay," he responded, his eyes on my own. He shifted his body against the rock. He seemed uncomfortable, but it was an uncomfortable topic—no movement in the mirror yet.

"Paul, I think you need to be on the rifle. I don't know if I could keep it steady." He nodded again. "So you have two choices."

"Go on," he prompted me.

"You either got to make them something they aren't, or you got to make yourself different. You've got to pretend." I wasn't sure he understood. "You either got to pretend that they can't feel pain or that you are the type of man that isn't bothered by shooting someone. Just for the moments that you are on that trigger."

"Does that actually work?"

"I don't know," I admitted. "It's like most things, you can either do it or you can't."

"I see," he said. He stared at the sky. There was no longer a cloud in sight. Crystal clear blueness for as far as the eye could see.

"So we wait," he said.

"Yep. Try not to overthink it."

We sat squished behind that boulder, neither of us saying a word. But with the pain in my shoulder and the excitement of being in yet another shootout, I could feel my blood pressure rise and my heart thump in my chest. My body felt restless and agitated, and I began to get anxious. A panic attack at this time could be deadly—a vicious spiral of worry building on itself.

I tried to breathe and send my mind backward to the beginning, tracing through each separate event to build a story that would fit. And I realized I still had so many questions, most of which I could not answer, at least not with me sitting behind a snowy boulder with a bullet in my shoulder.

There were a couple of things, though.

"Paul, I've been wondering," My voice was too loud, and I saw that I shocked the man, so I lowered it back to a whisper. "You were interested in the Chambers family right from the beginning. How did you know that they were part of this?"

Stanley let out a slow laugh. "I didn't. I just thought it was a coincidence because I had such a rough time with the father."

"You mentioned that." I turned my neck to face him. "What happened?"

Stanley shrugged. "Labor dispute." I wasn't sure if he was going to go on. He cast his eyes over the mountains. "It doesn't matter in the grand scheme of things, but in the moment, it was quite unpleasant."

Stanley kicked some snow with his boot, and we watched it roll down the steep bank. "I told you I played for St. Pat's in Toronto. A couple of guys, real good players, wanted to renegotiate their contracts. They weren't asking for much, a few extra dollars and better working conditions. They wanted to have some regulations about how often we practiced, how much time we spent away from our family, that sort of thing." He paused to see if I was listening. I was.

"They came to me because I was one of the younger players on the team. They figured that if we had diverse representation, then they would listen to us more. We made it to the doorway, and we were fired. Just like that. They heard we were coming, and they wanted nothing to do with it."

"Out of all the owners, Chambers was the one who was really in charge. And he didn't stop at firing us. He made sure that we wouldn't be playing hockey for anyone else. He barred us even from joining amateur teams by spreading out all sorts of scurrilous rumors. I could take it, but it was real hard on my family, especially my mother. It came out of nowhere. One day, we were heroes, and the next day we were bums. Fortunately, I knew someone on the force that would still recruit me. And that was that."

He sucked in, his heavy chest moving like a bellow.

I could tell that it still hurt.

"What's the chance of you being ordered to a town named after the man that ruined your career?" I asked.

Paul laughed. "Yes, the name leaves a rather sour taste in my mouth. But I don't think the town will bear the name much longer."

I had to agree, "Who's the bum now?" I asked, but Paul was silent.

"And the opium," I continued. "You had an idea about that since the beginning, didn't you?"

"It was the way you described Philip," Paul explained. "In Toronto, I'd seen others like him. I even had a friend who got addicted. The doctor was right. It can be terrible for some people."

I should have come to the same conclusion earlier. It was peculiar that Philip Chambers would be living alone, divorced from the rest of the community and the outside world. I should have looked into it, but I assumed Sergeant Deacon would have told me if he had misgivings about the man. How wrong I was.

****

People always think waiting is easy. All we had to do was to be ready for when they moved. But the mind does not want to be still. Minutes would pass, and I would realize my thoughts were drifting. There was a lot to distract me. The glare of the sun off the snow was becoming painful to the eyes, and then there was the bullet hole in my arm. Plus, there was a lot to consider.

The sickness that ran through the town. Where did it come from? Philip Chambers' addiction caused a lot of pain; one person's misery affected many others. For a drug that was supposed to reduce pain, it sure found a way to cause it. Was it an equation where both sides had to equal out? That there always had to be so much pain in the world? Reduce pain here only to watch it grow somewhere else.

But it wasn't just Philip Chambers. One person alone does not have that much power. There was Clayton's heartache, for example. He dealt with it similarly, lashing out at those around him. These men we faced, both above us and below, were also acting out of pain. Something was missing from them. Something they felt they needed. And they couldn't get it without causing the misery of others.

It was Paul's snoring that stopped my philosophizing. I guess he had found a way of not overthinking it. But the loud snort of his nose reminded me to look at my mirror, and I saw no Blood. I lowered it and found the men were already half the distance from us and coming on strong. Another ten or fifteen seconds, and it would be over. I elbowed Paul in the ribs, and he responded, waking with a deep gasp.

"Now," I shouted and gripped my gun hard to my chest. I dived on the ground, rolling sideways, my pistol before me. Paul rose behind the rock, and there was a rash of gunfire. Bullets, one, two, three, were aimed in my direction, all narrow misses, rebounding off the ground before me as I kept the momentum of my spin. I wanted their attention to be toward me as Paul shot.

I came to a stop, dizzy and in pain, with my gun pointed forward. I heard the deep echoing boom from Paul's rifle and saw Mitch Blood's hand come off at the wrist. A second shot, and the mayor fell forward, his hat rolling free as he collapsed face forward into the snow. I waited a millisecond before squeezing the trigger, and in that brief space of time, Larsen was smart enough to drop his gun.

Blood screamed. He grabbed at his wrist as blood sprayed him in the face. Larsen ran over and tried to staunch the bleeding with his toque. Blood kept yelling, "My hand, my hand, my hand!"

Paul walked out slowly, his rifle pointed out before him. He slid their guns down the hill toward me. Stanley checked the body of the mayor, but there was no blood. I was sure he was dead, but Paul rolled him over and placed his ear to his chest. He looked back at me, and I felt sorry for him. It's a hard thing to kill another man, whether you need to or not.

That's why I found his smile so inappropriate.

The mayor stirred, and I breathed out in relief. Paul fetched the man's hat and held it to show two bullet holes—one at the front of the crown and one out the back. Fox had simply slipped in the snow and was concussed when his head hit the ground. A one in a million shot. A Paul Stanley type of shot.

With effort, Stanley lifted the groggy mayor to his feet. Then he collected Larsen and Blood and made them walk to our little outcrop of rocks. Larsen steadied Blood as he continued to whimper and cry.

****

As Paul looked after our prisoners, I shuffled over to the chasm to spot the other fugitives. It was possible that during the gunfight, someone may have tried to climb the cliff face using those ropes we saw.

But as I peered into the gully, I saw only the waves of the river rush, a white froth building as it broke around the locomotive and its car. The train car and engine were free of men. Boxes and crates lay unopened around the locomotive, and there was no sign of motion. I scanned the length of the ropes and the nearest cliff face, but they were both empty. The men below must have found somewhere to hide or had moved off in an attempt to escape.

I stepped back to check on Paul. He was using his handcuffs to join Larsen and the mayor. Out of the corner of my eye, I saw something move, and a rush of panic coursed through my veins.

He must have just made it to the top. Out of breath and red in the face from the exertion, he came out from behind a boulder right where the bridge met the face of the cliff. I'd never met the man nor seen his picture, but the make of his Klondike hat, felt boots, and leather gloves meant he could only be one person—his service pistol pointed at my chest—Sergeant Deacon.

"Albright," he panted and took a tentative step toward me. How could I be so foolish? I did not expect any man would be able to climb so fast, and I failed to check the topmost knot of the rope.

"You're hurt," he sneered. "Your shoulder." All the blood was in my coat. I bent my elbow high to my chest in an attempt to dull the pain. "You're going to call over to the big guy and tell him to drop his weapon." Deacon was close now; the steam of his breath wafted in gusts toward me.

Was it the pain in my shoulder? The adrenaline from the gunfight? Or an irritation caused by yet another gun stuck in my face? There was not a shiver of panic in my nerves. I tested it, but all I felt was cold—cold as a February day.

I turned my head as if to call over to Stanley. His back was to us as he tended to our prisoners. I opened my mouth, but instead of yelling, I threw my good right hand at Deacon's pistol. I caught the barrel as he sent off a shot, the sound deafening as the bullet whipped by my ear. The weapon flew from his grip, and he was on me. He pressed down on my injured shoulder with his strong hand, then kneed me in the gut as he forced me into the snow. The pain in my shoulder was intense. Lights swarmed into my eyes, and I felt a sickness climb into my throat. The whole world swayed around me. His knee cracked me across my already bandaged chin, and I fell forward as he released me.

With all that was left of my strength, I lunged. I hoped to grab some part of him—my survival instinct in full force. Deacon would be after the gun, but I couldn't see it. Where was Paul? The world was now a sliver of light: the pain in my shoulder, the tears in my eyes, the panic in my heart. All I could see were Deacon's legs. His boots.

I fell forward, planting my face in the snow as I gripped his foot with both hands and set him off balance. Immediately, I felt his weight shift. The muscles in his boot clenched as he fell backward, slipping on the snow; his body struggled to maintain his equilibrium. His foot clipped my chin, but that contact failed to save him. No man may halt the rush of gravity.

I heard no scream, no sound of the body making contact with the rocks or the water below. I did not even know it was over, as my agony consumed me. My last thought was one of curiosity: Why was I holding a single boot?

****

Paul shook me awake and got me back to my feet. Before, I would be embarrassed by his help, but now I did not protest.

He guided me over to our little group of captured fugitives. Fox and Larsen were as grim-faced as me, and Blood was out cold, the blood leaking through Paul's improvised bandage. I sat with them, my pistol in my unsteady hands, as Paul retrieved food and drink from our packs. There was not a single word exchanged.

When refreshed, Stanley returned to the bridge to draw up the ropes. It was difficult to tell how far the men below would have to walk to get around us, but Paul was unconcerned. If the men were armed, they weren't soldiers—a greengrocer and a seventeen-year-old boy. When he returned to the group, he told me that Sergeant Deacon's corpse was caught facedown between the rocks in the rushing river. Then he got back to work. The only one of us that didn't look or feel defeated.

The rest of us sat, Larsen and Fox stone-faced. Blood whimpered as he fell in and out of consciousness. All afternoon, we waited as the sun melted the snow around us. Two hours before dusk, we heard the sound of a locomotive off in the distance, making its way toward us from Prince Rupert.

My earliest memory involved a train. My father took me and my sisters to Ottawa to stay with my aunt. It was 1904, and my mother was ill. She recovered from that bout but died two years later of tuberculosis. My father said the train had traveled across the country to collect us. I remember being overwhelmed by its sheer size and power, the industrial smell, and its shrieking whistle. In my memory, I am on the platform holding my eldest sister's hand as the crowd swirls around us. My father is carrying me on his shoulders, and I can see myself in the passenger car window, hatless and thick around my face. I am both excited and frightened that I will soon be swallowed into the belly of that beast. And my father's face is radiant.

That vision and its childlike sense of wonder flooded back to me when I saw the powerful face of the engine that came toward us. I had heard of such things but had never seen one at work. The behemoth that curled around the track toward us was not any ordinary engine but a twenty-foot-tall rotary snowplow. Its mild steel blades spun to launch a wild plume of snow thirty feet or more into the air as it swept the track before it.

As it rumbled onto the bridge, Paul tore off his fur coat to reveal his serge jacket and waved his arms to alert the train's engineer. When blades turned to blow the snow in the opposite direction, we knew the engineer had seen us, but the prevailing winds still sent gusts of snow that blinded us and our captured fugitives. At once, I panicked, sure that Fox might take this moment to attempt an escape. But as the mighty steam engine passed the bridge and came to a reluctant stop, the air cleared to reveal the same three defeated faces.

It took a while to sort things out. The engineer told us the plow had begun working from the Prince Rupert side when the snow cleared in the afternoon. It was slow, but they figured another plow would work westward from Hazleton. The locomotive pulled only a coal car behind it, so we came aboard the front cabin. Paul decided we could not wait for reinforcements, as Blood and I needed medical attention, and the sun was beginning to set. The engine would take us to the hospital in Chambers, Plateau, or Prince George.

But Stanley decided he would not come with us.

"I will keep an eye out to make sure those other two don't scramble back," he told me, "and then maybe assist in the search for them. I might also help to retrieve the contraband below." He looked pleased with himself and the possible adventure ahead.

I did have enough clarity to remind him about the horses. We found four more tied to the bridge rail, giving us six, but there was no sign of the last four, including my mount, Filch. They must have also wandered off in the storm. When reinforcements arrived, they would need to find and collect them. Poor Coot would be sick with worry if he knew what had happened to his charges.

I worried about Stanley staying the night here, possibly alone. But then I remembered the man's snoring, loud enough to scare off any bear. I checked the slopes to see if it was steep enough to cause an avalanche but saw no obvious danger. Besides, as I said, the man was committed to the task.

For me, the warmth of the steam plow's cabin was too tempting. Even then, I fought to stay conscious and did not have the faculties to argue with the recruit. So I let Paul Stanely go—to be his heroic self.

Chapter 13

Albright's Aftermath
1923-1924

Before he left, Paul helped the engineers pull the body of Mitch Blood into the cabin. The man had passed out, his face white with the blood he had already lost. They then helped the handcuffed Larsen and Fox aboard. Finally, I accepted Paul's help to climb the steps into the locomotive.

We discovered an astonishing display of engineering and modern technology inside the engine. A Toronto dentist had invented this technology just before the war. Now, every railway that traveled over snow needed to have one. The heat inside the cabin was pure bliss at first but soon became oppressive. The two plowmen and the engineer worked in grimy undershirts. Thankfully, they helped remove my furs and jacket. I watched as they did the same for the three fugitives, briefly unlocking Fox and Larsen from their handcuffs. They then chained them to a piece of metal pipe. They would spend the ride sitting on the floor.

The space in the cabin was small, but the men could still complete their duties if the three of us refrained from moving. The youngest of the workers was quite attentive to us, bringing us water and asking after our injuries. We talked about cauterizing Blood's hand in the fire to stop more bleeding, but Stanley's makeshift bandages effectively staunched the flow. Besides, none of us were eager to do it. I had heard enough of the man's screams already.

Besides, the hole in my shoulder and the sharp pain in my chin and head were making me feverish, and I drifted in and out of consciousness, sitting as immobile as I could on the hard, vibrating floor. The heavy engine chug and the powerful steam that heated even the windows and the metal frame of the cabin worked together to lull my senses. Reality became confused with flashes of dreams and memories, the present, past, and future tangled like a dark nest in the center of my mind. For a while, I let my body rest, floating in the security of the cabin.

I woke at one point to see Tom Fox staring at me. From the scowl on his face, I could see that his perspective on me had changed. I was no longer the doleful young lad he could jerk around on command. I was somebody who deserved enough respect to be hated. He was beginning to accept the enormity of his failure. The fantasy he patiently constructed over the last decade was now thoroughly undone.

I stared back at him. I was shot in the shoulder, but he was handcuffed to a train. My shoulder could be fixed, but nothing would fix the mess that he was in. I didn't need to take his pride any longer.

I knew he would speak if I waited long enough.

"You had to ruin everything, didn't you?" he finally said, but I did not answer.

"The town would have made it back if we figured out something to tide us over in the meantime." He shook his head. "If it wasn't for the snowstorm, you would have had nothing. You were lost in the dark, playing house with your little girlfriend."

He was trying to goad me—to make me lose my cool. But my silence was a better weapon. The power here was mine. I would be careful and not overplay my hand.

"We made a new deal with William Chambers," he continued. "Philip had been writing to him. There was new technology that could be used to drain the mine. We could have it in place by this summer if everything went right. And we weren't hurting anyone. Just moving things from place to place. Things that people wanted." His face was earnest, pleading.

"You don't have to take us in. What good is it for anyone if they lock us away? This is a death sentence for Chambers. Deacon understood it. He knew what was good for us. "

I shook my head, and he spat. "You don't look so good, Albright." He grinned. "I think you might not make it. Blood's bullet might be the end of you. It would serve you right for all the men you've killed. "For a moment, his face changed to show the pompous man I knew so well. And then it was gone. He was staring at the floorboards.

I waited a few beats more before I spoke. I kept my voice soft but with a trace of gravel. "The girl."

He coughed. I was relying on his anger. He had no real reason to tell me anything; he probably knew the mystery was eating away at me.

"The girl," he repeated. "She's a strange piece of work. She paid good money to them, to get her revenge on that poor idiot Clayton. Only God knows why. He was drinking himself to death anyway. And no one listened to a thing the man said."

"But they sent her my way and told me to make it happen. Told me I didn't have a choice. It was Deacon's plan to use her to fool you. To keep everyone looking the other way. He knew how weak you were. Command had told him about your fragility, that your nerves were shot."

His laugh was full of scorn. "And she, the girl, was right under your nose. She was inside the cabin when you went to Mitch Blood's place. I got you to head out in the middle of the woods at night. We could have made you dance a jig if we wanted to. And no one would miss you if you were gone." He was laughing loud now as if he was the victor.

He laughed so loud that he got a sharp kick in the ribs from the engineer. While I enjoyed the flash of pain on Fox's face, it startled him into silence.

I asked more questions, but his temper had dissolved. In its place was a melancholic little boy sulking in the corner. I decided to try again later, but soon, my fatigue overtook me, and I fell into a trance.

Eventually, the mayor's men were taken into custody at Hazleton, and we all were transferred to another faster locomotive. On our new train, three Mounties joined us, men I'd never met but brothers just the same. A doctor also traveled with us to Prince George, tending to our wounds as best he could.

I was worried that Blood's severed hand would end him, but he mended. Of course, he would live the rest of his life short-handed. For my part, I did not recover well. The wound in my shoulder became infected. The only treatment was serum therapy, as the injury was too close to the neck to amputate my arm. So I spent another few months in the hospital fighting off the infection and the pain. Morphine was administered and appreciated, but I was fortunate not to develop an addiction.

****

The superintendent visited me during the last days of my recuperation and offered me a citation for bravery and promotion to Corporal. I was to be detachment head in Smithers with three constables under my command, a position that suited me fine. Command had received my paperwork, and despite my anxiety, they never asked direct questions about the girl.

I did have other visitors as well. Two weeks before my dismissal, Genevieve and Millie came to see me. Together.

Genevieve, it turned out, brought sad news. Dr. Moody's health and mind continued to decline. She and Millie had brought the poor doctor to the hospital in Prince George to see a specialist. She was hopeful there was a treatment to stop the sickness from developing further. While I wished the best for Kenneth, I doubted the doctors could do much for him. But I did not say so to Genevieve.

While I was not at my best, it was wonderful to see two familiar faces. My sisters could not travel as they had young children, but Millie and Genevieve were excellent replacements. They split the task of giving me the news from Chambers, which I was anxious to hear.

Fortunately, Peter and Bea were not in command for too long. Around noon, on our first full day of travel, the telegraph began to work again. The Mounties in Plateau sent messages Eastward, so Prince George and beyond knew what was happening in the mountains. McClintock sent his last remaining constable in from Plateau to

Chambers to provide an actual police presence and to secure the prisoners we had captured. As they cleared the railway from the East, Command sent a dozen Mounties to the region. Of course, it was not until we arrived that headquarters learned about the last shootout. While I could not talk, Larsen gave the constables essential details and told them about Paul. He was hoping for some leniency in his sentencing. I remembered how he and his son helped me bring Clayton and Kayden Pickle out of the woods, never revealing the scope of the plan. So I hoped they wouldn't be too lenient.

Since then, Millie and Genevieve reported a steady exodus of people from Chambers. Some left immediately, not wanting to answer for their part in the mayor's plot. Others realized the town could not survive its new reputation and economic decline. I wondered how much land Bea bought in the last few weeks. I'm sure people were willing to sell it for beans. Bea's client would be delighted with her work.

And in all that mess, Clayton made himself disappear. Genevieve felt dreadful as the escape happened on her watch. They had removed the handcuffs so Clayton could bathe, and he did a runner. The fool ran out the back door, wearing only his hospital gown. Genevieve told me they convinced him to shave that lice-infested tangle he called a beard a few days earlier. Margaret was delighted to do the job. It was the first man she ever shaved, she told Genevieve, as if she had received a free ticket to ride a Ferris wheel. But now Genevieve wondered if he only let them do it so he would be unrecognizable. Most people figured he'd died of exposure. But I never believed it. Clayton was the resilient type. He wasn't built to thrive, but surviving was bred in his bones.

As for Chambers, it's still a manned stop on the way out of the mountains, but not much else. Contractors deconstructed the more valuable buildings and shipped their components to settlements far and wide. Fox's Grand Hotel chandelier now adorned one of the smaller dining rooms at a fancy hotel in Victoria. So you could say people still put all that silver money to good use. I'm not sure what happened to Chambers Lodge. I picture it languishing in the snow, its windows and doors open to the sanitizing breezes of the Pacific. I expect the Chambers family wouldn't sell it to Bea's client out of spite.

Millie went back on the train the next day, but Genevieve stayed in Prince George, renting a small apartment in the city so she could make more frequent visits to her husband. Each time she came, she visited me as well, and later, as I improved, we went to see Kenneth together. Dr. Moody often was unaware of our presence, sometimes for the entire visit, so the two of us chatted beside him, hoping our words and good cheer would spark his brain into remembering. Genevieve and I spent the afternoons walking together and watching Prince George's iconic rail bridge lift and lower for passing boats. Alas, I fear that Moody's brain had been too damaged by his time in the war to find its way back to healing, and he died only a month after they discharged me from the hospital.

Mayor Fox got fifteen years of hard labor at Oakalla for his part in the crime. Larsen and Blood each got ten. The Chambers family made some deal with the state and had their son Philip committed to an asylum because of his addiction. I know the way the world works. He'll probably be a free man before Fox is.

There was an investigation into the RCMP's involvement in the scheme, but they never produced an official report. Later, it came to light that three RCMP officers in Prince Rupert resigned without a pension, but no one received a criminal charge. And while there was plenty of evidence to point to the unsavory character of Amadeo Ricci and his many clients, he was allowed to continue his practice. Because of outstanding warrants, the Americans successfully extradited Yugoslavian Borna Selic and Brian "Bunny" Dix to the United States. They were both shot and killed on the steps of the Chicago courthouse as they were about to give sworn testimony.

All in all, the RCMP swept the entire affair under the carpet. While the various Prince Rupert papers did investigate and report on the train crash, they either never discovered or were forced not to address its connection to the opium ring in Chambers. Headquarters either kept the information from them or convinced them that it was an open case that would suffer from too much public input. Ultimately, the news moved on to a debate on the Chinese Exclusion Act, the discovery of insulin, and the Ottawa Senators' win over the Edmonton Eskimos in the second Stanley Cup.

****

Stanley was met at the bridge by five RCMP officers. Together, they descended into the gorge and discovered four bodies near the train. The first was Kyle Granderson's, squashed so flat by the engine he was recognized only by the items in his pockets. The second was Stewart Saunders. He had been thrown from the train and ended his life speared on the branch of a tree. It was unknown whether he died on impact or if his death took days. They found the bodies of two engineers in the cab of the overturned locomotive. I imagine they died knowing they had lost control. Whether they were going too fast or if there was some obstruction on the track could not be determined.

They never found the bodies of Cale Poulson or Robert Clack. Their wives held out hope that they had fled this dirty business while in Prince Rupert, but I had my doubts. Most likely, they were borne downstream or eaten by hungry animals.

Whether the pit train was carrying more women or girls was unknown. No bodies were found, and no one came forward to suggest anyone was missing. Though it was unlikely anyone in China would ever guess criminals had smuggled their daughters to British Columbia.

Stanley and the others followed the tracks of the remaining two gang members. They were a cagey pair and did much to cover their tracks. After five days of hard travel, Alexandr Dvorak, the greengrocer, surrendered. He had broken his arm and three teeth in a fall and could no longer continue.

Matti Larsen pressed on. They caught him after a whole month had passed. They came close twice before, exchanging gunfire from a distance. But both times, Larsen escaped. I would never guess the man would be so tenacious. Finally, he conceded the same way Dvorak did. The chase had not given him time to hunt, and harsh living in cold weather had broken down his body. When they captured him, he weighed less than a hundred pounds. I'm sure Stanley and the reinforcements had also lost much weight in that long pursuit.

For the next couple of years, Paul and I never shared the same room, though we wrote to each other and talked twice on the telephone. We didn't dwell on the events that brought us together; our conversations were often about the future. Already, we were on different trails. The higher-ups moved Paul back East, promoting him and using him as a spokesperson for the force.

My new position as Detachment Head in Smithers kept me quite busy. As an added benefit, Smithers had phone service as it was a larger center. As a result, I needed to hire a receptionist who would also do odd jobs around the detachment, including light cleaning and preparing meals. With some reservations, I hired Millie, who applied for the job as soon as I posted it. Her mother and brother had left to live in Prince Rupert, but Millie had a lady friend in Smithers who was happy to take her in. And so the two of us were colleagues once again.

****

There was one final piece of the puzzle that I needed to solve. I knew it might take some time.

I put feelers out to several of the other detachments in the area. I figured Clayton wouldn't go far. He would probably arrive at some place nearby, asking for a handout. He was almost recovered from his wounds when he ran, but he would not be the same man. I now had first-hand knowledge that a bullet wound was something you lived with your entire life.

It wasn't until the summer of 1924 that I got a phone call from our office in Creston in Southern British Columbia. The officer on the other end of the line told me he had located Clayton and wondered if he should arrest him.

I told him, "No, leave him be." It was something I

343

wanted to do on my own.

To my great surprise, a Christian organization had taken Clayton in. One of the first communities of American Mormons that had begun to settle in the interior. They got him sober and gave him an actual job—a real-world miracle for the man.

We met at the home of his pastor. It was a new build, with few decorations but clean as a whistle. We sat on opposite sofas and were served juice and finger sandwiches by our hosts, the pastor and his wife, along with four young daughters taught to smile and mind their manners.

Clayton was clean, shaved, and wearing a white shirt, black pants, and polished shoes. It was hard to recognize him without the beard, but his hoarse voice was unmistakable.

His manner was taciturn and guarded. Whenever he talked, he would glance at the pastor and his wife to see if his words were suitable. More than once, they gave him a subtle comforting nod. We talked about safe subjects, the long, hot summer we were experiencing, and the predictions for the annual crop yields. He measured his words, thinking through each statement before he said it. And he did well; not one curse escaped his lips.

After our refreshments, I prepared to leave but asked Clayton to come into the yard. He gained the nodded permission from our hosts, and we stepped out through the blazing sun and into the shade of a peach tree. As he stared into the branches, he took a deep breath.

"I'm sorry," he said, the words almost lost in the wind.

I let the moment hang until his eyes dropped to meet

my own.

"I'm sorry for my part in all this," he said, a hint of the old Clayton in his voice. He reached into his well-laundered pants and pulled out a note.

"You deserve to read this," he said. He took a breath and passed it over. I unfolded it, careful as the frayed folds showed he had read it many times. "It came by post three months ago." I read the name Clayton Cole at the top, and at the bottom, in a looping signature, a woman's name, "Emily." I looked at Clayton, and he nodded, and so I read.

Clayton Cole,

It has taken me time, but I can no longer live with the burden of anger I have for you. I decided to have you killed for what you did, and for that, I apologize. I see now that two wrongs don't make a right, and forever more, I will be forced to live with the shame of what I have done. My mother deserved so much more than to die through your negligence, but that is your cross to bear. Perhaps you can find some peace in this sad world. As for me, my life will always be one of loss.

Emily

I flipped the paper over, but there was no return address. I read it twice, the second time to feel the full weight of the words. "She forgave you," I said.

Clayton shook his head. "She was going to be my daughter." He paused. "Matilda and I. We were going to get married."

Grief was in his eyes—the pain he had been hiding in furs, beards, and booze. "She drowned," he croaked as the tears began to fall. "One night, when I was with her drunk. I couldn't even remember it. We were both so off our heads." He began to sob. The screen door opened behind us. The pastor stood there, his arms folded across his chest.

Did Clayton know he was walking into a trap? That's the heaviness of guilt; it sometimes makes people do what's against their best interests. He believed he deserved to die for his past mistakes. He had to know that it couldn't be Matilda's ghost that was haunting him, only her memory.

I waited until Clayton collected himself a bit. He couldn't look me in the eyes. So, I stared into the peach tree above us. There was a large nest, too big to be a bird's. Raccoon, I figured. When Clayton sighed, I asked my question.

"Did the girl come back to you that night? After I left?"

"I think so," he said. "There was some yelling, and then I think she kissed me."

For a moment, the memory of her came back clear—the girl's calm demeanor as if nothing could touch her. I wouldn't have left if I had presumed she was out for Clayton. It never once passed my mind that she would have anything against him.

Clayton's voice brought me out of my reverie. "She figured I was already dead or most likely dying," he murmured, "And so did I. Sin as it was, I wanted to die, right there. I knew it was what I was supposed to do, but I couldn't let go."

His wild eyes stared right through me. I wanted to calm him but didn't know what to say.

"She kissed you," I breathed. "And put that note in your coat."

He nodded.

"Listen," I said as the man brushed away his tears,

wiping his face with the backs of his hairy hands. "Are you going to give me any clues as to where to find her? Do you have the envelope that the letter came in? Was there a return address?

He shook his head.

"Well, what can you tell me? Where did her people come from? What was her mother's maiden name?" My searches through the records in Calgary and Vancouver provided no clues.

"Clayton," I pressed on. "I'm glad she apologized, but two men died. She may still be dangerous."

Clayton sent out a bubble of laughter, "Dangerous?" A wry smile played across his face. "Anyone can be dangerous. Aren't you the one that shot a man square in the eye at thirty paces after clubbing his brother to death?"

I stared at my shoes. They needed shining.

It was time to take stock of things. I could continue to search for the mother myself. But, of course, she could have come from anywhere. Esther's memory of her coming from Calgary could have been a rumor or even a lie. She could have been from British Columbia, Alberta, the Yukon, the Eastern provinces, or maybe the Northwest states. I didn't know where Clayton came from before he arrived in Chambers. For some reason, I couldn't picture him any younger than he was. Right now, I was having particular trouble with the image of him in a clean pair of pants and a shirt. If he wasn't going to help, finding this Emily Whithers would take a lot of luck. Somehow I doubted that was the name she still used. I guess I would have to keep that promise I made to her.

"All right, Clayton," I said. "All right." I handed him

back the note and gave a final wave to the pastor. Then, I let the man go. Who can say what is the price for any man's sins? I know I couldn't. Like Emily, I hoped we all could find some peace.

I walked back to the station the long way to town. It was built like a place should be—slowly—to keep the good things of the past and to let the others go, a history and a dream for the future living side by side. There were families here, just trying to live a life, carrying on. Maybe I would get there, too, someday.

****

The train was waiting at the station when I arrived—that pleasant smell of summer heat and engine fuel. As I climbed the ladder to the car, a little boy on the platform pointed me out to his mother, and I smiled back. Inside, I took off my jacket and Stetson hat and laid them on the bench beside me. For now, no longer a Mountie.

This train would take me to Vancouver, where I had decided to meet Genevieve like a schoolboy sneaking out of school. I hoped she was as excited about it as I was. She told me she would be waiting for me at the station. Even the thought of holding her hand gave me some sort of peace, but I truly longed to embrace her. Genevieve. Two tired souls in need of each other.

The train started with a lurch. Off and over the Rocky Mountains, we would travel like it was nothing—like there was nothing wrong with the world.

A word about the author...

Bowman Wilker is an author and children's poet from Ottawa, Canada. His poetry is featured in magazines such as Chirp, Chickadee and Caterpillar and in his picture book, Crackerjack Jack. This is his first novel. Please visit bowmanwilker.com to discover more The Weary Carry On content and samples of his poetry.

Thank you for purchasing
this publication of The Wild Rose Press, Inc.

For questions or more information
contact us at
info@thewildrosepress.com.

The Wild Rose Press, Inc.
www.thewildrosepress.com